Rain Line

Laurie Alberts, *Lost Daughters*

Laurie Alberts, *The Price of Land in Shelby*

Thomas Bailey Aldrich, *The Story of a Bad Boy*

Robert J. Begiebing, *The Adventures of Allegra Fullerton; Or, A Memoir of Startling and Amusing Episodes from Itinerant life*

Anne Bernays, *Professor Romeo*

Chris Bohjalian, *Water Witches*

Dona Brown, ed., *A Tourist's New England: Travel Fiction, 1820–1920*

Joseph Bruchac, *The Waters Between: A Novel of the Dawn Land*

Joseph A. Citro, *Shadow Child*

Joseph A. Citro, *Guardian Angels*

Sean Connolly, *A Great Place to Die*

Dorothy Canfield Fisher (Mark J. Madigan, ed.), *Seasoned Timber*

Dorothy Canfield Fisher, *Understood Betsy*

Joseph Freda, *Suburban Guerrillas*

Castle Freeman, Jr., *Judgment Hill*

Frank Gaspar, *Leaving Pico*

Ernest Hebert, *The Dogs of March*

Ernest Hebert, *Live Free or Die*

Sarah Orne Jewett (Sarah Way Sherman, ed.), *The Country of the Pointed Firs and Other Stories*

Lisa MacFarlane, ed., *This World Is Not Conclusion: Faith in Nineteenth-Century New England Fiction*

Anne Whitney Pierce, *Rain Line*

Kit Reed, *J. Eden*

Rowland E. Robinson (David Budbill, ed.), *Danvis Tales: Selected Stories*

Roxana Robinson, *Summer Light*

Rebecca Rule, *The Best Revenge: Short Stories*

R. D. Skillings, *Where the Time Goes*

Theodore Weesner, *Novemberfest*

W. D. Wetherell, *The Wisest Man in America*

Edith Wharton (Barbara A. White, ed.), *Wharton's New England: Seven Stories and* Ethan Frome

Thomas Williams, *The Hair of Harold Roux*

Rain Line

A NOVEL BY

Anne Whitney Pierce

UNIVERSITY PRESS OF NEW ENGLAND

HANOVER AND LONDON

Published by University Press of New England, Hanover, NH 03755
© 2000 by Anne Whitney Pierce
Printed in the United States of America   5 4 3 2 1

LIBRARY OF CONGRESS CATALOGING-IN-PUBLICATION DATA

Pierce, Anne Whitney

   Rain line : a novel / by Anne Whitney Pierce.

      p.   cm. — (Hardscrabble books)

      ISBN 1–58465–021–4 (cloth : alk. paper)

      I. Title.   II. Series.

PS3566.I38157R34 2000

813'.54—dc21   99–41911

for Al

AND IN MEMORY OF ALEX AND LUCY

Acknowledgments

I would like to thank Joe Umphres, Linda White, Alex Slive, Ann, Collette, and especially my agent, Lane Zachary, without whose help and support this book never would have reached beyond the sum of its parts to its whole.

Rain Line

chapter one

To this day, I wonder if Danny knew he was going to die. I some-how knew I would not, even as the car crashed through the railing and fell oddly quiet into the river. My life didn't flash before me. I wasn't scared. As we sailed through the dark, I thought clearly about how I'd get out of the car. Danny said, "oh, shit," and I said back to him, "I love you." It was a conversation we'd had many times before, in penultimate moments before lesser tragedies—Danny telling me what he was going to do—here to die—and me asking him not to.

We'd been at a party at Eddie Quintana's house just before. Eddie and Danny were long-time friends and hockey teammates, the only Cambridge boys in their Harvard senior class. They played Harvard down, played it cool, played it out. Asked where they went to school, they'd mumble, "down in the Square," or just "around." Solid stu-dents. Super jocks. Stuck together not so much by character or deed, but more by the ice-bottomed fate they'd come to share, Danny and Eddie held their ground, held their turf, held their own.

"We filled the quota," Eddie liked to say. "Token townies in the ivory tower."

"Only let us in 'cause we could skate," Danny would grumble, with a spit for emphasis.

And skate they both could—Eddie a lumbering bear of a goalie with mittened paws and voodoo mask, Danny, sleek and fast on offense, flying from one end of the ice to the other, slamming the puck into the net time and time again. Sticks raised in victory, grins and tousled hair laced with sweat. I'd seen the picture a thousand times—one Irish, one Italian son, heroes that night the Buick plowed into the river.

Harvard won the championship in the last period. Danny checked the Dartmouth forward against the boards and stole the puck. His stick hurled it from the crease into the corner of the net and he flew out of nowhere to catch it on the other side. Ice shards exploded in the air. Danny lifted his stick and made the shot in the corner of the net as the Dartmouth forward charged from behind and slammed into him. Danny's fist lunged into the forward's gut and Danny took a right to his eye.

They both took the penalty for roughing. As the 2 slid into a 3 on the scoreboard, the crowd rose to its feet, hoarse and wild. It was the go-ahead goal, Danny's third of the game. Hats came flying out of the stands—a cowboy hat and a curly blond wig, a sombrero, a baseball cap. The referee scooped them up in between his legs and dumped them into Danny's lap in the penalty box. Danny must have said something to make him mad. The ref's black and white striped arm started waving wildly and his thumb jerked Danny off to the dressing room. Danny stuffed the cowboy hat onto his head and stalked off to a standing ovation, skates stomping up the wooden ramp as the crowd chanted his name—McPhee! McPhee!—eyes never wavering. This was the kind of brooding exit Danny made so often—from the hockey rink, from his mother's house, from my bed.

After the game, the crowd streamed out of the rink into the parking lot near the river, whooping and shouting, dousing each other with beer. Danny and I hit the open air. It was an oddly warm winter night, a late January reprieve. A chorus of confused crocuses pushed its way up through the ground by the door of the rink. Above it, a ledge of ice slipped quietly away. Cries and whistles filled the pockets in the breeze. Beery breath hung steamy in the air. Some of the players took their shirts off and rode as bowsprits on the hoods of cars. Muscle-bound chests and gleaming grins shimmered in the dark. Eddie and Danny found each other by the pay phone and embraced.

"We did it, man," Eddie said. "Took care of business. The last deed. Like that painting on the ceiling. The last supper. The last god damned supper."

"Yeah," Danny said quietly. "We finally took the green boys to town."

I stood beside Danny as he held reluctant court. People clapped him on the back, slapped him five, ruffled his hair. He'd won the game for them. Everyone had said he would. Eddie let in two killer goals, but Danny had scored the hat trick. Without warning, he broke free from the crowd, strode through the rows of parked cars, shirt open, cowboy hat still atilt on his head, holding his skates by the blades, laces dangling. I turned on my heel to follow. The voices trailed behind.

"Hey, Danny, want a ride?"

"Hop in, McPhee. Got some smoke that will blow your brains out."

"You're the man, Danny. You're the fucking *man!*"

I slid into the Buick just as Danny's foot hit the gas pedal. Someone in a passing car threw a six-pack through the driver seat window. Danny caught it neatly, yanked a beer from its plastic yoke. We drove across the bridge and along Memorial Drive toward East Cambridge. The warm, wet air came up from the river through the window to brush my face.

"Congratulations," I said.

"Glad it's over." Danny took a swig of his beer. "Last game I'm ever going to play."

"Of hockey?" I asked him.

"Of anything. I'm tired of games. I'm almost a quarter of a century

3

old and all I've done my whole life is play games." Danny planted the beer can between his legs. "I just want to get on with it."

"On with what?" So often with Danny I turned into dumb inquisitor.

"Life. Plain old fucking life."

"Plain old fucking life as opposed to plain old fucking what?"

"Just life. Like like other people know it."

"I thought you were other people," I said, looking over at him. "Mr. Cambridge. Mr. Hockey. Mr. Golden Star."

"I'm just a fake, Leo." Danny took another swig as we passed the Hyatt and turned to me. "I thought you knew that."

I reached over to touch his bruised and swelling eye. "God, look at you." I said.

"Don't make a big deal." He winced as I pulled my hand away. "You know it's part of the game."

"I bet Bobby Orr didn't come home with black eyes." Bobby Orr was Danny's hero, some kind of deity sent down to roam the earth's ice patches on skates and spread the quiet word about superlatives— of body, spirit and mind. Danny told only one joke in a crowd, with a seriousness that made it more sacrament than humor, the one where Jesus saves, but Espo scores on the rebound.

"No one messed with Orr," Danny said. "You just don't mess with God."

I stuck my arm out the window, flattened my palm against the breeze. Spray dotted the windshield as Danny flipped open the top of his second beer. "What happened in the penalty box?" I asked him. "Why'd the referee kick you out of the game?"

"It was a bad call and I told him so," Danny said. "He thought I gave him the finger. I was scratching my nose. Can't even scratch my own god damned nose. It was nothing."

"Some nothings are more calculated than others," I said.

"What's that supposed to mean?" Danny ran the light at the corner of Prospect and Cambridge, passing by my apartment above the pizza parlor.

I didn't know and so I said nothing back. It was the kind of thing I often said to Danny when he was angry, words meant to distract or as-

4

suage, perplex or salvage an uneasy moment, but which only made him mad and me regretful, and then both of us sorry. "You could write a column," he said. "Right next to 'Ask Beth.' 'Dear Leo.' How do you play hockey and be a saint at the same god damned time?"

"Don't swear so much." I looked out the window as we headed west down Cambridge Street. "I'm sick of games too, Danny," I told him. "Sick of this game we're playing."

"What game?"

"X-rated sticks and stones."

"Break my bones, Leo," Danny whispered into a gulp of beer, as he careened around the corner of 3rd Street. "That Dartmouth jerk was trying to break my fucking bones."

We pulled up to Eddie's house just as the keg arrived. He lived near Lechmere Sales in East Cambridge, on the second floor of a triple decker, just above the railroad tracks on the Somerville line. Upstairs, an old door resting on two sawhorses made the bar. I poured myself a plastic glass of pink wine and sat down on a lumpy sofa backed up against a wall. An old poster of Janis Joplin hung crooked on the wall, baby face ravaged, a twinkle in her doomed eyes. Eddie's girlfriend of the hour, dressed in red high heels and a purple suede skirt, put on some girl groups and turned it up loud. She and two other girls formed a line, swiveling hips and swirling palms, fists to mouths. Doo wah. Danny and Eddie sat down to a game of Cardinal Puff, chasing beer with whiskey and whiskey with more beer.

Car doors slammed and more people tracked up the narrow rubber-trailed stairs to fill the empty room, bringing blasts of cool air and noise with them. The door table filled with bottles—vodka, Jack Daniels, Kahlua, Ripple wine—and the corners filled with coats—fake fur, leather, down, Army fatigue. The room was lit by a purple glow, and the rhythmic flashing of a yellow stop light hoisted from a street corner. Eddie got up and started to roam, swigging Jim Beam from a bottle, making introductions, making inquiries, making eyes.

I leaned back on the sofa and closed my eyes. I wouldn't miss these parties—the hockey crowd getting together to drown victory and defeat alike in buckets of beer—big boys acting like little boys with Tarzan bravado and girls who kept them small with cold shoulders, smoky lips, perfumed cool. The boys were a blur of muscle, mouth, smoke and sweat. They moved by me like the swells of waves. I had eyes only for Danny. But I watched the girls. I couldn't imagine where they'd all come from, who'd ever sprouted them. Some had a waxy perfection about them, straight white teeth and round breasts, thin hips melting effortlessly into strong legs, gently indented abdomens bared just above their beltlines, waterfalls of just-so honeyed hair. Some blew fine hair from their eyes with a puffed out lower lip. Others were freckled, hair-sprayed and tough. Some dressed to kill and were nobody's fools. A few would consider being anyone's. Some came alone. Others in gaggles. There were always plenty of girls.

Eddie's parties were open invitations to anyone who'd ever crossed his path—the drunk he'd once talked down off the railing of the Salt and Pepper bridge, the waitress who toasted his English muffins just so at the Tasty in the Square, his dental hygienist, and a retarded boy from grammar school for whom Eddie had looked out over the years. Most of these people had turned their memories inside out, felt beholden to Eddie where they might have considered revenge. In truth, it was Eddie who'd led the drunk up onto the bridge on a lark, Eddie who'd first dunked the retarded boy's head in a toilet at school before taking him under his wing. Who remembered that Eddie had given the Tasty waitress the clap, that he'd dumped the hygienist without so much as a phone call? Forgotten the kill. Remembered the kindnesses. Many years later, all these people would elect Eddie the mayor.

When Eddie Quintana opened his battered doors, everything was up for grabs—his apartment, his beer, his smoke, even his old girlfriends. On those nights, and only on those nights, was Eddie a generous man. The parties were wild, dawn-bound, filled with music and smoke, recklessness and booze. I'd seen the most unlikely couplings in Eddie's house—a Pulitzer pouring Boone's farm for a Somervillian beautician, a nice Jewish boy asking a nasty WASP to dance, a cheerleader arguing a Marxist into a dark, hot corner. I'd seen Eddie lead identical twin girls into an empty room, his arms curled around their waists like tentacles, and I'd seen Danny come looking for me after he was drunk, as if there were no one else in the room.

In Eddie Quintana's bleak house of noise and lust, metamorphosis was not only possible, but likely. In Eddie Quintana's bleak house of drink and blare, there was even room for me. Neither town nor gown really, but a swatch of both. I'd grown up in Cambridge, but so far up a hill in the city's northwest corner, so far from the subways or stores or real sidewalks, that the city only half-heartedly claimed Cobb's Hill as one of its neighborhoods, often neglecting to collect its trash or plow its streets in the winter. I'd gone to the neighborhood school, the first Baye in generations not to have stumbled through a private education. But so little had I made my presence felt, no more than a pale, black-haired phantom huddling in the back rows of class pictures, peering out of a tree costume in the "Save the Sycamores" school play, I couldn't say, with any conviction or pride, as Eddie's girlfriends did—that I was a Cambridge girl.

Music was all that distinguished me. I'd played the violin since I was six and was thought to have some talent, how much, no one knew, least of all me. As a child, I'd been eager to know who I was, composing paragraphs that would explain me in one paragraph in the *World Book Encyclopedia* after I died. LEONARDA BYEWORTH BAYE. Born 1960. Named after the great Leonardo da Vinci. Alphabetically, my entry would fall just after BAT. We had much in common, I thought, both nocturnal creatures and known to eat bugs, often misunderstood to be unfriendly or strange. Startled by passing shadows. Afraid of howling cats and white light. Prefer to be left alone, to hang upside down in dark, remote places. Not so much scary—as scared.

As I took a sip of the pink wine at the party, a curl of nausea rose up from a deep place in my stomach. I leaned forward and brought my legs up underneath me on Eddie's lumpy couch. Someone put on Sam Cooke. His cool voice slid over me. *At first I thought it was in-fat-u-a-tion. But oooh, it's lasted so long.* I sat and watched the smoky dream unfold before me, waited for the time when Danny and I could leave the noise and the smells and the hot, breathless confusion, make contact again

7

with the open air. I drank more wine. Danny leaned against the opposite wall, one leg bent straight back, beer bottle level with his groin. We
came and went together. That was all. What happened in between was
a mute and frenzied blur. This wasn't my way to spend an evening, but
for Danny, I'd made it my way, glad, sometimes, just to have a way.

I was somehow, curiously, Danny McPhee's girlfriend, and that fact
imbued me with powers and charms that weren't otherwise mine, as a
snake does a woman with a basket. I could have sat on that sofa forever. No one would have tried to move or shake or hurt me. Danny
McPhee was God's gift and I was his. He'd scored the hat trick, and
he'd be taking me home.

One of Eddie's old girlfriends came over, April, a tall girl with a
leopard skin shirt, all legs and beautiful green eyes, a gold chain riding
the lip of her tiny waist.

"You bored?" she asked me, fingering the links of her belt. "You
look bored, just sitting there like you do."

"Bored?" I straightened up on the couch. "No, I'm not bored."

"You always come here and you sit there all night on that couch
looking bored," she said. "Like you're too good for all this."

"No." I swept my hand around the arc of the room and tried to explain. "I'm just no good at this. That's all."

She laughed. "What's to be good at? You drink. You smoke. You
swing. You lean. You crash. All you got to be good at, girl, is being. Listen. You'll be all right."

"You think so?" I asked.

April tugged down her shirt, followed my eyes over to Danny. "You
better hold onto that boy," she said. "You don't look out, someone's
going to take him away from you. That boy's to die for." She took a
drag of her cigarette and warned me on the exhale. "The way I see it,
someone just might have to die."

I took a sip of my Kool-Aid wine, and hoped it wouldn't be me.

After a while, I got up and went over to Danny, who was still leaning
against a wall with his beer.

"Having fun yet?" he asked me.

"I wouldn't go that far."

"Just came to suffer, I guess."

"Let's go, Danny. You're getting drunk."

"Just be Leo, will you?" Danny raised his beer bottle to his lips. "And not the warden?"

"Okay, I'll be Leo." I turned away from him. "And you be the jerk." I was tired of arguing with the liquor after it had invaded Danny's bloodstream, after it brought the dull look into his eyes and the sneer to his face. I was sick of the ragged banter we let pass for conversation. We went on and on this way, strangely afraid of ourselves and one another, of our intimacy. We spoke in jibes and put-downs, interjections, inuendo, omission, shrugs, turns of the heel.

I went back to the couch. Someone passed me a joint. I took a why-not toke and coughed most of it back out into the air. Someone dancing by took the joint from my fingers. The music played on, disc jockeys rotating as the spirits moved—Airplanes, Beatles, Fish and Fuggs. Temps, Tops, Tammy. With George. And without. The mood changed with each flick of a hand. Eddie put on Van Morrison and came over to me.

"Hey, Lee," he purred.

"Leo," I said. "Nice game, Eddie. Good party."

"It's a waste, Lee." Eddie's hand brushed the nape of my neck. "Just sitting here, waiting for it to be over. Come on. Let's dance."

The hot breath of persuasion roamed my ear. I let Eddie pull me up onto the dance floor, where a few people moved in time. His arms wrapped around me, victory sweat still seeping. I pushed him away. But he drew me back and I gave in to the pulls of gravity and fatigue and Eddie Quintana alike. We dipped and swayed to "Moondance." I watched as Danny pulled a chair over to a table in the corner of the room, where a man sat alone, playing chess. Danny shook the man's hand and sat down across from him. The two of them bent their heads over the board. Slowly, a crowd gathered. People liked to be near Danny, to watch his hands and his murky blue eyes, to catch the muscles in his shoulders move under his t-shirt or one of his rare twisted smiles. Eddie's hands flattened against my back. I steered him toward the chess table. For a split second, feeling my eyes upon him, Danny looked my way. Finding me in Eddie's arms, his eyes went blank, and fell back down to the chessboard. As Eddie and I danced by the bar, I picked up a bottle of gin and took a swig.

For that blank look in Danny's eyes, I might have drunk whole bottles of gin, I might have stayed on the floor all night dancing with Eddie, followed him into a dark room, slid my shirt off my shoulders and my hand under his belt, breathed deep of his heady smell. But as Danny's forehead creased and the first pawn went out, as Eddie's thick fingers climbed up my spine, the sickness that had been riding my stomach all night shot up into my throat. I left Eddie crooning into his fist of a microphone, swaying in the direction of a girl with clocks on her tights, a girl he'd been watching in between twirls as we danced. In the bathroom, with no time even to flush away the froth of hockey player pee, I vomited. Once, and then again. Laying my head on the toilet seat, I closed my eyes and tried to think of nothing, until someone pounded on the door.

By midnight, Eddie's party had grown loud and frenzied. Smoke swirled and music blared. Couples slid lizard-like into corners and through half-open doors. I went over to Danny, who was still playing chess with the dark-haired man in the corner, both of them oblivious to the din. The dark-haired man wore one blue sock and one brown, a curiously insignificant detail, the catch of a hand that reaches in a drawer for the first two socks it can find and nothing more. I came up behind Danny, put one hand on his shoulder. He moved his rook, scratched his chin.

"Can we go now, Danny? Please. I don't feel well." He lifted his hand to silence me. I looked down at the board. "Looks like the game's over, anyhow," I said.

"What?" Danny's head jerked up.

"She's right." The dark-haired man looked up at me curiously. "It's mate with queen to bishop five."

"Shit." Danny flattened his king onto the board with his palm. "I didn't see that coming. I was going to attack your knight."

The chess player's fingers reached down to fiddle with the chess pieces. "This was your only move," he told Danny. "Back in the middle game. The bishop could have gone here, taken my pawn . . ." He rearranged some pieces, swooped up one of his knights. "You weakened your pawn structure back in the opening, left your king-side wide open."

"Damn. What an idiot." The liquor which Danny had cleared to one side of his brain during the chess game washed back over him, all those mingling shots of whiskey and beer causing him to sway as he ran his square fingers through his hair. "I'm so tired, man. So beat. I can't come up with the killer moves. I thought my pawn storm was going to do it. I thought I had the game."

"That's the thing," the man said. "When the attack is premature, the counterattack prevails."

Danny kept staring at the board, staring, trying to figure it out. "My pawn went here . . ."

"Danny, please," I said.

"Go on, take her home, man," the chess player said. "Game's over."

Danny didn't move, didn't speak.

"Hey." The chess player reached out to touch his arm. "I think she's had enough. I think you . . ."

"Who the fuck . . ." Danny flung his arm away.

"Danny, stop," I said.

"Lay off it, Leo. I mean it. Just lay off."

"Hey, easy, man," the chess player said. "Easy . . ."

"Easy?" The black had risen in Danny's eyes. "No. Whatever else it is, *man*, it is . . . not . . . fucking . . . easy." He raised the flattened edge of his palm, made contact with his fallen king as if it were a sitting puck, and with one fell sweep of his arm knocked the chessboard off the table. As the pieces rolled and scattered on the floor, Danny raised both arms as if in surrender. "Now the game's over," he said. "Now it's fucking over."

The chess player started to pick up the chess pieces and I knelt down to help him. Danny left the room without another word.

"I'm sorry," I said. "He's drunk. He's . . ."

"Don't worry about it," he said. "Why don't you just get him home."

Out on the sidewalk, Danny was waiting for me, hands in his coat pockets, rocking on his heels, still simmering. "What's the matter?" he said, really looking at me for the first time all night. "You look like you've seen a ghost."

"I needed some air, that's all," I said. "I can't believe what you just did in there, Danny."

"I lost," he said. "What can I say, Leo. I'm a loser."

"I guess you made that perfectly clear."

We sat silently for a while in the car on the way home, the dark cloud of Danny's blow-up at the chess table hanging heavy between us, postponing explanations and apologies because we couldn't make such gestures anywhere else but in my grandmother's dark, liquor-clouded bed. Danny drove fast along the river drive, still sure that nothing could ever really hurt him, and me suddenly aware that anything could. I held my tongue, knowing I had nothing to say that wouldn't make him mad.

"How'd you know the game was over?" he said finally.

"Your bishop was in trouble. I saw it a few moves back."

"So." He took a swig of his beer. "You play chess, too?"

"I used to play with my father," I said.

Danny put his beer can in between his legs. "I guess there's a lot I don't know about you, Leo."

"I could fill you in."

"It would take a lifetime," he said, reaching for a pack of cigarettes on the dashboard.

"That's right," I said. "It would."

Danny took a deep breath before lighting up. "That guy knows something," he said.

"What guy?"

"Kilroy. The guy I was playing chess with."

"What does he know, Danny? Besides the fact that some people are incredibly bad losers."

"Good, bad. A loser's a loser."

"What does he know, Danny?"

"If I knew, Leo . . ." Danny spoke so softly, I could hardly hear. "I wouldn't be smoking this cigarette. I wouldn't be driving this old shit box. And my hands wouldn't smell like fish."

"And maybe you wouldn't feel so sorry for yourself," was what I said back to him. But what I was thinking was, "and you wouldn't be here with me."

chapter two

*H*ours later, after the accident, after they'd pulled Danny out of the water and taken him away, I was released from the Mount Auburn Hospital into a grisly dawn. I passed Danny's father in the hall of the emergency room. It must have been after he found out that Danny was dead, because he looked half-dead too, no color left to his ruddy face, large body hunched forward. I stopped by a row of wheelchairs, steadied myself and started to speak, but he lurched by me and I had no chance.

I waited outside the hospital for my father to pick me up. The early winter morning was still and cold, the night before's warmth no more than a misty dream. I unfurled one fist, stretched out a trembling hand. The doctors and nurses had told me over and over again, as they held up fingers for me to count and asked me what day it was, that I shouldn't be alone, no matter how much I might want to be, that I should call someone to come and get me—that I'd need help.

My father pulled up in the Rambler he'd bought when I was a baby, in 1961, when he'd almost sold his idea for "The Musical Toothbrush" and still had hopes for the hopeless—my mother's good health, money in the bank. But by then, the shiny old car, an odd behemoth with its wood stripes and red wing tips, reminded him of lost time and failure, and he only used it for emergencies. As the car slowed, he waved. I slid into the front seat beside him and crossed my arms.

"Leo," he said. "I don't know what to say."

"Danny didn't make it," I said.

"I know."

"It happened," I said, glancing over at my father. "You never did invent that machine that could reverse time."

"I tried." He ventured a weak smile, put the car in drive. "Where do you want to go, Leo?"

"Home."

"Which home?"

I meant to say mine, of course, back to my apartment in Inman Square, my roost above the pizza parlor, where I'd lived for five years since I was seventeen, but a sudden panic seized me, of what I wasn't sure. I looked over at my father's profile, which was suddenly distorted and unfamiliar. "Take me to Cobb's Hill," I said. "Take me back to Cobb's Hill with you."

We drove down Mount Auburn Street along the still, gray river and wound our way up Cobb's Hill, where the trees grew gnarled and the grass unkempt and the silence of dawn complete. As the hill leveled, the old, shingled house rose before us in the mist. I slid out of the Rambler and made my way down the flagstone path, pushing aside the overgrown bushes. The front door opened with a groan. I started up the stairs and my father stood below in the chilly hallway watching me climb, swallowed by a fraying houndstooth check coat he'd worn since I could remember. He smiled and waved, as if he were sending me off to visit a distant aunt by train, though I had no aunts, and had never ridden a train. I waved back and climbed the forty-two stairs to my old attic room, where I fell into my childhood bed and the hole of deep, dark sleep.

* * *

In what I guessed to be the middle of that odd day, I woke up feeling utterly changed—a stranger to my looks and smells and ways. I remembered the accident clearly—the tilt of the car as we careened, the crash when we hit the railing, the ripping sound it made as it was torn from the ground, the dull thud of the car as it hit the water, and the pressure of the water building up around us like a wall. But I didn't remember how to swing my legs out of bed without tipping over, the noisy sounds of my own breathing or the angles of my crooked toes, how far one step should take me.

I sat up in the attic of my childhood home, dazed and bloated from the dark waters of the river, and looked at my face in the mother-of-pearl mirror my mother had given me for my thirteenth birthday, just one of many things I'd abandoned when I left home, no longer wanting them to describe me. In the mirror, I saw the familiar—freckles, thin lips and tangled black hair. I saw a long neck and high cheekbones, the sway of my crooked nose. But I couldn't connect any of my parts to the person who'd drunk the pink wine and danced a sweaty moondance with Eddie, who'd struggled in the river and tried to rub the life back into Danny's blue face on the pavement after they'd dragged him out.

And when I remembered that Danny was dead, really dead, I went to the bathroom where I'd played chemist as a child, a room which struck me as primitive at that moment with its dry sink and seatless toilet, its trickle of a makeshift shower which my father had installed with hurt eyes, some cheap gizmo from the hardware store, after I'd blurted out one day when I was about thirteen, "How do you expect me to live in a house where I can't even get clean?" I splashed cold water on my face, over and over again. I brushed my teeth with no toothpaste until my gums bled and took a hot shower which couldn't warm me, then sat down naked on the bed.

The mattress crunched beneath me as I landed, insides old and dried, blue-striped cotton cover ripped and stained. My tongue roamed the inside walls of my mouth. I savored the taste of lingering blood, its sourness and sting. The doctors had looked me over from top to bottom, pushed and prodded in search of cuts or bruises or tears. But they'd found nothing, nothing wrong, disbelieving, almost disappointed it had seemed. I was whole, unscathed. Like the glowing creatures of sci-fi flicks, I was rubbery, impenetrable.

The room smelled of must and damp cardboard, buttered toast. Books arranged in a colored pattern I knew by heart lined the dusty shelves, the bindings of those worlds to which I'd escaped as a child—Plum Creek, Narnia, a Wrinkle in Time. My damp clothes from the night before lay in a heap on the floor. I remembered how they'd clung dripping when I got out of the water, how they'd slowly dried on my body as the night wore on, how I'd peeled them like bark from my body at dawn.

I put one shaky hand up to my face, traced the bone that encircled the orb of one eye. Had I known how to cry, I might have. The tears would have run down my face and made hovering, dark puddles on the worn, pine floor. And I would have felt the spilling warmth of pain. But at that moment, I felt only cold, whole and strong. For one hovering dragonfly of a moment, my body was beautiful to me, a miracle of flesh and planes and moving parts. I ran my hand down the smooth ridge of my calf muscle, then sent two fingers to the inside of my wrist to feel my pulse, the pulse the divers had looked for frantically in Danny's neck just after they'd pulled him out of the water and ripped off their masks, before the blank look came into their eyes, and they slipped from fast to slow motion, crossing Danny's arms gently on his chest, a gesture made for me, I was sure.

And with that memory of Danny's limp arms and half-closed eyes, my body turned ugly. I saw the dent at the top of the wishbone of my ribcage and the bruises that forever adorned my knees, klutz that I was, klutz that I'd always be. I saw the scrapes on my stomach and sides and a burn scar on my forearm, the bumpy knobs of my wrinkled elbows. I felt the hard pain of a lump on the side of my head. My skin was green, my tongue patched and mottled. A clear, shed skin melted witchlike into a puddle beside the heap of my damp clothes, leaving me bony, scaly, hideously alive.

Rummaging through the bureau drawers, I came upon a dress I'd hidden in long-ago years, hoping my mother, Lydia, would forget she'd ordered it for me out of the Talbot's catalog. Dry brown and tentlike, scattered with yellow daisies, it was nothing her elegant self ever would have worn, but something she hoped might be more of an age, something I might like at fifteen. The dress was just where I'd left it so many years before, stuffed behind some old t-shirts, wrinkles left to set so long they'd become pleats. Nothing had been disturbed here. No one had thought to make order or put closure on my leaving by sorting or folding or packing things away.

The brown dress had a high neck and buttons. The few times I'd worn it to please Lydia, I'd felt like a silly, flowering triangle. Now it hung loose on me and covered most of my body in a way that made me feel shapeless and protected. I found some old brown shoes and clipped my hair on top of my head with a barrette that was already sprouting spots of rust. Opening the door, I climbed back down the forty-two stairs to face my mother.

"Claire." Lydia greeted me quietly as I came into the living room, though this had never been my name, except in her own clouded mind. She'd given in to my father's wish to name me after the great Leonardo da Vinci, but had never stuck to it, calling me instead by the name of an aunt she'd once loved. For as long as I could remember, I'd been Claire to my mother, and Leo to the rest of the world.

"Hi, Lydia." This was the revenge I'd chosen, I suppose—denying her maternal address.

Lydia was sitting on the sofa in ash blue silk, her hair arranged in poufs and layers and held together by the mother-of-pearl combs that matched the mirror upstairs in my room. I'd seen no trace of her when my father and I came in from the hospital at the crack of dawn. I'd never known Lydia to appear until late in the morning, and this was the only way to describe how she made her entrances—floating inward from out of the blue. And as often and noiselessly as she came, so would she disappear, sometimes without so much as a word or a sign, back into whatever haze it was that enveloped Lydia and kept her safe. The ghosts of childhood are said to roam mildewed attics and roost under cobwebbed porches. Mine had floated brazenly through my house from one deserted room to another, dressed in satin and silk, posing as my mother.

I walked toward Lydia, stepping into the frame of the picture I carried around in my mind of her— a tall woman dressed in pastel silks and crinoline, sitting straight on the sofa, the hum of the radio always by her side, ever ready for visitors or afternoon tea, though she rarely had either. The old chintz sofa was fraying badly, the chandelier tarnished nearly black. The grandfather clock stood silent in the corner, frozen for fifteen years at 4:31, since that time years before when my father had borrowed its pendulum for his "Magical Metronome." Had it worked, his invention not only would have kept the beat, but also tapped out a selection of popular tunes. "I Could Have Danced All Night." "Old MacDonald." My father's favorite, "Clementine." I thought today there might be a wrinkle in Lydia's dress, or a wisp of hair straying from the combs, a spark in the grey blue eyes, but as usual, she sat impeccable in the midst of barren disarray.

"I'm glad you stopped by, Claire," she said.

"Stopped by?" I froze on my way to her side, filling with an old and tired anger. So, my father was a gentle coward still, trusting that the gentleness would atone for the cowardice. "Oh my god," I said. "He didn't tell you."

"Tell me what?" Lydia squinted at the daisied dress, not waiting for an answer. "I just heard the forecast," she said. "Lows in the teens, chance of snow flurries later in the day." She spoke in a weatherman's patter. "Winds from the east, ten to twenty knots. That's a light cotton, Claire. It's high time you got out your warm things." Lydia dreaded the winter, though she'd weathered it year after year in that vacuous, drafty house, never abandoning her fragile silks or slippers. Of bitter cold and dire blizzard warnings, people walking ill-shod through the snow, stinging winds on soft cheeks—she had a real terror.

"Where on earth did that dress come from, Claire?"

"I found it in a drawer." I sat down beside her on the sofa. "Danny and I had an accident last night, Lydia."

"I heard the wind." She turned her head away. "A window broke somewhere. I must remember to tell your father."

"The car went into the river." I talked to her as I always had, with a bullet's aim, simple directness reserved for and by children, half to explain, half to jolt. "I got out but Danny didn't," I said. "He died, Lydia."

Lydia closed her eyes, which she often did, in mid-thought, in mid-sentence, so I couldn't be sure if she'd heard. She had long since perfected ways to twist and parry words which, when tossed together, conspired to bring bad news.

"Whenever I see Danny," Lydia said, "I'm reminded of Marcus Porter. He trained lions for the circus. He played the harp of all things. He'd come to the Conservatory for his lessons, then go back to sit in the lions' cages and play to them. They'd roll over and he'd tickle their bellies. As I recall, it didn't end well, though." Her hand went up to her cheek. "As I recall, Marcus Porter went to the dogs."

"Danny died," I said softly. It did me some good after all, this old exercise of trying to make Lydia hear. The second time, the words brought no particular imagery, no particular pain. "Dad picked me up at the hospital," I went on. "I'm all right. Nothing happened to me, Lydia. I'm fine."

"You look well, Claire, considering . . ."

"Oh, God, Lydia, listen."

"There's no need to raise your voice." Her eyes drew tight at the corners. "You haven't been here in such a long time."

"No." I drew the pain slowly back from Lydia's eyes with a practiced, steady voice. "Dad must have forgotten to tell you," I said.

"Oh, your father left you a note." Lydia got up and walked to the hallway, picked up a folded piece of paper from the embroidered linen cloth that had covered the front-hall table since I could remember, a woman's touch, though it had been neither Lydia's nor mine. On top of this cloth, now stained and crusted with time, had lain all of the papers of importance that had ever made their way into our lives. We'd always let these missives sit for longer than they ought, hoping the messages might self-destruct, or disappear.

The folded note read, in my father's spidery hand.

Dear Leo,
Coffee's on the stove.
Danny's father called.

People are gathering at the McPhees' house.
Only go if it will do you good.

I crumpled the paper in my hand. Four disentangled thoughts, written as they'd come to mind. This was how my father had always melted my anger, with a wandering train of thought that was hard to follow and tender last regard for me. I wasn't sure to what day I'd awoken, when the note had been written, when the gathering was to take place. I only knew I had to go. I picked up the pea jacket I'd slung over a chair at dawn and brought it up to my face. The coat was still damp, brushed with the smells of oil and fish. I threw it back on the chair and went over to the hall closet, where I took one of Lydia's old coats from a quilted hanger, one of many garments that had hung undisturbed over the years, clothes so fine they'd never answer to style, still in mint condition, because Lydia had only worn them once or twice.

"I'll wear this old tweed coat," I said, picking up a habit my father and I had of talking to Lydia whether she was listening or not, keeping the patter going.

"It's hardly old, Claire." Lydia's voice startled me from behind. "I got it for opening night at the Royal Ballet."

"You were in London. In 1948." Slowly, I turned to her. Every coat in the closet had a story. I knew them all. "You met the Queen," I said. "You were surprised. She wasn't at all stuck up."

"That's right," she said, in a voice full of wonder. "I thought, how on earth could she *not* be?"

I slid one of my arms into the coat sleeve. "I'm going now, Lydia. Will you be all right?"

"You never stay long, do you, Claire?" Lydia asked me.

The hurt in her childlike face could still make me say things I didn't really mean. "I'll be back," I said, though I had every intention of returning to my apartment, to my life in Inman Square. "I'll bring the coat back, soon, Lydia."

"Where is it you're going?" she asked. "Your father will want to know."

"I'm going to Danny's house. Dad knows. That's what the note was

21

about. People are gathering. Oh, God. I don't know if I can do this. His mother . . . all of them. There'll be a crowd."

"You two will patch things up, I'm sure. Sometimes, in the heat of the moment . . ."

"There was no argument, Lydia," I said in a weary voice. "We had an accident. Danny died."

"Take your time," Lydia said. "Walk slowly. Watch for hidden patches of ice."

"Lydia!" I said. "Stop. Please."

Her face stilled as she turned to me. "If you move slowly," she said, "you can outwit the cold. Some climbers lived in an ice cave in the Rockies for four days. They made a human pyramid, melted ice with their breath. One of them died, but they didn't eat him. In the end, they just couldn't do it."

"Lucky guy," I said. "I'll button up, Lydia. I'll be fine."

"Take your time," Lydia said again, and disappeared into a room for which we had no name or affection. Maybe she knew how I'd feel when I walked out the front door and slammed into a wall of raw, twisted wind, how I'd cry when a laughing boy threw a rock that grazed my foot halfway down the hill, how the trees seemed too high and the sky too low above me, the slope of the hill too steep, the pull of gravity too strong. Maybe Lydia understood that this trip to Danny's house was to be my last act of courage for a while. Maybe Lydia understood that all of a sudden, I knew I could die too.

chapter three

The wind pulled me down Cobb's Hill. I closed the top button of my coat and headed for the river. The WALK sign flashed three times at the Lars Anderson Bridge before I gathered the courage to cross the river drive. Walking the cement path under the barren sycamores, I looked out over the paraffin glass of the frozen river, watery in spots from the day before's thaw. A man jogged by in shorts and earmuffs, bobbing and panting. I kept my head low, and walked. One foot in front of the other. Walked and walked. Past the mushroom heaters where the street people huddled, past the basketball courts glazed with ice. Upriver, the smell of Sugar Daddies wafted from the Necco Factory and the subway rumbled over the Salt and Pepper Bridge. Some children were playing on the edge of the ice; a helicopter whirred overhead. All images came to me in slow, surreal motion, through a dull and purple haze. I saw the children fall through the ice, the train leap the tracks and tumble into the river, the jogger collapse and melt on the pavement—the DON'T WALK sign dripping blood.

At Western Ave., I headed north back into the city. Danny's family lived several blocks down, on Hampshire, in a house above their fish market, sandwiched by a florist and Ignatio's Pet Palace, where Danny used to joke they bought their filets at half price. A sign on the door of the market read, CLOSED. In the little patch of yard, I stopped by the plaster Madonna and Child, swathed in white against a basin of sky blue. Mary's vacant eyes lifted upwards—Mary on the Half Shell, Danny used to call her, kissing her brow as he came and went.

"Leave the Virgin Mother alone!" his grandmother would yell out the window at him. "God is watching you, Daniel! God is watching!"

I reached out to touch Mary's head, brought back my hand and made the sign of the cross, an act so second nature to Danny, he'd done it in his sleep sometimes, his hand finally flopping to rest at naked low center. As I climbed the stairs, I smelled the mingled odors of pet food and cedar shavings and fried fish. I'd only been to the McPhees' house a few times in the three years Danny and I had known each other, never feeling entirely welcome. Now, the door was ajar. In one corner of the front room, silent images danced on a TV screen, open mouths flapping, garish colors flashing, people playing a game of chance and fortune, spinning a glittering wheel. Flowers were every-where, in jars, vases, coffee tins, watering cans. The smells were strong and sweet—coffee, sugar, perfume. The walls of the front room were newly repapered, delicate flowers and stems, with a thought to spring. The southern wall, where the sun streamed in its dappled afternoon light, was covered with photographs of the McPhee children—Danny and his sisters and brother, a shrine of smiling faces—birthdays, tour-naments, communions, recitals—scrubbed, combed, ribboned, and posed, hair ribbons to bows and ties.

I passed through the front room into the kitchen and beyond into the living room. The house was full of people. Danny's family was dis-persed throughout the crowd—his father and mother, a steely, hand-some redhead, cousins, uncles and aunts, the middle sister Eileen, the twins, Mary and Molly, the oldest sister, Rose. The youngest child, the second son, was called Po. He was twelve, but slow, people said, more like eight. Danny's grandmother sat in silent vigil in an armchair by the window, waiting for Ireland to float her way. If you knew just where to look from the street below, you could see her brow and a thatch of white hair, catch a glimpse of her flashing eyes.

Danny's sisters were arranging food on trays, passing them through the crowd. His parents were huddled in a corner by the phone. Only Po, the younger brother, came over to me, but when I reached out to touch him, he ducked and ran away. My mouth was dry and sour. I poured myself a glass of thick, purple juice and sat down in a worn armchair. Food was laid out on a long table—sandwiches and chips, jello molds, cookies and casseroles. Danny's mother must have started cooking the moment she found out he was dead. I watched her move through the room. She might have been catering an afternoon luncheon, sleeves rolled up over her muscled arms, barking orders at her daughters, apron smudged with stains, mouth set with purpose, and not yet grief, winding through the crowd, a press of a hand here, an offer of food, a wiped tear or shared memory there.

Eddie Quintana worked the room in a fine black suit. I felt a rush of tenderness fuse with fury as he came toward me, smile curling his upper lip. "How are you, sweetheart?" he whispered, putting his arms around me.

"Numb." I held onto Eddie, knowing it would be the last time. "I can't feel anything."

"How could he do this?" Eddie whispered and I felt a tear fall hot on his face. "How could he fucking do this to me, man?"

"It was an accident," were the last words I said to Eddie Quintana. "He didn't mean to hurt you, Eddie."

People came and went, bringing more sadness and more food, as comfort found strength in numbers and sustenance. They ate and cried and ate some more. They found solace in their memories and ties, in bites of potato salad and deviled eggs, snatches of the past. They remembered Danny as a little boy, a hockey star, good brother, student, friend. They lifted forks and glasses to their lips and brought those same lips to the cheeks of those beside them. And when enough respectful, sober time had passed, they uncorked the bottles on the makeshift tables, not unlike the bars at Eddie's parties.

And with the first thirsty sips, they loosened their ties and their tongues.

"It should have been anyone but Danny," a woman standing near me said. "That boy was God's gift."

"It's Moira's loss," said another. "Heaven's gain."

"They don't come out of God's oven any more beautiful than that one."

"Troubled, though. A brooder."

"A drinker already, I hear, like his grandfather. The curse of St. Peter on him. So young."

"There was a girl in the car with him," someone said. "They call it the death seat. But I hear she got out without a scratch."

"Who was she?" I heard someone ask.

Who *is* she? I gripped the sides of the armchair, whispered inside. They could spare nothing for me that day. They didn't know yet that I sat heavy and bruised among them—one of the living, and when they found out, I knew they'd condemn me. Little would they think of the miracle of my still being alive—my pumping heart and the blood flowing through my veins, the soft breath that came from my mouth and my nostrils and the twenty-six bones in each of my feet which had led me there that day, all of them unbroken.

Who could blame them? Danny's god had failed him. He'd never missed a Sunday in church. I had never known one. He'd kept the faith. Religiously. I'd tossed it repeatedly to the wind. They knew. They were angry—at fate, at God, at Danny, at me. It was too soon that day to do anything but canonize Danny, and to push me behind a dark, confessional curtain. Forgiving God was one thing. Me another. I was the living, breathing reminder of their pain, their loss. I understood all of this. Part of me wanted me gone as much as they did. I, of all the people in that room, craved the peace of a different ending. There are still burning flashes, sometimes, of wishing it had been me.

The McPhees' living room grew crowded. As people started drinking, the mourning grew louder and more maudlin, more forgetful of Danny. Up rose the chatter of the living—weather, sin, sports and money. Healing stirred in the stuffy room. Danny's younger brother, Po, fell asleep on the couch. Bottles emptied and trash cans filled. The family moved in and out of the mourners, ever gracious, ever sober, no time yet to be anything but busy and grave. The grandmother sat in her chair by the window, weaving her fingers, keeping watch.

After a time, Danny's father bought a chair over and sat down next to me.

"Leo," he said.

As his heavy body landed on the seat, the wobbly legs of the chair creaked and groaned. I tried to sit up straight, as Lydia did effortlessly, the posture of a singer poised to break a pane of glass with a high note. Mr. McPhee leaned forward. A murmur passed like a shudder through the crowd. I'd been identified. The girl in the death seat. Sitting silent in the blue chair. Mr. McPhee cleared his throat. I saw how Danny might have looked in thirty years—square hands worn and lined, strong, muscled frame gone a bit soft, broad Irish face lined with care. Mr. McPhee smiled hard and I tried to smile back, the handshake before a duel of broken spirits. A father. Now minus a son. The girl in the death seat. Straight backed. Silent. Still alive.

"How are you then, Leo?" he said.

What was there to say but "fine"?

"We all know what you've been through," he said. "And thank God you're sitting here with us today, safe and sound. But I think I speak for everyone here when I say, well . . . we wouldn't be human if we didn't want to know . . ." A whisper of a brogue stole into his voice. "Just what happened down there last night."

Down there. For a moment, knowing him to be a religious man, I thought he meant hell. A hush severed the rising murmur and the room fell silent again. "Could you go over it for us one time? Would you be willing, Leo?"

I shifted in my seat. I knew what they wanted. They wanted to know if I could have saved Danny, to judge for themselves. I'd rehearsed my speech a hundred times on the walk over—a simple accounting of the truth. I thought I was prepared. But the first few sounds out of my mouth were no more than croaks. I took a sip of the purple juice and the liquid fell heavy and sickly sweet to my stomach.

My hands trembled. I saw only the white of the crowd's hungry eyes. Everything else was black.

"Danny said there was a party at Eddie's after the game." Mr. McPhee said gently. "Did you go then, Leo?"

I nodded. "We stayed until about midnight." My eyes found Eddie Quintana across the room, his arm draped around the shoulders of Danny's middle sister, Eileen. "Then we started driving home."

"Where were you going?"

"To my apartment."

"Was something wrong with the Buick? Was there ice on the road?" Mr. McPhee's voice gathered strength and speed. "Were any other cars around?"

"The car was fine." I took the questions one at a time. "And the road was dry. I don't remember seeing any other cars. Danny was driving fast."

"Fast?"

"As fast as he always did."

"Had he been drinking?" Mr. McPhee asked.

"Yes."

"How much?"

I lifted my palms, looked over at Eddie. "Lots. They were celebrating. They won the championship." I don't know why I went on to try to explain. "But it was more than that. Danny was mad . . ."

"Mad?" Mrs. McPhee's voice shot out from the other side of the room. "Mad about what?" I looked up to find her sitting on the sofa, Po's red head resting in her lap.

"A lot of little things," I said. "Being thrown out of the game. A dance at the party. A chess game."

"Chess?" Mrs. McPhee said.

"Danny was playing chess at the party," I said. "Just before we left."

"What happened next?" Mr. McPhee broke in. "On the road."

"Danny took the corner too fast and lost control of the car on the bridge." I put down my juice. "We smashed through the railing and went into the river. He couldn't stop."

"What happened in the water?" Mr. McPhee's voice grew hard.

"I tried to open the door," I said. "But it wouldn't budge. I climbed out through the window."

"Aye," he said. "You're a wisp of a thing. You slid right through. And Danny?"

"I don't know. I couldn't see." I shifted in my seat. "I came up for air and tried to go back down. But it was cold. And dark. I couldn't move. I couldn't stay down." My voice cracked. "I heard sirens. Someone must have called. They came and pulled Danny out. They wouldn't let me go to him. I had to fight my way. That's all I remember."

Danny's father let his big head fall into his hands. "Why couldn't he get out?" He spoke into his knees. "A big strong kid like Danny. Why not, for the love of God?"

We sat in the silence of the unanswered question until the grandmother spoke from her corner. "Too big, Sean. Too strong. Daniel thought he had a little bit of God in him, and God didn't take kindly to that."

"Hush, Mother," Mr. McPhee said. "It'll do you no good to speak of Danny now that way."

"And you no good to speak of him with what-might-have-beens," she said. "He's in a better place now."

"Let's hope it's so." Mr. McPhee looked up at me, crossed himself and touched my head with all five fingers in what I took to be some sort of blessing. "May God go with you, Leo," he said, the pressure of his hand increasing. "As He came to you last night."

The grandmother made a hissing sound, and the sloppy murmurs of Danny's lifeline swelled once more. I sat for a while longer in the armchair. Eddie and Danny's sister, Eileen, disappeared. A few people came up to me and spoke. I must have found my voice, though I don't know what I said. After a time, I got my coat and made my way to the door. I don't remember saying goodbye.

Outside, snow had begun to fall. I started walking toward my apartment, two blocks away. Halfway there, feeling dizzy, I landed on a bench across from Rosie's Bakery. The smells of almond truffles and chocolate orgasms drifted my way. Wet snowflakes stung my cheeks and eyelids, pelted the insides of my wrists. I shook my head, trying to relieve the pressure of Mr. McPhee's hand, shake off the dust of his blessing. A woman stopped and held out some coins. I waved the money away. I wanted to shed the cocoon of this nightmare right there on the sidewalk, leave it for the pigeons to peck at. I wanted the buzz in my brain to stop. I wanted to implode before I burst. I wanted to go home, but I was no longer sure where home was. Above all else, I wanted to sleep.

Leaning back against the slats of the bench, I shut my eyes and re-played the night without the accident, as I would do so many times in years to come. The film flickered in the darkness of my closed eyes. Danny and I would have gone back to my apartment. In the kitchen, after we'd turned on the light and the coackroaches had scuttled away, Danny would grab a beer from the six-pack I kept for him in the re-frigerator, always gentler when we were alone. He'd kiss me, a cold beery kiss, and smile. We'd make our way to the bedroom, to my grandmother's mahogany bed, his beer can pressed to the small of my back. He'd whistle a tune, the same one my father loved—"Oh, my darling. Clementine."

Some parts of the ritual never changed. Danny would sit down and take off his shoes, cross his arms on his chest and pretend to shiver. "This bed smells like dead people," he'd say. "Old Aunt Matilda and Grandma Moses and Great Uncle Fred. I can smell them, Leo. I swear."

"No, you can't." I'd sit down beside him and feel the cool, slippery dome of the bedpost beneath my palm and with it the first stirring of sex. To me the bed smelled of bark and the forest, of darkness and de-sire and deep sleep. Still, I'd waxed and polished that bed endlessly, trying to get rid of those dead smells, one of many silly things I'd done to please Danny.

"It just smells old." I'd pull down the covers while Danny took off his shirt, rub the smooth skin of his tight back with one hand. "We'll be old one day," I'd say.

"Not if I can help it." Danny would push me down on the bed with the same kind of blunt gesture his younger brother Po used to make himself understood. Easing down on top of me, he'd make his declaration with a tight kiss, then start to fumble with my clothes, yanking and pulling until he got so frustrated he'd stop and groan, "Why do you wear all this damn stuff, Leo?"

No answer would have satisfied him. I wore what I'd always worn, old clothes with buttons and lace and ties, things that gave a lover trouble. While Danny fumbled and muttered, I'd try quietly to help—slipping my tangled clothing down over my feet into a heap at the end of the bed. I'd look at Danny's muscled chest and follow the line of fair hair from his navel downward, shocked every time to think he'd soon be inside of me. I'd wind my arms around Danny's thick neck, and he'd whisper "Leo" into my hair, and then, with square hands that smelled faintly of fish and lemon juice, we'd make rocky love.

Danny's caresses were frenzied, jagged. Every time, I wondered how hands so skillful with a wrench or a piece of fish, which spanned a football or dealt cards with such grace, which hefted a hockey stick as if it were a wand and ruffled his brother's hair with such gentleness, could be so clumsy and rough with me. Through it all, his lips would stay shut, unwilling to get entangled. As we pressed together, naked and hard—in that one moment of silent, trembling heat—I always felt that we did this thing as children might, in perfect imitation, but without real understanding.

As Danny rolled off me into sleep, I'd lie still and silent, vowing the next time to tell him to slow down, to be gentle, to lie still with me for a while. I'd ask to hear the story of the hammer-shaped scar on his thigh, or make him tell me about the economics class in which he struggled so, about business at the fish market, plans for a day in the future we might share. I'd ask him to rub my back and stay for breakfast, instead of slipping away so early as he always did, leaving no trace or smell, before the dawn broke, as if to be caught in the light trap of a sunbeam would somehow inculpate him. Out on the sidewalk, he'd zip up his jacket and comb his hair with his fingers, and then, as I watched from the window above, he'd fly.

* * *

The sun made a sudden, lurching dip out of the clouds and I pulled the tweed coat tighter around me. A homeless man curled up on the bench beside me. He yanked his pants down over his thin legs, scabbed and bloated at the ankle, trying to get comfortable. His laceless shoes were crushed at the heel. The smell of chocolate, thick and warm, oozed across the street from the bakery. I felt a dark, wet presence at my back. Danny bent over and told the man to get up, to keep the blood moving through his veins.

"Danny," I whispered. "Danny. It's me. Here. On the other bench. Next to the old man."

But Danny couldn't see me, couldn't hear me. He saw only the old man, his scabby legs and gaunt face, saw only his misery. "Get up, man," he said. "You're going to freeze if you don't keep moving."

The man didn't move, didn't answer, though his eyes were open wide.

"I'll take care of him, Danny." I nudged the man's shoulder gently. "I promise. I will."

But the man wouldn't budge, and Danny wouldn't hear of it. Neither of them would listen to me. Neither of them could hear.

Getting up from the bench, I took off Lydia's tweed coat and spread it over the man's legs. I walked away from Inman Square and the McPhees' house and my apartment back toward my parents' house on Cobb's Hill, zigzagging the side streets until the three miles seemed like six. In the winter sky, a sliver of a moon waited its watch. As the day let go all light and the snow started to stick on the ground, I started up the hill. And slowly, as I walked, Lydia's villain cold took hold of me, wrapped itself around my body and crept inside to let loose its fever. And I was glad, glad to be sick, glad to know that someone would have to take care of me while I slept, at least for a while.

chapter four

What I remember most about those first days back in my parents' house were the hot forces that fought the cold in me—the fever that dipped and swelled and the morning sun that gathered in my feet and crept no higher than my knees, spoonfuls of hot liquids sliding down my throat and the heat of smoldering bad dreams. I slipped in and out of dreams filled with teaspoon faces—people thrashing in a swimming pool, checkout women at the supermarket, shoe salesmen, kids from grammar school. My father came and went. The spoons that fed me were by his hand—broth and tea, tea and broth. The smells of consommé and chamomile wafted in and out of my senses. Trapped in sickness and sleep, I tried to escape from my dreams to the places I knew I should be—my job at the music store in Harvard Square, my classes at the Conservatory, practicing my violin back in my apartment, working on my thesis. I slid endless coins into broken payphones, trying to get through, trying to explain that there'd been an accident . . . that I was on my way.

Danny's funeral must have come and gone. I never asked. I never heard. I didn't want to know what was going on outside of me, about the drought-stricken grapefruits in Florida or bombs lurking in airport suitcases, babies waiting for kidneys, wars on the brink. Had I been out of my bed, Lydia would have reported catastrophe brewing as she heard it on her radio, always the keeper of dire and timely news. But I didn't see Lydia during those days. As had long been our habit in this house, we kept to our own selves, our own spaces. She didn't come upstairs and I didn't venture down. I lay still. Time lost all context and meaning; light slipped into dark and back into light. I heard every moth's flutter, every page rustling, every drip, every creak on the stairs. I felt every tic of my body, every heartbeat, every twinge. The world rocked and swayed as I lay in bed, breathing softly, shivering, afraid for a time that death had designs on me too.

I slept for days, rolling in and out of bizarre dreams. Danny's hands wriggled in and out of them, shooting up after scoring a goal, snapping a hockey stick in midair, playing checkers with his younger brother Po, sliding hard up the sides of my body, pushing flesh to bone, my face losing all of its features at his touch. His long fingers moved chess pieces onto squares that swallowed them whole or spit them back out, broke off tape from a roll to seal the fish packages in the market. One by one, the customers would disappear, leaving us alone. We'd get tangled up in the tape, frantically trying to make love in a dark pool of wishing pennies, but sinking instead, flailing, sinking back to the place the fish had come from—deep, dark, underwater.

In the water dreams, *I* was the one who couldn't get out of the car. Slowly, we'd sink to the bottom of the river. Danny would slide ghostlike through the windshield. I'd smile and wave. He'd come around and try to help me, but my legs would be stuck under the seat, bent in an impossible way. "You go ahead." I'd motion him upward to the surface. "I'll fix my legs. I'll be up later. Go on. I'll be fine." I'd lie contentedly. It was all right. Relief. Dreamlike justice. Danny would fly effortlessly through the roof of the dream the way I'd seen him barrel over the ice to catch a spinning puck. In a cloud of bubbles, he'd disappear. Back to life. Back to *life*. Later, he'd send my violin floating down. I'd reach out to catch it but my arms would shrink back into themselves, back, back, slowly, until they were no more than stumps. The violin would twist and turn as it sank, scroll to chin rest and back to scroll, until it bounced silently on the murky, dark bottom of the river, which exploded in a muddy swirl at its touch.

Out of the dark water one night came the sound of my name being called. Danny had just spun up in a whirlpool out of a dream. My neck and chest were wet with sweat. No moonlight came through the attic window. I had trouble swallowing; my heartbeat tripped over itself. One of Danny's old hockey jerseys was bunched and twisted around my waist. I'd worn it for days, still believing it carried his faint odor, although I'm sure by then it reeked only of my own rank smells, the clotted perfumes of sickness and long sleep. As my eyes grew accustomed to the dark, I made out my father's slight figure by the door.

"Leo. Are you all right?"

"I'm fine." I pulled the blankets up tight around me. "What time is it?"

"Time?" He looked around for a clue. "Oh, it must be terribly late," he said. "Or terribly early, I suppose." I pulled my legs up into my stomach as he sat down on the edge of the bed, the feel of Danny's dream hands still on me. "I heard your voice," he said.

"It was just a dream."

"You didn't make it?"

I shook my head.

"I used to have dreams about dying."

"You were in a war," I said. "It's no wonder."

"What happened to you was like a war."

"Of my own making," I said.

"The accident wasn't your fault, Leo."

"I know, Dad," I said, looking up at him. "And the war wasn't yours."

I didn't want to talk about dying with my father. Or dreams. Or war. Most of all about blame. But I was curious, always, hungry for what he could tell me—about all of us, about the past. I knew that he'd been drafted into the Army and gone overseas. Beyond that I only knew that the war had changed him forever.

"Did you ever kill anyone, Dad?" I asked him.

"Kill anyone?" He straightened up on the edge of the bed and laughed. "Heavens, what a question. Accidental poisoning, maybe."

"Poison?"

"I worked in the kitchen, Leo. I cooked a mountain of hash, an ocean of scrambled eggs. Thank god, the Army never gave me a gun. I think they knew I couldn't use it."

"You would've done what you had to do," I said. "I know that now. When you're in danger, you don't have time to consult the rational part of your mind, or your conscience. You act on instinct."

"I've never really been sure about my instincts," my father said. "If it hadn't been for your mother . . . Anyway." He smiled. "Somebody had to do the cooking. We all had to eat. I made the soup out of whatever I could find. I got to know them all. Who liked cornbread and who couldn't stomach cabbage, who ate kosher and who was allergic to nuts. It always seemed so completely . . . absurd—to feed them and then send them back out." He brought his hand up to his temple. "And every time one of them didn't come back, I dreamed the soup boiled over me and I died."

I looked at his eyes, which I knew would be teary. "You still have those dreams?"

He shook his head. "I stopped feeding them, Leo. A long time ago."

"Feeding them." I pulled the covers up more tightly around me and shivered. "Okay, Dad. I'll bite. What do nightmares eat?"

"Fear," my father said, eyes narrowing in the dark. "Plain and simple, old girl. They eat fear."

The next morning, I went downstairs for the first time. The sun was low in a colorless sky and my fever was gone. Dizzy and weak, I reached the bottom of the stairs. From the kitchen came the smells of toast to steady me. I stood in the hallway and pictured my father, alone in the kitchen, buttering the barely warmed bread for Lydia, cutting it into triangle shapes and carrying it upstairs to her on a tray with a cup of lukewarm tea. So many times I'd thought to suggest that he make the tea after the toast, so that it would stay hot, but he wasn't the only one in our family who feared the revenge of broken ritual.

I stood by the door, face pressed flat against the hallway wall, the spy I'd been as a child. I peeked inside the kitchen and quickly back out again, my eyes chased by what I'd seen. The picture froze neon on my brain, twisted, glaring, all wrong. A giant box of cereal, bright blue with blazing orange letters, was centered on the old wooden table. That was not so odd. And my father sat in his usual chair by the window. But across from him, in a chair I'd always thought of as mine, sat Lydia, something I'd never known her to do before. My parents were eating breakfast together, pouring milk, lifting spoons, murmuring. I stepped over the threshhold into the kitchen to shatter the tranquil scene.

"Leo!" My father's chair tipped backward and fell as he rose. "You came down." He followed the course of my confused eyes, picked up the fallen chair, spoke carefully. "Lydia's decided to join us for breakfast, too," he said. "Isn't that wonderful?"

"I don't always feel up to it," Lydia said, as if she often did.

"Let me get you some coffee, Leo. Here, sit down." My father's voice shot out warnings, to be careful, to be kind, warnings that the winds had changed. He didn't need to tell me. This was the kind of small miracle we'd given up on long ago—Lydia sitting in the sunlight with a bowl of Cheerios, Lydia come down for a bite to eat. I'd always accepted the fact that my mother wasn't able to be part of the world as we knew it. As a child I'd been told, simply, that she wasn't well. Every wish that had ever come my way—on every eyelash, wishbone or star—had been spent trying to make Lydia well. But it only seemed like betrayal on this morning, to find her planted in my chair at the table which had been my father's and mine for so many years, on this day when I needed to find courage in the familiar.

"Sit down, Leo. I'll make you some toast," my father said. "How 'bout you, Lydie, another slice?"

"Maybe just a half, August," Lydia said, though her first piece lay untouched. "Your father says you haven't been feeling well, Claire."

"Marmalade, Leo?" My father's voice strained again.

"I'm feeling better," I told Lydia. "No. No marmalade. Thanks."

"What on earth are you wearing, Claire?" Lydia's hand took hold of the handle of her tea cup. This had always been her way of anchoring me, by tracking what I wore, as if a dress or a shoe could tell a lucid tale.

"It's one of Danny's old hockey jerseys," I said, pushing up the sleeves.

"CAMBRIDGE ROCKETS?" Lydia read the letters that arched across my chest in gold. "Danny was a rocket, was he? Then a Harvard man. Not the right boy for you, I think. I had a feather boa once, a gift from a Moroccan prince who came here to study. He confessed he'd bought it in Chicago. I wore it only once. It smelled like ginger. Still, to this day, when I smell ginger . . ." But she lost the thought then, no longer someone who tripped the light exotic—Pullman cars, princes, lace and ginger. "But then . . ." Lydia's eyes turned away. "Danny's not at Harvard any more, is he?"

My father shot me a dark look.

"No," I said. I wasn't strong enough that day to do battle with my father's pleading eyes, to get caught in Lydia's web of confusion. I sipped at the strong coffee my father had poured me. Lydia's radio murmured at her side, cord stretching in a taut line to the wall socket. After the news, the sports came on. Lydia got out a small spiral notebook she often carried, and made notes, murmuring all the while.

"Celtics 96. Sixers, 87. That's seven straight," she said.

"Seven straight what, dearie?" my father asked.

"Seven straight wins on the road."

"Is that a lot?"

"Not for the Celtics," Lydia said. "They haven't had a losing record on the road since . . ." She leafed through her notebook. "Oh, it's not so long after all. 1979."

Nothing Lydia knew or said astonished me anymore. To my knowledge, she'd never held a basketball or been to any kind of sporting event, and yet she knew all of the Boston team players, their names and heights, hometowns, birthdays, favorite foods. She knew their injuries and the names of their wives, their free throw averages and their shoe sizes. Many years later, when I had occasion to look through Lydia's notebooks, I'd find pages and pages of these statistics, recorded neatly on faint blue lines.

Lydia knew these facts just as she knew about evangelical trends and natural disasters, ways to fight off zucchini pests in the garden, who wore what to the Academy Awards. She'd gathered more trivia about the world she'd left behind than anyone who still tramped in it ever could. The voices on the radio were her contacts to the outside world—putative friends, mentors, devil's advocates—and she listened to them with careful interest, in return for their good company.

I looked at the woman who'd borne me twenty-two years before, as she wrote in her spiral notebook, once so beautiful, so talented, my father said, she'd had the power to shatter glass. I saw her robin's egg skin, almost like the blue in parchment, so long untouched by sun or air, there was no telling what might happen if she were to step out into a glare or a gale, if she might not crumple or scatter like ash. I saw the bones that poked through at every turning point in her big-framed body—in her cheeks, in the wings of her back, at her wrists, at the base of her long neck and forming the ridge of her chin. Had the flesh filled out the bones, she would have been a regal woman still, the way I'd heard she was before her breakdown, when she used to sing opera.

"The Celtics have a fellow named Larry Bird," Lydia said. "They say he could be the best ever. He earns millions of dollars. Can you imagine?"

"That's a lot of bananas," my father said cheerfully.

"They say Larry Bird could change the game of basketball forever," Lydia said. "Do you think so, Claire?"

"His name is Bird?" I saw a flash of light in Lydia's eyes and it scared me. "Well, can he fly?"

The doorbell broke the silence of Lydia's confusion. Her face went pale and her tea cup clattered onto her saucer. "Who on earth could that be?" she asked.

"I'll go see." My father pushed back his chair, patted Lydia's shoulder on his way to the door. "Sit tight, Lydie. I'll be right back. I'll take care of it. It's nobody, I'm sure."

"Who do you think it is, Claire?" Lydia asked, when he was gone.

I shrugged. Over the years, we'd devised so many answers to the riddle of the doorbell—who it might be, who had come, who would dare. The answers were meant to soothe—just a lost soul, Lydia, a misdelivered package, a girl scout selling cookies, no one at all. But on that morning, feeling betrayed by my mother's sudden appearance in the kitchen, I chose to sting.

"Maybe it's that Bird guy," I said. "The basketball player. Maybe he's come up here, to the highest point in the city, to look for his millions of dollars, to fly away home."

"You're joking, aren't you, Claire." Lydia fiddled with her tea cup. "You always were a cryptic child. People fly in nursery rhymes or movies or dreams. Or sometimes . . ." She looked over at me. "In songs."

"Or in a 1978 Buick," I said. "On wheels." I spread butter on my toast, felt an old rush of guilt as I let the words fly. "Floating out over the Charles River. On the wings of death."

"They say Larry Bird is always the first one on the court and the last one off," Lydia countered. "And that then he goes home and shoots baskets in his back yard. Such devotion to his game." She looked over at me, and said, "Do you think it's true?"

My father returned with an envelope in his hand.

"Who was it, August?" Lydia asked.

"The census taker." He took his seat again.

"The census taker? What did he want?" Lydia grew agitated. "Did you tell him that Claire was staying here? They may count her twice." The small piece of toast in her hands turned to crumbs under her fingers. "How did they ask the question? Did they say, 'How many people are living in this house?' or 'How many people are there in your family?' They should make the questions clear."

"It's a wonder someone's even keeping count," I said, imagining the census taker at Danny's door, the falter in Mrs. McPhee's low voice as she reported one less child.

"I explained everything, Lydie." My father spoke in a soothing voice. "He seemed like a fellow with a brain. I think he understood. I think he got it right away. They'll only count Leo once."

"They should only count me as half," I said. "That's what I feel like now. About half."

"Why?" Lydia looked over at me in alarm. "What's wrong, Claire? August? What's wrong?"

"Tell her, Dad," I said, giving him a pointed look. "Tell her what's wrong."

"Nothing's wrong, Lydie." My father patted her arm. "It's over, now. He's gone. Done and gone. Here. Have another piece of toast."

But Lydia had been undone by the coming of the census taker and could no longer sit with us at the table. She wandered away, muttering to herself. "It's February. The dead of winter. And they want to know who's living here. It's an intrusion, really. Couldn't they send it by mail?"

"You didn't tell her," I said to my father when we were alone.

"I couldn't, Leo. I just didn't know how she'd take it."

"You're the only one who can make her understand, Dad. I've told her a dozen times."

"She actually came down for breakfast, Leo," he said. "I can't believe it."

"What happened?" I asked.

"I don't know." A smile cracked the smooth, weary surface of his face. "I don't dare ask."

"She just appeared?"

"Just like that." The smile wobbled and broke, full and wide. "She walked right into the kitchen, plain as day. Asked for a cup of tea. It's almost as if . . ."

"As if what?"

"I don't know." My father's hand drew a circle in the air. "As if she's coming back to us, Leo. After all this time. Maybe she's coming back."

I lifted my coffee cup, lowered my eyes. To him she'd be returning. To me she'd be coming for the first time. Sitting there with my father, I tried to remember another time when Lydia had sat down in the morning with us for breakfast. But either I couldn't reach that deep into my memory or she never really had. My mother wasn't well. She didn't eat breakfast just as she didn't do so many other things. Over the years, my father had tried to explain why Lydia was different—in bits and pieces. In so many words.

Who knows how how much of Lydia's illness began as a lump inside her, how much she swallowed along the way. The only child of two classical musicians, she'd been born with a voice that would leave the world breathless, a once-in-a-century voice, I'd heard it called. From what I can gather, Lydia was a gifted but difficult child, pushed relentlessly by her parents, who gave up any ambitions they'd ever had for themselves, to foster hers. She had no childhood to speak of, no time to play or idle, daydream, giggle, swim. No time to do anything, really, but sing. Her wild mood swings were tossed up to the artistic temperament. No credence was lent to her unpredictable explosions, which seemed to have minds of their own and left her trembling and damp in dark corners. Shirley Temples with stemmed cherries, pretty new dresses, jeweled tiaras and silver dishes of creamy ice cream. These were the rewards for her hard work and good behavior, the remedies for her distress. No one paid any real attention to Lydia's odd lapses in memory, her fear of grocery stores and wide-open spaces, her mother's harsh voice, the thumping of a fearful heart.

Every night, on her knees at her bedside, palms joined and raised, Lydia prayed to be the best.

"*Tell God, Lydia,*" her mother would say. "*Tell God how you practice your singing every day.*"

"*I practice my singing every day,*" she'd say. "*Every day.*"

"*Tell God what a good girl you are, Lydia.*"

"*I'm a good girl, God,*" Lydia would whisper. "*Good girl. Good girl. I'm a good girl.*"

"*Of course you are,*" her mother would say. "*God's watching you, Lydia. God sees everything. God knows.*"

After prayers, Lydia's mother would cup her hands together and together they'd look through her wrinkled palms into a crystal ball.

"Do you see what I see?" her mother would ask. "A beautiful young lady, singing an aria on a shining stage. The crowd is cheering and clapping. Crying out for more. Can you see?"

"Yes," Lydia would whisper, shutting her eyes as tightly as she could. "I can see."

In Lydia's glass music box, her voice was the clearest, most commanding sound. No one ever thought to help her rid that box of its tiny demons, imps of the id that squatted in its corners and nipped at her toes when no one was watching. She learned to sing them out, to deafen and flatten and blow them through the cracks in the glass, back to the dark corners in which they lay in wait. And on those occasions when even her own voice seemed to frighten her, when she was found in a trance, or when she'd flee from a solfège lesson to a bathroom stall, when she just plain forgot the notes of an aria she'd sung perfectly an hour before, she'd be given a scolding and a sedative, a careful smile, a peck on the cheek, a long look back into the crystal ball of her mother's weathered hands, where the beautiful girl slowly melted into a puddle of black tears on the stage, while the crowd, now turned ugly, hissed and booed.

Lydia's career had been carefully charted. In her teens, she traveled all over the world, singing in small, private settings—garden parties, teas and soirées. War-torn Europe was the backdrop for her early triumphs. When she was twenty, she came back to Boston to prepare for her professional debut. It was then that she met my father at a concert they were both attending at Symphony Hall. He was seven years her senior, recently back from the war, working in the family export business. Music, he'd discovered, was the best remedy for the aches the war had left in him, the chill. He took to driving Lydia around—to voice lessons and concerts and costume fittings and rehearsals. Lydia's parents trusted my father. Nothing in his nature made him a threat. He became Lydia's chauffeur, bodyguard, confidant, masseur of tired feet, dance partner, amuser, consoler. He brought her flowers and made her chamomile tea when her throat was scratchy. No one considered him to be her lover. I doubt in those days that he even was. Prodigies didn't need lovers, after all. When and if they wanted, they took them. The Lydia's of the world needed admirers, promoters, protectors. And they had no flaws, only vagaries.

In November of 1949, Lydia was scheduled to sing a three-day engagement at Symphony Hall downtown, her first appearance on a big stage. The night before, she went to her mother. "I'm not sure I can do this," she said. "I really don't think I can."

And her mother is said to have answered her, simply, "You can, Lydia. And you will."

On opening night, as the curtains lifted, Lydia looked out into the crowd, put her hands over her face, and fled into the wings of the theater, before hundreds of people and thundering, expectant applause, chased by sheer terror, I suppose, a terror of the hushed voices and the tuning strings of the orchestra, her face drawn in caricature on the opera posters, bust heaving, mouth open wide—finally betrayed by a voice that just up and died.

The first time, it was called nerves. Warm potions were poured down her throat, careful words into her ears. She was young. Overworked. She'd had a cold. All she needed was a little rest. She went back on that same stage a few weeks later, in front of all the same people who'd come back to get their money's worth—either to hear her sing, or to watch her flounder again. The second time, it was called a crisis. A specialist was called in to examine her throat. The critics whispered; the headlines roared. I saw the newspaper article once when I was a child, tucked inside an old book in the attic, yellowed with age and clipped neatly at its edges. I read it through quickly, once, and then never again. The headline, I remember, was alliterative—DIVA DISAPPOINTS. DIVA DEPRESSED. DIVA'S DREAD. Something with D's. Whatever it was, I understood that it all spelled doom.

Lydia was sent off to rest, thought to have been pushed too hard, too soon. She spent several weeks with her mother's sister, her Aunt Claire, in New Hampshire, where she rested and read, got her appetite back, began to heal. Impatient for Lydia's career to resume, her mother brought her back to the city, where she was consoled and counseled, reassured and restored, but by those who read notes and not psyches, those who puffed her up when she needed to be bled.

The third time, months later, on a smaller stage, with no posters and the lights not quite so bright, Lydia sang the first three notes of an aria and collapsed, came to on the floor not remembering her own name. It was called a fiasco, a breakdown. And then it was called over. A waste. And a crying shame. In time, the story would take on the dark, glittering hues of operatic tragedy. Lydia had unwittingly upstaged herself, played out her own "Manon." Her mother refused to talk to her for several weeks. Her father developed odd facial tics and migraines. The starmakers retreated to find a new glimmer in the sky. And Lydia was left to live in a way she couldn't possibly understand—in the excruciating silence of the present, and no longer for a beckoning future.

My father married Lydia and took her to live on Cobb's Hill. His parents had recently died, leaving him the family home and a modest inheritance. But he was unable to let loose the happiness he felt at suddenly having all he'd ever wanted—independence, some means, and Lydia, to boot—because of her great shame and despair. Ever faithful and still in love, he continued to do what he'd always done—take good care of her. For a while, Lydia's parents came to visit on Sunday afternoons. My father would pull together dinner, cold cuts on a platter, a few baked potatoes and lima beans, always giving credit to Lydia for the meal. Her mother would sit stiffly, in silence and rage, and her father would tangle his fingers together, his left eye blinking helplessly. No one spoke of what had happened. No one spoke at all. Lydia became a married woman and my father set out to be an inventor, to come up with an idea that might turn their lives around, tilt wrong back to right.

For a while, Lydia could still manage. She'd walk down Cobb's Hill to the nearest corner store, speak to the grocer and to the mothers of the children who came once a week for piano lessons. For a while, Lydia sang as she puttered around the big house, tossing seeds into a garden plot which was never tended, washing dishes that never got rinsed, sweeping floors but never bothering to gather up the piles of dirt, making plans that floated to the wind with those who were no longer a part of her world— princes, divas, phantoms, czars.

"How are you feeling, Lydie?" my father would ask from time to time. "Are you feeling better?"

"Yes," she'd say, still with a stunned look in her eye. "I'm better, August. So much better. Aren't I?"

During the second winter, an especially cold one, the walks ceased and the children stopped coming for piano lessons, one by one, and Lydia sought out no more. Her parents no longer came for dinner on Sundays. In time, the piano slipped out of tune and stood silent in its corner, a great beached and blackened whale. Soon, Lydia's voice lost its precision and its power, its resonance and sheen. The arias became songs and then hums, and finally she sang no more. Unable to bear the silence, my father bought Lydia a radio, an impulse he regretted the minute he saw the relief in her eyes when she plugged it in. He'd had no way of knowing how Lydia would fall silent before that little brown box, with its gold knobs and speakers, its ceaseless patter and song, how it would become her ear, her confidante, her voice. Still, to my father's mind, fate had been more than kind. He saw all that he had and not a shadow of what he hadn't. He wasn't a greedy man.

All this I have learned in bits and pieces from the time I spent with my father as a child while he worked in his invention room. I'd sit on a high wooden stool by his side and ask him why things were the way they were, how they used to be, before I was born. My questions were impossibly simple, impossibly hard. Why was I an only child? Why didn't we have any friends? Why didn't Lydia ever look at me? Why wouldn't she go outside? His answers were direct, always honest. Sometimes they made him smile. Sometimes they caused him pain. Lydia's tired, he'd say. The light hurts her eyes. We used to have friends. Once upon a time. You were all we ever wanted. Of course, your mother loves you. Of course she knows who you are. Over the years, I've rounded out my own corners to the busted fable that is ours, filled in the cracks, lit candles in its darkest reaches.

I am, by nature, an embellisher.

chapter five

I was, by understatement, a surprise, arriving almost eleven years after Lydia's breakdown, when she was thirty-two and my father thirty-
nine, perched on the childless rim of middle age. Too shocked to do
anything else, my father once told me, not unkindly, I think, but in
truth, they had let me be born. Lydia went through the pregnancy un-
attended. At the last moment, a doctor was called in and Lydia bore
me quickly and without much ado. I was swaddled and cared for, a
wrinkled, un-asked-for gift. I took my place in the old Baye house,
alongside the fraying furniture and the tipply lamps. Lydia's parents
were both dead by then. I was the only child of two only children. I
had no grandparents, uncles, cousins or aunts. There was no one to tell
the news.

The three of us lived high up on the rise of Cobb's Hill near the
Observatory. The house was an old Victorian, ever shabby but neat in
its spareness. It sat across from Five Moon Fields—a great expanse of
dry, weed-ridden land, a land of unhappy trees and wind-ravaged
brush. The house was dark and musty, full of echoes and cobwebs and

family heirlooms which were stored in a careless manner in the attic and fetched periodically to be sold—to pay the electric bill or fix the refrigerator or to buy new shoes. By the time I left home at seventeen, there were only a few of the heirlooms left—the china plates, the portrait of my great-grandfather Temple Byeworth, the Paul Revere silver ladle and the piano, those possessions Lydia said she'd rather walk the plank than part with.

Ours was the house neighborhood children, had there been any, would have called haunted. It sat on a half acre of land and no others were visible from any of its thirty-two windows. The yard was an unkempt jungle where I went on safaris with a broomstick and a paper bag, to collect boarders for my "Animal Hotel," a tenement house made of plywood and tar paper and chicken wire. Over the years, I kept mice and toads and beetles, a raccoon and a crippled squirrel for a time. I gave them rides on the dumbwaiter, raced them in sand tracks under the chestnut tree. I knew every nook and cranny of the house. I hid marshmallows in the old musket closet and slid down the laundry chute into the cellar. My father rigged up a net off the stairs. From time to time, I'd tightrope-walk the banister and leap into the net, calling out for help, just to see the pleasure in his eyes as he lowered me down and said, "Good thing I put up that net, Leo, old girl. You might've been a goner."

The roof leaked and kitchen pots, spotted and streaked with rust, dotted the warped wooden floors, catching the drips until the brackish water hovered at the rims and started to spill over. When we needed one of the pots for cooking, we dumped it out, though we had few such needs, preferring to make do with foods that could be eaten as they came—sliced bread and spreads in jars and wrappers, fruits and vegetables in their own skins. The stove was used to boil water for tea or to heat up brown bread and baked beans, and I don't remember lighting the oven but once on my father's birthday, when I tried to make him a cake and served him sweet goop instead, the candles sinking like passengers on a doomed ship. Among my first self-appointed chores were to empty the water pots, to get rid of the varmints in the kitchen (I'd leave a trail of cheese and bread that led to my Animal Hotel), and to tell anyone who came to the door that we weren't at home.

The old wood house was warped with weather, neglect and time. The paint peeled and the floorboards popped up at the ends. As a child, I went about fixing things, nailing and taping and spackling, carrying my tools in the leather toolbelt my father had brought home for me from the hardware store where he worked, a belt made for the thick middles of men and not the stovepipe waists of little girls. I remember the motion of yanking the belt up over the place where my hips would later form, and the feeling of it sliding down over and over again.

The ants stayed in our pantry out of loyalty or maybe just habit, certainly not because they were well-fed. The sounds of the drips and the squirrels rustling in the eaves grew to be no more than the familiar, arhythmic music of home. It all added up to disrepair, but it was grand disrepair—grand weeds and grand leaks, grand ants. My ants. My animal hotel. My echoes. My dust. My silence. *My* disrepair.

Although there were six large bedrooms in the house, I chose as a child to live up in a small attic room, which led out onto the widow's walk, pentagonal, wooden railing all around. From the time April lost its rawness until October's chill set in, I slept outside on a mattress with an old goose down quilt which sent feathers into the wind, surrounded by Chinese lanterns dancing on a string. With an old telescope of my father's, which rested on a tripod he'd rigged up, I searched the heavens above and spied on the world below. Ursa Minor and Calliope looked down at me and I, in turn, looked down to see children hiding in the bushes, picking their noses, walking on the cracks of the sidewalks, breaking their mothers' backs with each flack of their sneakered feet. I saw lovers stealing kisses, and a robber once, fleeing into the bushes with a TV set—people caught in unsuspecting acts—small secrets on a dark and lonely hill. On a clear day, I could see the Bunker Hill Monument. 294 steps. My father and I climbed it once when I was eleven.

This was the life I'd led, not because I was given permission so much, but because I was left mostly to my own devices. My parents weren't neglectful, exactly, just preoccupied, with unraveling all that had come before me, trying to collect the scattered pieces of what sense they'd made of their lives after Lydia's breakdown and before I'd shattered it with my infant cries. For the first three months of my life,

I had the colic, arching my back and crying day and night. Recuperating from my birth and not able to bear the noise, Lydia hid in a far-off room while my father walked me on his shoulder, hour upon hour, trying to soothe me. He said I turned colors that made the roses look pale. "We thought all babies were like that," he said. "We prepared for a life of calamity and tears, and then one day, you just stopped."

As the story goes, I turned into a quiet child. I suppose there wasn't much point in crying in that vast and drafty house. The cries weren't always heard and the echoes were just too loud. I never saw myself as being deprived. I understood, as children do, that there was no one kind of love and that ours was probably no better or worse. But I also understood that I wasn't a beacon, as other children were to their families. I'd not been enough of a moon to turn tides, to shed new light on past darknesses, to make Lydia well or my father successful in his work. And though of course no one blamed me, I took these to be my weaknesses, my failures. Understanding that my mother required more care than I did, I took care of myself—believing this, for a long time, to be the work of all children.

I kept my family secrets from the world, about how I washed my underwear in the sink with bubble bath and drank black coffee with heaps of sugar, how I kept my father company in the nether hours, making magic potions in the bathroom while other children slept, how I wandered the house in my mother's old opera costumes, looking for secrets and stones unturned, gathering animals for my hotel, how holidays and birthdays passed without a whisper or a rustle, how my mother was a phantom of the opera and my father a wizard by night. I kept these secrets because I was afraid someone would find them out and take me away. It wouldn't matter how happy we were, or who was to blame. Either way, I'd be the one who'd have to go.

The attic was my kingdom. I kept a stack of crackers and a jar of peanut butter by my bed, a supply of water in my father's old army canteen. I read books. I wrote letters to ghosts and dead relatives, to the tooth fairy to let her know I knew she wasn't real. I dressed up in Lydia's old opera clothes—silks and taffetas with bodices and frills, hoops and empire waists and bustles, dresses she'd somehow managed to bring home with her from the theater, hardly ever worn. I fanned myself with a silk fan and sipped sherry out on the widow's walk, from an ancient, crusted bottle, pretending it was slow, deadly poison. I tried to make my voice shriek and flutter, the way I imagined Lydia's had before she lost her nerve on the stage that night. And then, with my arms lifted to the sky, I'd fall to the ground and die.

When I heard the stairs creaking, it was sure to be my father, come up to unearth one of the heirlooms from the boxes in the room next to mine, looking older each time he climbed. I'd peek in and watch him rummage, and when he saw me he'd smile and mumble something about the furnace or the faucet or some other treacherous, failing part of our old house which had sent him climbing, and meant one more tumble in our fall.

"We're not rich anymore, are we?" I thought to ask this question once when I was about eight. I was helping him search through some old boxes to find a silver salt shaker that had to be turned into new window sashes.

"Rich?" My father looked up at me in surprise. "When did you ever think we were rich, old girl?"

"We have such a big house," I said. "And all of Lydia's fancy things."

"Oh, Leo," my father said.

"Why are you looking at me that way?" I saw pity in his eyes and I couldn't stand it. "Why do you say, 'oh, Leo'?"

"All this time, and you so willing to call a little bit a lot," he said. "We could've named you Faith."

"I hate that name." In a flash, I saw how true it was, what it all meant, our bending down on our knees this way, pawing through the tarnished riches of the past. The meaning of poor. Not hungry. Or homeless. But poor of spirit, poor of courage. My father and I rummaged in silence. When I found the salt shaker, I blew the dust into his eyes.

For generations, the house had been passed down from son to son, tended by maids and gardeners and tradespeople well paid. But my father hadn't inherited the Baye knack for business, and made short work of the family fortune soon after his father died, eating through it with gifts for Lydia and parts for his inventions. When the money was gone, he'd had no choice but to go out and find a job. Ever since, he'd struggled along on what he made working at Burrow's Hardware Store in Davis Square. The house had slowly fallen to shambles. I was the end of the Baye line, and I was a girl. Had my father been a different kind of man, he might have made me feel that this, too, was my fault, my failure.

When I was six, I joined Mrs. Halligan's first grade class at the old Curley School, down on Chauncy Avenue. In Mrs. Halligan's class, on pain of being sent to sit in a corner wearing a pointed dunce cap, suns were to be painted yellow and oceans blue. The bathroom could only be reached in a straight line, and the word "ain't" was frowned upon, even if it was in the dictionary. The alphabet had twenty-six letters, no more, no less, no matter how much you were tempted, as I often was, to add a new squiggle or sound. Two plus two could only ever equal four.

I thanked whomever or whatever had made order from above out of all the chaos on earth. I saw how blissfully simple these rules were, how easy to follow, how saying please and not wandering over the lines of the coloring books brought praise, and how even the punishments for lesser crimes such as chewing gum or daydreaming held a kind of pleasant satisfaction—writing, "I will not dawdle in the lavatory line," one hundred times in your best penmanship, and not really having to mean it. School was not the place for playing cards or tricks, fidgeting, farting, acting out. School not was the place for having fun.

My other saving grace as a child, besides being what Mrs. Halligan called a good little worker, was my looks. Old ladies cropped up in un-likely places to straighten my collar or brush the hair from my eyes. "Poor dear," they'd mutter. "With a little work, she'd almost be pretty." They were able to fuss for a small minute, somehow knowing the work would never get done. I could make no sense of my looks— green, upturned eyes and unruly black hair, long neck and high cheek-bones. In my family, appearances were neither mentioned nor judged. I felt like a Martian when I lifted my hand to my heart at school to say the Pledge of Allegiance. To the Republic, one nation, under God. I had no sense of our nation and I didn't believe in God. I couldn't. I could only believe in what I could see and feel and touch. My shoes were too tight. My clothes didn't match. My teeth and my heart ached all the time. At school, I heard voices faintly through a long tunnel. I talked to the Eskimo girl on the UNICEF poster, asked her to tell me about the cold, wintry place she lived, to tell me what she saw when she looked at me.

I kept my fingers crossed and hoped it was true, what the old ladies said, that with time or care, my looks might change. And though secretly I laughed at them when they pinched my cheeks and I called them loco, to this day I look fondly and with some fear upon these alchemists who roam the streets and supermarkets, masquerading as old ladies with blue hair and gold-clasped purses, the ones who used to wipe the smudges from my cheeks and tuck the tags into the back of my neck, the ones that could have made me pretty, if they'd wanted to, with just that little bit of work.

My father felt only distaste for money and tried to avoid its use at whatever cost, acting in ways that made other people think him cheap or eccentric, drinking slightly sour milk, fixing the old boiler in the basement time and time again with wire and duct tape and spare bits of metal, wearing the same clothes year after year, chopping my hair underneath the rim of a bowl, using half a towel to dry himself, and making do with tiny bits of things—butter on toast, toothpaste on toothbrushes, pencil stubs and paper scraps. And this the same man who came home at night with perfume for Lydia, orchids and dark chocolate, fancy pears wrapped in crinkled lime-green paper.

We had no lawn mower or washing machine, no new fangled gadgets in our house. I always thought that it might hurt my father's feelings to own an invention that wasn't his own. I discovered television at Rosalie Parker's house. Rosalie Parker was my one childhood friend, although friendship wasn't really the word to describe what happened between me and Rosalie, more a grudging truce of misfits. We met in school in the fourth grade. I was quiet and shy. Rosalie was loud and hard. We fit no one's bill. We didn't dress right; our timing was off. Old shoes and nervous eyes gave us both away. We smelled peculiar, she of sour milk, me of mildew. People thought we were stuck-up, but we were just scared. And because for a time no one else would have us, Rosalie Parker and I took each other.

Rosalie lived in a beat-up modern house a ways down the hill. She, too, was living on the tail end of a once good thing gone bad. Her father had made a fortune managing a teen singing idol—Jackie Bo Breen—whom he'd later shot and killed with a gun in an argument over money. He'd fled the law soon after, leaving his family in the house he'd had built for them on the low rise of the good part of town.

There Rosalie lived with her mother, Lila, and her younger brothers and sisters and any number of different uncles, as they were called. I remember each one—Uncle Hal the chain smoker, Uncle Bob the whistler, Uncle Floyd the lisper, and Uncle Billy, the toucher. The TV or the stereo was always on. No one ever seemed to care if I slipped through the unlocked door and sat on the leopard skin couch, where a half-eaten bag of corn chips was sure to be leaning. I'd sit by the hour, mesmerized, watching "Leave it to Beaver" reruns or the Hillbillies or the witch who twitched her nose. I studied the TV mothers. They wore aprons and smiled. Soft music played. Laughter rolled from a can. They put their hands on their hips, shook their fingers, gave hugs, scoldings, caresses, advice. They curled their hair, dabbed perfume on the napes of their necks, chatted on the phone, opened oven doors and took out steaming pies. Humming mothers in a black humming box. As good as aliens to me. The only thing these mothers seemed to have in common with Lydia was that they never left the house.

Babies and children drifted in and out of Rosalie's living room, leaving trails of crumbs and toys, the aroma of warm milk and wet hair and half-filled diapers hanging low. Her mother, Lila, sat by the hour, legs twisted up underneath her in an old armchair, sucking butterscotch candies, filling out the quizzes in the *Ladies' Home Journal*—"Do You Really Know How to Please Your Man?" Patsy Cline wailed on the stereo; Kents burned down to the filter in the ashtrays. She'd get up to wash a dish here or there, fold a towel or a shirt. She'd slip off with one of the uncles into a room and reappear, mussed and crumpled, hug her children at every small tragedy, saying, "It'll all come up roses, sweetheart, just you wait and see," or "Here, honey, come and let me wipe that snot off your nose." If I were there, she'd hug me too, press me close to her bursting chest and murmur, "Sugar, you smell different from the rest."

I never thought to ask my father for a television, not so much because I was afraid he wouldn't get me one, but because a TV didn't belong in our house, just as washing machines and food blenders and hair dryers had all been bidden to stay away. Even the morning toast that became my father's ritual of love to Lydia was made on a four-sided wire contraption, which sat on top of the gas stove, long after toasters became affordable. The bread slices lay at an angle, backs to the licking flames, roasting like sunbathers against a granite slab. The laundry danced out on a sagging rope in the back yard and met the tips of the uncut grass, got soaked in the rain and dried by the sun over and over until it hung stiff and bleached and my father or I thought to collect it. The "Magic Pulley" that my father had almost invented lay in a tangled heap in the yard. The rusted "Space Shot Sled" leaned up against the back of the house. The only appliance that plugged into a socket in our house, besides a few old lamps, was Lydia's radio, which traveled with her everywhere. By keeping herself tethered to the wall, she was in no danger of getting lost. The radio was on day and night, a low buzz, like a pestering bug noise. When I didn't hear it, I worried.

Like my parents, the house was old and odd, but for a long time, I felt safe there, lost in a long-ago time when horses galloped and forests lay untouched, a time in which my family would have made more sense, been less of an anomaly. I was a Byeworth. And a Baye. I clung to the old, the rumpled, the weathered. As a child, I studied our family tree, framed in gold in the living room. I knew every great-uncle and cousin—men by the names of Jedediah and Ebeneezer, Nathaniel and Ezekiel. I knew all of the occupations and illnesses and skeletons to be found in our moth-eaten closets, the white sheep and the black sheep

.

alike. The women were named Verity and Hanna, Tryphena, Patience—even a Submit. I wondered how many of them had been happy. In the end, they'd all died young.

chapter six

 W hat Danny saw in me—or I him—I still can't say. The answer drifts in rusty, cragged pieces along the bottom of the Charles River. No question, we were an odd duck pair. By the time I met Danny, I'd grown strong in a twisted way, like a broken bone left to heal by itself. I'd gotten good at pretending that I wasn't the way I'd always felt—different, clumsy, and strange. In 1979, I was nineteen years old. The era was amorphous, indifferent. I wore high button boots and second-hand clothes, in an age when polyester and perma-press still knew no contenders. I had wild, thick black hair, a long neck and narrow, up-turned eyes. Almost everywhere I went, I carried a violin case. Danny would later say it made me look like a gangster. At nineteen, I had a high school diploma and was studying music at the Beacon Conservatory of Music. I worked at a music store in Harvard Square, kept an apartment in Inman Square, cooked my meals and paid my bills.

The McPhees' fish market was a few blocks away from my apartment. I'd bought fish there a dozen times before Danny and I even spoke. I found myself going back time and again, just to see his face and watch his strong hands wiping clean on the apron before he wrapped up the fish and tied it with string. I'd go to watch him as I went to the Orson Welles to watch Marlon Brando over and over in "Streetcar." I wasn't the only one. I saw the same look in other people's eyes. Danny could have cut them slabs of blowfish from the harbor. They'd have thanked him kindly and taken the bad fish home, remembering only the curve of his cheek and the blue of his eye. Danny spoke to every customer, about a snowstorm or a bad back or a Red Sox game. His younger brother, Po, never left his side. When the market was slow, Danny would sling one leg up onto the counter and read from a school book laid open on the counter, sometimes smudged with the brown stains of fish blood. He'd throw the trash into the barrel as if he were dunking a basketball, or pitch it underhand to Po. One day, he spoke to me out of the blue.

"You must eat a lot of fish," Danny said. "You come in here a lot."

"I live nearby." I felt myself blush as he wrapped up my halibut. "And I do like fish. Quite a bit."

"Quite a bit?" From the start, Danny liked to tease me.

"I live nearby."

"You said that already. I'm guessing you're an only child."

"How can you tell?" I asked.

"You're not used to being razzed," he said. "Your top lip curls all up, like this."

I pulled my top lip in with my teeth and took my package of fish. "Thanks," I said.

"Hey, I was kidding," he said softly. "You want to buy one of our t-shirts?" He pointed to a red shirt hanging on the wall. "I GOT SCROD AT MCPHEES FISH MARKET," it read.

"No thanks. It's clever though."

"You're pissed, aren't you?"

"Pissed?"

"Too pissed to go to a movie with me? I bet you wouldn't."

"You'd lose."

"You're serious?"

"I'm always serious. That's what people say."

He nodded. "People tell me that too."

"What was the bet for?" I asked him, as I turned to leave. "What did you lose?"

"Nothing." Danny's smile fell before it broke. "The way I figured it, I've got nothing to lose."

After the movie, Danny stood on my doorstep and asked if he could come upstairs.

"Why?"

"I like you." His arms slid around my waist. "You're not like anyone else I know."

"Meaning you want to sleep with me?" I turned away from Aphonse, the drunk man resting on the stoop.

"Sure he does," Aphonse slurred, with a flap of hand.

"I'd be a liar if I said I didn't," Danny said.

"He's no liar," the drunk said.

"And if I don't want to?" I asked.

"She wants to," Aphonse said. "Sure she wants to."

"Hey, I can do my own work here, pal, all right?" Danny said, and then lowered his voice to me. "Whatever you say, Leo. I'll respect it."

"Hey, he won't touch you, you don't want him to." Aphonse rose up out of his slump. "I know this guy. He's a man of his word. He's the fish man."

"Hush," Danny said.

"Hush!" Aphonse brought one finger to his lips, slumped back against the door. "Hush. Shhh. Zip it up. Mum's the word."

We went on this way for a while, under the flashing neon pizza sign. A police car skidded around the corner of Prospect, lights flashing, siren wailing. Aphonse nodded off. The liquor store closed its metal grate. I led Danny up the crooked stairs. We drank beer in the kitchen and pressed our fingers together, undressed and made quick stranger love, rushed and steamy. Afterwards Danny leaned on his elbow and traced the shape of a cross on my chest.

"You okay?" he asked me.

"I'm fine." I ran my hand along the rim of his chin. "I've been wanting to do that since the first day I saw you."

"Just like that." He gave a short laugh. "You can come right out and say something like that to me?"

"I just did."

"I never met a girl like you." Danny wound a spiral of my hair around his finger. "Where do you come from, anyway?"

"Cambridge," I told him. "I come from Cambridge, just like you do."

"Not the Cambridge I come from." Danny climbed on top of me again, pressed his hips against mine. "The McPhees are old Irish—ornery, proud, stubborn as mules. What about your family?"

"My family's proud, too, in its way." I wrapped my hands around his neck. "Eccentric," I sighed. "Well-meaning. Creative. In the end, we've all had some trouble settling on this planet."

Danny's head dipped down. "So have I," he said with a moan.

For the first month or so, everything I said seemed to please him.

Like the needle of the "Magical Metronone" he'd once tried to invent, my father came and went that winter that Danny died. My presence under his roof after so many years didn't jostle or disturb him. He went on as always, working at the hardware store by day and into the nights at home in his invention room on the second floor. We met at the breakfast table, murmured in passing on the stairs. I slipped back into the groove that had been so roughly carved out for me over the years. There were no expectations, no need to talk or inquire or plan. I was his daughter, just as I'd always been. Nothing more. Nothing less. As always, this was as comforting as it was unsettling.

As a young child, I'd loved my father dearly. He'd been older than other fathers, and different in ways I couldn't put my finger on, but which hadn't mattered for a long time. He was the one who'd raised me, who'd taken care of me. No one ever argued this. But when my second grade teacher, Miss Butler, told my father at PTA night that I should be brought out of my shell, he was shaken.

"What shell do you mean, Mrs. Cutler?" he asked.

Miss Butler never really forgave my father for butchering her name that way. I can imagine how her voice rose shrill like a teakettle whistle when she corrected him. "That's Butler. With a B! And it's Miss!" I was painfully quiet and shy, she said. Frankly, she was worried. She couldn't get me to speak in more than a whisper. Was this expected of me at home?

"No." I can imagine the kind of troubling answer my father gave in innocence and truth. "Nothing is expected of her at home."

Miss Butler probed. Was there anything my father could tell me that might shed some light on my behavior? Did I have any physical problems she wasn't aware of? Was I anxious or depressed? Was there anything going on at home? A crisis in the family? An illness?

Lydia's name rarely came up. Neither of us would have lied, but no one ever asked directly. My father came back from school that night, eyes full of remorse. "Miss Cutler says you whisper, Leo," he said. "I suppose it's all my fault."

"She's a witch," I said. "Don't listen to her."

"She says you're too quiet. I don't understand. Would she rather you were too loud?"

"She's loco," I told him. "She talks to herself at recess, and she drinks mouthwash at lunch." I tugged on my father's arm. "Come on, Dad," I said. "Let's go up and work on the 'Electric Earmuffs.' I got this great idea. You know how the fur on lucky rabbit's feet is so soft, but it's not real?"

But Miss Butler had put the fear of something into my father that night and perhaps I owe her no small debt, for thus began the era of our outings. My father would take me over to the Fresh Pond Reservoir, where we'd slip through the holes in the fence and skip flat stones, walk the wooded trails up on the high ground above the golf course, looking for bones. We'd go to Burrows Hardware Store, where my father worked, and pick out a tool, or to the auto store to get a part for the Rambler, for a swim at the War Memorial Pool, to watch men pouring cement or working the cranes at a construction site. On cold days, we'd stop at Baileys for hot soup with oyster crackers, and then sit in the leather chairs at the Cambridge Public Library and quiz each other on the Ten Commandments etched in stone above the door. THOU SHALT NOT COMMIT ADULTERY. THOU SHALT HAVE NO OTHER GODS BEFORE ME. HONOR THY FATHER. AND THY

MOTHER. If you obey these commandments, the engraved letters cautioned, you will be happy. If you don't, sorrow will rain upon you.

We made these journeys only when Lydia could spare us, when she had what my father called one foot over the rain line, when she dwelled in a warm, sunlit place in her mind, when the closing door didn't fill her with panic, when she was napping or reading, occupied or distracted enough to be left alone. I took these pleasures when they happened, and accepted the times when they couldn't, when my father would take one look into Lydia's worried eyes, slip off his coat and hang it back on its hanger, and I would do the same. And although I'm not sure I ever came out of my shell, these are good memories, and they are of my father.

Year after year, day after day, my father worked at the hardware store, where the young Mr. Burrows made him dust the shelves and keep inventory and lug heavy loads down off the delivery trucks. It was only my father's love for the tools and the coils of wire and chain that kept him there, the smells of paint and turpentine and the sparkling grit of the key machine as it spun through metal, the nuts and bolts and wire he was able to bring home at a discount for his inventions, and finally his loyalty to the elder Mr. Burrows, whose last act of kindness before he died had been to hire my penniless father, with no more than an anxious face and hungry family to recommend him. This was my father's job—his livelihood—and he was of an age and a generation that stuck to the bargains it had made with life, quite literally, to the death.

But for as long as I could remember, my father had spent all of his spare hours, night and day, in the invention room upstairs at Cobb's Hill, under the stark light of a naked bulb, puttering with wood and wire and batteries and springs, as he tried to perfect the "Easy Grapefruit Peeler," or the "Really Safe Safety Pin," or the "Last a Lifetime Napkin." When he'd finished an invention, he'd call me down from the attic, if I wasn't already sitting on the wooden stool by his side, no matter what the time, and we'd drink ginger ale and call it champagne, planning the trip we'd take to Bora Bora when our ship came in, the passion fruits we'd eat, the diamond ring we'd buy for Lydia and the new coat of paint we'd put on the house—purple or maybe lime green— toasting a life where Lydia would be well and might sing again, where my father could pluck ideas from his brain and turn them into gold, where I could sit with a book and a coconut on the hot sand, where nobody cared who I was or what I did, what operas my mother had or hadn't sung, where the breadfruits grew like weeds.

And when the "Electric Ribbon Tie-er" jammed or the "Collapsible Camera" sprang apart or the "Automatic Pillow Fluffer" smoked and wheezed, my father would shrug and say, half singing, half sadly, "Well, Leo, Rome wasn't built in a day and neither was the 'Disposable Fishtank.'" I'd climb back upstairs to my room, not having seen the failure, but only the closeness of the failed moment and all the hours we'd spent together before it came. I somehow felt safe in the secret knowledge that as long as my father's inventions flopped, nothing good in my life would change. For a long time, I was proud anyway of a father who could make things that almost worked, sure that the next invention would be the one that would bring great heaps of money to our doorstep, that would set us asail on our raft, that would buy me a star finder and an ant farm and roller skates, that would pay some doctor or wizard to make Lydia well, that would give my father the chance to tell Mr. Burrows, Junior, exactly to which hot place he could go, and he didn't mean the South Sea Islands. This would be the fortune that would buy us happiness, though Miss Young, my fourth grade teacher, said it couldn't be done.

But as the years passed, and Bora Bora drifted farther and farther out to sea, my old gnome of a father grew to embarrass me, with his rumpled clothes and gentle shrugs, the way he stumbled over his feelings and his words and his feet, the way he cried at the drop of a hat. I stopped telling him about PTA nights, told my fifth grade teacher, Mrs. Peabody, that he had a night job, and my sixth grade teacher, Mr. Graham, that his legs were bad. Questions were asked; notes were sent home. I signed them and brought them back to school. When asked about my mother, I said she was an invalid, my conscience never troubled by a lie. People nodded their heads in sympathy. They'd heard as much; they weren't surprised. For a while each year, the phone would ring and the doorbell would chime. And gradually, over time, they'd give up the ghosts they'd been sure they would find.

In the sixth grade, I fell in love with a dark-haired boy at school, Thadeus Fletcher, lean and pale and curved like a bow. He wore a perpetual scowl and drew Escher-like designs in his notebooks, stairs melting into storm clouds, birdtails sprouting champagne glasses in the sky, a formation of y-o-u d-i-e jet planes turning into bats. There was always something gruesome in Thadeus's pictures—some steely weapon or grisly body part dripping blood. He'd leave his notebook masterpieces, with their frizzy, torn edges, on top of his desk, the warnings dire—BEWARE! NO TRESPASSING ON MY MIND! TO DIE! The teachers would study the drawings, turning them around and around, shuddering before they crumpled them up in tight balls and threw them into the wastebasket.

One day I told Thadeus that I liked his drawings.

"Yeah, right," he said. "Girls really love blood and guts."

"I do." This might have been my first, yellow-bellied lie.

His eyes narrowed with a dare. "Okay, prove it," he said.

"How?"

"Cut up this worm. Into six, juicy pieces." Thadeus produced both a worm and a jackknife from his pocket and flashed the blade in my face. The worm squirmed pink and grotesque in his hand. He dropped it onto the floor.

"Go ahead," he said. "Make mincemeat out of Wanda the Worm."

I knelt down and took a deep breath. I made the first slice, then the second, chopping the worm into two, four, then six pieces, sick to my stomach as the worm sections quivered where they lay. This was the first living creature I had ever harmed, and there was no question in my mind—this was murder. I stood up on trembling legs, looked Thadeus in the eye, and gave him back his knife. "You call that blood and guts?" I said. "I don't see either."

Thadeus collected the pieces of the worm and put them back in his pocket, looking up at me from his crouch in a new way. "Are you sure you're a girl?" he asked me.

"Positive," I said. And for the first time that day, full of lust and shame, I really was.

I went home to find that my father no longer looked like a man, only someone who'd been mistakenly endowed with the male sexual organs, the thought of which made me wince from then on. Nor did Lydia look much like my new-found picture of a woman, which was something akin to a vampire-faced mermaid on the bowsprit of a ship—thick, ruby lips, breasts covered with an iron plate. By the next year, mine were huge at thirteen. I hated them, squished them down with layers of tight shirts. But Thadeus Fletcher looked often at my breasts after I cut up his worm, and one day they appeared in one of his drawings, perfectly round with small nipples at the center, two flowers below, and a knife stuck in one. I caught him off guard for one second that day, staring at me, pen still in his hand, mouth slack. The worm segments writhed in front of my eyes and I felt sick to my stomach all over again. I understood that if I could melt the steel in Thadeus Fletcher's eyes and make the ink in his pen bleed, then I had some power after all. But I could never forgive myself for what I'd done to that poor, brainless worm, the first misgivings I had about how far to go for love.

Except for her occasional morning ventures into the kitchen for breakfast, Lydia was unchanged. She'd aged little over the years, having long since removed herself from the dirty-workers of time—the wrinkle-makers, the heart-wrenchers, the bone-crackers—weather, contagion, noise. She was still beautiful in a cragged way, still something close to regal, though she ate hardly a pea. She passed the days reading the newspapers and listening to the radio—music and call-in shows, news, sports and weather, sometimes up in her room, sometimes down in what she still called the parlor.

Lydia, too, seemed to accept my being back in the house, once in a while asking how my music was coming along, to which I'd reply that it wasn't coming along at all. I'd talk to her, knowing she wouldn't hear, remembering what the doctors had told me, that silence could be my worst enemy. I told Lydia how I felt changed, interrupted, as if my life had come to a screeching halt, that a shaky hand was redrawing me and that I was at the mercy of that hand. Halt. It reminded her of a policeman who'd once stopped traffic for her in Austria. A more handsome man you'd never laid eyes on.

"It happened so fast," I said. "The car tipped to one side. I still can't believe it. I have these terrible dreams." I somehow couldn't get on with my own grief until I saw a glimpse of what I was feeling reflected in Lydia's eyes. "I got out, Lydia," I told her, breathless. "I got out of the car."

Her eyebrows crumpled, as she answered in steady non sequitur. "I saw the moon." "A boy ran a marathon with one leg. Sawed off at the knee by a train." "It's the Ides of March." "What's that smell, Claire? I could swear it's lilacs. But how could it be. It's only February."

We sat, the two of us, wrapped in winter's chill, day after day, while between us, Lydia's radio spun out its news, patter and song. John Belushi collapsed dead in a heap and Claus Von Bulow got thirty years for killing his wife. A strange virus slid into a young man's body and swiftly did him in. A crow squawked incessantly in the back yard. The last working clock in the house stopped ticking. The days somehow passed. Like the needle of the "Magical Metronone" he'd once tried to invent, my father came and went.

One morning in late February, Lydia rose up from the breakfast table. My father turned his head to watch her go. I looked at him hard for the first time since the accident. Now left with only clownlike clumps of hair on either side of his head, he wasn't a handsome man, but an earnest man still, with some measure of passion lurking still in those quiet eyes. He sipped at his coffee and stared in the direction in which Lydia had gone, up the stairs away from us, back to her private room and her silent, impassable world.

"Seven times, Leo," my father said. "She's been down to breakfast seven times in three weeks."

"Lucky number."

"Something's changed," he said. "Ever since you've come home.

She's different. I remember . . . She used to light up a room. It's been so long. Do you think she could really be coming out of it?"

"Coming out of what?"

"Her . . ." His hands whirled round and round. "Fog," he said.

"Maybe," I said. "But don't get your hopes up, Dad. I've been spending time with her these past few weeks. It doesn't feel that different."

"I hope you'll stay for a while, Leo," he said. "That's all."

"I've already stayed too long," I said.

My father nodded and turned to a large Leonardo da Vinci book that always rested beside him on the table, the bible of August, Lydia called it. Every morning, he'd leaf through the book, settling on a page to study, his way of saying grace at a meal. As Leonardo's namesake, I, too, had spent many an hour exploring da Vinci's world through his drawings. I knew them all, the bird pages, the war pages, the water pages.

Pulling a pencil from behind his ear and a scrap of paper from the book, my father began a rough sketch—arrows, numbers, dotted lines.

"What are you working on?" I asked him.

"The 'Automatic Page Turner.'" He showed me the sketch. "So a person can read comfortably in bed. Da Vinci had a similiar idea." He turned the book my way. "See? Mechanical arms. One to hold the book. One to turn the pages."

"Make this arm moveable." I pointed. "So you don't get stiff reading on just one side."

"Right." He added a few lines to the sketch. "It could slide back and forth on a pulley. Attached here."

"Only thing is, it's a lot of hardware to take to bed." I reached out a finger. "Have it start here, and go up. Make the frame out of plastic, maybe." For a moment, I slipped back onto the stool where I'd sat by the hour as a child, inventing with my father. "You could put on a small lighting track," I reached over to trace a line with my finger on his drawing. "For reading in the dark."

"Right." My father started sketching again, drawing more crude lines, forgetful of me and even Lydia for that moment, as the idea took shape, of the cereal growing soggy in its pool of milk, butter hardening on his cold toast.

I put my coffee cup in the sink and went back upstairs, where I took off Danny's hockey jersey that day, finally conscious of its stink and its sweat-filled weight. I tossed it on top of the pyramid pile of dirty laundry on the floor, which had been building since the accident. I showered and dressed, dressed so that it made some kind of sense, so that the socks matched and the shirt reached down to tuck into my pants. My hair was so tangled, a brush wouldn't run through it. Since the accident, it had been falling out in small clumps. I'd find them on my pillow, drifting down my side, clinging to my shin. I took a pair of scissors, rusted from the pelting of umpteen rainstorms, and chopped my hair off above the shoulders all around, in three crunching clips. The hair fell to the floor, a sodden pile of seaweed. My head felt relieved of a great weight. I'd been wanting to cut my hair for a long time, but Danny had liked it long.

I collected the clumps of fallen hair and went out onto the widow's walk, goose bumps rising to my skin, breath snatched by the cold. I looked out over the city. Below me the shadow of a whistling man passed down the road. A crow let out its mocking cry. Everyone else was moving forward in time. But I stood still, trapped in old footprints, old stances, ankle-deep in murky dreams. With a shiver, I realized that it was almost March, that I'd done absolutely nothing for three weeks, that I'd suddenly broken a sweat. I understood, then, what would happen if I stayed too long in that house, if I didn't keep moving forward. Soon, I'd be a child again. I opened my fists and let go of my hair. The soft wads swirled up into the February wind, as I inhaled deeply and took back my breath. Maybe denial ended there. I still don't know.

chapter seven

March was a month I'd never liked, with its stinginess of warmth and light, its blustery winds. In its early days, I squeezed myself back into the simpler rituals—brushing my teeth and hair, drinking endless cups of coffee and washing out my cups and spoons in the sink, doing laundry in the sink and hanging it out on the line. With the practice of old ritual came an uneasy sense of rhyme. Glimpses, ripples, echoes of the familiar. I felt a bit stronger, better. This must be healing, I thought. Still, I wasn't ready yet to return to the blare and hustle of my old life—to the Conservatory, to my job at the music store, to my apartment in Inman Square. The strangest fear had come over me, the fear of being alone.

My father drove me over to my apartment one evening in the Rambler to pick up a few things. My fingers played with the door handle. I thought about asking him to come upstairs with me, to keep me company. But there was no precedent for such an urge, such a question.

"Are you all right, Leo?" he asked me.

"Yeah, I'm fine." I swung the car door open wide. "I won't be long, Dad," I said.

As I climbed the crooked stairs, the smells of port wine, pizza and hairspray wrapped tightly around me. The key turned easily in the battered door. I slipped inside, hoping that my kitchen would reclaim me, as kitchens will do, that I'd fill the tea kettle and open my window wide, breathe deeply of exhaust and stale beer, yell down to my father to go on home without me.

But it was cold and still in the tilted kitchen. The echoes of my desertion ricocheted off the brown panelled walls. I stood on the edge of a cracked pea green tile. A cockroach fandangoed by my feet. A back-page MAD magazine cartoon came to mind—a giant cockroach sitting at his kitchen table with a foaming beer, watching the little humans scuttle up the drainpipe and under the sink, and I felt as if I were shrinking, soon to be one of those tiny people fleeing underfoot.

In the bedroom, I waited for Danny to pounce from under the bed and grab my leg. But if he were there, he stayed hidden, silent. As I smoothed the quilt on my grandmother's bed, the dead smells rose in dust, Danny's now among them. I cupped my hand over the wooden bedpost, felt old silences simmer, the faint stirrings of sex.

On the bedside table lay a thin strip of photos. I picked it up, held it curling at the edges like a fish that tells your fortune in my palm, looked down through its glossy finish back through time. Danny and I had slipped behind the curtain of a Woolworth's photo booth downtown one day in the fall. He was unlike himself, in a playful mood. He'd pulled me onto his lap; his hands slid up under my shirt. The red light flashed four times, catching us in bizarre twisted close-ups—Danny's shoulder and collar bone bared, my arm winding around his face, his mouth pressed to my neck, the rise of one breast exposed and Danny's hand pressing. A child had lifted up the curtain and stared.

Walking over to the window, I looked out to the west. A few blocks away, I could see the corner of the McPhees' fish market. Down below me, my father sat waiting in the Rambler. I stood in what Danny used to call the shallow end of my apartment, the cars honking below, my landlord's family, the Favolis, pounding above me, and tried to talk myself back into the place I'd called home for five years. I took a deep breath and closed my eyes. How long, I remember wondering, do you wait for a sign. And what form might it take—an itch, a thunderclap, a voice from above?

"*Derek!*" A woman's voice came in through the window, loud, weary, impatient. "*Get over here! Right now! If you know what's good for you!*"

If you know what's good for you.

I threw the strip of pictures into the trash, collected the rest of the garbage and tied it up in a bag. I gathered my music and my violin, my checkbook and a few more clothes. Writing a check in the amount of almost all that was left in my bank account, I slipped it into Mr. Favoli's mailbox upstairs, sure that I'd be back before he rapped on my door for April's rent—with a new strip of photos, Leo with a new haircut, Leo in a new shirt, Leo with one foot back over the rain line, heel rising from a rainbowed puddle.

Back on Cobb's Hill, I carried my violin up to the attic and unlatched the case on my bed. The smells that flooded forth—mingled wood and velvet and rosin—steadied me where I stood. The violin lay in its bed of deep green velvet, a smoky red brown, scroll rounded, strings loose on the bridge, chin rest tucked into its compartment, a square of shiny rosin next to the tuning fork, limp bow attached to the top of the case with metal clips, a few horsehair strands straggling. These were the objects around which my life had always revolved, those that would lie in my glass case in a museum after I died, with bat bones and a lace-up boot, and one long, black curl.

I took the violin out and held it up by its neck, amazed all over again, as I had been when I first held one as a child, by its delicate beauty. Asked at the age of six what instrument I'd like to play, I'd chosen the one that would always be beautiful, no matter what I could or couldn't do with it. Ettore Danza, an old friend of Lydia's, took me on as a student at the Beacon Conservatory of Music. For twelve years, twice a week after school, I'd taken the subway to Harborside for my lessons. From "Baa Baa Black Sheep" to Scriabin, every Tuesday and Friday, we'd toiled. He'd fussed and banged, scolded when I fumbled, clapped and cried when it came out right.

Ettore's devotion to me was his gift to Lydia. He'd known her in better days.

A trail of cold air snaked in through the crack in the window of my old attic room. I attached the chin rest, hit the tuning fork to the bookshelves and tuned up the strings. G-D-A-E. Good Day, Abbot Earl. Gina's Dogs Ate Eggs. Goodness, Darling, Ask Ethel! The verses I'd made up as a child swirled through my brain. With a shaky hand, I tightened my bow. Curling my fingers around the neck of the violin, I ran them through a few simple scales. The pads of my fingers flapped on the cat-gut strings and the notes wailed shrill and lost—E flat too low, C sharp too high. I walked the room as I played, floorboards creaking beneath me. My fingers fumbled, stiff and sore. I stepped outside onto the widow's walk. The moon was half full. I found the Big Dipper. Orion. Venus. I played the scales over and over, until my hands started to loosen up. In first, then third, then fifth position—in the major keys, and then the minor. As the strength crept back to my bow hand, the tone rose up from the strings. The notes flew out into the sky. The silences fell below. My fingers found their pace, my bow hand its stride. I played to the night, and, for the first time, to Danny, as he ripped through the Milky Way on Eddie Bauer skates, cutting a new constellation in the sky, never looking down.

I went back to the Conservatory on a Friday—the most relenting day, weekend waiting in its wings. Waking early, I got dressed, and walked outside through the kitchen door to the back yard, a jungle of bush, brush and vine. The yard was centered by an ancient, twisted chestnut tree, bare still of all green. I stood near the tree and waited for the air to settle around me, for my eyes to get used to the dull brightness of the morning light. Making my way down the flagstone path to the front of the house, I started down the hill to the bus stop.

The noises of the world shook me at close range—cat screeches and the shouts of construction workers, the cries of children and the rumble of underground trains. I hummed Vivaldi, the spring season, as I walked—down Whitney, up Dickinson, down Warren. My breath came from a shallow place under my ribcage. A light flashed in the far corner of one eye. I walked slowly, with a jerky gait, as if each step might land me in a pit of eels. The clouds lowered above me. The ground pressed from below.

The #22 bus came and I was proud like a child when I finally slipped into the plastic dish of the speckled orange seat behind the driver, proud to have gotten to the stop on time, not to have tripped on the steps or dropped my violin, to have counted the coins and put them into the gargling fare box without mishap, deeply relieved to have a destination.

"Hey, Stradivarius!" The bus driver's voice startled me. "Long time no see."

I looked over into his broad, warm face. "Are you talking to me?"

"Don't you remember?" The bus driver beamed. "Name's Phil. I never forget a face. You and that fiddle of yours used to ride my bus all the time. Then you disappeared."

"I moved away," I said. "Five years ago. To the other side of town."

"Back up on the hill again?" he asked.

"Yes," I said, watching the crest of Cobb's Hill disappear behind us. "Just for a while."

At the kiosk, in Harvard Square, a girl with purple cowboy boots and long black hair sang Dylan too sweetly. I put some change into her guitar case and headed down the subway stairs. Underground, I paced the platform, rainy day women let loose in my brain. Numbers twelve. And thirty-five. A rat swaggered across the third rail. My body stiffened as the train's headlights pierced the darkness, rushing toward me with a clattering hiss. Making my way into the crowded subway, I took hold of a pole. As the train picked up speed, a heat rushed up from my gut to the back of my eyes and pressed. I closed my eyes. The pole grew slippery under my clenched fingers. The blackness of the tunnel closed in on me as I imagined the water above exploding through the walls, bodies floating and flailing. I may have made a noise, low and last-ditch. This time I wouldn't be so lucky. I wouldn't get out alive.

At Harborside, I ran breathless out of the station, up the stairs and into the cold March air. The Conservatory rose, a great stone structure, to the east. I walked along the boardwalk, waiting for my heart to slow, for my breath to ease. I stood for a long time by the boatyard, arms wrapped around a wooden pole on the dock, looking out over the harbor and beyond. The water kept changing, now wind-whipped, then motley brown under clouds, and then for a split second, the beguiling, far-too-blue of a cunning eye. In the distance I could see the runway at the airport and the bold, painted splashes on Sister Corita's gas tanks, the bobbing masts of a few sailboats. A plane took off at Logan and I watched it soar until I couldn't tell it from the birds. And when a seagull dove into the water to catch whatever it might scrounge living, I thought for a minute that the airplane had silently crashed, until the bird came up again from under and rose awkwardly, wings struggling, flapping, into the air.

The bird found its wings and floated effortlessly away, as Danny did in my dreams. As I took the time to place myself, at that building, on that ocean's edge, a memory slid up into my throat with a vile rush—my hand clutching Danny's arm in the Buick just before we hit the water. The feeling of his skin breaking under my nails. His flinging my arm away. The thought to say something, a thought sliced in half by a slam and a wail. If you think fast enough. If you just . . . I leaned over the railing of the dock and dry heaved the memory back into the harbor. Just . . . Just in time.

Ettore met me at the door of the Conservatory, as if he'd been waiting patiently since the day after Danny died, four weeks before, when I'd gone to the gathering at the McPhees' house and missed my two o'-clock lesson. He stood in rumpled silence by the entrance to the stone building, smoking a filterless cigarette, face and hairline thick in profile as he looked out over the harbor. In all the time I'd known him, Ettore hadn't aged. He could have been fifty or one hundred; I'd never asked. I climbed the granite steps toward him and raised my hand in a wave.

"Leo." He turned as if just unfrozen in time, picking up the dangling thread of our last conversation. "You catch me in my act. Still blowing smoke out of my ears."

"You have to quit, Ettore."

"*Domani.*" He took my hands. "Today, you're back."

"Whatever's left of me," I said.

"Come." He took my violin and led me inside. The old smells of sheet music and wood and rosin and stale cigar smoke hit me head on. We walked down the long hallway, boards creaking beneath our feet, snatches of music swirling out of the cracks of doors—cello, oboe, trumpet, flute.

"First, tell me, Leo," Ettore said as we walked. "How is your mother?" He paid Lydia a visit once a year every spring at Cobbs Hill, bringing flowers and delicate conversation. He sat with her as if she were still the rising star of the opera world, sparing him a precious moment, a well-turned word.

"Lydia's fine," I said. "The same. You know. Actually . . ." The picture was still surreal, Lydia sitting at the breakfast table with a cup of tea. "She may even be better, Ettore."

"Better?" His eyes rose in surprise. "I'm so glad."

My legs shook underneath me, rusted at the joints, tired from all the walking and the jostling on the subway and the stairs. Sweat leaked from my brow. I put my hand on the door of Lesson Room D to steady myself. "Ettore," I said. "I have to explain . . ."

He raised his hand. "Your father told me everything."

"Everything?"

"He told me about the accident. That the boy was killed. You've been ill. I know. I'm sorry."

My breath started to come short and fast. My hand trembled on the doorknob. "I don't know if I can do this," I said. "I need air. I get sick sometimes. I have to move. I'll try. I'll do what I can, Ettore. But I can't make any promises."

"Promises?" Ettore scoffed. "For the birds. Don't make promises, Leo," he said. "Only make music."

I followed Ettore into Lesson Room D as I had so many times before. He sat down on the piano bench and I set my music on the wooden stand. He closed the door; I opened it again. He turned the music stand east; I turned it west. While I tuned up, he played swirls of Chopin on the piano. Slowly, my stomach settled. I set my chin on the chin rest and my bow to the strings, and we began.

For an hour I played scales, first the major, then the minor. My fingers moved up and down the neck of my violin from first to third to fifth position until they nearly bled. I kept at it, trying to make sure I'd lost nothing else in the river, the feel of distances between notes, the bend of the wrist and the touch and tilt of the bow on the strings. After a rest, when the purple ruts in my fingers had softened to pink welts and the throbbing had stopped, I started again. Ettore rounded my fingers and straightened my arms, shook the tightness from my bow hand and the stiffness from my fingers, pounding the piano at the crescendos and crystallizing the sharps, honing my staccato, impatient most of all with my sluggish sense of time.

"Two! Three! Four! " His hands crashed on the piano keys as I slowed a measure. "This is not a waltz, Leo. We are not in Vienna. Sorry to say. It's Boston. Nineteen eighty-two. Four four time. Simple like ABC. Don't forget when you fall off your bicycle."

I took the violin out from under my chin. Ettore whirled around on his stool. "Why do you stop?" he said.

"I didn't fall off my bicycle, Ettore." I rubbed the crease in my forehead where a deep ache had lodged. "There was no bicycle."

"Aye, me. I'm sorry." Ettore put his hands up to his temples. "I'm an old man. I talk too much. Too loud. The boy is dead. Half of you goes with him, Leo, I know. But I am sure, dead or alive, this boy does not like to see you lose your face."

"Face, Ettore," I said. "Just lose face."

"Yes." He reached out a hand, let it fall again. "Such a face."

I straightened my aching shoulders and played the measure again, as unlike a waltz as Brahms had intended it to be. I wove through the études until I no longer felt the pain in my fingertips. I played another. And another. And when I was done, I started all over again.

After two hours, Ettore closed the piano lid. "*Basta*, Leo," he said. "Enough for today."

"No. Don't stop. It's coming back. I can feel it. Please, Ettore. Keep playing. If you stop, I'll lose it. I don't want to lose it."

"No." Ettore took the violin from my hand. "You do yourself in, Leo. Go home now. And rest."

* * *

But I'd rested for too long, and home was no longer a clear notion. Slathering my fingertips with tiger balm, I headed for the Conservatory's library, a modern, cement hunchback on the old stone building, which edged into the harbor, backside hoisted up on steel stilts that crept underwater at high tide. Retreating to a sofa in one corner, I pulled out the heap of books and papers that so far comprised my senior thesis. Spreading it out onto a low table in front of me, I began to sort and skim and cull. It was my final year at the Conservatory. I'd spent most of it working on this paper, a study of Aurelio Macaux, an eighteenth century Austrian composer. One of his most difficult works, "Cascade," "The Waterfall Symphony," was to be my performance piece that spring, and later my audition tape for city symphonies.

But my work had suffered that year. I'd accomplished what Lydia would have called precious little. It was tempting, now that he was gone, to blame Danny. Like a bird shown an open gate when I met him, I'd flown. Slowly, I'd come to resent the demands music made on my time. I'd chosen to watch a hockey scrimmage rather than practice Mozart. I'd come breathless and late to my lessons, with no better excuse than having been lost in a daydream at my kitchen table, or tangled in Danny's arms, pressing flesh and bone. On those days, Ettore's brow would crease and he'd look into my eyes and say, "Where have you gone, Leonarda?"

"Don't call me Leonarda," I'd say. "Don't be mad, Ettore. I'm here."

"The body is here. The spirit is off in the bushes."

"I'm not off in the bushes." I'd protest half-heartedly, tighten my bow. "I'm a little late, Ettore, but I'm here. I practiced. I know the piece. Listen."

"You know the music, but you don't feel it." Ettore would wave his arms. "Something's taken you away. It's love. *Amore*."

"How do you know?"

"In hell there is a great fury, Leo. And her name . . ."

"Hell hath no fury . . ." I'd begin the proverb again and he'd break in.

"Music. The first lover. You scorn her."

"No. I don't scorn her." I'd start to play, try to woo him back to calm. "Listen. Danny's good for my music. Can't you hear it? He makes me happy."

"Happy?" Ettore would scoff. "Happiness isn't real. Only music, Leonarda."

"Don't call me that."

And on and on we'd go.

The mess of thesis papers on the library table read senseless and fragmented now, a mass of strange, undecodeable data, a language I'd known in another life. The heap of Aurelio Macaux. A brilliant composer, but a man so vile his own mother had renounced him on her deathbed, ashamed in the end to have made such an offering to family, country, and God. The father of some dozen children by three different wives, Aurelio alternately doted on and beat the members of his family, showering them with gifts and abuse, even stabbing one of his sons once in a quarrel over a pomegranate, or a woman, it was never clear. Lewd, contentious, often violent, Aurelio made a scene wherever he went. Arrested many times and dragged off to prison, he railed at the stupidity and injustice of the world, writing bleak music in his velvet-covered cell—stark, violent strains laced with slicing knives of poignancy, the passages of his remorse, I was sure. Anathema in polite society and soon in any society at all, he was banished first from the courts, then from the concert halls, and finally from the history books in any more than a cursory mention. He'd died in a debtor's prison, ranting, alone, unmourned.

I'd questioned the fairness of Aurelio's obliteration, his lonely and pathetic end. Who wasn't fascinated by the spiderweb boundaries between madness and despair? Who drew the fine lines of the id, and who really stayed between them? Some said Aurelio had been, quite literally, out of his mind. But his crimes weren't always proven, the motives unclear. The music was brilliant and his children had known some love. Wasn't everyone entitled to have his whole story told?

I took off my shoes and pulled my legs underneath me, reread a chapter in Aurelio's biography about his early years. The eldest of five children, he'd been the only son of a blasphemous, hard-drinking father and a pious, ailing mother. A bad beginning. A lousy lot. We were all victims—of circumstance, character and time. It was far too muddy and sprawling a question—evil, born or bred?

I read on, seeking the softer sides of the man. Aurelio had practically raised his four younger sisters, early resorting to a life of crime, feeding them swiped bread and bruised fruit from alleyway garbage piles. I imagined him soothing these sisters when they were sick, as their mother lay dying, warming them milk, singing them lullabies. Maybe he'd protected them, shielded them from the hand of their drunken father. He'd felt the force of that hand himself many times, and the stick, and a hot poker once—a grazing scar on his cheek told that tale.

I thought I knew how things could go awry. How easily. How swiftly. I'd cut up a worm for what I thought was love and turned out to be nothing more than desire. I'd treated Lydia badly because I so desperately wanted her to change. I'd scorned my father because I thought he was cowardly and weak. Good intentions twisted like pipe cleaners into steely snarls. Aurelio's fate could have been anyone's. Even mine. If things had been that much worse. If there'd been more children. If my father had been a drinker. If Lydia . . .

Dozing off to the soft hum of library murmurs, I woke to find the sun fallen halfway into the harbor. When I tried to read again, the words blurred and the gnawing in my stomach grew worse. A girl with thick-rimmed glasses passed by and I asked for the time. And when quarter-of-three didn't seem like enough information, I asked her what day it was. The girl looked at me strangely. "It's Friday," she said.

"What day of the month?

"Friday the twelfth." A pencil stuck through a bun in her hair. Green ferns sprouted on her shirt.

"The twelfth of March?" I asked.

"Yeah, March," she said. "Hey, are you all right?"

I must have told the girl I was fine. She went about her business and left me to mine. I didn't always hear my voice in those days after the accident, sometimes catching the echo hours later. "I'm fine," I'm sure I told that girl with ferns on her shirt that day. I gathered up my papers and got wrapped up in a gabardine coat Lydia had once worn in Copenhagen to a royal tea, and walked back down the subway stairs, one half of a day back into the world.

chapter eight

Getting off the subway one stop early at Central, I headed for Harvard Square on foot. The old landmarks passed me by—City Hall, the Orson Welles Cinema, the Old Cambridge Baptist Church. I bestowed a sort of silent blessing on each building as I left it behind, grateful for solid fixtures in a spinning world. At Plympton Street, I paused in front of Hartman's Music Store, where I'd worked part-time since I graduated from high school. When I saw my boss through the window, handing a customer some sheet music, I turned away.

I paced myself, kept my eyes steady. I saw Danny in every blond head, broad back or thin lower lip. The man selling papers and candy at the kiosk had his hands. I looked hard into his face—long nose and droopy mustache, deep-set eyes. I had to resist the urge to engage with this man in some way which would have alarmed us both, apologize for something I hadn't done, ask him for something he didn't have to give me. As I passed the man two quarters for some life savers, my hand trembled. Pulling away, I slipped it safely into the silk pocket of Lydia's gabardine coat.

The day, risen cold and grey, had grown almost balmy, as a dry wind cast a lightness into the sodden March air. I cashed my last paycheck from the music store at the bank and went for a cup of coffee at the Cafe Trocadero at Brattle Court. Slipping some change into a panhandler's palm, I followed the smell of baking bread into the café, then brought my coffee and roll outside to sit at one of the tables facing the street. A group of Morris dancers formed a circle in the brick courtyard and started to dance, hands on hips, sticks clashing in mid-air. A few tables down, a man and a woman sat playing chess. A sign was taped to the edge of the table and flapped in the breeze. "Play the Chess Master—$1." Wooden pieces moved in fits and starts; a chess clock ticked rhythmically, marking time. The chess master swooped up the woman's bishop. She shook her tightly permed head, made a noise in her throat, thought for a long while. I watched the man's tapping foot, saw mismatched socks sticking out of brown hiking boots. A streak of déjà vu spilled over me like black ink. Before. Just before Danny died. The memory seared me when it reached focus, so brilliant and clear. Following the socks up to the pants and legs and then over the table to the chest and neck, my eyes came to rest on the face of the man who'd been playing chess with Danny in the corner at Eddie's party.

My breath slowed. The chess player's face was interesting, not handsome in its parts, but compelling in its whole—thick black curly hair, dark eyes, full lips and a broad, almost simian nose. He sat patiently while the woman thought, studying the board for a long time. I watched his long, slender fingers resting on his arm. I was struck by his stillness and utter calm, as he sat amid the swirl of people and honking cars. A dark haired man. Sitting at a chessboard. The last one. The last one to talk to Danny except for me.

Kilroy.

I slid into the hard-edged arc of memory. The smaller details of that January night were slowly crystallizing in my brain—the brand of wine I'd been drinking, the reading on the gas gauge in the car, the color of Eddie's shirt at the party, the chess player's name.

"Kilroy?" I said it out loud.

The chess master looked up at me slowly, a look that first meant to silence and which then showed surprise. Cocking his head sideways, he nodded. The woman glanced upward, tugged at a wandering curl, and castled. Her edginess closed in on the game. I took a sip of my coffee. The woman punched down the button on her clock and Kilroy's hand went to his black queen. Slipping it onto a black square, he said quietly, "Mate."

The woman tipped her white king on its side. Taking an accusatory look at the board and then at me, she dug in her pocket and threw a dollar bill onto the chessboard. "Well, I guess that's why you're the chess master and I'm Assistant D.A.," she said with a tight smile. "That's justice for you."

Kilroy put the dollar into his bulging back pocket. "Thanks for the game," he said.

When the woman was gone, Kilroy smoothed his hand over the chessboard. "Man. I can feel what she left on the board."

I reached down to brush the squares. "What is it?"

"Angst," he said.

"Angst?" I slid into the woman's seat, picked up her fallen white king. "It's hot," I said. "Sticky."

"I know you from somewhere," Kilroy said.

"A party at Eddie Quintana's. You were playing chess."

"I usually am." He started to set up the black pieces again. I helped him with the white. Someone came up to the table, hesitated, then turned away.

"Should I go?" I asked him.

"No, stay." He leaned back in his chair. "It's the first day of my outdoor season. My stamina's low. I could use a break."

I sipped at my warm coffee, offered bits of my roll to my churning stomach. "You must be a good chess player," I said.

"Not good enough."

"To do what?"

"Make a living," he said. "Only a handful do."

"Music's the same," I said, pointing to my violin case.

"You a friend of Eddie's?" he asked.

"Not really," I said. "I came to the party with a friend of his. You played a game of chess with him, actually."

83

"I played with a few people that night," he said.

"He was the guy who knocked your chess pieces off the table," I said.

"Ah, yes," he said. "That guy. He'd had a few too many. You get him home all right?"

"No, not really." I spoke to ward off the panic I felt to hear Danny spoken of as if he were still alive, hiding in some small town— Malden, Fitchburg, or Braintree, still playing hockey and selling fish, as if Lydia's way of thinking was right, that people didn't die, they simply vanished into thin air.

"You two break up?" Kilroy asked.

"Not exactly," I said. "He died."

"What?" Kilroy's hands froze on the rook.

"Danny died in a car accident. Two months ago."

"Wait a minute. Was he the guy who went into the river?"

I nodded. "Danny was thinking about you, and that chess game," I said. "Just before we crashed."

Kilroy's eyes tightened. "You were with him in the car?"

"We were coming home from Eddie's party."

"Oh my God. You were the girl in the car?"

I wrapped my hand around my coffee cup. "I am the girl," I said. "Who was in the car."

"God, I'm sorry. I didn't know." Kilroy started to line up the black pawns. "I'm really sorry."

I lined up the white pawns, one by one, facing his. "It's okay," I said.

"I remember you now." Kilroy looked up. "His bishop was in trouble. You knew. You look different."

"I've been sick." I set up the last white pawn. "I've lost some weight."

"Eat," he said, pointing to my roll.

"I'm trying," I said.

"You got out of the car," he said. "You saved your life."

"Just mine," I said.

"You were dancing with Eddie."

"Eddie dances with everyone."

"Van Morrison. 'Moondance.' I know what's different. Your hair."

"I cut it all off," I said. "It was in my way." I reached up and tugged a bunch of hair down on the nape of my neck. "Men seem to notice people's hair," I said. "More than their eyes or their clothes or their hands. Do you think that's true?"

Kilroy shrugged. "If you cut it all off they do," he said.

By the time I'd reached the grainy mud at the bottom of my coffee cup, the balminess had vanished. As the wind picked up, a man came up to the table to play chess. I reached down to center the white queen on her own square.

"You play?" Kilroy asked me.

"My father taught me when I was young," I said. "He once tried to invent a fold-up leather chess set."

"He was the guy who did that?"

"No," I said. "Someone beat him to it." The man waiting to play chess cleared his throat. "I should go," I said.

Kilroy looked up at me. "I like your hair short," he said. "Come back some time."

As I got up and the man slid into my chair, I ran my finger over the rise of a vein in my neck, searched for the bump where my pulse thumped below. Kilroy brought out the first pawn and the two men bent their heads in that dipping motion that would always remind me of unanswered prayer. With a lurch in my gut, I saw Danny's head make the same dip as he passed by Mary in the Half Shell in his front yard and crossed himself, the same dip as he pushed himself into me, just before the come. For an instant, I remembered the feel of the back of Danny's neck, where the hair met the skin and bristled, sweaty and soft under my fingers, the taut stretch of his tendons and the indentations at his temples. And all I wanted was for him to come back alive.

The satin lining of Lydia's coat pocket rippled under my fingers. Across the street, at Nini's Corner, the headlines blared. As I walked, my violin bumped against my leg. I smelled meat sizzling in Buddy's Steak Pit, coffee brewing at the Cafe Algiers. At the arc of Brattle

85

Street, Brother Blue spun a tale to a crowd. A juggler juggled fire-spewing bowling pins. Local author books lined the windows of Reading International.

At Story Street, I broke into a run, dodging the parking meters and the bricks that popped up out of the sidewalk, the pedestrians and the dogs. As the sky grew mauve, I picked up speed. Dashing across Mt. Auburn just as the traffic light turned green, I ran into the line of oncoming cars. I lost my footing and stumbled. The traffic came to a jagged halt. My violin case flew out of my hands and landed on the street, bursting open as it hit the pavement. I watched the violin sail into the gutter. A woman came out of nowhere and helped me to my feet. I felt the sting of scraped palms and knees. Standing in the middle of the street, I looked over at the violin, heard the murmurs of onlookers, saw Danny all over again, lying on the ground when they pulled him out of the water, strangely limp and turning blue. A hand reached into the frame of the picture to pick up the violin.

"No, don't touch it!" I yelled.

I went over and knelt down in the gutter. The violin lay tilted, neck lodged in a pot hole full of gravel and trash. I picked it up, turned it this way and that, checked for cracks or gashes. Miraculously, there was only a flattened bridge, two busted strings, a tiny chip on the scroll. The line of traffic straightened and pushed forward again. On shaky legs, I made my way back onto the sidewalk, carrying my violin in one hand. A man collected my rosin, tuning fork, and chamois cloth from the street and followed with the case.

"Hey, Irene, play us a tune," someone yelled out.

"You want a ride, honey?" A man's voice rolled past me.

"Hey, what were you trying to do, little lady?" a voice called out. "Kill yourself or something?"

"No!" A voice shot out and I didn't know it was mine until it had spoken, its tenor so strong, its message so clear. I held the violin tightly at the neck. Couldn't they see I was just trying to stay alive?

I hurried up the rise of Cobb's hill, the last leg in my race with darkness, which now sat smug in a smouldering, orange glow. As the last shadows died, I reached the overgrown walk. And though I'd found strange and simple pleasure weaving in and out of the garbled world by day, by dusk I was glad to be back under my parents' roof, bowing to the night in passing at the door, as it stepped out to dance.

"You don't look so good, Leo," my father told me at breakfast a few days later. I could remember his telling me this sometimes when I was a child, always a bit too late, after sickness had won the arm wrestle with denial, when the chicken pox had begun to run rampant or the poison ivy swelled my eyes nearly shut. My father and I had kept sickness away on a dare, as we did other unwanted intruders—the man who read the water meter, candidates looking for a vote, flushes that threatened to be fevers, cuts that needed to be stitched.

"How do I look?" I munched full circle on a piece of toast, just the way Lydia did, I suddenly realized.

"You're a little gray around the gills, old girl." My father poured himself another cup of coffee. "Maybe you should see a doctor."

"Doctors cost money." I reasoned with him in terms we could both understand. "I'm fine, Dad. Really."

He put down his coffee and stared.

"Don't look at me that way," I said.

"What way?" my father asked.

"As if I'm not here. Not long for the world. I'm fine, Dad. The doctors checked me out at the hospital. There's nothing wrong." I made a muscle with my arm. "See? Strong like bull."

"Okay." My father picked up the da Vinci book, turned his eyes away. "It's just that you don't look so good, Leo."

But my father was right. Something *was* wrong with me, something more than waterlogged grief. I was weak, distracted, tired beyond any understanding I'd ever had of the word. Before I left for the Conservatory that morning, I reached for the mother-of-pearl mirror on my bureau. It was me I saw, only more so, a fairy-tale hag, my hair a black bush around my head, giving a sunken look to my thin face and a sharp point to my chin. I ran the hand mirror down the length of my body. Everywhere, bones stuck out. I saw the sharp bend of my elbows and the slight swell of my belly from underneath my ribs, full of all the liquids I poured inside me, always parched, always thirsty. I still could only keep little bits of food down, had lost more weight than I could afford. My breasts were the only round and fleshy parts of me, and they hung full and pendulous, an absurdity on my beanstalk of a body.

As I ran my hand over the soft skin of my belly, a shiver slid through me, a shiver I experienced as sex inverse, arousal inside out. I hadn't been touched by a human hand since Danny's father blessed me that day after the accident and sent me away. I touched my body now, pinched it and rubbed it, slapped it at its softest parts to make it move or tingle or ache. I grazed the inside of my thigh with one finger, found the crease of my leg, brushed the fold. Softly, I tried to caress, to arouse. But I felt hollow, sexless. I felt nothing.

As I pulled on my underwear, my eyes saw blood where there was none, spurting, clotting, dripping down my legs. But it wasn't red, the blood. It was black, the black of an oil spill, of a cold, cold night. My periods had always been irregular; I couldn't remember when I'd last had one. I knew that stress and shock could sabotage a woman's cycle. And so maybe the woman in me was gone. Maybe it didn't matter any more who or what I was. What a relief it would be, not to have to answer to any description—fat or thin, soft or hard, pretty or plain. To have my mirror image fade and my feet cease to leave footprints in the snow. If I spent enough time in that time-warped house, maybe I, too, would become androgenous. Maybe I, too, would become invisible.

But it was easier simply to say, as my father had, that I didn't look so good. There were powders and pills and a thousand ways to chase illness away. A sick body had a chance to get well, but a shipwrecked soul might sink forever in a moonless swamp. And because part of me worried that I might be dying, in some slow, incomprehensible way that would leave me ashen and stiff in the attic and baffle even the shrewdest coroner, I decided to go back to Dr. Early, the doctor who'd put in my IUD just after I'd met Danny. I couldn't remember her face, just a cool voice and a lumpy body, gentle lotioned hands and a no-nonsense way.

* * *

Danny'd had no patience with the diaphragm I'd been using when we met. One night as I fumbled in the bathroom with the slippery dome and jelly, he flopped back on the bed and called out, "Christ almighty, Leo. Do we have to go through this rigamarole every time?"

I remember the small, sarcastic *we* that rose up in my throat but never made it to my lips, the thought to say, "sure, I'll just have my father whip up a magic potion. And you can drink it." But, as I'd done so often with Danny, I'd held the thought, and taken it upon myself, in the early practices of sexual martyr, to get out the phone book and find a doctor.

Dr. Eleanor Early was the first woman doctor listed in *The Yellow Pages* with a Cambridge address. I went alone on a winter's day. It was done in half an hour. She asked me a few questions, felt no need to chat. I lay myself down and spread my legs, and she put the shiny looped thing inside me. I paid the bill and took some aspirin for the cramps, threw my diaphragm away. And the next time Danny and I made love, when he raised himself up, waiting for me to slip away, I pulled him back down again and said, "It's all right. I took care of it."

In what turned out to be one of Danny's more tender moments, he thanked me.

chapter nine

I stayed late in the Conservatory library on the day of my appointment with Dr. Early, working on my thesis. Getting off the subway at Central Square, I walked down Prospect to Broadway, stood for a while outside of her house and office on the sidewalk, my hand resting on the chain link fence. It troubled me now, this mesh of work and play space, to think of the doctor roaming in her nightgown among the specula and urine cups, stirring her coffee with a throat stick. It bothered me in the same way it made me shiver to think of a mortician watching TV in his carpeted living room while the powdered corpses lay below in a chilled basement, waiting to have their smiles arranged.

I climbed the sagging porch steps and rang the bell. The house didn't comfort me, as it had three years before, with its rickety tilt and guise of homeyness. This time, it looked dirty, run-down, the yard full of weeds and litter, covered by patches of dirty, pock-marked snow— unprofessional, a place you'd sneak to get a coat-hanger abortion. For a minute, I thought of going back to the clinic at the City Hospital where I'd gotten the diaphragm when I was seventeen, to walk the shiny floors and smell the sterile smells, but before I could finish the thought, the door opened and Dr. Early stood before me. Under a white lab coat, she wore a liberty print dress, blue with flowers, the same one, I was sure, she'd worn on my last visit. Her hair was straight and coarse, sliced in an even line just above her shoulders, gone to white and pulled back tightly at the temples with silver barrettes, like a child's. Thick at the wrists and ankles, she looked older than I remembered, dowdier, less crisp.

"Nice to see you again, Leonarda."

I shook her warm, puttied hand. "Just Leo," I said. "Hi."

"Come on in." She led me over threadbare carpets to a desk piled high with papers, a heap that, given the weight of one more sheet, might have crashed to the floor.

"My secretary's on vacation," she explained. "As you can see, I'm lost without her."

I looked back at the door. "Am I the only one here?" I said.

"You're my last appointment of the day. Then I'm off to a conference in Chicago. Don't worry. The medical care doesn't suffer here when Sheila's gone," Dr. Early said. "Just the paperwork." She motioned me to a chair and sat down at her desk. "Let's see. You were here three years ago, in 1979. We fitted you with a Copper Seven IUD." She leafed through my file. "So, what brings you back today, Leo?"

"I don't know. I've been feeling lousy."

"Lousy how so?"

"I'm tired. Always tired. I get short of breath. My heart races. I'm sick to my stomach and I can't eat. Sometimes . . ." I said. "I get this feeling that I'm dying."

"What of?" she asked quietly.

"Nothing specific," I said. "Nothing real. It's not such a strange feeling, I guess. I mean we're all dying, aren't we, basically, from the minute we're born?"

"That's one viewpoint," Dr. Early said. "A rather morose one in my opinion." She wrote some notes in my file. "How long have you been feeling this way, Leo?"

"A month or so."

"Have you seen your regular doctor."

"You're it," I said.

She looked up. "I'm it?"

"I mean. You're her. You're she?" I leaned back in my chair. "Grammar's not my strong suit," I said. "What I mean is, I don't *have* a regular doctor."

"I'm it, then." Dr. Early smiled. "Come this way." She led me to the examination room, which was reassuringly clean and spare, no crumbs to be seen and brightened by a child's drawings on the walls.

"Who's the artist?" I asked her.

"My granddaughter, Halley." Dr. Early pulled fresh paper onto the examination table. "She's six years old. She lives in Texas." She pointed to a picture of the state of Texas in rough outline, two human legs sticking out of a tooth-studded, cake-piece mouth. TEXAS IS EATING HALLEY, the caption read. "As you can see," Dr. Early said, "she's not crazy about being there."

She handed me a paper johnny and disappeared into that hole of discretion where doctors linger while you disrobe, calling out over her shoulder, "Give me a urine sample, please. Cups are on the bathroom shelf."

A few minutes later, I sat waiting on the examination table, my legs swinging back and forth, feeling faint and very young. My inch of pee sat steamy in its plastic cup beside me. The paper coat crackled when I moved. I wondered if I'd put it on backwards. My palms and feet were sweaty. One of Halley's drawings was of A BEAR GOES SHOPPING FOR CARROTS. The carrots were bigger than the bear, which wore glasses and a green, plumed hat. Dr. Early knocked on the door as she reappeared, brusque and formal as she began to examine me. She took my pulse and my blood pressure. I tensed as she shone a light into my eyes. She put the stethoscope to my chest. "Deep breath," she said. At least there was no phony smile. Her fingers pressed against my ribs. I thought of Kilroy's long fingers wrapping around the shaft of a rook at the chessboard, breathed deeply and then again. Dr. Early took the stethoscope away from her ears, tested my reflexes, thumped my back, felt my glands. I followed the motion of her fingers, and though I knew I was being touched, I could barely feel the pressure of her hands.

"IUD given you any trouble, Leo?" she said, as I lay down.

"IUD?" I'd almost forgotten about the metal object she'd put inside me three years before. Now I felt its cold and foreign presence and with it a rising hope. Maybe this was the problem, a piece of corroding metal, which, once removed, could do me no more harm. "It's been fine," I said. "But I'd like to have it taken out. Today, if you can."

"What about birth control?" Dr. Early asked.

I shifted on the table. "I don't need anything right now."

"You're not having sex?" Her fingers started to knead my belly.

"No."

"No chance that you might?" Her fingers moved up to one of my breasts, moving in circles outward from the center.

"Ouch," I said.

"Sensitive?"

"Yes."

"Sorry. I'll go easier. No chance that you might have sex any time soon?"

"No."

"My notes show that on your last visit you were sexually active."

"I had a boyfriend then." I tensed as she started in on the other breast. Had I told her such private things? How many times a week Danny and I screwed? When and where? "I don't now," I said.

"Nobody new on the horizon?" Her fingers bunched in one of my armpits, then the other. "It's just been my observation over time that most young people don't jump from a bed of passion to a nunnery, unless . . ."

"He's dead." I found an odd pleasure in watching her eyes jolt. "The guy I was sleeping with died."

"I'm sorry." Dr. Early's hands drew away. "That's tough." She wrote some notes in my file and put a dropperful of my urine onto a glass slide on the lab table. "Okay, let's do the internal exam and I'll remove the IUD." I put my heels into the cold, metal stirrups and slid my body forward until the base of my spine met the crack in the table. The air brushed my skin as I opened my legs and let them flop to the side. From the knee up, one leg trembled. Dr. Early calmed it with a steady hand. As she flicked a switch, the heat of a clamp lamp flooded down. She slipped on her rubber gloves, took a speculum from a drawer.

"You know how this feels," she said. "Cold at first. A pinch, a slide, then a click."

The speculum's metal tongue scraped up along the dry walls of my insides. I felt the tightening and the click as its jaws opened me wide. Dr. Early sat down in a chair by the light. "Have you been checking for your IUD string, Leo?" she asked. "To make sure it's in place?"

"Not for a while." I lied badly, for I did it rarely. Lying there, wide open and exposed, I pictured all of Halley's crayoned creatures swooping off the drawings and climbing inside me. "Since I'm not having sex," I said, "I didn't think it mattered."

Dr. Early bent her head. "Still, the IUD shouldn't be left to roam around," she said. "There's always the chance of infection or perforation. You'll feel my finger first. Good. Now a push. Good." Out came her finger. Her head bent down again. "Now I'm going to insert this plastic rod. The idea is, the hook on the end will catch the curve of the IUD. You may feel it poking." The rod started upward. When I winced, she stopped. "Does that hurt, Leo?"

"A little." A crack inside me widened. I thought I might cry. It all hurt. The indignity. The invasion. The questions. The bloody hook. I held onto the sides of the table as I would grip the seats of moving cars for years to come, and turned my head to one side.

"Breathe, Leo," Dr. Early said, putting her hand back on my shaky leg. "Breathe."

Another of Halley's drawings was called, A TV GIRL WHO IS MAD AT HER MOTHER. The girl was almost all head—square, with a screen and knobs and antennae. She wore a frown that reached from one side of her face to the other, fangs hanging nearly down to her knees. The mother stood in the corner in a cage, a spindly, stick figure, with wirebrush hair, clutching the bars. The rod pushed higher and higher, until I thought it might come bursting out through my navel. I stared at the TV girl, my fists clenched tight.

"Why's the girl mad at her mother?" I asked on an in breath.

For an instant, Dr. Early's eyes traveled up to the drawing. "For leaving her," she said.

"Where did she go?"

"Just away," Dr. Early said. "To a place no child can understand. You'll feel the rod moving to the other side. Halley lives with her father now."

"Is he your son?" The hook still roamed.

"No. My daughter's the deserter, the one in the cage. Halley wants to know why I made her such a bad mother. You may feel some pressure here, over your ovary."

"What's taking so long?" I asked her.

"The IUD string's not within reach," Dr. Early said. "I'm trying to . . ." Just then I felt a tug. "Ah," she said. "There it is."

A quick burning pain went through me as Dr. Early gave one last tug and the IUD slid out. I saw it, shiny and bloody, in her hand for a second before she opened the trash can lid with her foot and tossed it in, peeling her gloves from her hands in the same motion. My legs gave in to the tremble and collided at the knees.

"Done," she said, sliding out the speculum. "Sorry that took so long, Leo. The IUD had wandered pretty far."

As I tried to sit up, my stomach buckled.

"I think I'm going to be sick," I said.

Dr. Early helped me off the table and guided me to the bathroom, shut the door gently behind. After I'd wretched, she knocked and said, "When you're dressed, Leo, come on out to my office and we'll talk."

I sat for a while on the bathroom floor, looking at a picture of A WHALE DRINKING ROOT BEER WITH A STRAW. I thought of the strange toilets I'd thrown up into lately, how surreal my life had become. When I was dressed, I walked back out to Dr. Early's office, where she sat with her overflowing piles.

"What's wrong with me?" I asked her.

"Sit down, Leo."

"No. No, thanks. I'll stand. Just tell me what's wrong."

"There's nothing really wrong." Dr. Early leaned back in her chair. "But you are pregnant, Leo."

"Pregnant?" It was a made-up word, a word Halley might have used in one of her drawings, for a moose or a bird or a kangaroo. "Pregnant?" I said.

"About eight weeks, I'd say, judging from the size of your uterus. Does that make any sense?"

"No." A heat charged up from my feet and flooded my head. "It doesn't make any sense at all."

"When was your last period?"

"A few months ago. I don't remember."

"And the last time you had intercourse?"

"Intercourse?" My brain raced to make sense of the word. Sex. She was talking about sex. I fumbled in my memory. Two nights before Danny died. In my grandmother's bed. The neon Z of the PIZZA sign flashing green on his back. A cut above his left eye. A pool of sweat on my belly. The big game coming up. The last game against Dartmouth. The last game.

"January," I said. "January 26th."

"Then it's all too possible," Dr. Early said gently. "This would account for the nausea, tender breasts, fatigue, all common complaints of early pregnancy. The rest of your symptoms . . ."

"But the IUD," I said.

"The IUD wasn't in place, Leo. I found it halfway up to your ribcage. You weren't protected."

"I thought I was."

"Ah. If conviction only did the job." Dr. Early lifted the stethoscope up from her chest, spoke softly. "I take it this doesn't come as good news."

"I can't believe it," I said. "I can't believe what you're saying."

"You need some time, Leo. For all of this to sink in. And then you should consider your options.

"Options?" Another ridiculous word. I saw squealing women picking doors on quiz shows, executives buying stocks by phone, ribbed socks and pointed shoes perched on the edges of desks. The steam of panic shot up from my toes. I was in trouble; I was pregnant. I had no options.

"If you're considering abortion," Dr. Early went on. "You'll need to act in the next couple of weeks. After the first trimester, it's not such a simple matter."

"Abortion?" My mouth went dry on the word. I plunked myself down in a chair.

"Or," she went on. "If you decide to have the baby . . ."

"Have the baby?" I could only echo her dumbly. "Oh, my god."

"You should have an ultrasound test to make sure there's been no damage from the IUD. It's unlikely. The fetus is tiny, well protected. I'm sure you . . ."

"Fetus?" The language she spoke became more and more foreign to me. The room spun in wobbly circles. I had trouble focusing, keeping upright, even in the chair. The upper parts of my eyes were in darkness. I thought I might pass out. A voice came out of the void. It was mine, hoarse and haggard. "*Fetus?*" it said.

Dr. Early's voice came through a tunnel as she touched my arm. "Leo, listen," she said. "I want you to sit here for as long as you need to. I wish I could stay with you. But I have to catch a plane. I'm going to give you the number of a counseling center in Central Square. I hope you'll talk to someone there. Soon." She pushed some slips of paper into my hand. "Meanwhile, no matter what you decide, you're anemic and should pick up some . . ."

"No!" I didn't hear the rest, lost for a moment thrashing in my grandmother's bed with Danny, trying to remember how that last night might have distinguished itself, how the sex might have been different, something Danny might have said, how this possibly could have happened. Danny, moody and restless. Rough. Turning me over, pushing hard inside me from behind. My face pressed against the pillow, my protest thick and muffled. "*Stop. You're hurting me Danny. I can't breathe.*"

"Leo, please," Dr. Early said. "Just sit for a while. Breathe deeply."

"No!" The walls tilted forward. I struggled out of the chair. "I have to get up. I have to go."

I made my way back to the hallway, picked up my violin and put on my coat. Dr. Early's voice caught my hand on the doorknob. "Leo. Please. Wait."

I turned around, forgetting for a moment where I was and who was speaking to me.

"Whose baby is this?" she asked.

I thought she was testing me, making sure, before I left, that I was of sound mind, that I'd understood what I'd been told. "It's mine," I told her. "I know. It's mine."

"Yes, but the father." She spoke slowly, carefully, the way my father did to Lydia, the way Danny had to Po, the way the loving spoke to the lost. "Is the father the man who died?"

I nodded. Strange. Dr. Early spoke of Danny as a man. I'd always thought of him as a boy. "Yes," I said. "He was."

"Aah." Her voice turned gravelly again, the backthroat voice she used when she spoke of her granddaughter, Halley, in Texas. "Then you have to make a decision for two people," she said.

"Yes," I said. "And one of us is dead."

For the next hour, I wandered the side streets off Broadway, up Bigelow, down Hancock, up Ellery, and down. Everywhere I looked, I saw children, always before just a blur of color, limbs and squeals. I saw them playing in the park, sitting on porch steps, wriggling out of cars. I headed down Quincy Street past the Fogg Museum. College students strolled in the dying spring light, fresh-faced and smiling, books tucked under their arms. I could no longer place myself in the context of time or age—in one hour, I'd come from being a young girl swinging her legs on a doctor's examination table to a pregnant woman trudging through Harvard Yard. I passed the Lamont Library, the Henry Moore sculpture, Widener Library. It wasn't until I reached the gates at Dunster Street that I saw where my feet had landed me, across Mass. Ave. from Brattle Court, where the chess players gathered at the stone tables in front of the Cafe Troc.

A panhandler lay in wait for me on the street side of the gates. "Hey, lady, you got a cigarette?"

"Smoking's bad for you." I looked down at him, crouched low on a piece of cardboard. "Don't you know it causes cancer?"

"Yeah, sure, forget it." He waved me away with his hand. "You must be the Surgeon General, right? Right here in Harvard Yard. And you know who I am, lady? I'm the Night Watchman."

I pulled a rumpled dollar out of my pocket and held it out to the man. "Here." I stared at his grizzled face, saw him suddenly as a gurgling baby, cradled in his mother's arms. I made a gesture Danny would have made, gathered words he might have spoken. "Take it," I said. "Take it and buy some food."

The man took the money and put in in his pocket, but waved me away impatiently with his hand. "Hey mister!" he hailed the next passerby. "You look like a philanthropist. You got a butt?"

Crossing the street, I stood behind a telephone pole and watched Kilroy from a distance. He sat alone at his table, head bent over a book. Lydia had told me stories she'd heard on the radio about people arriving mysteriously at places that had cropped up in long-ago dreams or conversations, at the site of a reported UFO landing, the temple of a Buddhist monk, the house of a long-lost lover. Revenge. Salvation. Enlightenment. People making meccas, trancelike, with no earthly idea of their destinations. And there I was, pregnant and stunned, come from a doctor through Harvard Yard to Kilroy's dollar-a-pop chessboard, with no earthly reason why.

Next to me, a man etched the solar system on the sidewalk with pastel-colored chalks. I watched the powdery planets form. A swirling Saturn. A marbled Mercury. A polka-dotted Pluto. I watched Kilroy. Again, his stillness struck me most. He had no tics, no special postures or gestures, except for the hand that ran from time to time through his thick, curly hair, causing it to bounce back in odd configurations. He wore a Celtics jersey, which swung my thoughts against will to Danny, man of a thousand sports shirts. But for the first time, the pang of recognition didn't knock down the dominoes of panic. All similarity ended there.

When I came close enough to touch Kilroy with the reach of an arm, he raised his head.

"Leo."

"You don't know me very well."

He leaned back in his chair. "You play the violin and you got yourself out of a sinking car. You think men have a thing about long hair. I've been thinking about you."

I sat down across from him. Some of his calm washed over me. "I don't even know your last name," I said.

"Brimmer." He set his book face down on the chessboard. "How are you?" he asked.

I looked at Kilroy for a long while before I answered, slowly releasing the words, butterflies into a cold wind. "Actually," I said. "I'm . . . pregnant."

"Pregnant?"

"I just came from the doctor. I thought I was sick. But I'm not. I'm pregnant."

"Did you want to be pregnant?" Kilroy picked up a bishop from the chessboard.

"No."

"You don't get pregnant out of the blue, do you?" His eyes retreated as they met mine. "Or is that where you've been?"

"I had an IUD," I said. "It wandered."

"Wow." Kilroy tipped the white queen back and forth. "What are you going to do?"

"I don't know."

"What about the father?"

"There is no father."

"Immaculate conception?" Kilroy pulled his chair closer. "Come on. How does the guy feel about this, Leo?"

"It doesn't matter," I said.

"How can you say that? He's the father. He's got a right to know. He should be involved. He should help." The light dawned on Kilroy then. "Oh, my god. It's McPhee's, isn't it?"

I nodded.

"Damn. He left you a little something to remember him by all right."

"I don't know what to do."

"What are your choices?"

I liked Kilroy's word better. Choices, I could make. What shirt to wear, what cereal to buy, whether to eat one or two pieces of toast. To change the course of my life forever or leave it be. "If I want an abortion," I said, "I'd have to do it soon."

"You could walk through the doctor's door and out again," Kilroy said. "It would all be a dream."

"There's adoption."

"They find good homes for these kids."

"Do they?"

"I don't really know," Kilroy confessed.

"But if I had a baby and it was mine," I said. "Could I let it go?"

Kilroy shrugged. "You could keep it," he said.

"I don't have the slightest idea of how to be a mother."

"You have one, don't you?"

"One what?"

"A mother."

"Sort of," I said.

"A sort-of mother?" Kilroy said.

"I have nothing to give a baby, Kilroy."

"What does a kid really need?" he said. "No shoes for a while. No toys. A chess set, maybe."

"No, a kid needs parents who can take care of it," I said. "A kid needs a real family."

"Kind of a luxury these days," Kilroy said, starting to set up the pieces on the board. "Isn't it?"

c h a p t e r   t e n

A little something, Kilroy had called it. A little something Danny had left me to remember him by. After that day, I understood that if I had the baby, I'd be keeping Danny with me forever, in more than just the smells in the bed, the jarring faces on the streets, or in the water dreams—but in a small face that might be the spitting image of his, a brooding spirit or square hands that might forever remind me of hockey sticks and fish, a brow that might furrow deep. To have the baby, knowing all of this, seemed dangerous, even self-destructive. And yet it was finally this same reasoning which began to seem as good an argument for keeping the baby as against. Not to lose Danny completely. To fight for what was left, the floating scraps of memory, feeling, even pain. Not to let death win.

Over the next few days, I went over and over it in my head—lying awake up in my bed at Cobb's Hill or practicing Aurelio's "Waterfall Symphony," out on the widow's walk, rumbling over the potholes on the #22 bus, holding my breath on subway trains in dark tunnels underground. Part of me wanted to be rid of everything that might remind me of Danny, the part that had cast off his dirty sweatshirt and cut my hair, steered clear of the fish market and turned deaf ears to all voices that might have spoken of him. Abortion was every woman's right and I was glad to have it, but I began to question whether it could be my choice this time around, given the odd twist of this life's beginning and its father's end.

Indecision bore inertia. I didn't call the counseling center, didn't fill Dr. Early's prescriptions. At night I fell into dreamless sleep. I told no one. Two weeks passed, and still, I'd done nothing. I looked at a calendar and saw the pregnancy in thirds. The first trimester would soon be over. Come May I'd be showing, In August, I'd start to waddle. If I relinquished all control, by Halloween, I'd be a mother. The baby could grow. Nothing I could do would stop it. Time would pass. And maybe it would close up a few, gaping wounds. Disbelief and terror were slowly diluted by a seeping, guilty elation that grew faster than the seed inside of me. I wasn't dying after all, nor was I barren. Neither killer nor jinx, not only had I been spared, I'd been graced. There was a baby inside of me and we were both alive. A faint voice spoke to me. Keep it, Leo. Keep it that way.

Lethargy slowly turned inside out to drive. I stopped at the drugstore on Brattle Street and filled Dr. Early's prescription for prenatal vitamins, big as horse pills. I forced down cereal with milk for breakfast, sliced peaches over cottage cheese. Apricots for iron. Bananas for potassium. Cheese and dairy for calcium. I walked and I walked. I played music and I played more music. I studied in the library, read and wrote about Aurelio. Page after page. When I was tired, I slept. When I couldn't sleep, I practiced some more. Over a time I couldn't gauge, I made peace with a decision that had somehow made itself. And one morning when I woke up, the sickness in my belly was gone.

A week later, I got off the subway at Central on my way home from the Conservatory and walked to Brattle Court to see Kilroy. This time I didn't pretend to be going there for any other reason—coffee, exercise, a change of view. I bought a muffin at the Cafe Troc and sat a few tables away while Kilroy finished a game of chess. When he'd pocketed a dollar and shaken his opponent's hand, he got up to stretch and saw me.

"You must think I'm a spy," I said.

"When I'm here, I'm public property," he said. "A dog even took my leg for a fire hydrant once."

I smiled. "I just wanted to thank you," I said.

"For what?" He corralled the black chess pieces on the table, started to set them up on the board.

"For talking to me the other day," I said.

"Forget it. If you thank me for talking to you, then I'll have to thank you for listening to me, and things will start getting out of hand."

"I've made up my mind, Kilroy." For the first time I said it out loud. "I'm going to keep the baby."

"Good," he said.

"I'm not doing it to be good."

"I only meant good, you made a decision, good," he said carefully. "That must be a relief."

"It is," I said. "But it was a passive decision. And that worries me."

"Why?"

"I didn't really make it. It made itself."

"But you let it be made," Kilroy said. "Passivity inverse is forward motion. And everything is partly its own opposite."

"Not pregnancy," I said.

"Think of it another way," he said. "You decided against what you couldn't live with."

"Which was what?"

"Not knowing. Never knowing. Who this person would be."

"But how do I know if I can live with this person?" I asked.

"You don't." He slid his pawn across the board toward me. "That's the heat, Leo—the mysterious, the unknown. That's what makes the butter melt, the ice flow. That's life."

"But what if I screw up?" I handed him the last of the black pawns.

"Hey, Kilroy!" A bearded man hailed him from a few tables down.

"Hey Lex!" Kilroy said. "How'd you make out at the chess club last night?"

"Got smushed in the middle game playing the French Defense."

"Been there," Kilroy said. "Check out Capablanca-Lasker, 1921, Game Four." He turned back to me. "How'd your family take the news, Leo?"

"I haven't told them yet."

"Hmm." He lifted his queen. "Seems like your father should have known before mine."

"Your father knows about my baby?"

"We talk a lot on the phone. Did you know that if you shrunk the earth," Kilroy said, "it would be smoother than a cueball?"

"I don't play pool," I said.

"My father told me he was feeling old." Kilroy retraced his thoughts. "Said soon he'd be bald as a cueball. I reminded him of a time we were playing pool once in a bar and we heard a baby crying. The noise was so out of place. We tried to find the baby, but we never did. I told him that Yul Brenner had no trouble with women, and then I told him about your baby."

"What did he say?"

"He congratulates you," Kilroy said. "I think he was disappointed that it wasn't mine."

I smiled. "What about the mountains on the earth?" I asked him. "The volcanoes and the oceans?"

"With a magnifying glass, you'd see tantamount things on a cueball," Kilroy said.

"Tantamount?" I said.

A lanky boy slid up on a skateboard, tipped neatly off it and put it under his arm. "How 'bout a game?" he asked Kilroy.

"Sure," Kilroy said, starting to set up the white pieces. "Have a seat."

The boy wiped his face with his t-shirt and plunked himself down in the chair. "So what ever happened to Bobby Fischer?" he asked. "I heard he got reborn in Southern California and rides a Greyhound bus all day."

"Yeah, I heard he and God got tight." Kilroy shook two straight fingers in the air. "I don't know about the bus, though." He turned to me and his dark eyes leveled. "You won't screw up, Leo," he said. "You won't."

A few days later, Dr. Early's voice found me in the downstairs hall closet where I kept the phone, coiling the wire around my finger, the smells of old pine and mothballs enshrouding me.

"Leo? Is that you? Are you there?"

My heart started to race. When a doctor called, it could only be bad news. Something was wrong. Wrong with the baby. Worse yet, there *was* no baby, after all. I'd read how women could talk their bodies into pregnancy—nausea, bloating, cravings and cramps, breasts bursting with milk—women who'd lost children, who couldn't have children, women who kidnapped babies from supermarket carriages—madwomen.

"I'm here," I said. "Hi, Dr. Early."

"Is this a bad time?"

Yes, it was always a bad time for bad news. "No, it's fine," I said. "Is anything wrong?"

"No. No. I just wanted to check in, that's all. See how you're doing."

"I've decided to have the baby." I ran my hand over Lydia's ermine stole. "I'm sorry. You were so nice that day. I should've called."

"Congratulations, then," Dr. Early said. "How are you feeling?"

"I don't feel much of anything. The nausea's gone, finally. I'm tired."

"That's to be expected," she said. "So. Eat well. Get your rest. Moderation is the key."

"Another one of my not-so-strong suits."

"Make it one," she said. "At least for the next six months. And find yourself a doctor, Leo."

"Can't I keep you?" I asked.

"Sure." She laughed. "You can keep me, if you like. Let's schedule an ultrasound at the hospital to make sure there's been no damage from the IUD."

"Damage?"

"It's very unlikely. And I'll want to see you in my office once a month."

"So often?"

"It's routine, Leo. Have you always been such a worrier?"

"No, it's recent. Recent me."

"Understandable. By the way, how's your head?"

"My head's fine," I said. "Hard as a rock."

"Nothing else you want to talk about?"

"I'm not much of a talker." I fingered a silk scarf dangling from an elephant tusk hook in the closet. "Thanks, anyway."

"Just so you know," Dr. Early said. "It's Halley's doing. I've just lately become a good listener."

It's not something you can describe, the feeling of being followed, nothing as definite as a noise or the cast of a shadow or a change in the wind, the shift of molecules around you. It's more the sudden, if subtle, absence of these phenomena—a glitch in the normal cadence of light, rhythm and sound. On an overcast April day, I came up from the subway at Harvard and walked toward the bus stop. The clock above the bank flashed 2:11 in neon green. An aproned boy arranged bricks on the newspaper piles at Nini's Corner. Cars and buses rumbled over the ravaged streets. Everything was as it should be, as it had always been, though images still came to my eye at a lag, slightly blurred, the world off balance with Danny gone from it.

As I walked, I turned around several times to shake the feeling of some distraction, some encumbrance, something unfinished, forgotten. It wasn't until I crossed Brattle at Church that I saw Danny's younger brother, Po, peeking out from behind a lamp post. When I lifted my arm, he ran down Story Street toward the trolley car barns.

"Po! Come back!" I cut through the alleyway at the Casablanca, tried to keep him in sight. He was far from home. I knew how his mother worried, how she called him her slow, sweet boy and kept him close, how she'd only trusted him with her husband or Danny.

I found Po in the car barns across Mt. Auburn, huddled behind one of the broken-down trolleys, its antennae busted, wires dragging, tires slung low. As Po raised his tousled head, my stomach heaved. He had Danny's light eyes and the same slight nose, his mother's pale, freckled skin and red hair. One ear was slightly lower than the other, one eye a bit crossed. Wispy hair flew in all directions, giving Po the look of a sprouted onion. Still, he was Danny's brother, make no mistake. He was a McPhee.

I crouched down in the dirt, eye level with Po. We were both wearing Danny's old hockey sweatshirts. Po's reached down below his knees; the gold letters "NATICK CONCRETE" hung at his waist. Mine read, in silver pitchfork script across my chest, "MEDFORD DEVILS."

I leaned against the tilted trolley. "Po," I said. He looked up at me, plugged his ears with his fingers. "Po." I tried to speak gently, the way Danny always had, not to shout as people often did, thinking him to be deaf, or dumb. "I'm glad to see you." I eased his fingers away from his ear. "I just want to talk to you. Say hello. That's all."

Po started to yank on the tongue of his sneaker.

"How'd you find me?" I asked him.

Po steadied himself in his crouch, in the shadow of the old trolley, knuckles planted square on the ground. "Where's Danny?" he finally said.

"Danny's dead, Po."

"He's never coming home." He rubbed his nose with one knuckle, smearing his face with dirt.

"No," I said. "He isn't. Come on. Get up, Po. Let's walk."

Po got up and dusted off his knees. We walked through the trolleys on the hard, rutted mud past the post office, back around the arc of Brattle.

"Where's Danny, Leo?" he asked me again as we walked.

"I really don't know." I had no religion and didn't want to confuse Po, didn't want to ask where Danny had been buried, if he'd been buried.

"Is he at your house, Leo?"

"No, Danny's not at my house, Po."

"I know where you live," Po said. "Near the pizza parlor. I saw you and Danny. Take me there."

"That's my apartment," I said. "I'm not living there right now. I'm staying with my parents, up on Cobb's Hill. Your mother will be worried, Po. Come on. We can catch the bus. I'll take you home."

"No," Po said. "I don't want to go home."

"You have to, Po. Your mother . . ."

"No." He pressed his palms flat to the wind. "Take me to your house, Leo. Take me there now."

My bus pulled up just then. And because I was tired, and maybe because now that he'd found me, I couldn't let Po go just yet, I motioned him up onto the stairs of the bus and put money in the fare box for both of us.

"Don't take me home, Leo," Po said, as we made our way to the back of the bus. "Promise."

"I won't," I said. "Not for a while." Po's face relaxed. We sat in sun-baked seats, way in the back. I gave Po a handkerchief to wipe his sweaty face, strangely comfortable by his side. I guess it's simple, once you've wondered if there's murder in you, to be a mere and kindly kidnapper.

Lydia was reading the newspaper in the living room when we came into the house. I went to the phone and Po made his way over to her on the couch.

"What are you doing, lady?" I heard him ask.

"Reading the sports page," Lydia said. "The Red Sox are four and one in spring training. Three more games to go."

"I love the Red Sox," Po said. "I know all their names. Dave Stapleton. First Base."

"Jerry Remy. Second," Lydia said. "I love them, too."

"Carney Lansford. Third," Po said. "He led the league in batting last year."

"I know he did," Lydia said in a purring voice. "I know."

I dialed the McPhees' number. Mrs. McPhee's voice was dull on the other end of the line. "Leo? Leo who? What's that you say? Porter's where?"

"He's here, with me, Mrs. McPhee. At my parents' house."

"What are you talking about. Po's with his sister, Rose. They went off not an hour ago to do errands."

"He followed me in Harvard Square," I said. "I found him in the car barns. I brought him here." I heard a door slam on the other end of the line and Rose's voice calling out. "Mother? Did Po come back here? He ran away from me at the market. I've looked everywhere."

"Oh, good Lord." Mrs. McPhee's hushed voice slid through the receiver. "Don't let him out of your sight. My husband will be right there to fetch him."

"53 Cobb's Hill Road," I told her. "Off of Peabody Square. Way up the hill. A big house with vines. It's hard to find. People get lost . . ." My voice trailed off into a loud buzz. She'd already hung up the phone.

On the couch, Po and Lydia were looking at a photograph on the front page of the newspaper. "Dog Leaps Seventeen Stories from Burning Building," the headline read. The dog had been caught by the camera just before landing on the firemen's trampoline, fur raised, legs scrambling in air, terror in its beady dog eyes.

"Dogs can't jump that far," Po said. "He'll get hurt."

"No," Lydia explained. "He didn't get hurt at all. He landed on all fours and trotted away. He ate a bone from the butcher shop half an hour later and went on television."

"He's hurt," Po kept saying. "His legs got broken. Smashed."

"No." I stood by the grandfather clock and watched from a distance. "It happened just the other day." Lydia's voice was gentle and firm. "The dog is fine. He went on the Johnny Carson Show."

"Did you watch him?" Po asked.

"I don't have television," Lydia said.

"Everyone's got television," Po said.

"Everyone?" Lydia said, suddenly noticing me. "Who is this boy, Claire?"

"Who's Claire?" Po asked.

"That's me, Po," I said. "It's sort of a nickname."

"Who's she?" Po pointed at Lydia.

"That's my mother," I said. "That's Lydia."

"Do I *know* this boy, Claire?" Lydia's voice grew agitated.

"This is Po McPhee," I said, putting my hands on Po's shoulders from behind. "Danny's brother."

"I'm looking for Danny," Po told her.

Lydia nodded. "We haven't seen him in a long time. Maybe it's just as well . . ."

"Danny's dead," I told them both.

"I brought extra money for the bus." Po took some coins out of his pocket.

"How much does the bus cost nowadays?" Now that Po had been identified, Lydia was more at ease again. "In my day, it was a nickel."

"Quarter for grown-ups." Po held one out to Lydia. "A dime for kids. Are you old?"

"I'm ancient," Lydia said. "As old as the hills. When I was born, there *was* no television. Imagine."

"When I was born," Po said, "I was blue."

"My favorite color," Lydia said. "I see you didn't stay that way."

Po grinned. "No way," he said. "I'm not blue anymore."

I sat down on the couch and said, "Danny's dead," again. And Po and Lydia talked some more, about the leaping dog, and the bravery of firemen, the colors people might turn if they had their way—purple, polka-dotted, striped like a zebra.

When the doorbell rang, Lydia rose from the couch and vanished. Mr. McPhee stood on the doorstep in a bowling jacket, his apron from the fish market still on underneath. I saw how Danny's death had done real damage, a slow crushing of body, spirt and bone, and wondered how it had changed me.

"Here's our little wanderer, then." He went over to Po, knelt down and pressed him to his chest, before he pushed him away and took him hard by the elbows. "You mustn't ever run away like that again," he said. "Your mother's had enough to bear lately. Never again. Do you hear me, Porter?"

"I was looking for Danny," Po said.

"I know." Mr. McPhee ruffled Po's red hair and got to his feet. "Still thinks his brother will turn up somewhere. Can't say as I blame him. I catch myself doing the same thing, sometimes." He spoke past me, as if I were a stranger. I wanted to remind him that I, too, still looked for Danny in unlikely places, that I, too, did battle with memory and dreams, that I'd touched his softest places and seen his ugliest spots, felt his hardest words, the strength of his hand. I wanted to tell Danny's father, "I miss him too."

"Well," Mr. McPhee said. "Thanks for your trouble, Leo. We'll be on our way."

"Wait." As Mr. McPhee walked towards the door, his arm around Po, I felt an intense desire to have the telling done, a grisly wish to see his face clench in pain once more. "Could I ride back with you?" I said. "I want to talk to you and your wife. It won't take long."

I saw Mr. McPhee's eyes retreat, as his mind searched for words to keep me at bay. "It's fairly mad at our house about now, Leo," he said. "Moira will be cooking dinner. The twins will be wanting help with their homework. Rose is alone in the fish market. It's still got to be cleaned. I left in a hurry. Supper will be on." He lifted his dirty apron. "There's a delivery tomorrow at dawn. It's fairly mad." The reasons came spilling out, one after another, all of them painfully real and true, why this wasn't a good time, for me to come, for me to speak, why I must stay silent, stay away. "Maybe another time, Leo," he said. "Maybe another time."

Lydia called out from somewhere. "Who is it, Claire?"

"No one," I called back.

Mr. McPhee craned his neck. "Who was that?" he asked.

"My mother," I said. "She was just saying goodbye."

"And we'll be doing the same, Leo," he said, excuses spent, a spark of apology in his eyes. "Moira will be wondering . . ." He looked around the house for the first time—at the hanging net and the tarnished chandelier, the broken newel post on the stair. "Where on earth we've gotten to."

chapter eleven

*T*wo girls were talking on the subway one day. They sat knee to
knee, snapping bubbles with their gum, sharing a forbidden cigarette
in the nearly empty car. The subject was their friend, Darlene. Darlene
went with Kenny. She thought she was such hot shit, that Darlene, and
look what happened to her. She and Kenny went all the way, and she
got herself knocked up. Darlene was so fucking stupid, the girls said.
So fucking brave, so sort of fucking lucky, their mascaraed eyes and
tapping toes told me. Darlene was going to have a fucking *baby*. The
word exploded in a puff of smoke.

I pressed my hand to my stomach as we came up from underground
over the Charles River. The John Hancock building rose flat and
metallic in a powder blue sky. The Esplanade was splashed with green.
A few small sailboats tilted in the wind. I felt a strange tug at my
cheeks, the first reaches of a smile. I was probably the first Baye ever to
get knocked up and somehow that pleased me. As a child, I'd tried to
imagine what happened after sliding down the hole that swallowed little girls and turned them into women. A strange place, the wonderland

of sex and marriage to a child such as I had been, where people never touched, where eggs didn't drop and semen didn't spill, where babies simply got made. Mysteriously, in a cloud of smoke, on a noiseless night, in a hot whirlpool of confusion. The rabbit died, they said. The rabbit died. Why, I'd wondered. Who killed it? I pictured a bow-tied rabbit doing slapstick on a stage in a top hat, the crack of a gunshot, the rabbit falling, a trickle of blood oozing from its temple, a baby, pink and powdered, popping out of the overturned hat.

As the train slid back down under the ground, the ember of the girls' cigarette gleamed. I took a deep breath and closed my eyes, as panic enveloped me in the dark of the tunnel. No, I'd sooner have been knocked up—me and Darlene—by a pimply, big shot named Kenny or a moody ghost on ice skates, knocked up good, and no turning back. Darlene never did know her ass from her elbow, one of the girls said, as she took a last drag of the Marlboro. That Darlene had really fucked up this time. The girl smushed out the butt with the bottom of her spiked heel as the train screeched to a halt at Park. My palms were full of sweat. I raced out of the train. Fucked up but good.

I ate suppers alone at the kitchen table, food I'd picked up at Sage's Market on my way home, paid for with the little that was left from my last music store check, and the spare bills and change my father emptied into a glass bowl on the hallway table each day when he came home from work. My appetite was huge and strange. Cravings rolled through me like waves. I ate sardines and yogurt and apricots and nuts and even a hamburger once from Bartley's Burger Cottage—suddenly wanting meat—foods full of calcium, potassium, protein, iron, Dr. Early's list of edibles, a diet which made me feel slow and sticky, on which unborn babies thrived.

After dinner, I practiced the "Waterfall Symphony" in my room, methodically—measure by measure, page by page, movement by movement. When I'd mastered the adagio, I began on the allegro. When the allegro was done, I started in on the andante. One night when I'd had enough, I pulled some old sheet music from the shelves and played what I used to call the pretty music as a child, untroubled melodies that bent the heart and not the fingers, long before I'd come to understand how much more there was to music than prettiness. The notes of an old Corelli piece crept back into my fingers. I turned away from the music, played it by heart. As I played, I felt my neck and stomach unknot, my fingers relax on the strings. And as my mind relented, I gave in again to memory.

I remembered a night, the winter before, when Danny had gotten dressed up in a tuxedo to receive an award at a hockey banquet downtown.

"Good heavens, Daniel Rory McPhee, look at the likes of you." His mother had fussed over him before we left. "You could be right up there on a movie screen, right next to Robert Redford, so handsome you are." She purred softly, reached out a hand to brush his hair from his forehead, as if I weren't there, standing by Danny's side, dressed in midnight blue, not right for the occasion though I'd tried.

"Cut it out, Ma." Danny thrust her hand away, brought up phlegm from his throat. "Just lay off, okay?"

"The likes of you," she murmured, and turned away.

Later that night, in bed, after the banquet, I made the mistake of asking Danny if he thought I were pretty. The room was dark, the bed still damp and warm from our lovemaking. His back was to me, his voice slurred and cool. "You look like Leo," he said. "Isn't that enough?"

"It's all there is." I traced the letters of my name one by one across his back. L-E-O-N-A-R . . ."I was just wondering. How I look to you. What you see when you look at me."

He gestured to the mirror. "Take a look," he said.

"So many pieces are missing," I said. "They always have been."

"I could tell you you're the most beautiful woman in the world."

"It would be a lie."

"What started all this, anyway, Leo?"

"Your mother gushing all over you that way," I said. "As if you were some sort of movie star." I came to the final A in my name, started in on his. D-A-N . . .

"She's my mother, Leo," Danny spat out. "What the hell do you expect?"

"Nothing." I trailed a finger from behind down his thigh, to a point that made him shiver. "I expect very little from Lydia," I said. "Anyway, your mother's right. You are beautiful."

Danny flung himself on me, or maybe it was off me, in such a way as his hand whacked my face and I bit the inside of my cheek. "What the hell does any of it matter, Leo?" he said, sitting up on the edge of the bed.

"It doesn't." I rubbed my stung cheek, ran my finger along the line of my jaw, feeling foolish and enraged. "It doesn't matter at all. You're ugly, all right? You really are when you get this way. You're Frankensteinian. Jeckyllish. Draculonian."

"Don't make up words, Leo. I can't stand it when you play smart ass with me."

"It's your game, too." I wiped a trickle of blood from the corner of my mouth. "Playing dumb."

When Danny saw the blood, he winced. "Oh, sweet Jesus. What did I do." He wiped what was left with one finger, took my face in his hands. "I'm sorry, Leo. You know I am. You're the pretty one. God. You're the only one. I swear."

I remember what went through my mind as he buried his face in my hair—it was the blood made him say it. It was the blood.

I met Dr. Early on a Tuesday at the hospital for the ultrasound test. I'd drunk a quart of water that morning and couldn't pee until the test was over. I sat in a waiting room full of Norman Rockwell pictures and pregnant women, and read about Kegel exercises and how to get your uterine muscles back in shape after your baby was born. A dozen times I looked at the clock, trying to concentrate on keeping the dam of my bladder from bursting. Near noontime, in a small room, Dr. Early squirted cold jelly onto my stomach and brought out a round metal disc attached to a tube. As she moved the disc around my belly, crackling noises came out of a small black box. When she found the right spot, she dug into my skin and a thumping sound came out of the box's small speaker, awash and aswish.

"Oh, my god," I said. "What's that?"

"That's your baby's heartbeat, Leo," she said. "Coming in loud and clear at 102 beats per minute."

"Won't it explode?"

"No it's perfect," she said. "Listen."

The office filled with the galloping thumps of my baby's heartbeat. Never had such a perfect sound frightened me so. I remember wondering, as I lay there, belly up, how I could have been so cavalier about what was growing inside of me. No more than an inch, the baby was already sure and strong.

"And now for the video portion of our show." Dr. Early turned on a TV screen and the baby appeared, spinning in a black void full of milky ways, galaxies of thigh, brain and bone, planets of brain, heart and muscle. I lost a breath as my eyes focused on the screen. I saw the curve of the baby's spine and one tiny arm flex. The heart pumped, a bat's wing rising and falling. Ears and fingers were forming; tongue and toes wiggling. Already that thumping voice spoke loud, that curled up, translucent crablike creature made its sure way in a warm, dark river inside me.

"That's my baby?" I whispered.

"That's your baby."

I let out a breath. "Oh, my god. Is it a girl or boy?"

"I can't tell from this angle. We could try . . ."

"No." I put out my hand. "I don't want to know. It doesn't matter. Just so long . . . as it's a baby."

"You were expecting an alien, maybe?"

"Maybe." I sat up on the table and swung my legs around. "So everything's okay?"

"Everything's fine, Leo."

"What do I do now?"

"You rest," Dr. Early said. "You take good care. And surround yourself with the people you love."

I straightened my shirt, reached for my shoes. "Funny advice from a gynecologist," I said.

"I've been at this a long time, Leo." For the first time, I noticed the weariness in her voice. "I'm sort of a funny gynecologist," she said.

So long an expert at severance, I now began the task of reconnection, to all the people and places from which I'd shied away since the accident and maybe long before—city parks and drugstores, policemen, pedestrians, popcorn vendors. I tried for small changes at first, trusting that one would lead naturally to another. When the #22 bus driver said, "hello, Stradivarius," I said back to him, "good morning, Phil," whether it was or not. I made myself speak to the druggist who filled my prescriptions, the children who jousted at the bus stop, the woman who cleaned the bathrooms at the Conservatory, the clerks in the grocery store, the old people who roamed the supermarkets. These were the people on whom I'd depend, after the baby came. One of those children might someday be my child's lover, give him a job or a break, bring her some news by mail, fly her in a plane to see me. And some day, I would be one of the old people who hovered in the produce aisle in the supermarket, searching for a firm, fairly priced tomato and a sympathetic ear. And in truth there was nothing I liked doing more in those days than to run my thumbs over the skin of a bumpy avocado and listen to tales of far-off grandchildren and how the time did fly by, breezy Muzak bouncing off my ears in soft ripples.

Heal thyself, Leo. A voice spoke to me from a deep place inside. Old instincts stirred. Surges of hows and whys. Ripples of anger and with it drive. Anger at what Danny had called God and I'd always left at fate. He'd fallen into a black hole and I was clinging to its smoking, ragged edge. I wanted to level doom. If people could make themselves sick, couldn't they make themselves well again? If people dissolved slowly in grief, surely they could solidify again with work and time. I hadn't died. I *hadn't*. I remember how hard it was at the time to accept that it was all right for me to be alive.

My second self-appointed task had to do with visions. From then on, whenever I saw a part of a person that reminded me of Danny—a broad back or the ripple of a satin sports jacket or a blond head, a brooding scowl or a square knee, I fought down the heat of panic that rose to curl my ears. Breathing deeply, I'd go close enough to see the rest of the person's parts—crooked tooth, green pants Danny wouldn't have been caught dead wearing, forearm too long, part on the wrong side of the head. One day, when a man in line for coffee at the Cafe Troc found me too close behind him, breathing down his neck, he flung me an accusing stare. And I just said to him, in a voice as clear as running water, "Excuse me. From the back, you look like someone I used to know." The man lost the ridge in his scowl then, the edge to his voice. He nodded his head. I'd made it right somehow. He seemed to understand.

On the good days, I'd see my child as the one who'd finally cement our feet in time, enmesh us in the present. She'd throw me a ball, sing me a song, draw me smoke-breathing creatures never before imagined. He'd fill the Cobb Hill halls with echoes, run a red crayon down a white hallway wall, make cambric tea with hot milk and sugar for imaginary friends. There'd be birthdays, bedtimes, riddles, racket, rhyme. Diddle diddle dumpling. My son John. Went to bed with his stockings on. Silly boy. Where's my mother? this child would say. Over and over. Find her for me. *I want my mother.*

On the bad days, when my body felt sluggish and cramped, when the "Waterfall Symphony" music on my stand roiled an angry mess of black and white notes, blurring in front of my tired eyes, when Danny's hands made their way back into my dreams, wringing, strangling, ripping me apart to get at the baby—*his* baby— I'd consider the darker possibilities—that the baby would be deformed or crazy or without compassion, an unlucky mix of bad genes, that she'd be just another skeleton in the closet instead of a bright new leaf on the family tree, that he'd be a brooder like Danny, or plumb insane, a murderer maybe, annihilating the entire Baye family from the earth, making sure there was no one left to mourn the loss—a bad, bad seed.

But the sun rose time and time again to clear away dark clouds. My belly swelled and the life inside me was giving, without rage. Surely this baby would have Lydia's voice and my father's good heart, Danny's athletic grace, and my . . . I didn't know what of myself I would have bestowed on this child if I could have—my empathy maybe, my way in water, a light touch and a tough stem, an occasional sparking eye.

"Look at this belly," I said to Dr. Early on my next visit to her office in late May. "Have you ever seen a better one?"

"Never." Dr. Early ran the tape measure from my rib cage to my pubic bone. "Fifteen weeks. Fifteen centimeters. Right on target, Leo. How are you feeling?"

"I wish you wouldn't keep asking me that," I said. "You make me nervous."

"You make me nervous by never saying anything but fine."

"Would it be better if I felt suicidal, maniacal, vomitous still?

"Vomitous?" Dr. Early's eyes widened.

"I make up words," I said. "Danny called me Mrs. Funk & Wagnalls."

"Danny?" she asked.

"Danny was . . ."

"The father," she said. "Say it, Leo. It might feel good. Danny was the father."

"Yes, Danny was the father." I looked her straight in the eye, maybe for the first time. "And there's something else you should know. I was in the car with him when it crashed. We went into the river. I got out," I said. "But he didn't."

"Oh, Leo."

I ran my hand over my stomach, remembering how Danny had liked it—hard, flat and smooth. "God, look at me," I said, pulling down my shirt. "I'm turning into a blimp."

"This is no time for vanity, Leo," Dr. Early said. "Eat."

The list of strangers who knew about the baby began to grow—Kilroy, the druggist, Kilroy's nearly bald-as-a-cueball father. To most of the world, I looked unchanged. Had I not been so thin, the rise of my middle might have gone unnoticed until summer. But some knew. Women with children knew. They looked at my belly before they met my eyes and smiled. By May Day, even Phil, the bus driver, knew. He was like a woman in some ways, soft, chatty.

"Secret's out now, I guess, Stradivarius," he said.

"It is?" I slipped my coins into the fare box as we rumbled down Prospect.

"Can't wait to be a grandfather myself," he said. "Your parents must be tickled pink."

I laughed.

"What's so funny?" Phil grinned.

"Tickled and pink? You'd have to meet them, Phil. Anyway, they don't even know yet."

"They don't know yet?" Phil's face fell. "Ah, you got to tell them, Strad. Right away. A parent waits a lifetime for this. You tell 'em. I guarantee, they'll be tickled pink."

chapter twelve

Back at Cobb's Hill, I felt the old reluctance to speak aloud what felt safer kept inside the vault of my soul. I was so long in the habit of keeping secrets—getting my period in the seventh grade, finding the bird man's dead body in Five Moon Fields, hitchhiking clear to Buffalo to hear a Nina Simone concert and back in one night, dozing in the cab of a ten-wheeler while country music wailed on the radio. I still kept the secrets of a game my friend Rosalie had played with one of the uncles in a dark closet, where both the prizes and the penalties were forbidden touches. No one ever knew about the snake I'd taken from a boy I met wandering the streets with it wrapped around his neck, a boy whose mother had ordered it out of the house. The snake—Charlie was its name—lived in a special annex of my Animal Hotel for two years until it squeezed through a hole in the screen and swallowed all the resident mice, then slid off in search of a more exotic life, ending up in an alleyway in Harvard Square on the six o'clock news.

I'd always seen secrets as my private property, even persuaded myself that their keeping was a daughter's kindness, one of few I could afford. But by the end of May, as the baby drew tiny bits of me away from its center, I felt more human in a flesh and bone sense than ever before, more scattered, more vulnerable. The harboring of my live and growing secret began to seem selfish and self-destructive. Both the baby and the secret pushed and pulled at my seams, threatening revolt. It became clear to me that I couldn't keep both.

I decided to tell my father first about the baby, then hope he'd find a way to tell Lydia with his close-to-whispering words, a way that wouldn't drive her away from the breakfast table again, for I couldn't be responsible for reversing the one spare miracle of the last twenty years. And if my father saw pain in Lydia's eyes or she said, "baby?" with a glassy look in her eye, if he came back to me with shrugs of apology, then I'd have to use my own blunt ways to make Lydia listen and hear, that she was going to be a grandmother.

On the night I decided to tell my father about the baby, I brought Lydia some tea on my way to the invention room. She sat at her desk by the window, listening to the radio. A woman's uncertain voice sang along to a strumming guitar. Outside, the chestnut tree stood broad and twisted in the center of the yard. Through the dwindling purple dusk, a few irridescent leaves shone. As always, I felt like an intruder in this room, someone who saw these images of Lydia through a one-way mirror. To my eye, she sat serenely at her desk by the window. But behind the glass, I imagined Lydia stretched out on a divan, silk slipping from one round shoulder, eating grapes, making love to a sun-drenched stranger, singing high notes or playing blackjack with the mailman and my old grammar-school teachers, even Danny. At night, she left her windows open and the mice and the voles and the crickets and all of the admirers she'd ever had, all of the hags and jesters and tyrants and kings from Shakespeare and Puccini, crept in to make music and merry in the nether hours.

My father and I didn't tread often or long in Lydia's room, for fear we'd shake the fragile walls with the rough push of our clumsy selves, for fear of ruining Lydia's private life behind the glass, which we had to believe was better than her life with us—the fates wiser and more patient, the lovers more passionate, the animals lighter on their feet in a waltz. For it was here that Lydia spent hour upon hour with her radio, in a room that swallowed anything louder than a whisper, a room that never seemed to change or need care, where the wallpaper didn't yellow or peel and the dust bounced endlessly in the sunlight, where the roses kept their soft crimson on the ivory wallpaper and the patches on the quilt never dirtied or faded, even those that gulped the sunbeams.

In one corner of the room stood a four-poster bed, my father's father's bed and all the Baye men before him. I suppose it had once been my parents' bed—the bed where I was made—although I couldn't imagine them sleeping there together, let alone in the throes of passion. For as long as I could remember, my father had been the keeper of the night, working until dawn in his invention room at the other end of the hall. My only picture of him at rest was a lumpy form stretched out on the cot in his room full of metal scraps and tools, fully clothed, mind running in another direction from his bloodshot eyes. Lydia, too, never seemed to rumple or soil the bed clothes, resting on top of the quilted coverlet, fully dressed, ankle bones touching, still and waxen as a poisoned fairy-tale queen. All my life I'd kept watch on my mother through the crack in that door, after school on my way upstairs, or at night when I'd come down from the attic, restless, roaming, to eat spoonfuls of peanut butter from a jar, or to sit with my father on a high stool and watch the slow, creaky wheels of his inventions and our lives turn.

These riddles of prudery and sleeplessness and suspended time—why we never cried or slept or collided in this house, why I rarely heard a cough or a toilet flushing, or smelled the smells of shaving cream or sweat or chocolate kisses, why all that lay between these walls hadn't crumbled with time and neglect, were all still mysteries to me. What was the black magic of preservation that had kept time at bay? What formaldehyde wind had kept us all those years from slow ruin? As a child, I'd wondered if we'd live for a thousand years.

"Lydia?" I knocked softly, twice, before I entered. "I brought you some tea."

"The chestnut tree," she said, turning slowly. "It just bloomed."

"Just?"

Pressing my face up to the window, I felt a sudden wrench of fatigue. For a moment I considered a life that allowed the watching of a blooming tree, leaf by unfurling leaf. Maybe I'd give in to it all. Maybe I'd pull up a chair beside Lydia, let my eyes glaze over and my mind go blank. What would it feel like to sit down with my mother and listen to the sound of my own voice going dull?

"Yesterday, it was no more than a tangle of bare branches, Claire," Lydia said. "Today, it's a tree again."

And when, I wanted to ask her, will you be a person again? I felt the hot wax of frustration drip over me where I stood, modern and pregnant, in my purple Fruit of the Loom t-shirt and hacked-off hair, holding a cup of Salada tea whose fortune read, *"Dracula is a vein man."*

"Let's go outside, Lydia." I put the tea down on the desk. "Let's go outside and see the tree. We'll walk to the bench. We'll sit for a while." I'd always thought that if I could only get Lydia out to that tree, something would change —the wind would shift or a chestnut would fall on her head and zap the sense back into her. On that day, we'd open the lid of the piano and the nesting bats would whoosh out. Lydia's voice would rise and soar out through the night and the music would heal us all.

"Go outside?" Lydia's voice echoed in a hard and crumbling memory. "Sit for a while?"

When I was young, a devil girl lived inside me. She snuck out from her corner sometimes to prance and play. From Lydia I'd learned the word sadist, as it described us both—me a little girl with two tight braids, hands stuffed into the pockets of my corduroy pants, her a specter in silk and lace. How many times I'd cajoled and dared my mother, pleaded for her company, even when I knew it wasn't really hers to give. I remembered a hot, hot summer day. I'd gone to find Lydia. She kept to herself in a dark room, sitting in a straight-backed chair, beads of sweat glistening on her brow.

"Let's go outside and have a campfire, Lydia." The devil girl pulled her by the hand. *"Let's go toast marshmallows, out in the back yard. I'll make them perfect. Golden brown. Come out with me. They'll taste so good."*

"*No!*" Lydia pressed her palm flat my way. I watched the panic rise to her cheeks, watched her lips pucker. Marshmallows weren't good for children, she said. They got stuck on the vocal cords, rotted the teeth. As I listened to her, my insides tightened. My heart withered and then turned hard. I let go of her hand. If it were true, what she said, what did it matter? I could buy marshmallows anytime I wanted. Eat them ten at a time for breakfast. Nobody was watching. Nobody would care.

"*Come on, Lydia.*" Once the devil girl had started, she couldn't stop. "*I know how to make a fire by rubbing two sticks together. Let's pretend we're the Girl Scouts.*" It was just a matter of time before she'd go too far, before I said the wrong thing. Fire. Sticks. Girl Scouts. Lydia rubbed her hands and wiped her brow, as words gathered speed and order in her brain. Hadn't I heard, about a bonfire at a girls' summer camp in Boise, Idaho, that had gotten out of hand? Just that week. On Tuesday. The flames had caught the tip of a girl scout's scarf and charred her through and through. A ringful of people standing right there and not a one was able to save her, the fire swallowed her so fast. Not a one.

"*Imagine, Claire. Bringing a little girl in ribbons to camp and taking home a pile of bones.*" I remembered my stomach turning, my courage spilling, my ten-year-old braids falling limp on my sloping shoulders. The cackle of a bird came through the screen door, and out in the back yard where I'd lain a ring of rocks for a fire, the crickets roared. I remembered feeling a fear so deep it ached. I remembered the echo of Lydia's voice as it chased the devil girl back inside me. "*Fire isn't a toy. Marshmallows are too sweet. Remember the girl scout, Claire. Remember the poor, poor girl scout.*"

"How 'bout it, Lydia?" I pushed the tea cup toward her. "I'll get you a coat. Maybe the green wool jacket. With the beaded edge. You wore it to the picnic in Central Park with the Westerlys. Remember?" I kept talking. Talking. "I'm sure the coat still fits you. We'll just walk to the tree. It's such a nice, warm day."

Wrinkles formed in Lydia's brow. "We may still have another frost," she said. "I learned a long time ago, Claire, that May just can't be trusted." She slid her fingers through the handle of her tea cup. "Colorado just got hit with a blizzard. An avalanche killed seven people in the Rocky Mountains. I remember an Easter snowstorm in Chicago. There was a raging fire at the arena. Eighty-three people were crushed to death. Twenty-six of them were children. Or was it twenty-seven? . . ."

"I don't know." I shook my head, let the idea of the walk go. "Drink your tea, Lydia. Drink it while it's still hot."

"Did I tell you about the man, Claire, who was weeding his garden in Ohio, just last week, minding his own business?" Lydia put down her tea cup. "A tornado hit from out of the blue, lifted up his house and turned his head clear around . . ."

"It's all right, Lydia." I raised my palm to stop the mudslide of tragedy, details of strewn tomatoes, twisted necks and broken lives. "We'll walk another time."

Lydia closed her eyes and turned her head back to the window. "Another time," she said.

"Good night," I said.

"Where are you going?" Her head jerked back around.

"Just down the hall," I said. "To talk to Dad."

The confused look came into Lydia's eyes, something that happened most often when the seasons were changing and when I said the word, Dad.

"You're staying here with us now, aren't you, Claire?"

"I am." Remorse slid through me then, for my intrusion, for the moment of serenity I'd destroyed. "Just for a while."

"You came in the dead of winter," she said.

"That's right."

"You wore my tweed coat. You came back with a fever. Danny wasn't so lucky."

"No," I said. "He wasn't lucky at all."

"He wasn't right for you, Claire. I often thought . . ."

"He's dead now, Lydia. It doesn't matter anymore."

"Are you leaving again?"

"Again?"

"You moved out. In June of 1977. You'd just graduated from high school. Elvis died that summer. The whole world mourned. His little daughter, Lisa Marie. That pretty, young wife he kept, like a jewel in a glass case. They said for years, he didn't even touch her."

"I was seventeen," I said. "I had a job. A new apartment. Elvis had a death wish. I wasn't surprised."

Lydia smiled. "At seventeen I was still in my mother's fold," she said. "I traveled to San Francisco and met the great Italian opera singer Pucelli."

"He kissed each one of your fingertips," I said. "And gave you a ruby red ring."

"Elvis shot his television with a gun. Can you imagine? You can see the bulletholes at Graceland." Lydia's left hand went to feel the bare knuckle of the ring finger on her right. "I had to take that ring off, Claire," she said. "It was just too cold."

"Good night, Lydia," I said, making my way to the door. "I'll see you in the morning."

"When you left, Claire . . ." Her voice trailed after me. "You said this house was like a morgue."

"What?" I turned.

"That's what you said. In June of 1977. When you moved away."

"I don't remember."

"Maybe you were right." Lydia's eyes burned silver. "Maybe it was."

"You say a lot of things when you're seventeen," I told her. "And do you know why?"

Lydia looked at me hard, shook her head. Fiercely. Eyes clear. For the first time that I could remember. Lucid. Listening. Really wanting an answer. "Why, Claire?" she asked. "Why do you talk so loud?"

"Because sometimes," I told her, "it seems like no one's listening."

The years had changed little in my father's invention room. I lingered by the half-open door for a few minutes before he saw me, paralyzed by cold sparks of déjà vu. For this room—a selfless, barren wasteland, piled high with hardware and books and paper and bottles, peeling walls and empty coffee cups, the old cot and green army blanket, a room with no pretense, no order and no grace—described my inventor father as well as Lydia's rose-covered room did her.

"Dad?" No other word reminded me so much that language was nothing more than human invention.

"Leo." The smile when he saw me was always real and I felt like a traitor that night, not because of the secret I'd been keeping, but because, somewhere along the line, I'd lost my passion for him. He motioned me in. "Come in. Come in."

"God." I ran my hand over the worn seat of the old stool. "This room takes me back."

"Back where?"

"Back to when I was little. I used to sit here on this stool with you. Hour after hour." I slid my leg over the stool, rocked my hips to find my balance. "Remember?"

"You were a night owl, all right." My father's head tilted up from his screwdriver. "I suppose I should have put you to bed at the proper time. That Mrs. Cutler wanted to tar and feather me. But you would have just popped up again. You didn't seem to need much sleep. And you kept up all right at school."

That was my doing, I thought. Not yours. I'd dipped my bubble gum in instant coffee and chewed it on the way to school, pinched my cheeks and propped up my sagging eyelids with riddles and rhymes and self-threats at my desk. I'd kept myself awake with sheer determination, the sheer terror of not being allowed to sit with my father anymore in the night, of losing my freedom, my self in family. I hadn't been a tireless child. Like the rest of my family, I simply had never been able to trust myself to sleep.

"Five years ago, I came down here to tell you I was moving out," I said. "In June of 1977. Lydia just reminded me."

"She never forgets a date." My father pretended to tidy up the table, gathering papers and making piles. "I didn't think you'd ever come back, Leo, not in any real kind of way."

"I probably wouldn't have," I said. "If it wasn't for the accident. If Danny hadn't died."

My father looked up from his pile. "Are you leaving again?"

I picked up a coil of wire. "No," I said. "Not yet."

His face relaxed. "I'm glad. Your being here has been so good, Leo, for Lydia, for me, for all of us. I can feel it. In the air. In my bones. Things are changing."

"More than you know," I said.

"What do you mean?"

"I'm pregnant, Dad."

"Pregnant?" My father's hands let loose the debris of screws and wire and duct tape back onto the surface of the table. "A *baby*, Leo?" The softness of incredulity stole into his voice, a hoarse cracking of tone and peaking of pitch, a sharp drawing inward of breath, and I had my first glimpse of a child's power, to make a man drop everything. And then my father's eyes teared, the way I'd feared they would, the way they did in love for Lydia or at a sad story in the newspaper, or in what I'd always thought was pity for me—a helpless pity I'd come to hate, because it seemed so passive, so undiscriminating. His voice came out hoarse, in a cracked whisper. "When?" he said.

"Halloween." I put my hands on my stomach, spread my fingers wide. "Boo."

My father's eyes filled with tears. "Oh, Leo. I don't know what to say."

"It's Danny's baby," I said.

"Yes."

"He won't be bringing home the bacon or changing any diapers. No little white house with a picket fence. I never would have done it this way. But it happened."

"Things do."

"I'd like to stay here if it's all right. Until the baby's born, until I come up with some sort of plan."

"Of course you can stay."

"I'm going to keep up with my music," I said. "I'm probably out of my mind."

"I wouldn't have you any other way." My father smiled.

"I want this baby, Dad."

"You're sure." It was neither question nor statement.

I looked over at him. "How sure were you?"

My father took a few steps, sat down on the sagging cot. "Oh, Leo.

You have to understand. We were stunned, completely unprepared."

"So was I."

"We were terrified. We had no money. I'd squandered it all away. Lydia wasn't well . . ."

"I'm on my own," I said. "Twice as poor. Three times as scared."

"We didn't feel fit to be parents," my father said, lifting his hands.

I raised my hands in the same helpless gesture. "And how do you think I feel?"

"I don't know." He smiled, looking as close to haggard as I'd ever seen him. "How *do* you feel, Leo?"

"I feel enormous," I told him. "And I feel scared."

My father nodded, fiddled with a rusty hinge, speaking more to the worn, pine floor by then than to me. "Some things take too long," he said. "The unraveling of old knots, old riddles. You try to be careful, but all you do is waste time. I'm so slow sometimes. So dense. And this contraption I'm working on . . ." He gestured down to the table. "All of it. I begin to wonder."

I walked over to the end of the table and picked up something that looked like a primitive, mechanical arm. The "Automatic Page Turner?" I asked. He nodded. I remembered the day at the breakfast table in February, when I'd first came down from the attic after the accident, when my father had been newly full of this idea, eagerly drawing the first sketches, the da Vinci book at his side. Now, three months later, there before me, assembled in ragged, disconnected pieces on my father's work table, it looked like some ghastly aide for an amputee.

My father flapped the hinge back and forth on its post. "Could it be a worthwhile thing, Leo? A useful thing? Or am I just a ridiculous old man, trying to make ridiculous toys?"

"Some people don't have the use of their arms." I spoke slowly, forming the answer as my brain parceled out its parts. "A lot of people read in bed, Dad. Sick people. Paralyzed people. People in bubbles and iron lungs. Tired people. Oblomov. He spent his whole life in bed. People who like to do more than one thing at a time. Like you."

He smiled at me. "Like us."

"I think it could be a useful thing." I picked up the bulk of the mechanical arm. "I think it could change someone's life."

My father tossed the rusty hinge in the direction of the wastebasket across the room near the door. Falling short, it landed on a heap of trash that had never made it into the bin. He ran a hand across his brow and looked at me long and hard.

"But not like a baby, Leo," he said, reinventing an old, rueful smile. "Nothing like a baby."

"Getting close to the half-way mark," Dr. Early said at my next appointment. Her house was being painted by two cheerful boys blasting loud, dismal music from a radio. Sheila, the secretary, had returned from a beachy place where she'd grown tranquil and brown. The rugs had been vacuumed and the dust banished. The piles of paper on the office desk had been tamed. The coffee maker was purring.

"How are your spirits, Leo?"

"Spirits?" For a moment, I thought Dr. Early was asking after Danny. I hopped up onto the table. "They're chasing me, I think. I cry a lot. About nothing. Nothing at all."

"Must be plenty on your mind, besides the baby."

"No, it's just a family thing, something that's caught up with me." I lay down and pulled up my shirt.

"Lot of criers in your family?" Dr. Early took the cloth measuring tape out of the pocket of her lab coat and measured the swell of my belly.

"Just my father," I said.

"Crying's a healthy, natural release, Leo. Don't you remember how good it felt, when you were little, to really let it all go?"

"No," I said, shifting on the table. "I don't, really."

Dr. Early unfolded her stethoscope. "You can't change what's happened, Leo, but you can try to change the way you feel about what's happened. Work through it. I'm trying with my daughter. It isn't easy. I'm so mad at her. She walked out on her marriage; she abandoned my grandchild. And somehow, I feel like it's *my* fault. I can't bear to think that I raised a person with no backbone, no heart." She put the stethoscope to my belly and listened.

"Maybe your daughter's scared," I said, when Dr. Early took the stethoscope out of her ears.

"Scared?" she said. "I've never known Susan to be afraid of anything. Baby's heart sounds fine."

"Good." I pulled down my shirt and sat back up on the table. "Maybe it was all just too much for her. Maybe it all crashed down and she didn't know what else to do but run."

"Coward's way out, don't you think?" Dr. Early jotted down some notes in my folder.

"Maybe," I said.

"You've had a rough time of it, Leo. And you're coping."

"Cowards mean well," I told her. "Cowards aren't evil."

Dr. Early looked up at me before she spoke. "So, you're crying rivers, Leo?"

"About the most ridiculous things," I said. "Yesterday, I was watching this half-dead beetle trying to right itself, and I broke down in tears."

"Flailing beetles, eh?" Dr, Early smiled. "Well, your hormones do go slightly crazy when you're pregnant."

"Mine are out of control," I said.

Dr. Early looked at me hard. "Blame it on your hormones, Leo," she said. "But only if they're at fault."

Looking back, I see how badly I needed scapegoats at the time.

c h a p t e r   t h i r t e e n

No more than a soft peal of chimes, the Cobb's Hill doorbell still made me jump from my skin. Washing dishes at the kitchen sink one June evening, I heard footsteps on the flagstone path, or could I have? I froze the way wild animals do at the first sounds of encroachment, a snapping twig or the rustle of dry leaves. Soapy water dripped from the plate in my hand. A buzzing noise started up in my head. In the back yard, swallows swooped from tree to tree. Plum dusk hovered.

Wiping my hands on the back pockets of my unsnapped jeans, I pulled Danny's Bruins jersey down over my thighs. As I made my way down the hallway, I took a moment to place my parents—my father in the invention room and Lydia in the rose room upstairs. The soapy dish came with me, as proof that I was busy, that I couldn't be disturbed.

Kilroy Brimmer stood at the front door, arms wrapped around his broad chest, cheeks flushed, curly hair sticking straight up from his head. "Leo," he said. "I found you."

"How?" I asked.

"I've been Baye hunting." Kilroy held out a page ripped from the phone book. "No Leo to be found, so I started at the beginning of the alphabet."

"I'm not listed," I told him.

"I met an Albert Baye," Kilroy said. "Over on Linnaean Street. And an Audrey. On Upland. Audrey was nice. She asked me to stay for dinner. This is my third stop." He pointed to a line on the phone book page. "August M." He caught his breath. "Is that your father?"

"It is." I held the dripping plate to my belly. "You're sweating, Kilroy."

"I just ran up Cobb's Hill," he said. "It did me in. I used to run up here all the time and when I got to the top, I'd just keep on running. I remember this house. People said it was haunted."

"Maybe it was." I dabbed my bare toe into the puddle of soapy water on the floor.

"I used to come up here to Five Moon Fields with a pair of binoculars," Kilroy said. "I even camped out there a few times. There was this old guy, a birdwatcher. He had a tent in the woods. I'd bring a chess set and we'd play sometimes. I always wondered what happened to that old guy. He just disappeared."

"He died," I said. "He died one day in his sleep."

"He did?"

"I found him," I said. "He was curled up under a tree."

"How did you know?"

"I used to watch him, with a telescope. Out on the widow's walk."

"Wow," he said, catching a drip from the plate and handing it back to me. "And now you're a widow."

"Why did you come, Kilroy?" I pressed the wet plate flat against my stomach, hoping I didn't sound like Lydia, paranoid or unfriendly.

"I wanted to see you." Kilroy said simply. A rising blush inside me died.

"Technically speaking, you can't be a widow." I ushered him inside as the door closed behind us. "Unless you've been a wife."

* * *

135

As I led Kilroy through the house, he whistled low through his two front teeth. "Man, they don't make 'em like this anymore," he said. "High ceilings, post and beam, wainscoting . . ." He looked up the stairs. "A net?"

"For a while I considered the life of a trapeze artist," I said, as we entered the kitchen. "My father thought I'd tumble to my doom. Would you like something?"

"Sure. Anything." Kilroy pulled a chair out from the table. "What have you got?"

"Coffee. Milk." I poked my head into the empty refrigerator. "Some dried apricots."

"Coffee would be good," he said. "Maybe an apricot or two."

We sat at the kitchen table with warmed-up coffee and a bowl of dried apricots. Kilroy chewed one slowly.

"I tried to ask you out the other day," he said. "At Brattle Court."

"Out where?" I asked him.

"Out on a date."

"There's no such thing anymore, is there?" I asked.

Kilroy rubbed his palms together. "Maybe not."

"How far did you get?" I asked him. "It wasn't a good day. And I'm kind of dense."

"Not very far," he said. "I was going over this chess position and a B.B. King tune was stuck in my head. That kid on the skateboard came up and wanted a game. I never really got a chance. So I thought I might try again. You want to go out with me, Leo?"

"Out where?" I said.

"Anywhere," he said. "Are you always this difficult?"

"I guess I am," I said. "Do you mean now?"

"Now's good for me," he said.

"Could we go to Fresh Pond?" I said. "To the reservoir?"

"Sure." Kilroy paused for a moment, confused. "How did you know?" he said.

"Know what?"

"I live at the reservoir," he said.

"You do?"

Kilroy nodded. "It's my other job," he said. "I take care of the golf course and fish balls out of the pond. In exchange, they let me live in a little house in the woods, rent-free."

"My father and I used to go there and look for bones."

"The old looking-for-bones date," Kilroy said. "One of my favorite kinds."

I got up to get my coat from the closet. Kilroy followed, eyes grazing all that was ours, his fingers trailing walls and furniture, brushing moldings, lifting up a silk jacket in the closet.

"Whose are all these clothes?"

"My mother's."

"Is she an actress?"

"In her way. She used to sing. Opera. A long time ago."

"Does she live here?"

"She does."

"It's so quiet." Kilroy looked around. "Where is everyone?"

"It's a big house." I struggled with the buttons of my coat, felt Kilroy's eyes upon me. "What are you looking at?" I said.

"Every once in a while, I remember there's a baby inside of you," he said. "I think about it, oh, maybe three percent of the time. You must think about it more like . . . seventy-three percent."

A button popped off the coat as I tried to wedge it through its hole. "Seventy-three percent is too much time to spend thinking about any one thing," I said, sliding a silk scarf off a brass hook and draping it around my neck. "Even a baby."

I put my hand to my belly as the door closed behind us. Ninety-three percent was probably more like it.

We walked in the dusk down the hill. The river was a restless, chilly blue under the rising moon, the first, sketchy reflections of the street lights and the boathouses flickering in the water. To the west, the downtown skyscrapers rose up into the sky, the Prudential Building looking misplaced where the river took its broken bone bend. A Red Line train rattled over the Salt and Pepper Bridge. The sweet, chalky smell of Necco wafers wafted from the candy factory in Kendall Square.

At the footbridge, a troupe of geese honked and scattered. We cut back through the city, down long, tree-lined streets of triple deckers with overhanging porches and lingering supper smells, children playing in the clinging jade light. A warm wind blew in fits and starts. We tripped over bulging bricks and roots and bicycles and bits of trash as we went, heard rock music rolling from a speaker perched on a window ledge, a woman's voice calling to her children from the door.

"I like this place," Kilroy said. "I know why I live here."

"Why?" I asked him.

"It's all here," he said. "The ocean, the park, kids, old people, Cheapo Records, chess, Emma's Pizza."

"I just live here because I live here," I said. "Because I've always lived here."

"Where would you rather be?"

"Bora Bora," I said. "Where it's always warm and the breadfruits grow like wildflowers."

"Too small," he said. "Too hot. No jazz clubs. No Fenway Park. I don't swim. I'd get antsy on an island. I'd run in circles and make myself crazy. No way out."

"I love to swim," I said. "I used to anyway. I'd bring the music. Surrounded by cool, blue water. It would be heaven. You could float and float. No one could touch you. And I could learn to live without pizza."

"Sure, you *could*," Kilroy said, cocking his head as we turned the corner at Prescott. "But why?"

Kilroy jumped into the driver's seat of his car. I leaned my head back against the seat and closed my eyes. He shifted into first gear and put his foot on the gas. We headed down Garden Street, past the fire station and the old dump. The evening was warm, and I kept my window half open, needing the air, but wanting part of the pane raised. I took long, deep breaths. Kilroy drove carefully. He slowed down at yellow lights and took the corners wide. He let pedestrians pass before him, used his blinkers faithfully. But still, fear drifted in through the half-open window and slowly made prey of me. It all started to cave in— the roar of the busted muffler, the sweep of the plastic dashboard, the smells of gas and oil, and the speed with which this rusty box of metal was whisking us down a busy street. I pulled my fingers into fists and stared ahead down the endless broken white line of the road, willing the car to stay on course, not to careen off onto the sidewalk or a person or a tree. I clamped my eyes shut as the heat of panic flooded my brain, and waited for it to be over, one way or another.

It was only when I felt one of my fists unclenching that I realized Kilroy had pulled over to the side of the road, that the car was in neutral, idling quietly, that I'd broken a sweat.

"What happened, Leo?" He rubbed the ruts my fingernails had made in my palms. "I lost you there for a minute. You made a weird noise. You scared me."

"I'm sorry." I pressed my legs together, took a deep breath. "It's just that I haven't been in a car for a while."

"Car. Car." He spoke to himself. "You haven't been in a car . . . Ah." He looked up. "Since you went down with McPhee."

I nodded. "I shouldn't feel this way. It wasn't the car's fault. A car's an idiot."

"No, I'm the idiot." Kilroy closed up my palm. "Let's ditch the car and walk. It's a warm night. You should've said something, Leo."

"I can't stay out of cars forever."

"You could."

"No. Keep going. I want to go to the reservoir."

"Bones?" he said. "You and your dad used to look for bones?"

"We found an animal skeleton once," I said. "Untouched. Perfectly in tact. My father thought it was a squirrel. I thought it was a chipmunk. Whatever it was, it died peacefully, in its sleep, maybe, like the bird man did, just as it lay."

We pulled into the reservoir parking lot where my father and I had parked the Rambler on our expeditions when I was a child, where by day, children and dogs spilled out of station wagons onto the sun-drenched hill with bikes, frisbees and balls, in winter with sleds and skis. That night, there were only a few scattered cars parked and no other signs of life. The full moon was slung in a hazy mist above us, completely round to my eye, lighting the reservoir like a spotlight from the eaves of the sky. We started down the path that wound its way around the water's edge, passing some night fishermen, crouched low on the stony beach near a hole in the wire fence.

The smells of maple, mimosa, and pine wove through the cool, night air. The winding path was so thick with trees, the moon's light couldn't penetrate. As we rounded the first bend, the golf course stretched out before us, a neon stretch of green under the inky sky, empty of all else but the rises and falls of the mounds and the weeping willows and maples and oak trees, an earth emptied but not dessicated, a velvet carpet laid. Far back, beyond the marsh reeds and the smooth hillocks, lay the backdrop rows of lit-up houses. We walked up one side of the green onto a dirt path that wound its way into a wooded area, bumping headlong into a cabin that belonged on an Irish hillside, or in a fairy tale in which a wicked witch was brewing a potent stew.

Kilroy opened the door to the cabin. A sign in the small foyer read, in bold, black letters—"No Humping."

I looked over at him quizzically.

"Trains," he said. "Not people, Leo. I found it down by the tracks."

We went through a second door, the weight of thick cardboard, which led into the two-room cabin. Danny's room had been full of pucks and trophies, broken hockey sticks and team pictures, dense with the mixed aromas of leather, gum and sweat. Kilroy's cabin didn't speak right away of either sex. There'd been an axe stuck in a wood stump outside. Maybe I'd expected to find a moose head on the wall or a gun lying on the table. My eyes took in the stuff of Kilroy's life—a jar of pennies, a cactus and a tea pot, a bowl of apples, a picture of Einstein on one wall. Another wall was covered with bookshelves, brimful to the edges with colorful bindings, sagging low with the weight. I scanned a few titles: *Think Like a Grandmaster*, *The French Defense*, *The Best Games of Capablanca*.

"What are all these?" I asked him.

"Chess books." Kilroy picked an apple out of the bowl and went over to the shelves to run his hand along the bindings. "This shelf is all tournaments. This one is the games of individual players—Alekhine, Morphy, Fischer. These talk strategy, these are openings, and these are endgames. And these . . ." He took out a book from the third shelf, crunched his teeth into his apple, and lost his train of thought. I scanned the titles of the books that were scattered around the room, *Topology for Fun, Baseball Encyclopedia, Autobiography of Nikita Krushchev, Mobius Strips and Penrose Triangles.*

"Have you read all of these books?" I asked Kilroy.

"I've read almost all . . . of almost all of them," he said. "I have a problem finishing things." He took another bite of his apple. "How do you stand on ends?"

"You talk in puns."

"Not intentionally. Do you save the best for last?"

"Sure. Get the hard things out of the way first. It's a natural instinct."

Kilroy shook his head and bit into his apple again. "But if you do the easiest things first," he said. "Then you're always doing the easiest thing at any given time."

"But that's only relative," I said. "It doesn't actually make what you're doing any easier." I started roaming the room again, picked up a book called *Black Holes and Bug Eyed Monsters.* "Where do you fit all this information?" I asked him. "I picture this big, huge card catalog in your brain."

"I just cram it all in," he said. "There's always a way to eke out a little more space."

"Eek?" I said.

His eyes came to rest on my breasts. I crossed my arms. "Eke," he said softly.

On Kilroy's desk, no more than an old door resting on two sawhorses, I found a stack of papers filled to the brim with numbers and nothing more, endless numbers tripping off one line and onto the next, page after page.

"What's all this?" I asked him, leafing through the pages.

"Just a problem I've been looking at."

"What's the problem?" I asked.

"They're looking for a new prime number," he said.

"You mean they haven't found them all?"

He shook his head.

"What kind of number will it be?" I asked.

"It will have thirty-three thousand digits, be divisible only by itself and one, and fill several computer pages."

"And what will they do when they find it?"

"Start looking for something else." Kilroy shrugged. "The number will have no practical value. Just another fact."

I shook my head, reached for an apple to reconnect us. "I have enough trouble finding my shoes in the morning," I said.

"Ah, but shoes are devious." Kilroy poured dry cat food into an empty bowl by the door. "And lazy."

I picked up an old black and white photograph with crinkled edges, a woman in pleated pants and a man's shirt, leaning against a fence. "Who's this?" I asked

"My mother."

"What's her name?"

"In this life? Aurora. In her last life, Phoebe."

"How many lives has she had?"

"Just two. She got reborn a few years back. On a mountaintop in Colorado. At dawn."

"Maybe that's what my mother needs. A new life." I bit into my apple, put the photograph back on the shelf. "What about your father?"

"He's a school teacher up in New Hampshire." Kilroy took a knight from one of the many chessboards laid out around the room and moved it onto a black square. "I talked to him on the phone today. He asked after you."

"He doesn't even know me."

"He remembered. Because of the baby. Today, he wanted to know when *I* was planning on having a baby."

"Could be difficult," I said.

"Right. I told him I wasn't sure I could swing it." Kilroy looked down at my stomach. "How big is the baby now?"

"About two inches," I said. "It's got a profile and all of the bones in its feet. The lips open and close. The forehead wrinkles. The eyes are still closed." I quoted verbatim from a book I'd gotten out of the library. "'The black pigment of the retina shimmers through the skin.'"

"Can you feel anything yet?" Kilroy asked. "Inside?"

"Not much," I said. "I have to pee a lot and I'm always hungry." I reached under my jersey to scratch my belly. "And I itch."

Kilroy's hand landed on my stomach just as my hand left it. I would soon get used to people patting my belly, even strangers. "Must be great," he said, taking his hand away. "Swimming around in there, all day and night. I wish I could remember that part."

A black cat came in through a flipflap door in the wall and rubbed up against Kilroy's leg. The cabin was warm with the day's store of sunlight. "Hey, Boris," Kilroy said, bending down to pick up the cat. "Where's your sister?" As if on cue, a tiger cat batted at the door with its paw before squeezing through and sauntered over to Kilroy, jumped up into his arms. "Natasha!" he said. Kilroy held both cats, rubbed them together, hung them by the scruffs of their necks. They dangled limp and serene, purrs filling the air.

"Boris and Natasha?" I reached over to stroke the tiger's fur.

"I was a Bullwinkle fan," Kilroy explained, as he dropped the cats gently to the floor.

"Who's Bullwinkle?"

"Who's Bullwinkle? You're kidding, right?"

"No."

"Bullwinkle and Rocky, Mr. Peabody and the gang? Fractured Fairy Tales? Television classics, Leo."

"There's something you should know about me," I told him. "I didn't grow up with a TV."

"No idiot box?" he said. "That could make you the eighth wonder of the modern world. How have you come this far?"

"I love TV," I said. "I used to watch at a friend's house." I pointed to his portable on the floor. The Bruins jersey slid off kilter on one of my shoulders. "Let's watch."

"No." Kilroy reached out and slid the sleeve of my jersey back to center. "There're enough of us idiots in the world," he said. "Come on back outside. Let me take you for a ride."

Kilroy took a book from the table and put it into his back pocket.

Boris and Natasha raised their tails and followed him out the door. Beside the cabin was a small golf cart with a fringed awning. Kilroy climbed in and motioned me to follow. As he started up the cart, Natasha's tail started to switch back and forth. As we pulled away, her green eye caught mine and she howled.

c h a p t e r   f o u r t e e n

Kilroy and I made our way in the cart down the bumpy path out of the woods and down onto the golf course. The silhouettes of the night fishermen darted along the path, as they headed back to the parking lot with their poles dancing in the dark. We rolled up and over the green, across the velvet field, swept under the bows of the weeping willows and up once more. The shadows of small field animals bounded in front of us. In the distance, the muffled sounds of traffic and the city echoed. The cart came to a stop on one of the mounds. Kilroy jumped out and took the book from his back pocket. I could just make out the title from my perch in the seat. *Vicious Circles and Infinity: An Anthology of Paradoxes*. He opened the book and started to read.

"'A sadist is a person who is kind to a masochist.' Think about it for a minute. Here's another. 'The chicken was the egg's idea for getting more eggs.' Ah, deep. 'You cannot step into the same river once.' How true. 'The word "dog" does not bite.' Now, here's one for you, Leo," he said.

Kilroy lay down and propped the book up on his chest. "A crocodile snatches a baby from its mother and offers to return it if the mother can correctly answer the question: 'Will I eat your baby?' Now, if the mother says 'No' . . ."

"She has to say yes," I said.

"Why?" he said. "If she says no and she's right, then the crocodile won't eat the baby."

I got out of the cart and sat down next to Kilroy, pulled my knees up to my chin. "But if the crocodile were to eat the baby and prove the mother right, then he'd be going back on his word about not eating the baby if the mother answered correctly. So she has to say, yes."

"Just keep your baby away from hungry crocodiles," Kilroy said, looking up at the sky. "So, you really can read by the light of a full moon. It's been on my list."

"What list?"

"The see-if-you-can-really-fry-an-egg-on-the-sidewalk, or fit-two-basketballs-through-a-regulation-hoop list."

"Don't keep me in suspense."

"Over easy at 120 degrees, and the net *is* big enough, though your eye would tell you otherwise."

"What else is on this list?"

"Go to Mars. Become a grandmaster. Settle down. It's not a milk and cat food kind of list. It's the big list. The cosmic list." Kilroy turned to me. "What's on yours?"

"I don't have one," I said.

"Start one."

I thought for a minute. "Have a baby," I said.

"Have a baby," he said quietly.

I watched the lights of the houses in the distance and the swaying of the tree branches and the cat tails in the marsh. Feeling Kilroy's eyes on me, I turned my head. With one hand, he reached out and lifted the hair away from my neck. Under a vein I knew well, a spot I'd made a habit of touching since the accident in a ritual of reassurance, my pulse leapt and fell. He moved his hand to the side of my neck.

"This is the part of you," he said, the pressure of his hand increasing just slightly, "that I first really looked at. When I met you at Brattle Court, when you first told me about McPhee. I was staring, right at this spot and wondering, how does life change for her now that he's dead."

I pulled a blade of grass from the earth, looked over at Kilroy. "That's my paradox," I said.

We sat quietly for a while. Kilroy lost himself in his book and I grew drowsy in the quiet stillness. When I yawned, Kilroy looked up.

"You're tired," he said. "Come on. I'll take you home. Or you can take yourself home. Or . . ." He closed the book and looked over at me. "You could stay here, with me, Leo."

I looked into the light of Kilroy's steady eyes. Exactly where he meant, on that soft mound of damp green grass, or on the mattress in his cabin, side by side, belly to belly, naked or clothed, I didn't know.

"One of those three things will happen," I said. I made a pillow of Danny's hockey jersey and lay down on the grass on my back. Kilroy's shadow fell over me as he brought one finger to the space where the top button of my shirt was open. I lay still, watching Kilroy's broad shoulders and the slight heft of his chest with each breath. Bending low, he kissed me, a brush of a kiss from one side of my mouth to the other.

"Now that I've done that," he said, taking a deep breath, "it's hard not to want to fuck you."

I laughed. "Such polite lust," I said. "What's so hard?"

"One kiss and greed sets in. Sex is the ultimate touch, I guess."

"And without it?"

"Without it's fine, too. I was just telling you . . . what I was thinking . . ."

"About my body." I reached up to touch his face. "You speak your mind."

"Too much so, my mother says." He held my finger and traced it over the ridge of his cheekbone. "God, you feel good."

"God has nothing to do with it," I said. Strange laughter brought tears to the corners of my eyes.

Kilroy drew away. "What's so funny?" he said. "Or did I make you cry?"

"You made me laugh," I said. "And then I made myself cry. I cry all the time these days. It's so strange. It's not something I'm used to doing."

"I can tell," Kilroy teased. "You're not very good at it."

"I know." I brushed my fingers upward against the grain of his shaven cheek. He bent down again and kissed me on the neck and shoulders. His hands slid under my shirt and this time, I felt the heat of his touch.

"Wait." I sat up and began to unbutton my shirt. My fingers worked methodically, plucking the buttons from their holes. What I was doing didn't shock or scare me. Touching Kilroy was less risky, less entangling than what little we'd already exchanged in gestures, glances, words. Making love had its own time frame, its own momentum. Your body picked up from the last time—the last sensation, the last smell, the last syllable—no matter where you'd been, whom you'd been with. My fingers slid the buttons from their slivered holes, one by one. I didn't know anything about paradoxes or prime numbers or Bullwinkle, but I knew the music of Shostakovich and the feel of the night wind, and I knew my own body and how the buttons on that shirt worked. My body guided me and my mind held no sway. I looked into Kilroy's ready eyes and I knew he'd do nothing to hurt me. For the first time, with a man, I considered my own powers of destruction, what I might do to harm him.

The ring of haze disappeared from around the moon. The chatter of hidden night creatures rose. The tips of the weeping willows swept the green. Warm winds blew hot, or maybe I only imagined that. As I undid the last button of my shirt, my breasts fell forward. Kilroy yanked off his black t-shirt and knelt by my side, one hand pulling his belt slowly out of its loops. As he slipped it from the last one, he held the belt in his upturned palms, as if it were a dead snake. I slid the shirt off my shoulders and it dropped, a white fish in a sea of moss. We knelt facing one another on the grass, naked from the waist up.

"You're beautiful," he said.

"So are you." I ran my hand across his smooth chest.

He dropped his chin, looked downward. "Why do men have nipples, anyway?" he said. "They're useless."

I laughed, circling Kilroy's chest with one finger. "Pleasure," I said.

Slowly, I brought the circle inward with my finger until it landed on one nipple. Kilroy's belly heaved. "Doesn't that feel good?" I asked.

"Yes." We were close enough then, to taste one another's breath. "But I swear you could have touched me anywhere," he said. "And it would have felt that good." We slid off the rest of our clothes.

Kilroy brought his hands forward, ran them down my sides. He bent his head and brought his mouth to my breast, swirling his tongue, sucking gently. A warmth spread through me, even and full. When the good feeling reached a fine point of pain, I pushed him away. I saw his face twist and I remembered a baby I'd once seen wrested from its mother's breast on the bus when their stop came, the confusion and outrage on that tiny, screwed-up face. A thousand strands of memory followed. A bottle full of sour milk, a bottle that was never full enough, never warm. A mother far away. The moon was suddenly too bright. The houses too near. My breath ran short. I pushed Kilroy away.

"I don't know if I can do this," I said, crossing my arms over my chest. "It's too easy."

"What's too easy?"

"Sex," I said. "It's the aftermath that's hard. What happens afterward, Kilroy?"

"It hadn't crossed my mind," he said. "I'll take on the aftermath when it comes. Right now, I'm just in this moment. And I can't argue with it. It feels good."

"It does." Kilroy's calm logic floated over me like a warm fog. My body relaxed. My pulse slowed. I stretched out on the grass again, like one of Kilroy's lolling cats, and reached up one thin, white hand to touch his face. "It does feel good."

Kilroy climbed on top of me. The grass was damp beneath my back and legs. The smell of wet earth hovered. We slid and turned, got used to the feel and fit of one another, rocked from side to side. Kilroy's hands roamed. Mine danced lightly on the small of his back.

"What if someone else is out here with a cosmic list?" I said, coming up for air from a kiss. "Counting how many people make love on golf courses, or if the sperm count rises with the fullness of the moon?"

"Then it will be our contribution to science." Kilroy landed full weight on my stomach. I pushed him a little to one side. His hand ran up my leg, along the ridge of my thigh, stopped when it reached the swell of my stomach.

"God," he whispered. "I've never done this before."

"Never made love?"

"Not to a widow. To a mother-to-be."

"I'm Leo," I said. "Forget the rest."

"Can you?" he asked.

"Most of it," I said. "Most of the time."

"Are you all right?" he asked. "Should we be doing this?"

"Yes," I said. "I want to. Fucking *is* the ultimate touch."

"I won't hurt you?" he asked, my center found, the trip begun. "I won't hurt the baby?"

"The baby's far away, down low, safe and sound." I shifted my hips and felt Kilroy start inside me. "Probably laughing at us." I rubbed his warm back with my palms. "We must look ridiculous."

With a breathless sound, Kilroy pushed hard inside of me. I felt a warmth and a fullness as he reached the deepest part of me. We rolled over and I sat on top of him, the tips of our fingers meeting in a high arc. He caught my head and rolled me back down again underneath him. As he moved back and forth, my insides tightened in one, maybe two quivers, so shimmering and quick, I hardly caught them, a pleasure born not so much of what Kilroy had done, but what he hadn't. He pressed into me, deep, deep and steady, came soon after, with no moan or spasm, just a sudden level breath and then a stillness. I felt something stir low inside me. Kilroy looked up at the moon and then back down at me, smiled as a crow cawed cranky from a tree. "I want to do that all over again," he said.

"Starting from when?" My hands ran through his hair as his head moved in circles.

"From the beginning." Kilroy dipped down to kiss me. "You play the violin and I'll play chess. You come to Brattle Court. I'll notice your neck and you go back and wash that plate again." He buried his face in my hair. "I'll run up the hill and ring your bell. You answer the door. I wasn't sure you would."

"I'll offer you an apricot and warmed-up coffee." I raised up my arms. "I think I knew it was you."

"And you can tell me how you used to spy out on the widow's walk, before you were a widow."

I turned my head away. "Don't call me that, Kilroy."

"I'm sorry." He kissed me again. "God, you feel good. We'll get my car and come out here under the moon and undo ourselves all over again."

"Is that what we just did?" I asked him.

A muffled "yes" fell into my hair. Kilroy started into me again. I held onto his neck, looked out over the flickering lights in the distance, felt the smooth ridge of his shoulders. This time, as our bellies met in a thin layer of sweat, I slid out of my body and watched. I saw Kilroy spread-eagled over me, the thick mat of hair at his neck, the clench of his buttocks and his feet bumping together at the ankle. I saw myself lying beneath him, my hair spread out on the grass.

Looking out into the night, I saw two little girls, in two separate houses. One was a girl I didn't know—with apricot-colored hair, being tucked into bed by her mother, read a bedtime story, sung a good-night song. The other little girl was me—black curls and rubber boots, sitting out on the widow's walk on a mattress alone, with a bottle of root beer and a book of nursery rhymes, reading to herself out loud.

Rapping at the window.
Pounding at the lock.
Are the children in their beds?
For now it's eight o' clock.

As Kilroy's back arched high, he groaned. Both girls heard the sound and looked up from their books. Peering into the night, each caught the glimmer in the other one's eye—and both mistook it for starlight.

chapter fifteen

June was gentle and steady—day after day of mounting sun and warmth, the slow, steady tilt of the earth from spring to summer. I heard hammering and scraping one night and came downstairs the next morning to find the kitchen opened wide to the yard, the lilacs and the weeds and forsythia lunging inward, a new plate glass window running the length of the southern wall. This was another of my father's acts of faith, made in the dark of the night—this, in celebration of Lydia's return to the kitchen.

I sat over toast crusts and milky coffee before I went to the Conservatory that morning, my belly a small cat ball in my lap. A lover was said to put a bloom in your cheeks and a spark in your eye, but I'd never known it to be true before. Others had left me pale, without appetite, on edge. Three days had passed since I'd spent the night with Kilroy. And there was nothing in my lexicon to describe the way I felt—lopsided, detached, surreal.

My thesis was due in two weeks. The audition was scheduled for three. These facts no longer drove me. They simply existed. Cause and effect might as well have blown to the wind. Time, if I'd ever had any hold on it at all, had slid completely out of my grasp. Spring was full blown and the baby was growing inside of me. I was not in love, on that pale-lit morning in June, but I'd opened the door to persuasion.

The sun streamed in through the plate glass window. Out in the yard, two sparrows squabbled. A mix of soft new greens sparkled in the rising light, and a come-and-go breeze set the tree tops shivering. The birds' spat came to an impasse and they flew off in separate directions. My eyes followed one of the birds to a branch in the chestnut tree where it landed and caught a flash of red. The flash bled into the blue of a shirt sleeve and then the pale flesh of an arm. Slowly, onto the curved lens of my eye formed the shape of Po McPhee, crouched in the Y crook of the chestnut's low branches, stuffing something into a hole in the tree.

I put my cereal dish into the sink, picked up a piece of buttered toast with one hand and my violin case with the other. The back screen door closed with a soft thwak behind me. Po stilled himself in the tree as I came toward him.

"Hey, Leo." He watched me carefully, spoke without inflection, as if, like the birds and the squirrels, he came every morning to roost in the tangle of my back yard.

"What are you doing here, Po?" It pained me still to see him. I wanted him to go away. "What's going on?"

"The birds were fighting," he said. Only with his eyes did he ask me how much I'd seen.

"I know. I saw them from the kitchen. What was it all about?"

"A worm," he said, jumping down from the tree.

"Ah, it often is with birds," I said. "People, too."

"Why?" he asked, and I remembered that with Po, there was always a why.

"It's a long story. I once did something terrible to a worm."

"Worms can't hurt you, Leo."

"I know," I said. "It wasn't really about the worm." I picked a leaf from the chestnut tree, twirled it by the stem with my fingers. "How'd you get here, Po?"

"The bus. Number sixty-four." He drew the number with his finger in the air.

"It's Tuesday." I sat down on the bench and put my violin case in between us. "Aren't you supposed to be in school?"

"I hate school," he said.

"All the time?"

Po put his head in his hands and shook it slowly back and forth. "Arithmetic," he said. "Arithmetic hurts my head."

"It hurts mine, too," I told him.

Po took the chestnut leaf from my hand and tore it in jagged half. "What do you think about all the time, Leo?" he asked.

I didn't know and told him so.

"Everyone thinks. All the time." Po shook his head again. "Unless they're dead. I think all the time. I can't stop."

"Me either," I told him.

"So what do you think about?" he asked again, dribbling an invisible basketball between his legs.

"I think about music," I said. "And Danny. And these days . . ." My hand rose to my stomach. "I think about the baby."

"Baby?" One of the birds returned cautiously, looking for food or foe. "What baby?" Po said.

"My baby," I said. "I'm going to have a baby, Po."

"There's a baby inside you?" He twirled the invisible ball on his finger, looked over at my stomach "How do you know?"

"Doctor told me." I handed Po the piece of cold toast. He took a bite and threw a piece to the bird.

"How does he know?"

"She. There's a test."

"I hate tests," Po said.

"You don't have to do anything for this test," I said. "Just pee."

"Cinch." Po shot the invisible ball into a basket of air. In mid-grin, any resemblance to Danny ended, so full rose the simple, fleeting pleasure in his face. He unlatched my violin case and opened the lid, eyes widening as his thick fingers slid over the cherry wood up to the rounded scroll. Danny had never once opened that case, never been curious about what was inside or what I could make it do. Po plucked the strings, one by one. "Who made the baby with you, Leo?" he asked.

I looked at the still hungry bird, jerking its head to and fro, waiting for more toast, down at Po's orange head, and then back at the house. I wasn't a good liar, had no reason to trust deceit. "Danny did," I said.

"Danny?" Po's expression didn't change. The heel of one foot kicked the ground rhythmically. His hand lingered on my violin. "Can I take it out?" he asked.

"Carefully." I showed him how to lift the violin up by its neck. "What do *you* think most about, Po?"

"Heaven," he said, without pause.

"You think heaven's a pretty great place?" I tightened the bow and handed it to him.

"Danny's there. I'm going, too."

"Not soon, I hope."

Po shrugged. "When it's my time." He brought the bow up to his eye as if it were a rifle and took aim at my face. "If they let me in."

I pushed the tip of the bow away, told him what I thought everyone who believed in heaven should know. "They don't give tests to get into heaven, Po."

"Danny tell you that?" he asked.

"No," I said quietly. Po placed the violin under his chin. I helped him line up his fingers on the bow and lay it on the G string. "Draw it slowly across," I said. A ghastly, cat gut sound squeaked forth. "Gently," I said. "Don't crush the string, Po."

"I can't do it," he said. "I'm stupid."

"No," I said. "A stupid person . . ." I put my hand on Po's and we played the low G note together, back and forth, rich and deep. "A stupid person can't count or take buses or, or play G like this . . ." I let go of his hand. He played the note by himself, back and forth, back and forth. "Or be such a good brother," I said.

"I'm not a brother any more," Po said.

"To your sisters, you are."

"I don't *have* a brother anymore." Po put the violin back down in its case. "It sucks," he said.

"It does," I said. "But you'll be an uncle soon."

Po's head lifted. "What do you mean?"

"You'll be the uncle of my baby. The father's brother. That's the uncle."

Po's eyes narrowed. "Am I the only one?

"You are."

"No one told me," Po said.

"No one knew." I latched up the violin case. "Come on, Po. I'll take you to school."

Po shook his head. "I can't go," he said. "I don't have a note. Write me a note, Leo. Tell them I'm not coming back to school."

"I can't do that, Po," I said. "I have to take you home."

He put his head into his hands again. "They'll be mad," he said. "I'm too tired. I don't want to go home. I don't want to go anywhere."

I brought my hands down and lifted up Po's head. It was the look of resignation on his face that pained me most. A boy too tired for arithmetic, too tired to fight back, was a boy who'd have no yearning, no courage to be a man.

"They'll be even madder, won't they?" I said, "if you don't go home?"

Po threw one last look at the chestnut tree and got up from the bench, followed me through the weeds and the cattails to the back of the house. Lydia stood behind the screen door as we passed by, a checkered blur, a whiff of almond oil and rose petals.

"Who is it, Claire?" she asked. "Who's there?"

"It's Po," I said. "You remember. Danny's brother."

"Who was playing the G note?" she asked. "It went on for so long. I began to worry."

"Po was just trying out my violin," I said.

Po went over and spoke through the screen. "Hey, lady, did you ever see that dog again?"

"Dog?" Lydia brought her face closer to the screen. "I had a dog once. A dalmation. Covered with spots. He was deaf. Dalmations are, you know. He had no sense. He was hit by a passing car. The driver didn't even stop. I could never bring myself to replace him."

"No, not a dog with spots," Po said. "The dog who jumped out the window. In the fire. Remember? The one who went on TV?"

But Lydia was already gone, gone from the door, gone from the kitchen, gone to a place where no bounding boy or dog could ever find her.

"Where'd she go?" Po asked me.

"To rest," I told him. "She gets tired easily."

Po rubbed his nose back and forth against the screen. "What happened to that dog, Leo?" he asked.

"He's probably back home now," I told him. "Happy as a clam. Digging up bones."

"That's your mother?" he asked, pressing his hands up against the screen, peering inside.

"That's my mother," I told him.

Po and I walked down the hill and waited for the #22 bus to take us to the Square. Phil was at the wheel.

"Who's this, Stradivarius?" he asked, as we put our fares in the box. "Your brother?"

"No," I said. "Just a friend."

"I'm Porter Sean McPhee," Po said.

"Is that a fact?" Phil said. "Glad to have you aboard, Porter. Find yourself a seat."

We staggered to the back as the bus started up again, flung ourselves down beside an old woman in tight blue curls.

"I couldn't help overhearing," she said to Po. "You have a very grand name."

"Yeah, well . . ." Po wiped his nose on his sleeve and worked his crooked charm. "You got nice shoes, lady."

Opening the door of the McPhees' fish market, I caught my breath and held it. The smells came rushing at me—fish, sawdust, lemon, brine. Mr. and Mrs. McPhee stood still and without expression, him with a broom, her with a piece of fish. The oldest McPhee daughter, Rose, was working behind the counter. The grandmother sat in her chair in the corner. Po and I stood before them, knee deep in our separate pools of fear. They stared at us with questions and no kindness. Against my will, my mind filled with pictures of Kilroy, and me writhing beneath him, the two of us wearing only the smiles of conspirators. Mrs. McPhee wrapped up the piece of fish and took it over to the register to ring it up. When she opened the cash drawer, a bell dinged and I felt the baby kick for the first time, a swift jolt to the underside of my ribcage. A thrill rolled through me as I brought my hand up to my belly, and caught my breath again.

"What's all this, then, Porter?" Mr. McPhee said wearily, after the customer had gone. "You've been at your disappearing act again, have you?"

"You little demon, you." Rose spoke from behind the fish case, where she was spreading fresh ice. "I took you to school not two hours ago."

"Did you walk him to his classroom, Rose?" her mother asked.

"Just to the door. He makes a scene if I go in. He's a rogue, I tell you. There's more than a bit of the devil in that one there."

"He's only a child," Mrs. McPhee said. "A poor, dim child." She came from around the counter and took Po by the arm. "Next time, Rose, you'll see to it that the seat of his pants touches the bottom of his chair. Good lord, Porter McPhee. You look as if you've been in a cave."

Po squirmed free and ran to his father's side.

"Porter!" His mother stood angrily, waiting by the window.

"You can't keep him on a leash forever, Mother," Rose said. "He's not a dog."

"No good will come of it," the grandmother said from her corner. "The boy's not a dog."

"Go." Po's father pushed him gently forward. "Go to your mother, Po," he said.

"No." Po locked his legs and looked over at me for courage. I sent him what little I had to spare. He ducked under his father's arm and went behind the counter, picked a dripping yellow sponge out of a white bucket. After squeezing it, he began to wipe the fish counter with long, smooth strokes, counting slowly, out loud, "one, two, three, four." After each fourth count, he dipped the sponge back into the water and started all over again, idle hand holding a tight fist. "One, two, three, four." He counted. The counter glistened, wet and shiny. So did Po's eyes.

"Squeeze harder then," Mr. McPhee said. "It's a countertop we need, not a swimming pool. Now listen to me, son."

"I can work here," Po said, still wiping, wiping. "I'm going to work here. I can."

"Sure and that you will, when you're a bit older, Porter, in the afternoons," his father said. "But the place for you to be working now is school."

"I don't need school." Po shook his head, back and forth. "I don't need it."

"Ah, you sound like your brother now, you do," Mr. McPhee said. "But I guess that's the whole point, isn't it?"

"School sucks," Po said. "Danny said."

"Don't use such words," his mother said.

Mr. McPhee got down on creaky knees, bent Po gently at the shoulders. "Danny stuck with it, Po. Danny didn't quit."

"Yes, he did," Po said. "He did quit. He died."

Mr. McPhee looked up at the ceiling and then bent his head back down again. "Tell me now, Lord," he said. "What would you have me say to that?"

"The Lord giveth," the grandmother whispered. "And the Lord taketh away."

"Amen." Mr. McPhee crossed himself. "Where'd you find him this time, Leo?"

"In my back yard."

"I'd like to tell you this won't happen again."

"It's all right if it does," I said.

"We can't keep him locked up. He may be a bother for a while."

"The boy's not a dog," the grandmother said again. "God have mercy."

"He's no bother," I said. "None at all."

"Wait and see," Rose said, from behind the counter. "Just wait and see." Pausing in her work, she rested her hand on the back of her hip, a gesture that had newly become mine that month, as my center slowly shifted. Through the glass case, I saw the rise in her apron and the sway to her back. And I knew.

"Congratulations, Rose," I said. "I didn't know you were expecting."

A silence fell with Rose's eyes. Mrs. McPhee slammed the register shut. "Take Porter back to school, Rose," she said. "When you get back, you can start the dinner upstairs."

"And shall I raise the roof as well?" Rose glared at Po as she came from around the counter. "Little monster."

"Hush!" Mrs. McPhee said. "Off. The two of you."

I watched them as they made their way to the door. And so, the angel Rose had fallen from grace—after Danny, the family's second pride and joy. Hair and heart of gold, secretary in a big bank downtown, Rose went to business school at night and helped out in the fish market when she could. She brought home money to her family, took beach vacations once a year and came back with gifts—palm tree nightgowns and exotic shell ashtrays, whiskey from the duty free shop, t-shirts, ceramic Virgin Mary's for her grandmother. She'd often had a good-looking, foot-tapping man at her side.

My father had gone soft and stuttered when I told him about my baby. And then he'd simply beamed. I'd felt first cheated of his outrage, his jealousy—the fierce inquisition I thought to be part and parcel of love—and then comforted by his sweeping acceptance of all that had been and might be. No sins of the forebears would be visited upon my child. In my family, mistakes could be reinvented, or turned inside out, turned back into a creaky wheel, or just the little bit of confusion they'd started out to be. The McPhees saw the dark of black and the glare of white, color-blind to the greys—reincarnation, reinvention, forgiveness. With Danny sainted and Rose shamed, the McPhees had been stripped of their shining stars, robbed of their most promising saviors. My family had never had either to lose.

The door closed behind Po and Rose. An empty moment in the fish market lingered, just the four of us now—Mr. and Mrs. McPhee, me, and the grandmother in her chair in the corner.

"Thanks for bringing him home, Leo," Mr. McPhee said. "We're in your debt once more."

"There's no debt." I felt the way I often had in conversation with Lydia, flooding with a frustration that pounded its head against brick walls of denial. "I'd like to spend more time with Po. Plan a day together, if that's all right."

I might not have spoken at all. Danny's parents went about their work. Mr. McPhee took over the sponging, sopping up the glistening surface Po had lain with his smooth strokes, and Mrs. McPhee put more ice in the fish cases. A swell of anger rose in my throat fit to burst. The shop lay strangely empty of people and noise and I saw how rare was the collision between courage and chance. I did what I'd done so often with Lydia to blast through those mortared walls of denial—I called the bluff of silence to stun.

"You should both know," I said. "I'm pregnant, too. With Danny's baby."

"What?" The quickest flash of light passed over Mr. McPhee's face before his wife's eye caught and flailed it. "Danny's baby?" He squeezed the sponge into the bucket with one massive hand.

I nodded and turned to Mrs. McPhee, knowing she'd speak next and what she'd say. "How can you be sure?" she said.

"There was no one else," I said. "I'm sure."

"Holy Mother of God." She nearly whispered. "If you had to have been a sinner, why not at least have been a smart one?" She wouldn't look at me, wouldn't call me by name. "They have ways, pills and creams. A thousand evil ways to keep this from happening."

"Moira, stop," Mr. McPhee said. "Stop in the name of God."

"No, Sean. They had no God. Sex before marriage. Heaping shame upon sin. And now look what's come of it."

"We were careful," I said. "I was using birth control. But it failed."

"It failed now, did it?" Mrs. McPhee winced.

"It was an accident."

"Another accident?" she said. "They say there's no such thing, really, now don't they?"

"Moira!" Mr. McPhee's voice grew sharp. "Enough!"

"Don't they?" Mrs. McPhee hissed.

Something vital oozed from the hole she'd made in me. "Danny didn't want a baby any more than I did," I said.

"He'd have done the right thing," Mrs. McPhee said. "He'd have married you. Sure and that he would have."

"I don't know," I said.

"Danny never shirked his responsibilities," she said. "Never once . . ."

"Neither of us was ready to get married," I said.

"So if Danny were alive," Mrs. McPhee said. "You'd have gotten rid of it?"

"I didn't say that."

"What's stopping you now?"

"Moira!" Mr. McPhee said. "I won't hear it anymore."

"Speak," the grandmother said from her corner. "Let the girl speak."

"What is it you're after?" Mrs. McPhee's voice trembled. "Money? Revenge?"

"I'm not after anything," I said. "I want the baby. It's all I have."

"All you have?" Mrs. McPhee sputtered. "All you *have*? You've your whole life ahead of you. Your whole blessed life. Don't fool yourself. A child is no savior. A child is a burden, as well as a gift. There's no turning back. They worry you; they wear you thin. They shame you, or they die. But still and always, they are your children."

"For the love of God, Moira," Mr. McPhee said. "It's Danny's baby, too."

"It's hers," she spat out. "Danny's dead and gone."

"It's your grandchild." The words wobbled as they flew. "I think Danny would have wanted you to know your own grandchild."

"You have parents, don't you?" Mrs. McPhee asked.

"Yes, I have parents."

"Then let the pleasure be all theirs." She turned away, tight-lipped and teary, and headed for the back door that led upstairs to the house.

A bell jangled and an old woman walked into the market. "What looks good today, Mr. McPhee?" she asked.

"Haddock just came in, Mrs. Jamison." His eyes turned away from his wife as she disappeared up the stairs. "Would you like a piece?"

"I had haddock last Wednesday," Mrs. Jamison said. "Or was it Tuesday? I thought maybe some nice scrod."

"Scrod's nice and fresh, too," he said. "I'll be right with you, Mrs. Jamison." Mr. McPhee led me to the door and said in a hushed voice, "Try to understand, Leo. A mother can never completely give up a child."

"Why can't she understand, then, that I can't give up mine?"

"She doesn't mean it. She'd never have you get rid of it. Never in a million years. Give her time, Leo. She's been crushed." He put one hand on my arm. "Be patient. Let the baby be born. Time heals. Things change. God willing, it will be a boy."

"A boy?"

"A son for Danny. What better gift?"

"A daughter, maybe."

"Aye. Girls are lovely and loyal, Leo, but a son . . ."

I stood by the door as Mr. McPhee went off to get Mrs. Jamison's scrod. A son for Danny. I hadn't yet thought of the baby as a boy or girl, not since the ultrasound test when it was only clear that I didn't want to know. I hadn't thought it mattered. But of course it did. Someone would always be there to pick up the pieces of a boy, but a girl would have to pick up her own. What was it I'd once read about babies in China? How they sent the girls floating down the river on a raft. Kept the boys and taught them how to row. My first maternal instinct, as it came to me at the door of the fish market, nearly curled my hair on end. What would I do to protect my baby, to empower her if she were born a girl?

As I reached out to open the door of the fish market, Po burst back through, nearly knocking me over. Rose arrived on his tail, breathless, her hand on her full belly, eyes sparkling their old blue now, with a gleam of malice or pleasure, I couldn't tell.

"What's happened now, Rose?" Anger shot up into Mr. McPhee's grey eyes. "Do you mean to tell me you're no match for one simple lad?"

"See the light of day, Dad," Rose said. "He's no poor, simple lad.

He's fast as a jackrabbit and cunning as a fox. He broke away from me at the bus stop. I can't be chasing him any more. Not in my condition. He says she's going to have Danny's baby. Sweet Mary, Mother of Jesus, is it true?"

"It's true," I said.

"I'm the uncle!" Po flung his arms around my waist. I planted my hands on his sweaty, orange head, felt the heat rise up through my fingertips into my palms. "I'm the *only* uncle," he said.

Rose and I stood face to face by the door. She smiled, the smile of a child who's connived for another to share the blame for a prank that was her idea to begin with.

"Aren't we a fine pair then, Leo?" She spoke in a whisper to me—only to me. "A fine, fine pair."

chapter sixteen

I rushed into Practice Room B, half an hour late for my lesson with Ettore. He sat waiting at his piano bench, said nothing as I took off my coat. We were scheduled to run through the entire "Waterfall Symphony" that day from beginning to end, a dry run for the audition. I got out my violin and put my music on the stand.

"I'm late, Ettore. I know. I'm sorry."

Still, he wouldn't speak. He played the first note. I put my bow to my strings, and we began. For a half hour we played, without any breaks, any words at all. When we were done, Ettore turned on his stool.

"Ears and fingers are working fine," he said.

"Don't give me the cold shoulder, Ettore."

"Cold shoulder?" He worked to unravel the phrase.

"Talk to me, please. What's wrong."

"Inside . . ." He tapped at his chest. "What is missing, Leo?"

"I don't know. I can't hear it. You've got to tell me."

"Spill your beans, Leo," he said, looking up at me hard. "What is different about you? You think I don't notice?"

I put my violin down. "You won't forgive me."

"Forgive you?"

"I'm pregnant, Ettore. I'm going to have a baby."

"Ah." He let his hands fall on the piano keys with a crash, mumbled in Italian before he spoke to me in English. "I did not think you had such a big appetite. All right. When does this baby come?"

"October."

"October. I see."

"What do you see?"

"That you have decided."

"Decided what?"

"To throw down the bath towel."

"No. I'm not throwing down the bath towel," I said. "The baby's not due for four months. I have time."

"*Tempo?*" he said, and let his hands fall to his knees. "Time for what, Leo? You will play at the symphony with a violin in one arm and a baby in the other? Where is the third arm, *il braccio terzo?*"

"The baby won't interfere, Ettore. I swear."

"No," he said. "A baby does not interfere. A baby is helpless, but all powerful. A baby does not ask for sacrifice. But he gets it."

"This one won't."

Ettore shook his head. "Nothing changes. Why should it?"

"Your son?"

"He's a lawyer. In New Jersey. A bigwig, now, a big shotgun in the courtroom."

"You made sacrifices for him."

"Of course." He spread his hands matter-of-factly. "I am here."

"Yes." I put my hand on his arm. "I'm glad you're here."

"What do you have, Leo?" Ettore said quietly. "What do you have that the others do not?"

"I have the baby," I said.

"It will be difficult, Leo," he said quietly. "The others will quickly fill your shoes."

"They're my shoes," I said. "I want to keep them."

Ettore smoothed back his hair, brushed his rumpled cheek, looked at me long and hard before he spoke. "Then let us begin again, Lydia," he said softly. "You are late. And the 'Waterfall Symphony' does not wait."

I thought of Kilroy that morning at the Conservatory, as Ettore knit his brow and pounded the keys, having called me by my mother's name, his shoulders slumped, both of us feeling more than a little bit betrayed. We waded through Aurelio's rushes, sank into quicksand, sailed his murky seas, swept through a gail to the bottom of his mountain. The notes flew by. I'd cleared room in one corner of my brain, a clean bin for sweet and strange new memories—Kilroy's fingers lingering on a chess piece or his chest in sleep, the feel of his hands on my body as they explored. I stole glimpses of him on the moonlit grass. I thought about the paradoxes he'd blown into the night like bubbles from a child's wand, the willow boughs trembling in the breeze. As Aurelio led me a dance through a meadow, I remembered the feel of cool, matted grass under my naked legs, the warmth and weight of Kilroy's body on top of mine, the rough-grained curve of his jaw, the slight give to his belly. I remembered Kilroy's gentleness, his even breath in sleep.

As I made my way down from the heights of the E string, I brought the night to a close. We'd driven the golf cart back to the cabin and made love again, slept on and off until dawn. The moon had vanished in the pale morning light. I'd slipped off the mattress and gathered my things. Kilroy caught me at the door and took me in his arms.

"Call me, Leo," he said, bending to kiss me.

"When?" I slid my palms over his warm back, swallowed the taste of his kiss—coffee, wet earth and sweat.

"Whenever you're ready," he said. "There's no time too soon or too late. As long as I know there'll be another time." He tugged at my shirt, slid his hand across my belly, and murmured, "How about now?"

"No." I'd broken away, walked out into the still morning air, where I stood still until my skin cooled and Kilroy's smell slowly evaporated.

Call me, Leo, he'd said. *Call me.*

Strangely comforting at the time, Kilroy's parting words only confused me in the days that followed. Danny had done most of the calling, the casting and cuing of our life scenes together. I'd wound my life around his like a snake, scheduled classes and practices around his school and work hours and hockey games. I'd somehow thought it was my responsibility, my job, to keep us together. Danny was moody, unpredictable, unreliable. He came and went at what seemed like whim. Days would pass and I wouldn't hear from him. When he came, he came hot and needy. A piece of the night was all he could ever spare, ever dare. After he left, I'd wipe the sticky insides of my thighs, straighten the bed sheets and wait for him to call again.

Call me, Leo, he'd said.

As the days went by, I began to see Kilroy again as I had early on, in passing through a rain-spattered bus window, a man bent over a chessboard with mismatched socks, an air of gentle mystery around him. The other Kilroy grew dim, the one who'd unfurled my clenched fist in the car and rubbed two cats together, the one whose hands had first lured the aches from my body and then roused it, who spoke in riddle and paradigm. This wasn't courtship as I'd ever know it—no clash, no greed, no jagged edge. Kilroy didn't push or pull, didn't seem to want or need or expect anything of me. This made me feel both too ordinary, and too strong. It would be different with Kilroy. There'd be no goals, no checks, no saves—no masks, no power plays. Life with Kilroy would be more paradox than hockey game.

A week passed. Came lurking were the feelings I'd been afraid of—vague longing and nagging doubt. Another week passed and I began to be afraid of losing something I didn't even have. I made my way through the days—played music, walked, studied, and slept. I ate tahini and banana sandwiches and stopped dreaming altogether. Ankle caught in a crack between uncertainty and desire—I waited.

When I wasn't practicing, I worked on my thesis, wandering through Aurelio's eighteenth century Vienna, on its cobblestoned streets, in its concert halls, its balconies and its cafés, in Aurelio's palace of stone, in his dungeons. I sat in an empty second floor room at Cobb's Hill, not far from my father's invention room, typing at the old "Lickety Split Typewriter," on which he'd once tried to rearrange the letters of the alphabet—"*The Way Your Fingers Would Want It If They Had Their Say.*"

Much of what I'd written about Aurelio before the accident puzzled me now. I crossed out whole passages as I went, ripping up pages, confused by the logic I'd used, the theories I'd put forth, the crooked halos I'd drawn. In September, I'd started out on a limb for Aurelio. "Maestro Misinterpreted," had been the early working title of my thesis. Convinced there'd been more to his story than met the outraged eye, I'd set out to plumb his life and psyche. Surely monsters were bred and not born—neglected, beaten, fed spider soup day in, day out, and made to walk on nails. In the garden of pain, I'd thought, could be found the seeds of madness. Aurelio's bleak family life—an abusive father, a mother sick and dead so soon, all those sisters to take care of, a talent too strong. Genius and hopelessness mixed in one bruised and hungry body, fed by a wellspring of rage. What could anyone have expected?

But slowly, as I worked that spring, my logic began to swivel on its axis of facts. I started to see Aurelio head on, as the ogre he'd been painted—without heart or scruple, lewd, unconscionable, violent, a brute of a man who'd held pissing contests with beggars in the dead of night, who'd sliced the index finger off a rival and half his thumb, who'd made women crawl on their knees to wash between his toes with their tongues, who'd clearly time and time again abused the powers of his talent and his sex. "He beat his wives." It was said, point-blank, in tome after tome. What had *I* been reading? I'd bent it all backward. The wives must have been selfish, I thought, besotted, greedy, jealous, dim-witted, bored. Women of that era had no voice, no occupation, no spine. They'd loved him too much, or not enough, badgered him, pleaded for his attention and his time. They hadn't understood his gift. They'd fed his madness.

But in the end, what did it matter, about the wives—their motives, character, moral fiber? He'd beaten them. More than one. More than once. With a wooden spoon, maybe a belt, a hot fire iron. The wives hadn't asked for it. They'd simply gotten it. I hadn't asked for Danny's roughness. I'd slid into it, weathered it, and, in the end, every time, let it go. A playful nip in foreplay became a bite in full-blown passion, a caress, a scratch, a squeeze, a near choke. I'd born the next-day aches and bruises with quiet denial. The look of anguish in Danny's eyes had always been apology enough. I knew Danny was no Aurelio, but by the end of June, in an empty pea-green room at Cobb's Hill, sleeves rolled up to the elbow, my hands dancing on the keys of a confused alphabet—I'd been given pause.

In a twilight ritual, I burned my thesis in the back yard. Gathering stones, I made a ring of rocks on a patch of bare ground near the chestnut tree and tossed in the pile of dog-eared papers. The flame of the first match swallowed the corner of page 47. The number shriveled and was lifted by the breeze, a floating silver cream puff. The fire bore down into the pile, untangling, lifting, burning, until all that remained was a smoking heap of spark and crackling ash. I felt the heat rise up my neck and through my nostrils. I smelled the smoke of old memories and dreams—burning sugar, wood, and sadness. I felt a swelling urge to spill and cry. It was the fire I'd never made in the back yard— for Lydia, for my father, for me—the fire that would have roasted the marshmallows a perfect, bubbling brown, that would have swept our lives black and spare and clean. It was the fire I'd never dared to light before, the fire that had swallowed the poor, poor girl scout whole.

My thesis got rewritten—not much more than the standard encyclopedia entry expanded, filled with my own vehemence and confusion, honest at best, garbled at worst. Beat. Blood. Bruises. Brute. I flung the words onto the page. I wrote about Aurelio's madness, the trail of havoc he'd wreaked through history, about his women—battered and beloved—his sisters, his mother, his daughters, his wives. And then I wrote about his music—the beauty, the recklessness, the reach. And finally I wrote about the waste of it all—talent, mind and time. In one tangled week, the work took new and crooked shape. "Aurelio: Terribly Talented Man."

Another week passed. Absence had made my heart grow curious, if not fonder, and out of sight led to backflip frames of mind. Everything was partly its own opposite, just as Kilroy had said. What was logical in one sphere, left to run loose in another, became senseless. I remembered Kilroy vividly and not at all. No sooner did I wish him evaporated, then I'd will him to come crawling back under my skin. The days rushed by and never ended. The distance between us struck me alternately foolish and wise, the silence protective one day, barren the next. I was only too ready to follow a clear voice that spoke to me finally one morning in bed.

"*Get up*," it said. "*Get up and go find him.*"

Kilroy sat alone at his chess table on that drizzly day, head buried in a chess book. I tapped his shoulder from behind.

"Leo," he said, twisting to one side.

"You didn't call," I said.

"I asked you to call, remember?"

"You shouldn't have done that." I sank down into the chair across from him. "I wanted to be strong."

He closed his book. "About what?"

"Seeing you. Not seeing you," I said. "Coming here. Not coming."

"You came," he said. "Does that mean you're feeling strong?"

"No, I have a weakness for you, I think. I'm not sure I like the feeling."

"So strength is power?"

"Partly," I said.

"It's also a state of mind," Kilroy said. "A farmer can lift a calf on the day it's born, right? What if, as an experiment, every day, he lifts the calf as it grows? The months go by. The calf becomes a cow. The farmer gets stronger. Every day he lifts the cow. When will he finally drop the cow, and when he does, will he be called a weak man, or a strong man?"

"If I know this farmer . . ."

"You don't," Kilroy said.

"This farmer will find a way to avoid that day," I went on. "Something will happen. The cow will die or wander off or kick the farmer in the teeth, giving him an out. Or the farmer will get sick or busy with the crops. It won't be his failure. He'll still and always be the man who could have kept lifting that cow if he wanted to, if he had to."

"Maybe you do know this farmer." Kilroy laughed.

A steady rain began to fall. I leaned across the chess table and brought my face close to Kilroy's, the steam of his wet breath meeting mine. "I'll try it with my baby," I said. "I'll lift it every day. My arms will get stronger and stronger . . ."

"And one day," Kilroy said. "When the kid's sixteen. He'll say, 'Okay, Ma, time to put me down.'"

"Ma?" I brushed the green velvet bottom of a black queen against his cheek. "Will he call me Ma?"

As the rain dripped down his face, Kilroy considered the question, considered the kiss. "If you want him to, he will."

Later, as we lay face to face on Kilroy's mattress, he leaned up on his elbow. "You're quiet, Leo," he said.

"I'm all talked out," I said. "Danny called me the mime. And he didn't talk much more than I did."

"That's a conversation we should probably have one of these days," Kilroy said, curling my hair behind one ear. "The one about Danny."

"We can talk about Danny. Any time you want."

"You're sure?"

"I'm sure."

"Is he here with us?" He took the hair out from behind my ear and put it carefully back again. "Here on this mattress?"

"No," I said. "Danny was very particular about where he screwed."

"Maybe I don't want to have this conversation after all." Kilroy pulled his hand away. "He seemed like such a hard guy."

I propped my head up on my hand. "What do you mean?"

"Hard to figure. Hard to deal with. Hard to please. He made a big impression on me that night at the chessboard."

"You saw him at his worst," I said. "Danny had a temper. But he tried to be careful with it. He was upset that night. He was . . ."

"Hard," Kilroy said again, running his hand along my collarbone.

172

"Maybe he was hard," I said. "But so was I."

"No, Leo." Kilroy traced the swell of my breast with one finger. "You're not hard." He brought his hand down to my stomach, and flattened his palm over my belly button, which had begun to push outward. "You are incredibly, incredibly soft."

Danny waited until Kilroy had dozed off to appear. I lay wide-eyed and ready as the ghost of him, weightless and grey, slid down onto the mattress. "Who's that?" he asked, flinging his arm in Kilroy's direction.

"No one," I whispered. Kilroy didn't stir. I curled up into a ball to face Danny. "It's no one, Danny."

"It's the chess guy, isn't it?" he said. "You're sleeping with Kilroy."

"You liked him, Danny. You said . . ."

"You cut your hair," Danny said. "Why?"

"It's just hair," I said. Slowly, the room began to fill with water, lapping up against the sides of the mattress. "It will grow, Danny."

Danny stood, ankle deep in the water, arms crossed, firing questions at me, not waiting for answers.

"You're fat, Leo," he said. "Why are you so fat?"

"I'm not fat."

"It's revenge, isn't it? You're trying to get revenge."

"For what? No. That's what *she* says. Your mother."

"Fat!" He swooped around me, poked at my belly and breasts, waited, waited for my answers. "Why are you so fat, Leo?"

"You know why, Danny," I said. "Don't play dumb. *Don't.* You know why."

Beside me, Kilroy lay deep in sleep, one arm flung over his shoulder. I kept Danny busy, occupied. I danced for him, wrapped my naked legs around his neck and fucked with him over and over in the rising water, letting him bend me in half till my back nearly broke, as he yanked at my hair to pull it out of my scalp, to make it longer.

"*Why? Why? Why?*" Danny's why's echoed, burning in my ears.

"Because I didn't die," I told him. "Because I'm still alive."

173

chapter seventeen

The week before my audition, Lydia came to breakfast three days in a row. On the first morning, I was going over the music of the fourth and last movement of the "Waterfall Symphony," the one where Aurelio sent you up a mountain and then tumbling down over the falls, the one that could unravel me at the audition if I let it. The passage had no theme or core, was only powerful in the rhythmic pulse of its chaotic swirl. I'd always heard in this movement the pain Aurelio must have felt after the sudden death of a favorite child. Now I sensed only a fury that must have burned day and night in the crater of his soul.

I sat over a bowl of oatmeal with my sheet music, trying old tricks of memory and rote—pairing notes and breaking down measures, assigning key note roles, identifying break points, oases. But the waterfall passage scorned gimmick and logic. As my tea grew slowly cold, my doodling became more elaborate—clef signs unfurling, a chorus of thirty-second notes wearing wings. I was drawing mustaches on whole notes when Lydia appeared in the kitchen. Her hair was different that day, not arranged in its usual fragile sculpture of poufs and wisps, renegade tendrils curling down her back. It hung loose in a silvery sheet down past her shoulders. I watched her come through the door. From a distance, she looked eerily young, but as she came closer, the skin on her face crumpled to sag and wrinkle, as burning wood does finally to ash.

"Lydia," I said. "What did you do to your hair?"

"Nothing." A frail hand went up to grasp a few strands. "I did nothing, Claire."

"Living dangerously," I said quietly.

"What do you mean?"

"It looks nice, Lydia. That's all. Your hair looks nice."

Lydia walked slowly to the kitchen table. "I was thinking, Claire," she said.

Thank God, a cruel voice inside me said. After all these years. You're thinking. "About what?" I asked carefully.

"That walk to the chestnut tree." Lydia's head turned. "When we might take it."

"Now." I caught my breath after the word was flung. "Let's take it now."

"Now?" Lydia tightened her grip on the chair. "Oh, I don't know. It's chilly still. What would I wear? I only meant . . ."

"You'll wear a coat," I said. "A coat and a scarf." My mind raced to keep ahead of her fears. "The sun's coming up strong. Have some toast. It's all made. I'll be right back, Lydia. Just sit." I rushed up from the table, knocking my sheet music to the floor, but didn't stop to pick it up. "Stay right there." I kept Lydia in place with a raised palm and made my way out to the hall. "Don't move," I called out. "I'll be right back."

My hand dove into the closet and found mink. I slid the full-length coat off its hanger, one I'd never worn, even in play, always reminded by the bristle in the softness, of the animal who'd worn it before Lydia. As I slung the coat over my arm, the satin lining rippled cool against my skin. When I got back to the kitchen, Lydia was kneeling on the floor, slowly gathering up the pages of my scattered music, lost for that moment in a pool of light and remembrance, her face partly hidden behind the silver strands of hair.

"Aurelio's 'Cascade.'" She leafed through the dog-eared pages. "I heard Giovanni Piato play it in Zurich in 1949. It doesn't seem so long ago."

"It's my audition piece," I told her. "I've been practicing day and night. You've probably heard. The fourth movement's giving me a hard time."

"Of course it would," Lydia said, slowly getting to her feet. "Nothing was ever easy with Aurelio."

I held out the mink coat and Lydia slid her arms through the satin-lined sleeves, an act not practiced for years, but still second nature to her. As she adjusted the coat on her shoulders, I ran ahead to open the screen door. Lydia stood on the threshhold in halting mink, and blinked in the late June sunlight, breathing in and out quickly, the way I imagined a person might stand on the railing of a bridge, waiting for wind and courage to converge at the precise right moment for the leap. I took Lydia's arm and tugged her gently out the door, feeling the soft air envelop me, as if for the first time, as cool and sweet as I hoped it felt to her. The birds greeted us with scolding chatter. Lydia's foot hit the brittle earth and she winced. She wore embroidered satin slippers beneath the fur coat, a gift from a horn player in the orchestra in Madrid. Her anklebones poked out of her skin like bolts. She tapped the ground with each foot before taking a step, as if it might give way to quicksand beneath her.

The chestnut tree was no more than thirty feet away from the house. We took each step slowly, a long journey and no turning back. Each time Lydia hesitated, I'd put my hand to her spine to brace for the backward lean. Finally nearing the wrought-iron bench, Lydia stretched out a shaky arm to touch it, as if staking ground on a strange, new planet with gravity to spare. Sitting gingerly down on the bench, she stared back at the house with a scrounged look of wonder, as if the house were the earth seen from that other, distant planet.

"Here we are," she said.

"You made it, Lydia." A wash of almost hysterical gladness spread over me, as I slid onto the bench beside her. "You made it."

"I always loved this tree." She ran her hand over the bench's rounded arm. "This bench."

"I knew you could do it, Lydia. Now, don't you see? If you can do that..."

Lydia raised a hand to silence me. She brought the collar of the fur coat tight around her neck. "I thought if I wore my hair down," she said, "It might help to keep me warm. Do you remember that story, Claire? About the woman who sold her hair to buy a watch chain for her husband and the husband who sold his watch to buy combs for the wife's hair?"

"O. Henry," I said. "All those trick endings. I always wanted to jump in and turn everything around."

"She only wanted to please him," Lydia said, her eyes darkening. "There was no way she could have known."

"It was a story, Lydia," I said. "Just a story."

We sat in the last warm puddle of light, as the sun slid behind a bank of dark clouds. In the gray morning quiet, the crowning moment slipped away into uncertainty. After all, we were only a mother and daughter sitting in our tangled back yard, with no one else to call our journey a victory or triumph. Marooned on the wrought iron bench, we listened to the mounting sounds of morning and the city below us. We watched the weeds sway and the scrawny squirrels scrounge. Lydia breathed in and out carefully, turning her head slowly from side to side, but never too far in either direction, never looking back over her shoulder past the tree to where the yard bled into the woods and the city skyline beyond, where the river led out to the sea.

"The yard's grown wild," Lydia said.

"It's always been this way."

"No, not always, Claire. I can remember..."

"What?" I leaned closer, startling her, spooking the memory, it seemed, for Lydia gripped the bench, her eyes glassing over once more. "What about the yard, Lydia." I spoke too loudly, too late. "Was there a garden here once? Who took care of it? What did you grow?"

Lydia raised one hand and twisted her palm side to side. "I thought I felt it," she said. "The wind's shifting, Claire. It's time to go back inside."

* * *

The next morning, swung by an unfamiliar silence on my way down-stairs, I poked my head into the invention room and found it deserted. I wandered the second floor until I heard a faint stream of water coming from the bathroom in the east end of the house, a room with a tilted floor and a distorted mirror, one we rarely used.

"Dad?" I put my face up to the crack in the door, saw him sitting on the closed toilet seat, head in hands, fully clothed, his elbows propped up on his knees. "What are you doing in there?"

"Just sitting, Leo," he said.

"Why are you sitting in the fun house bathroom?" I asked him. "That's what we used to call it, remember?"

"I remember," he said. "I just thought I'd like to sit here for a while Leo. I never really have."

"The water's running, Dad."

"I know."

"Turn it off, okay?"

"I will."

I pressed my face closer. "How's the 'Mechanical Arm' coming along?"

"You were right, Leo, I think," he said. "It's too much hardware to take to bed. I've put it aside for a while."

"It probably just needs some fine tuning," I said. "Maybe it could attach to the ceiling or the headboard on a track. Come out of there, Dad. Please. Turn the water off."

"I'm all right, Leo," he said. "Go on. I'm all right."

My eye narrowed at the crack of the door. I saw the water fill the bowl of the sink, overflow, spill, rise and start to cover my father, inch by inch. "We should paint this bathroom, Dad. A brighter color," I said. "Maybe an orange or a blue. Stripes or polka dots, maybe. Really make it live up to its name."

My father said nothing.

"Don't you think so? Dad?" *Dad? Dad? Dad?*

I banged my forehead silently against the door—once, twice, three times, before I turned away.

* * *

When I got down to the kitchen, Lydia was standing by the new plate glass window, hair up and arranged once more with the tortoise shell combs, but not as neatly as usual, a straggling clump on one side all but forgotten. She stared out into the yard. There was the damp, mushroomy smell of a lovers' quarrel in the air. I'd known the feel of its clammy hands. Something had passed between Lydia and my father in the night and I had no clue. I slept soundly through those late spring nights, heavy, dreamless sleep, undisturbed by Danny or rushing water or footsteps—no dreams at all.

As I came closer to the stove, and Lydia finally turned to me, I saw heat rise in her eyes, a roiling wave of silver cresting over the center of the pale, blue pupils—my eyes, I saw suddenly, lighter and less piercing in their vacancy, but my eyes in anger.

"What's happened, Claire?" she said.

"We walked to the chestnut tree yesterday," I said.

"No," she said. "I mean, what's happened to you?"

"To me? You mean the accident? I've told you so many times, Lydia. Danny and I crashed into the river. Back in February. I got out, but he died. I was sick for a long time. You know all this."

"Danny was a troubled young man," Lydia said. "Anyone could see. He had a secret. I worried for you, Claire."

"Secret? What secret?"

"He was scared," she said.

"Danny, scared? Scared of what?"

"Himself," she said, nodding her head. "It's no surprise."

"It's a moot point, now," I said. "He's dead."

"Do you know what they call stage fright, Claire?" Lydia turned back to the window, not waiting for an answer. "They call it death."

"That's not death," I said. "*That's* fear, isn't it?"

"Fear on the stage *is* death," she said. "I had a baby brother who died when he was two weeks old."

"What? Oh my god, I never knew that," I said. "What was his name?"

"Edward."

"Edward," I held the name gingerly and let it fall. "What happened to him?" I asked

"He just didn't grow. He was a tiny, crooked soul not meant for this world, I'm sure. He must have known it right away."

"My uncle." A tiny, wizened man with Po's face flashed into my mind. "You must have been so sad."

"I was four at the time," Lydia said. "Only old enough to be glad it wasn't me." She pressed her hands together at the fingertips and her voice grew higher, childlike. "That's what children do, she said. They think only of themselves"

"Who said that?" I asked.

"I told her I couldn't do it. She said I was selfish. That I had to."

"Your mother?"

"She said I had a gift, but it wasn't mine to keep."

"Your voice."

"She said I had to give it back to the world. But it was mine, Claire. It *was*."

"Yes, it was yours," I said. "It *was*."

"So, tell me what's happened," Lydia said, as if all she'd said had led naturally back to this question.

"I'm going to have a baby, Lydia." I looked her straight in the eye. "In October."

Lydia smoothed her dress at the stomach and raised her head. "I had an inkling," she said. "You were a beautiful baby. Fretful at first. I didn't quite know what to do with you . . ."

"You're going to be a grandmother, Lydia," I said. "How does that make you feel?"

Lydia put her hand to her cheek, and turned back to the window. "It makes me feel warm," she said slowly. "Warm and rather . . . old."

I looked at the piece of bread I'd mangled with my hands, suddenly tired beyond all understanding. I gathered my music and my violin and left Lydia sitting at the kitchen table with a cup of tepid tea and all that had been said between us in those ten minutes, more than we'd said, in bulk and truth, in all of our years together. And though she looked no different that day than from any other of years past, she was no longer the silent, waxen queen of fairy tale stuff, more a shaky sorceress risen back up from her melted self, one who kept silver magic in a jar and the blackened seeds of wisdom in another. Outside, Po's bag still rested in the Y crook of the chestnut tree where he'd hidden it, and the morning birds still squabbled.

That evening, I was led again by my father's silence to another room that had lain unused and dust-shrouded for years, painted a sickly, mewling yellow, musty and peeling—the spider room, we'd always called it. As a child, I'd gone there to make wishes and cast spells. I opened the door to find my father in a Lydia-like pose by the window, staring out into the yard.

"Dad?" Nothing would swing his eyes my way, not my voice or a cough or even the first steps toward him. I was disturbed to find him that way again, idle and lost by the pane of a dirty window, the gentle look on his face gone to Lydia's vacant stare. "You're in another empty room," I said.

"We have so many of them." He finally turned to me. "I see you got Lydia out to the chestnut tree."

"How?" I wiped a circle of the dirty window clean with the end of my sleeve and peered out through the peephole.

"I was watching," he said. "Here. From this window."

"Weren't you at work?"

"No," he said. "I didn't go to work yesterday."

"What did you do?"

"I went to the beach," he said.

"The beach?"

He nodded. "I had a mission. But first, I was here, a spider on the wall." He smiled. "And I saw you and Lydia walking."

"She wore her hair down."

My father's face lit up. "She looked beautiful, didn't she?"

"Different," I said. "What's going on, Dad? Lydia's acting so strangely."

"Strangely?" My father turned back to the window. "She came to talk to me last night, Leo. After all these years. And I wasn't ready. To-day I'm going over the conversation again as if I had been."

"I do that with January 28th," I say. "But January 28th has a mind of its own. And Lydia does too, I suppose."

"She thought you were in some trouble, Leo."

"I told her about the baby," I said. "I think she heard me."

He nodded. "She's coming around," he said. "She's remembering things. Things that happened a long time ago.

"How long ago?" The back side of my knees ached. I slid my back slowly down against the wall and landed on the floor.

The moonlight shone through the peephole and filled a knotted column of the pine floor. "Light years," my father said, sitting down on the floor beside me. "Eons, it seems."

"After her breakdown?" I asked.

"Yes." He nodded. "Before you were born."

The empty years, I'd always called them, the ones between the opera and me, the ones that might not have existed for all I'd been able to find out about them, the years whose questions my father avoided, whose truths had brought the sag to his jowl and the wrinkles to the corners of his eyes.

"It was an odd thing, Leo." With nothing but the spiders and peeling walls as witnesses, my father set out to tell me the story. "Someone slipped a note under our front door one day. It was typed, addressed to me. I was never able to track the author down. The note said did I know that my wife was leaving the house at night, that she stood on the streetcorner, never warmly enough dressed, waiting for a car that came to pick her up. They saw no signs of me, and knew she'd been ill. They signed themselves, *Concerned.* "

"Spies," I said. "I wasn't the only one."

"The terrible thing was, Leo," my father said. "I *didn't* know. I was always working upstairs. I just assumed that Lydia was asleep in her room. She'd never been one to say goodnight. I'd come to think of her as an invalid, a child."

"Where was she going?" I asked him.

"To visit an old friend, a cellist. He lived in Harvard Square. She was going there to sing, she told me. Anton was helping her to get her voice back."

"Anton?"

"That was his name."

"What did you do?"

"I let her go, Leo," he said. "I would have done anything to get her voice back, and what did the rest matter? I made her promise she wouldn't keep any more secrets from me. I told her she could do anything she pleased. That's all she needed to hear, Leo. That she wasn't a prisoner. I understood it then. It was so simple. When she lost her voice, she thought she'd lost her will."

My father stretched out his legs, settled more comfortably into the story. "From then on, whenever Lydia asked, I'd drive her to Anton's house in the Rambler. He lived above a shoe repair shop in Dunster Alley. I remember the smells so well, mink oil and leather. She'd call when she was ready to come home, and I'd go pick her up. Sometimes it was midnight; sometimes it was dawn. We'd sail back home in the Rambler. The Square would be empty except for the vagrants. Lydia would be in high spirits. She'd make me stop the car and give them coins and she'd sing to them. They waited for her. They called her 'the good witch.'"

"Oh, my god," I whispered.

"For a while," my father went on, "Lydia seemed more like her old self. I'd hear her singing out in the yard. She started a garden, planted seeds. We had candlelit dinners. I made a pot roast once, I remember. And macaroons. I was grateful to Anton. For a while, I was hopeful." He looked over at me, as if the story were coming to a close. "And then Lydia got pregnant with you," he said with a smile. "That was the happy part, old girl. The rest, as they say . . ."

"No. You can't stop there," I said. "That's not fair, Dad."

My father sighed. "About a year later, soon after you were born, Leo, Anton killed himself," he said. "Lydia collapsed all over again. They wanted her to identify him at the morgue. Of course," he looked at me hard, "I couldn't let her go."

"You went," I said.

"I did."

"Were they lovers?"

"I don't know."

"You never asked?"

"What good would it have done?"

"It was your right to know, Dad. You should have asked her."

"She was happy again, Leo. For a while, she was happy."

"She got pregnant and you didn't even know whose baby it was?"

"After all that had happened, it didn't seem important. Either way, I knew you'd be our child."

"You really don't know?"

My father joined his hands at the palm. "I really don't know."

"Lydia must know. We've got to ask her."

"She may," he said. "But I wouldn't be the least bit surprised, Leo, if there's no answer to the question."

"Of course there's an answer," I said. "It's just a matter of finding out the facts."

"Facts." He threw up his hands. "Half are with a dead man, Leo, and the rest are with Lydia." His hands landed gnarled in his lap. "Facts," he said softly. "The truth is, I never really wanted to know."

"I have to know," I said.

"Ask her then, Leo," my father said quietly. "Ask her."

"Oh, god. Half the time she still doesn't even know what day it is."

"She walked out to the tree."

"That took her twenty years," I said. "How long before she walks down the hill, before she buys a carton of milk, before she can answer a question like, were you screwing this guy, Anton?

"Screwing?"

"Screwing, Dad. It's not just something you do to a piece of wood."

"Right." My father got to his feet and dusted off his pants. "I think your mother may finally be getting well, Leo." He didn't often refer to her this way.

"You don't sound very happy about it."

"It's all I've ever wanted." I heard a slight tremor in his voice, and understood suddenly that he was scared. "I just want Lydia to know that she can still trust us," he said. "That's all."

"Why wouldn't she trust us?" I asked.

"She's slipping back over the rain line, Leo. She's at the edge. She's walking slowly. We have to be careful."

"We've spent our whole lives being careful of her," I said.

"It's true," he said. "Maybe we had it all wrong. But still, walk softly, Leo. Please. Take care."

"I'd never hurt Lydia," I said. "You know I'd never hurt her."

"I know, old girl," my father said. "But right now, you're the one that can."

chapter eighteen

On the third morning, I was maybe more hopeful than sure, as I came down the stairs, tired and out of sorts, that Lydia wouldn't appear. We all needed time to recover, freshly scraped by the jagged edges of rocks discovered while turning over the earth of change. But she was there before me in the kitchen again, and yet with more changes on her—a new shirt, rayon, maybe, shimmery, mustard-colored, tucked into the waist of a blue velveteen skirt. Statuesque at the stove, pot raised in hand, she smiled.

"I'm making you an egg, Claire," she said, as I sat down.

"Making me an egg?"

"A soft-boiled egg," she said. "I ate them by the bucketful when I was pregnant with you. Three minutes from the boil. Or is it two?"

"I don't know," I said. "I've never made one." I didn't tell Lydia that I stayed away from eggs for the same reason I did fur coats, every yolk seen as the beakless blur of a chicken, the white its colorless blood.

"Eggs have great healing powers," Lydia said. "Long ago, I drank raw egg potions. With a dash of vanilla. And a teaspoon of sugar."

"What for?" I asked.

"Clarification," she said. "To clear the throat."

"Ugh," I said. "I'll make some toast." I didn't understand what we were doing there in the kitchen, Lydia and I, acting out this charade of three mornings, while my father roamed the house like an amnesiac in search of his name. My mother stood before me, draped in memory and mustard yellow, making me a soft-boiled egg. It was a breathless moment, terrifying and comical both, the moment before the parachutist jumps out of the plane, a moment at all costs to be left alone. I dared not breathe too hard, say anything that might jolt Lydia or dissuade her from her course. I watched her, more fascinated by the play of her hands and the dance of her eyes than by any book I'd ever read, any fantasy I'd ever spun. I would be careful, as my father had asked. I would just make toast.

Time moved in slow, wobbly motion. I turned on the flame under the wire toast maker and separated the frozen slices of raisin bread. Lydia filled the pot with water and turned on the burner next to mine, staring fiercely at the water as it heated, a speckled, brown egg in her hand. I stood next to her, turning the bread slices, tiger stripes lining their backs. I watched the egg water gather heat and strength in the old, dented pot, bubbles climbing its tarnished walls. I buttered slice after slice of toast that would never get eaten, piling them high on a saucer.

"They say a watched pot never boils, Claire," Lydia said. "But, in the end, of course, it does."

I waited for the story about the child who'd pulled the pot off the stove and was left with no scalp and no fingerprints, but it never came, the boy who cried wolf and cut off his nose to spite his face, the girl who licked an icicle and pulled off part of her tongue. Lydia's big hand released the egg into the rapids and pulled back into a fist as the boiling water hissed and spat. She counted Mississippi's under her breath, clutching a long-handled silver spoon, long past a hundred. And when the counting was done, she took the pot off the stove and ran it under cold water in the sink, bottom lip tucked behind her front teeth.

Lifting the steaming egg out of the cold water, Lydia placed it in a china bowl, where it rattled fitfully as she brought it over to me at the table. I sat with the stack of toast before me and took the bowl from her shaky hands. Lydia stood beside me as I had once stood beside her out on the widow's walk as a child, with a maple leaf mud pie and an acorn and twig sandwich, waiting to make sure that the offering was, if not edible, admired—that at least it would be praised.

Cracking the eggshell with my knife, I sliced through the thick, watery white, which wobbled and quivered as it split. I placed the egg's cap on the plate beside me. With a battered spoon, I dipped inside and pulled up some of the yolk, thick and gooey, the filmy white of the egg still clinging. I choked back the kind of spilling-over nausea that had come to me in the early days of pregnancy and wondered where my father was, why he wasn't there to help me. Looking back and forth from me to the egg, Lydia examined her work for imperfection. "Looks about right," she said. "Don't you think, Claire?"

"It looks good." The lie puckered my mouth. I took a swallow of the egg, ordered it to descend and be still. A bite of toast helped to chase it down, and a gulp of coffee doused the whole, squalid mess.

"Well," Lydia said. "How is it, Claire?"

"Fine," I managed to say. "It's just fine."

"It tastes all right? Really?"

"Really. It does, Lydia. It's the best egg . . . you've ever made me."

Lydia nodded, took a long, deep breath. The silver spoon clattered into the sink. Her hands trembled slightly. "I couldn't remember if it was two or three minutes from the boil," she said. "So I split the difference." She headed for the door, her back damp, with what I wasn't sure. Halfway there, she turned around. "Have you seen my radio, Claire?"

"No," I said. "I haven't. Not for a while."

"The Red Sox are playing Seattle this afternoon," she said. "Bruce Hurst is on the mound. He's due for a win." Lydia paused at the door. "All of a sudden, I'm so tired."

"Wait." I didn't want to let Lydia go until the egg ritual had explained itself, until I could ask her about Anton, until I could look at her face and see there my mother. I thought if I didn't speak at that moment, my voice might crack, if I didn't act, I might not move for a hundred years. "Let's walk again, Lydia," I said. "Maybe a little farther this time. Down the hill. The lilacs are out. It's even warmer than yesterday."

"Not today, Claire." Lydia said. "I couldn't walk again today."

"But you did, Lydia," I said. "You walked to the chestnut tree with me yesterday, didn't you?"

"Yesterday," she said, "was the fifteenth anniversary of Anna Fitziu's death. She was a great soprano. She . . ."

"You did, Lydia, didn't you," I interrupted. "Tell me that you did."

"All right then, Claire." Lydia's voice evened, as if to humor a petulant child. "I did."

When she was gone, I took my bowl over to the sink and rinsed it clean with a stream of hot water. "Thanks," I said out loud, needing to speak. To someone. Something. "Thanks, Lydia," I said, "for the *fabulously . . . awful . . .*" The words slid down the drain with the steamy, orange mess. "*Incredibly . . . generous . . . inedible . . .* Egg."

The egg danced a lurching jig in my stomach all day. I sat at the typewriter, drinking water by the cupful, trying to make sense of Aurelio's last word, uttered without context on his deathbed— "More!" He'd cried it out. Once. Then again. "More." More of what, I wondered— more time, more music, more relief for his pain, more of whatever vision came to you right before you died? I ate Ritz crackers, one by one, slowly calming my churning stomach. In the evening, Kilroy appeared again at my front door. He slid sideways over the threshhold, as if through prison bars, and kissed me.

"My mother made me an egg today," I told him.

"This is news?"

"Yes." I smiled. "In my family, this is big news."

"How 'bout you introduce me to your family one of these days?" he said. "Anyone around tonight? A brother who sleeps on a bed of nails? A mad uncle? A sorceress or two?" He poked his finger through a spider web in the door jamb.

"Sorry," I said. "I have no mad uncles. No two headed brothers. Only my parents, Kilroy."

"Are they human?"

"I think they qualify."

"Do they speak?"

"They speak," I said, as Lydia appeared at the top of the stairs.

"English?" Kilroy's eyes rose.

"Of sorts," I said.

"Can I meet them, Leo? I'd like to meet them."

As if in answer, Lydia floated down the stairs, a specter of the old opera, long skirts trailing, hair arranged with combs and lace, a feather boa flung over her shoulders.

"Who is it, Claire?" Lydia asked, pausing on the landing.

"A friend of mine. Kilroy Brimmer."

"Hello, Mrs. Baye." Kilroy stood mesmerized, the way people always did at first before Lydia, before they understood how much of her was an apparition.

"Mrs. Baye?" Lydia gave Kilroy a blank look, and I was glad to have her show him this side of her right away, and not the Lydia who'd made me the egg that morning in rayon. "Oh, I suppose you mean me. Nobody's called me that in years." She smoothed her dress at the ribcage. "No one's ever really called me that. I was a Byeworth, you see, before I was a Baye."

"I'm sorry," Kilroy said.

"No need," she said. "Just call me Lydia, please. Everyone does."

Kilroy walked over to the bottom of the stairs and shook her hand. "Nice to meet you, Lydia."

"You're Kilroy, you say?"

"Yes."

"Kilroy was here." The fingers of one hand rose to her cheek, tugged at the skin under her eye. "I remember."

Kilroy gave Lydia back her hand. "You've heard about Kilroy then."

"Yes," Lydia said. "I heard."

It was a moment before their eyes unlocked and turned back to me. I felt an old dip of strength, the bottom drop from my well. Somehow, it didn't surprise me that, right from the start, Kilroy would understand my mother better than I did.

Afterwards, Kilroy and I drank tea alone in the kitchen. The crickets began their Buddhist chant and the June bugs zapped fitfully against the screen door. We sat across the table from one another, sliding over the details of the time we'd spent apart—music, chess, chatter about nothing at all. When the tea was drunk and the moon fully risen, I brought the cups to the sink. Kilroy came from behind and put his arms around my waist. I felt his breath on my neck, the warm reach of his grasp. The cups clattered in the sink. I turned around and wound my arms around his neck. "Stay with me," I said. "Stay the night."

We climbed the stairs to the second floor. The door to the invention room was nearly closed, and I had to open it, suddenly, oddly afraid of what I might find, my father slumped in a chair, smoking gun on his lap, blood dripping from his temple. But he was there, in a worn shirt stained with shellac and paint and grease-stained pants, working away at his table. The floor was dusted with sand, and more bags of sand stood propped up against the wall. Beach towels were spread all about, bright stripes and baubles lighting up the barren room. The work table was littered with bottles and brushes and spray cans.

"Looking for the perfect wave?" Kilroy said.

"What?" My father's eyes rose, startled. "Oh, I didn't know we had company, Leo."

"This is Kilroy, Dad. Kilroy Brimmer. This is my father, August Baye."

They shook hands and looked one another in the eye, lover to father, father to lover—in that one glance, making not only a connection, but a pact. I felt the green envy I'd known sometimes as a child, the collosal, unswappable gyp of not being a boy. The meeting of men and boys was so simple, so clear. A truce for any foreseeable battle was immediately part of the deal. Boys met and tussled like puppies. Girls met and steeled themselves, either to love or to suffer. It made me wonder, what did girls have to lose that boys didn't?

Kilroy and I left my father in his wasteland beach and climbed the last fourteen steps to the attic. My room seemed suddenly too small and private to fit anyone but me. I opened the door of the widow's walk and led Kilroy outside. I showed him my father's old telescope, still set up on a tripod by the chimney. He swung the lens across the clear sky.

"What were the three most amazing things you ever saw through here, Leo?"

"A comet in 1967," I said. "Spinning right through the sky, dragging two burning tails. That's one. A man playing the bagpipes naked in Five Moon Fields one summer night. I swear to God. Buck naked. That's two. And I told you about the bird man, how I watched him that day under the tree. I checked him every hour. By nightfall, he hadn't moved. And I knew he was dead."

Kilroy took his eyes away from the lens and shivered. "I'm cold," he said. "You have something I could wear?"

Back inside, I picked up the first warm thing I saw, a pink sweatshirt draped over a chair. Kilroy slung the sweatshirt over his head, the black mop of his hair emerging curly and mussed. He scoured my room as I had his, reading the book titles, fingering the objects, leafing through the music on my stand. He found my violin on a chair and ran his hands over the bumpy black case. "Play something for me, Leo," he said.

"No. Not now."

"Play me anything. Pretend it's the audition. I can't be any scarier than those people at your music school."

"Yes, you can," I said. "I care what you think. I only care what they hear."

"But they're the ones who can make or break you."

"And what will you do?"

"I'll listen." Kilroy's hands rose up. "I'll just lie here and listen."

Kilroy unlatched the case and held the violin up to me. I took it from him and put it to my chin. I played the forest stream passage from the "Waterfall Symphony," the one I knew inside out, the one that tricked you into believing there must have been infinite kindness and purity in Aurelio's dark soul. Kilroy lay on my bed, beautiful in my sweatshirt and his reverence. He shifted his hips as I played. My fingers felt the softness of his skin and not the hard cat gut of the strings. He lay quietly, weightless except for his heavy boots. He dug the back of his head into my pillow and ceased to squirm.

When I was done, I put the violin back in its case and went over to sit down beside Kilroy on the bed. He lifted his hand. I wove my fingers through his.

"Man," he said, shaking his head. "I didn't know you could do that."

"You knew I played."

"But not like that," he said. "Come on, Leo, not like that."

"You're easily impressed," I said. The look in his eyes filled me with a sort of anguished pride for what I'd managed to accomplish over the years. "Someday I'll take you to hear Itzak, or Stern. Then you'll hear great music."

I leaned forward, pushing my pregnant belly into Kilroy's pink one. He slid the edge of his palm over the upswing of my cheekbone. At his touch, I began to melt. I wondered if it was wrong for a woman in my condition to be so insatiable, if all this sex were bad for the baby, who was spinning, lying in wait, witness, always watching.

Sex with Danny had left me sobered and spent, with a few nameless others, strangely chaste and dull. Sex with Kilroy made me feel kind and brave for no reason. Kilroy found as much pleasure at the bone of my ankle as he did at the swell of my breast. He made a game of undoing my buttons and ties. He liked to fuck with the light on, to watch me lean and arch and turn. Kilroy made love with all of his senses. He really wanted to see me.

Kilroy unbuttoned my shirt. I unzipped his fly. I pulled him down on me, around me, through me. I guided his hands, made him writhe with my hands and my tongue, spoke to him without shyness, off the top of my head. "Move. Slowly. Over. God. Does that feel good? All right. Stop. Hold on. Oh god . . ."

"I've never met anyone who was so into sex," Kilroy said afterward, hovering above me, steamy and spent, in a voice I couldn't read.

"I know," I said. "Something's happened to me." Suddenly embarrassed, I pulled up the sheets over my swollen body. "I didn't used to be this way. I'm sorry."

"Sorry?" Kilroy pulled down the sheet, turned my leg outward and licked the crease of my thigh. "It's fantastic," he said. "I like sex. I like you. What could be better?"

"You like everything." I laughed as his tongue hit the ridge of my hip bone, and I pushed it back up into the air.

Sometime later, in the deepest reaches of the night, I thought I heard noises outside the door, the rustling of skirts, maybe, and then soft footsteps on the stairs. Kilroy stirred beside me, flung an arm my way. The next morning, we woke naked to a chill. My parents ate breakfast with us at the kitchen table, a breakfast over which we talked of the weather and the squirrels and the coming of summer, as if we were a long-sitting family, embarking on an ordinary day. And the people who came to Brattle Court that day to give Kilroy a game of chess were surprised to find him off his game, and in pink.

chapter nineteen

I woke up at Cobb's Hill on the morning of my audition, unnaturally calm, clear on what day it was, and that it would pass like any other. As the first light stirred, I lay in bed with my hand on my belly. The baby flipped and hiccupped and twirled. In the east, an orange glow brushed the sky. Rolling to the edge of the bed, I dropped my legs and feet to the floor, after which my body had no choice but to follow. I straightened up slowly, hands spread around the back of my hips. Looking down, I saw only the tips of my toes. I slipped on a t-shirt and walked with my boots and socks to the top of the stairs, rubbed my swollen belly, stretched tight and riddled with veins. I'd become part penguin, walked with splayed feet and a side-to-side tip.

It had become habit, as I made my way through the house now, to peek into doorways, curious, slightly fearful, never sure of who or what I might find, in what ghastly predicament or posture. Once again, as I had as a child, I felt the house's vastness and my infinitesimaltude, the possibility for evil deeds to go unnoticed, for the clever to outwit time. Out of the invention room that morning came the smells of suntan lotion and burned coffee. I stuck my head inside, saw my father at work, and withdrew quietly.

Further down the hall, Lydia's bedroom door was ajar. I slipped inside the empty room. The sun had risen ankle high in the sky. I moved across the floor in my bare feet, opened the window a crack. A ribbon of cool air slid inside. I looked around, at the lace curtains and the standing glass lamp, the cherry vanity and the oval mirror above it, its table scattered with pins and combs and small framed pictures, of the young Lydia and my father, a myriad of beaming strangers, arms entwined. I picked up a photograph of me as a solemn, bonneted baby, and could see, oddly, through those dark, tunneling eyes, both my mother and my child—but not me.

Walking over to the closet, I fingered some of Lydia's old clothes, all of them soft and lovely to the touch—taffeta and cashmere and peau de soie. By then, most of the garments on the hangers were far too big for the bony, brittle Lydia. Though the photographs of her in more robust days stood before me in their frames, I still couldn't picture her at the end of a floodlight, head risen, throat full and trembling, bosom heaving, a body that would have given shape to those clothes, whose voice would have filled every crack and a thousand souls in one concert hall. I took out one of the smaller dresses and held it up to the light. It was simple, silver, empire-waisted, a scoop neck and long sleeves, mid-calf-length. Lydia wore it in one of the photographs, a laughing girl of sixteen or so, standing by a piano. I slipped off my t-shirt and stood perfectly still. The air I'd let in gathered hubris and steam, curling around chair legs and mirror edges, snooping, caressing, invading corners, rearranging odors, shifting planes, tickling the insides of my feet and running up my thighs, cool ribbons of pure, uncut fear.

For the first time, standing paralyzed in my mother's empty room, I had a glimpse of how Lydia might have slipped away from the world without being aware, how one raw moment as a child had led to that last terrible moment on the stage. I saw how the demons might have gathered force and taken hold, gathering strength as parasites, first on Lydia's mind and then on her body and soul. I saw how trauma could lead to delusion and a fear of all that had once seemed simple—buying milk or chatting to the mailman, going to the dentist, a fear of your own reflection, your own thoughts, your own heartbeat. And I saw, for the first time, how like Lydia I might be.

Don't feed it, Leo. Don't feed the fear.

I'd always assumed that if I were to succeed in music, it would be because of hard work and the kindness of whatever powers hovered above me, although I had little faith in such powers any more. I'd seen it as my destiny, maybe even my job, as Lydia's daughter, to plunge into my own musical vortex to find her lost voice. And because this was as much a burden as it was an honor, I'd hoped, at least, to be spared the disgrace of failure.

Fear's hungry, Leo.
It's like a cat.
If you feed it once,
it keeps coming back.

What happened to Lydia on the stage would never happen to me. I'd sworn it, all my life, over and over. Anything else, bad or good, but not that. It wouldn't happen to me. It couldn't . . .

Starve the nightmares, Leo. Starve them.

The silver dress slid haltingly down the length of my body. Were it not for the lump in my center, it would have fit me well, narrow in the shoulders, full busted, long in the waist. I ran my hands over the flickering scales of the dress. In the mirror above Lydia's dressing table, I saw the blue of my eyes against their dark rims, black hair shiny and full and down to my shoulders again, rich and fuller than it had ever been before, cheeks no longer hollow, mouth set firm. I looked solid and whole, almost matronly, I thought, and this made me shiver. No matter who my father was, I was Lydia's daughter, no doubt. And today was the day I proved it, one way or another. I sat on the bed and laced up what Danny had called my witch boots—black, pointed toes with steel eyelets. I took one of the mother-of-pearl hair pins and put my hair on top of my head. Let them see me the way I really am, I thought. Let them see whose daughter I am, and whose I'm not. Let them see all of me.

197

I heard the murmurs of my parents' voices as I passed by the kitchen. For one moment, I hesitated. Should I go in? Tell them where I was going? Wouldn't they want to know? How many secrets had I kept in that house and what good had their keeping ever done me? I stood there in the hallway for what seemed like a long, long time. Had it not been for the silver dress shimmering on my belly, the sudden curl of Lydia's laugh from the kitchen, or the broken grandfather clock reminding me with its stillness of lost time, I might have gone in and sat down with my parents to a piece of toast. I might have asked my father for a pat on the back, a good luck charm from Lydia, a bit of advice. As it was, I crept out the door and down Cobb's Hill, bought a soft pretzel from a street vendor and fed the birds as I walked, threw the last of it to the gulls when I got off the subway at Harborside.

Still early for the audition, I walked the cement path along the shore, watched the dark, oily water lap up onto a strip of grey sand. The beach was littered with bottles and trash, an occasional dead fish, silver eyes bulging. The scum-ringed motor boats rocked up against a rickety wooden dock. The signs said DANGER and meant it. Sister Corita's rainbowed gas tanks stood out in the distance, bold strokes streaking the smoggy sky. The seagulls came for the pretzel pieces and then flew far away. Only a few still bothered to scavenge there.

Ettore stood on the granite steps of the Conservatory, thick profile to the sea, the wispy smoke of his cigarette etching silhouettes above his head. I saw him for an instant as a brash young man—hungrier, happier, more ambitious, a head full of hair and idioms off by more than the inch. As I walked toward him, he crushed the butt of his cigarette with his heel.

"Leo," he said, spreading his hands. "Today's a day."

"Today's a day," I said. "It's true."

We walked together down the creaky wooden hallway and sat outside the concert hall in two fold-up wooden chairs. Inside, a cellist played Beethoven. We listened in silence. It was played flawlessly, but without conviction. Still, the cello was such a seductress. I let the music wash over me, rich, lilting and cool. Ettore tapped his foot nervously. I put my booted foot on top of his to still it. In those last few moments, I tried to empty my mind of all its clutter, all the scattered notes and bars. Clean sweep.

The door opened, and the cellist, a girl with a hairlip and golden braids, came out of the concert hall, followed by a woman who thanked her too kindly, I thought, and said, "Miss Baye? We're ready for you now."

Ettore clapped my arm with one paw. "Go on, Leo," he said.

"Come with me, Ettore."

"No, go on, Leo. Break your legs."

"Break *a* leg," I whispered. "Please, Ettore."

"If breaking one is good, then two is better. Go on, Leo. Go on in and play."

The concert hall was in the new wing of the building, underneath the library, offering the same view of the water and the airport and the harbor islands in the distance. One of those islands had once housed a hospital for infectious diseases. On another, a lighthouse keeper kept the Castle Island watch. The sky was a smouldering blue and the clouds slid in wisps and clumps, moving too fast to form the scalloped edges of animal shapes children find in the sky. The water was strangely flat that day, the color of dry ice, a faint, steaming gray, dotted with barges and sailboats, a few squat tugs.

A music stand was set up facing away from the window. The eyes of the man who'd endowed the new wing stared down from out of a portrait—a modern, green-eyed man, looking out of place in a turtleneck and gilded frame. Five judges—three women and two men—sat to one side of the room in fold-up wooden chairs. They were dressed to what was surely, for each, a T—an argyle sweater here, a seamed stocking there, a pressed linen shirt, a mustache trimmed. All five were poised on the edge of their chairs, all ears. They'd been chosen with an eye to variety and fairness—a Bach impresario and a Schubert scholar, a flutist, a viola player, a conductor. They all lived and breathed music; they held my future in their fine, rumpled palms. My heart raced as I tuned up my violin and tightened my bow. One of the judge's eyes bounced off my bulging center and traveled to my ringless fingers.

"You will be playing, Miss Baye?" She peered over her bi-focals.

"Aurelio Macaux's 'Cascade,'" I said. "The 'Waterfall Symphony.' All four movements." I turned the music stand sideways to face the window. Better to watch the water and the airplanes than to stare at those five doughy faces and that metal door, up into the benefactor's steely green eyes. Better to be looking backward at a moving world than forward into the eyes of those that might bring it all to a grinding halt.

"Whenever you're ready," the woman said.

I put my violin to my chin, smiled what I hoped was a valiant smile. My leg itched uncontrollably and I had to pee. I took these as good omens, never having played well when I was comfortable. I put my bow on the D string, played a trumpeting G and started down the adagio slope of Aurelio's hills, the funeral slide of the first slow measures into dark, discordant valleys, where the notes trudged heavy and long, a dirge. For a long time, I wound my way down Aurelio's familiar, well-trammeled paths, through the *pianissimo* forest, across a *crescendo* meadow, through a *piccato* stand of birch. My fingers were steady and sure on the strings. The pressure of my bow was right. The notes tumbled into those ten well-tuned ears. They leaned forward in their chairs. I stole a glance. They could hear what I'd never catch at such close range—glitches, lags, rushes, *pianos* not soft enough, *fortissimos* too strong. So far, at that last glance, I thought—so good.

I barely glanced at the sheet music, though I reached out at the right moments to turn the pages. I slid through the third movement with ease, back through the meadow and into the dark woods. I tried to keep eye contact with the music on the stand, knowing that at any moment, I could lose my focus, my stride. One lapse of thought, one note played just a bit to lee, one too many dips of memory—Kilroy's soft lips, Lydia's god awful egg, the swipe of a seagull's wing, Danny's hard body pressing, pressing, pushing me away from him in the car toward the door . . .

* * *

By then, it was too late. I'd bobbled a measure at the bottom of Aurelio's mountain, and scrambled to pick up the lost notes before the beginning of the next bar. Knocked off balance, I wasn't ready for the climb. The notes blurred suddenly into streaks of black and white. The judges' faces grew freakish—one's lips a gila monster's, another's flushed face a cooked lobster red, these the judges that lay in wait in the chambers of Po's heaven, to see if you could do arithmetic or carry a tune. The last sound I heard was Danny's voice calling out to me from where I'd left him, and then its echo. "Leo!" "*Leo! Leo! Leo!*" The silence that followed was the deep, pressurized silence of underwater, the music interrupted, time and reason suspended, while behind my closed eyes, the circus of my life had the nerve to unfold.

First, Kilroy bounced into the ring, doing cartwheels, reciting paradoxes and Red Sox batting averages, humming TV theme songs, spouting rock and roll trivia, all in the high-wired voice of an AM dee-jay. Under the moon, a yellow ball hanging from a string, Kilroy did a strip tease, revealing a body with chess pieces sticking out of all its orifices. Sweat beaded the ridge of my upper lip. Kilroy reached for the silver dress and started to rip. I pulled the tattered pieces back over me, pleaded with him, telling him, no, not now, not now. The farmer and the cow. The farmer and the cow. Go away, Kilroy. I've been playing this music every day, shifting, balancing, lifting. I won't drop it, not for sex, love or money. Go away. I tried to lift my bow, to push him away . . .

Not for anything.

Then came the McPhees—first Po, a lopsided clown leading a band of clown fishes, sad-eyed, wise, wispy-tailed, the strong grim faces of his parents following, whipping and hissing at the tigers. And then came the sisters, handsome, long-waisted and sequined, the giggly twins in leotards riding prancing horses, pregnant Rose walking poodles in tutus, pushing a baby carriage, the wail of an infant straining to the rafters, the grandmother in a wheelchair holding a giant rubber cross, and finally Danny standing tall and pretty on a float, cloaked in a red vampire cape and cracking a whip.

An elephant picked me up from the stands with its truck, tossed me onto a trampoline, where I bounced and flopped and splat. A cannon shot Danny on top of me. He made short work of what was left of the silver dress with the whip and speared me through the navel with his forked tongue, sucking, yanking, jabbing, hissing like the tigers. "Just do it, Leo!" His teeth sank down into my neck. "Just play the fucking music." The grandmother came up in her wheelchair and clobbered him with the rubber cross. A dwarf clown jumped out of Rose's baby carriage and shook rattles in my face. My violin smashed to the floor in a thousand pieces. The laughter grew deafening. No one heard me cry.

The ring began to fill with water, which rose first to drown the clowns, then Po and the sisters and the horses, until it reached Danny's neck up high on the float, a neck that kept stretching to keep its head above water, until it broke through the roof of the arena and could not be seen for the sky. And as Danny's neck grew and rose up through the heavens, the voice that had been his, calling out to me—savage, cracked and dry—turned into Lydia's lost soprano—rich, lilting and strong.

"Miss Baye?" Another voice, faint and strained, reached me from the other side. "Miss Baye? Are you all right?"

It was one of the judges, the kindly Schubert scholar, in a green cardigan, argyle socks, and red sandals, come to my side, her puzzled face peering into mine. I looked around, at her and the other judges, still in their seats, out the window, back at the music. I felt the sweat on my neck and brow. I didn't dare ask how long it had been since I'd stopped playing, how long I'd been standing there in a daze. I couldn't feel my heart beating; my hands were numb . . .

"Are we finished?" I finally said.

"No," the Schubert scholar said, gently. "We are not."

"Right." I brought a finger to the sheet music, slowly, carefully. "I'll just pick it up . . ."

"Here." The judge pointed to the beginning of the fourth movement. "Are you sure you're all right, Miss Baye?"

"I'm fine." I smoothed the silver dress over my belly.

"If you like" the judge said, "we could reschedule . . ."

"No," I said quickly. "There's no problem at all. I'll continue."

Putting my bow back on the strings, I stood at the bottom of Aurelio's mountain and started to climb, my fingers moving at hand-splitting speeds, sixty-fourth notes spread all over the strings without pause. I had no sense of how this frenzied interlude sounded to the human ear. It wasn't the most difficult part of the "Waterfall Symphony," but it was the most tiring. I reached the plateau safely, trembling on the misty ledges, a light staccato, dawn breaking on shallow rapids, dancing to the falls. I took a deep breath, middle finger steady on a two measure F, and plunged down into the falls.

Even in the midst of chaos, Kilroy said, could be found order. I'd finally made sense of the final waterfall passage by making connections to the people around me. The first gentle downward stream was my father, the steady rolling sequence of A, B, C, and back to A, leading the way stoically, but without much hope. The stream bumped into a rift of breathless trills as the water grew agitated. The frothy peaks at the crest of the fall were Lydia, the notes that soared and then dropped into oblivion, never making contact with one another, but vital and riveting, nonetheless. An eerie dance followed—the first, raw, burnished swells as they broke, haunting, broken chords—the earnest, misshapen Po. The downward plunge of the falls was Danny—thundering, dark, steam rising, swells swallowed up by themselves. The pool at the bottom of the falls, which slid into whirlpools and eddies and currents, notes spiraling in never-ending concentric circles, was Kilroy. And toward the end, where the water drifted silently into a dark, bottomless pool—the part I'd finally just had to memorize—was me.

The last scorching B flat ripped through the hall. My arms fell and trembled at my side. A barge groaned in the distance, the groan of a man who can't get far enough inside you. I put down my bow; someone's chair scraped the floor. The judges shifted in their seats. The faint blue of the ocean had been lifted from the deep by the midday sun and replaced by shimmering silver. The baby kicked low and hard. Someone blew his nose. A paper rustled; a foot tapped. I put my violin back into its case and took a deep breath.

"A very difficult piece of music, Miss Baye," one of the judges said. "Is there anything else you'd like to tell us? Anything else you'd like to add?"

"No," I said. "Thank you. The music speaks for itself."

"Indeed it does," the judge said, as she ushered me to the door. "Thank you again, Miss Baye. We'll certainly be in touch."

Outside in the hallway, Kilroy was sitting next to Ettore in a wooden chair.

"Kilroy, what are you doing here?" I said.

He stood up and kissed me. "That was incredible," he whispered.

Ettore stood up and kissed me on the cheek. "Who is this, Leo? And why does he sit next to me in this chair?"

"This is Kilroy, Ettore," I told him. "He's sitting in this chair because he's a friend of mine." I smiled. "I didn't know he was coming."

"Nice to meet you," Kilroy said.

"Pleasure, I'm sure," Ettore said stiffly.

"It sounded great, Leo," Kilroy said. "But then, what do I know?"

"Exactly," Ettore said.

"Ettore . . ." I said.

"A long silence before the fourth movement," he said. "What happened, Leo?"

"I got tired. I had to stop for a minute. But the rest of it, Ettore. If they forgive that. How do you think I played?"

"It was good, Leo. Very good." He nearly took my breath away with a squeeze. "I think you make the grades."

chapter twenty

On that day, it became summer, the kind of summer I hadn't known in years—those long, endless days on Cobb's Hill when the day slipped into night as an afterthought, where time lost all meaning, where crickets and field mice and owls made the day's jabber. As a child, I'd loved summer—untethered, unschooled. Summer made your hair thick and your feet tough. Summer had no rules.

Up in my attic room, after my audition, I took off the silver dress and hung it in the closet. I dressed for comfort now, reaching for an old skirt with an elasticized waist I'd made in home-ec class years before, red bric-a-brac running around its green denim hem. It hung absurdly over my belly, inches higher in the front than the back. I went downstairs and out into the back yard. The air was steamy and the field mice lay low. Flowers pulled back into themselves. I paced a garden plot with my bare feet, starting where the shadow of the chestnut tree ended, marking rows for tomatoes, impatiens, wild strawberries, cosmos, kale, herbs, popcorn at Kilroy's request, and breadfruit for me, a garden started too late, in which I was determined to make stubborn things grow. I'd given my father the last of my money from my job at the music store to buy me some garden tools at the hardware store—a rake, a hoe, some string, dowling, a trowel, and seeds.

All afternoon, I tilled the earth on my knees in the sun, my hair in a messy braid, face streaked grey with dirt, my stomach hanging low. As I was pounding in poles for the cosmos, Kilroy startled me with a hand on my sun-baked back. He looked down at me with an eye he might have plucked from my father's socket for all its softness, and I remembered a poem I'd once read, about how a daughter looks for her father in the back of her lover's eyes and if she can't find him there, she turns away.

"You should see yourself," Kilroy said.

I squinted at my spoon-faced reflection in the trowel. "I look like a weed."

"A beautiful weed." Kilroy knelt down in the dirt with me, put a chess book he was carrying on the ground, took the mallet from my hand and put his arms around me clumsily, picking the strands of hair from my face and trying to stick them back into the black braid, kissing my mouth, sucking it rather, finishing neither the kiss nor the breath.

"I planted your popcorn." I touched the folds of his cotton sleeve, wondered how long the lovemaking would last, the need to cast it all in touch and feel.

"I'll always remember you this way," he said. "Kneeling down in the dirt, in your garden like this."

"You sound as if you're heading off into the sunset," I said.

"Just for a while," he said.

I stuck my trowel upright into the earth and leaned back on my knees. "Where are you going?"

"New York," he said.

I sprinkled the cosmos seeds into their waiting holes, filled the holes back in with their own dirt. I often didn't see Kilroy for a few days at a time, but I'd come to count on his being near, within reach. "What's happening in New York?" I asked. "Besides murder and mayhem, Shakespeare in the Park?"

"Chess," he said.

"Ah, chess." I tried to wipe the smudges off my face with the edges of my hands.

"I'll be staying at the Biltmore Hotel and playing chess in a big banquet room. With dozens of other people. People just playing chess all day, all night long."

"Sounds like your idea of heaven," I said.

"I'll be gone five days."

"Five days in chess heaven." I patted the mounds of earth, smoothed them level. "How can you go wrong?"

Kilroy turned my face toward his, making me lose my balance in the dirt. "Don't go blank on me, Leo."

"I'm not going blank," I said. "I'm just no good at goodbyes, that's all." In the distance, I noticed Lydia, lingering behind the grey mesh of the kitchen screen door.

"You don't have to be good at them." One of Kilroy's eyes twitched with a force I didn't yet know. "You just say goodbye." He rose up out of the dirt and dusted off his knees. "Here. I'll demonstrate. Goodbye, Leo."

I looked up at him. "I'm sorry," I said.

"Sorry for what?"

"Not giving you what you came for."

"I just came to tell you that I was leaving, Leo. That I'll be back."

"Order room service for me," I said. "A five dollar grapefruit with a silver spoon and charge it please. Like Eloise. At the Plaza."

Kilroy waved as he made his way through the weeds to the stone path that led out to the crumbling sidewalk. I ran my fingers over the bumps of my braid and waved back. And if I said goodbye, he couldn't have heard me.

After Kilroy was gone, Lydia came out through the screen door and walked to the bench, moving cautiously still, as if on a quaking earth, but a bit faster by then, steadier on her feet. "Who was that, Claire?" she asked, arranging herself on the bench.

"Kilroy."

"Kilroy was here? Again? Did he leave?"

"He left."

"People come and go," she said. "So few stay anymore."

"There's a whole world out there, Lydia."

"I like it here," she said. "Here in the yard."

"It's nice here." My fingers spun holes through the earth like a top. I let the breadfruit seeds fall from my fingers, one by one. Lydia sat near me for a while. We grew warm and sleepy in the dropping sun. I went for lemonade and we sipped it in jelly jars under the chestnut tree, ate almond crescent cookies and called it supper.

"You're living here now, Claire," Lydia said.

"Just for a while," I said. "Until the baby's born."

"The baby," she said, creasing her brow. "Ah, yes, there'll be a baby soon. And everything will change."

The garden waited only for sun and rain. I waited only for a call. If I passed muster at the Conservatory, a tape of my audition would be sent out to symphony boards for preliminary screenings. With luck, I'd be called for an audition. It could be anywhere—Buffalo, San Francisco, Cleveland, Timbuktu. Wherever I was summoned, I'd decided to go. Until then, I had no prospects, no means. I'd quit my job at the music store. There were no nest eggs, no stocks or bonds. All the money was gone.

By the next Tuesday, I'd had no word from the Conservatory about the audition. Ettore called to say he thought it was a good sign, then called again. What was taking them so long?

"*Que sera*," I said. "You always say, Ettore. Whatever happens, it's not the end of the world."

"*Que sera*," he said. "Ha. Not the end of the world. Easy for you to say."

Strangely enough, it was.

The phone call came one afternoon. Who knows if we'd missed others. I slid into the closet to answer it after four rings, coiled the cord around my finger. Was I Leonarda Baye, a thin voice asked me. Yes, I was quite sure I was. I'd passed the audition, the voice told me. With commendation. I'd receive notice soon in the mail. I thanked the voice kindly, later wished I'd done more. Ettore sent me a Hallmark card, for the graduate, who has made it to the top, and now no one can stop. Inside, he'd written in a flourished scrawl, "*Bravissimo*, Leo. Your colors are flying!" My father's eyes filled when I told him, and he picked me black-eyed Susans from the back yard. And Lydia said, "you see, Claire?," though I didn't see at all. I cradled the praise with stiff, uncertain arms, as I supposed I might my new baby, trying to imagine it to be the product of my actions, my will.

My thesis came back in a big Manila envelope covered with illegible red scribbling. I made my way through to the final comment, littered with sprawling question marks and exclamations:

Miss Baye:

Your thesis proposal indicated that you held some less-than-orthodox views on Aurelio and his music. (!!!!) We didn't find them here (????). What you offer is a fairly standard treatment of his life and times, and a rather disorganized one at that. The discussion of his relationship with women and his mother was interesting (!!), but not fully developed (?!?). C+. Best of luck !!!"

C+ and the best of luck. I pushed the silver tabs back down on the envelope and put the thesis away. Just desserts, as Lydia would say. As good as Aurelio and I both deserved.

Five days had come and gone. Kilroy was still playing chess at the Biltmore.

It was time to let my apartment go. My father and I went one late afternoon to move my things. I cleaned out the rooms, took apart my grandmother's bed, packed my books and clothes and left everything else behind—the lamps and mirrors I'd found in street-corner trash, my rock heavy file cabinet, the peeling green Formica table in the kitchen. I left the last month's rent in cash with my landlord's wife, Mrs. Favoli, and tried to thank her, though her English was not so good.

"You getting married?" she beamed, pointing to my stomach. "*Menino belo*? To the beautiful boy?"

"No, I'm not getting married," I said. "Not to the beautiful boy. Not to anyone."

"Where is he?" she asked. "Where did he go?"

"He's dead." I raised my hand in prayer and pointed to the sky. "*Morto*. He's gone."

"*Nao*." Her hand clutched her heart. "*Nao permita deus*."

"*Sim*," I said. "*Morto*."

As my father and I pulled away, I saw a help-wanted sign in the window of the Portuguese restaurant near where the bus used to let me off, mid-way between my apartment and Danny's fish market. The owner, a bald man with a full mustache and father to many children, used to come out to sweep the sidewalk and arrange shellacked foods in the window. He'd often greeted me as I stepped off the bus, a friendly, steady presence in the neighborhood. The smell of roasted potatoes and steamed fish trailed behind us, garlicky and rich. That night, as my father and I unpacked the Rambler at Cobb's Hill, I decided to go back for the job.

I caught the #22 bus to the Square the next afternoon. I'd come to think of this bus as my roving home, with its orange plastic seats, its signs for cigarettes and correspondence schools and mortuaries lined up in a row, the gargle of the fare box as it swallowed the coins, the roll and tilt of the bus, the chatter, my well-worn seat behind Phil, the driver.

"Hey, Stradivarius," Phil said. "Did I ever tell you that my mother used to call me Mozart? I had quite a set of pipes, you know. I used to make up songs, belt them out in the shower." He ventured a half-hearted do-re-mi. "She had high hopes for me," he said.

"Mothers do, I guess," I said. "I didn't know Mozart sang."

"He did it all, didn't he?" Phil said. "The guy was a genius. Wrote his first symphony when he was four. Hey, you haven't given up on that fiddle, have you?" he asked. "I'm still counting on that front row seat at Symphony Hall."

"No, I'm still at it, Phil," I said.

"That's the spirit," he said. "Don't let the baby take over. My wife and I always said, a kid comes to live with you, and not the other way around."

"Is it true?"

"Not for a minute." He grinned. "The kids rule the roost. Especially the first one. No doubt about it. So, what'll you do when the baby comes, Strad?"

"Keep on playing, Phil." I rested my chin on the metal bar. "Just keep on playing."

I got off the bus in front of Rudy's Liquors and walked toward the Portuguese restaurant, where the bald man was sweeping his sidewalk, whistling and fit, his mustache aswirl. He recognized me at once, took in my belly and followed my eyes to the empty window.

"You come for the job?" he asked.

"Yes."

"Job taken," he said. "Anyway," he pointed to my belly. "You busy now."

"I need the work," I said.

"No." He shook his head. "You go home. Put your feet up. Papa take care of you."

"No," I said. "No papa. I need a job."

"Try fish market." He shrugged. "I see the sign. Help wanted."

I stopped dead in my tracks. The fish market. There was only one. I'd all but banished the McPhees from my mind—forgotten my promise to make a plan with Po, to call Rose and see how she was feeling, not to let Danny's parents forget, about me, and the baby I was carrying. A flash of guilt slid over me, as blush and searing burn. I was brazen to be out in the world again so soon, in flipflops as if I had no cares, with no money, joking with bus drivers, looking for jobs, making love on a golf course to a man who could make numbers dance but couldn't even match his socks. How well could I ever have loved Danny, or he me?

Help wanted. A chance for atonement. Engagement. For work. The McPhees needed help. I could give it. Many hands. Turn the other cheek. No time like the present. I turned around and headed in the direction of the fish market, counting my steps. Eighty-five brought me to its door. In the clean glass window hung the help-wanted sign, handwritten letters squeezing to the right, the labored work of a child. The shop was full of customers. I stood at the back and watched. Mr. McPhee worked without pause, plucking fish, wrapping, tying, reaching, ringing in, counting change. Po was sweeping the floor. The grandmother raised a finger and tried to place me. When Po saw me, he put down his broom and came over, wiped his short fingers on an apron that reached nearly to his ankles, even though it was folded over at the waist.

"Hey, Leo," he said. "You're getting fat."

"And you're getting skinny." I tousled his red hair. I waited for Mr. McPhee to acknowledge my presence, which he did as the last customer arranged her fish in her shopping bag and then her hat on her head, and walked to the door.

"How are you feeling then, Leo?" Mr. McPhee asked me. "You're looking well. I've been meaning to call."

"I'm doing fine," I said. "It looks busy in here."

"Aye, it's a busy time, and just the two of here to mind the shop." He clapped Po on the back. "Don't know what I'd do without my right-hand man."

"Rosie's in the hospital," Po said.

"She chose quite a time to have her baby, Rose did," Mr. McPhee said. "Two and a half months early."

"A preemie." By then, there was nothing Po couldn't say. "His name is Patrick Michael. Just like my grandfather. He's in an incubator. Three pounds . . ." He looked over at his father.

"Five ounces," Mr. McPhee whispered. "God look after his tiny soul."

"They sliced up Rose's belly." Po ran his finger along his waist. "The scar's gonna be this long."

"Porter," Mr. McPhee said. "Don't be telling Leo such things now."

"My mother watched," Po said. "She saw Rosie's guts."

"Moira's been over at the hospital night and day," Mr. McPhee said. "The baby's no bigger than a field mouse, Leo. They say they'll pull him through, with all of their new fangled machines. It'll be a miracle, really. In my day, the wee bairn wouldn't have made it, and it would have been called God's will, God's way."

"Maybe it's not always the best way," I said.

"It's been good enough since the beginning of time," he said.

"Since the beginning of mankind," I said.

"God made man," he said. "From one of Adam's ribs. On a wish and a prayer. Never forget it, Leo."

"God's an invention," I said.

"Hush, now," Mr. McPhee said. "You'll be needing all the help you can get from God soon enough."

"Soon enough," the grandmother echoed from her chair.

"I came about the job," I said.

"The job? Are you serious, Leo?"

"I need the work."

Mr. McPhee thought before he spoke, above all else, a practical man. "I'd need you right away," he said. "And I can't say for how long."

"I can start right now," I said. "And I'll only stay as long as you want me."

Po went to get a clean apron for me.

"Man, you're huge," he said. "You'd better take one of Dad's."

"Show Leo where to hang her coat, Porter." Mr. McPhee began barking orders. "Show her the ice and the sponges. Show Leo the cash register and where the brooms are, Porter. Then come help me unload the truck."

"Come on, Leo." Po led me behind the counter. "I'll show you the ropes. Like Danny showed me."

Tying my apron, I followed Po behind the counter and let memory spill. Danny had once shown me a rope, a rope he'd brought up from the car. On the way upstairs, I kept asking what he was going to do with it, what it was for. He wouldn't tell me. He wouldn't budge. Later, in bed, the rope had appeared suddenly between us, a snake waiting to strike. He'd uncoiled it, teased me with it, wrapped it around my waist, pulled it in between my legs, tied my hands and turned me over on my stomach. "Down, Leo," he said, not wanting me to see as he came at me. "Keep your head down."

"No."

"Show you the ropes . . ." Po's voice drew me back to the day, back to the fish market, back to the light. He tugged at my sleeve. His face was open and warm. "Come on Leo," he said. "Wake up. And I'll show you the ropes."

When I came down for breakfast the next morning, both of my parents were in the kitchen. Lydia stood at the stove, waiting for the tea kettle to boil. She wore a pair of grey, tweed bloomers which ballooned out from the thigh and tapered at the calf. Her breasts filled out the eyes of a smiling yellow face which had come to roost everywhere in those days, on billboards and buttons and t-shirts and ties. Her hips swung the bloomers to and fro as she brought her tea to the table. As Lydia sat down, my father's hand brushed her shoulder. He looked over at her with such a hunger that I felt suddenly invisible, unborn. In that one touch of the arm, he had inhaled her—soft shoulders and strong arms, the heavy breasts, the gentle curve of the neck, the mossy, unkempt hair. His fingers lingered on her arm until she said, "Unhand me, August."

I stood still by the stove, dangling my tea bag from its string. Waters deep inside me stilled. I knew. Moreover, they wanted me to know. They were making love again, after all these years. There, finally revealed at the kitchen table, was my parents' hidden love affair, the conspiracy that had made me, but beyond the fact of the making, had very little left to do with me. Is this what I had missed as a child, I wondered, the dawning one day of exactly where you have come from, an understanding which offers you all of your comfort and all of your loneliness in one fell swoop?

"So, Leo . . ." My father finally let go his hand, his gaze. "How does it feel to be a real musician?"

"I was as real a musician yesterday," I said. "And the day before. It's such an arbitrary line."

"Now the real work begins," Lydia said. "Now, they'll be watching you."

"Who?" I asked. "Does the CIA have musical spies?"

"Let her rest on her laurels for a while, Lydie," my father said. "It's nothing to sneeze at, what Leo's done."

"No one's sneezing, August," Lydia said. "Soon the symphonies will be calling."

"With any luck," I said.

"I knew the conductor of the Boston Symphony," Lydia said. "Albert Wexler. Not the most refined man, but he worked wonders with the strings, which were dismal at the time. We should give him a call, August. Albert Wexler. Wasn't that his name?"

"Albert Wexler?" My father thought for a minute. "Yes, I think it was."

"That was thirty years ago," I said, making my way to the table with my tea "He must be gone now. Dead, maybe."

"Dead?" Lydia said. "Oh, heavens, no."

As I sat down at the table, my father chuckled.

"What's so funny?" I asked him.

"You're beginning to look like a pear, Leo," he said. "Isn't she, Lydie?"

Lydia smiled. "Your father has always looked rather like a pear himself."

"Well, you know what they say," my father said. "The old pear doesn't fall far from the old pear tree." He took a sip from what turned out to be his empty coffee cup. "Not far from the old pear tree."

Lydia's eyes suddenly darkened. "Albert Wexler couldn't be dead, could he, August?" she said.

"Oh, I don't think so, Lydie. I think we would have heard."

The teasing wind passed and a silence fell over us. My father's eyes lost their light and Lydia fingered a button on her shirt. I got up to make toast, leaned my belly against the cool white Formica of the stovetop. Time passed, though the old grandfather clock stood still.

We sat stuck and taut, as do people who wait out disasters together, huddled in the lee of Lydia's rattled memory and the pear joke gone cold.

As the bread slices on the toaster swallowed the flames, I watched for more change as I'd watch a drop of water waiting to drip. Lydia was wearing red, not the kindest color, she liked to say, but always a challenge. My father chewed on his thumbnail and drummed the table. It wasn't like him to come to the table without a sketch or an idea, with nothing but the empty space in front of his eyes. The da Vinci book had disappeared from its perch on the chair beside him. I didn't dare ask where it had gone, as if Leonardo were a favorite uncle whisked away by sudden illness, his condition best left undescribed. Just as I'd always felt that all would be well if a warm wind blew Lydia out to the chestnut tree, so had I always believed in Leonardo as the patron saint of our kitchen, of our lives. With my icons uprooted and my credos up in smoke, how could I possibly pray?

Without warning, my father rose abruptly from the table.

"August?" Lydia's voice caught him at the door.

"What is it?" My father turned around.

"You're leaving?"

"Yes, I'm off to work." He came back to her then, patted her arm, the avuncular touch of old, not the caress of breakfast. "I'll see you at five thirty. Like always." He turned away again.

"August," Lydia said again, pleading, firm.

"I have to go, Lydie." A ripple of irritation rolled through his voice. "It's nine o'clock. I'll be late for work."

I saw Lydia's eyes pale and I knew he'd gone too far. I couldn't bear his lapse, his stupidity. His head had swelled too quickly with relief and passion. He'd jumped ahead in his thinking; he hoped for too much. I ached for my mother as I waited, for him to say something, to make it right.

My father looked back and forth from me to Lydia. "What's wrong?" he said. "You're both looking at me as if I'd just done the butler in."

Lydia looked over at me.

"You didn't kiss Lydia goodbye," I said.

"What?"

"You didn't kiss me goodbye, August," Lydia said.

"How strange." My father bent down and kissed Lydia absently on the cheek. "I was quite sure I had."

"What about Claire?" Lydia said. "My father gave me kisses for every perfect note I sang."

"He did?" I said. "Why?"

"Why?" Lydia said. "Because he loved me. Because my mother told him to. Go on, August. Kiss Claire goodbye."

"Leo?" My father looked over at me, eyebrows arched, uncertain.

"You better get going, Dad." I waved him away with my hand. "Go on. You'll be late for work."

"Your father's got something on his mind," Lydia said, when we were alone. Her face was white, her lips a pale blue.

"People do," I said softly. "They get over it."

"He's gone somewhere," she said.

"He'll be back," I said.

We left the conversation dangling, the hole into which my father might have plunged himself half dug. We were both unwilling to look too closely at who or why or what strange place might be luring my father away from us—a lure so powerful it had made him forget to kiss Lydia goodbye.

Lydia rose from the table. The sides of a pit in my stomach gave way like sand. I wanted to ask her what her plans were for the day, to have her ask me about mine. But neither of us had any plans, and, in the end, maybe this was simply too hard to bear. The questions between us were too large and frightening, the confusion too profound, the chasm of silence too old and far too deep. By the time I thought to ask Lydia if she wanted to go for a walk or have another cup of tea, she'd already slid on her Chinese slippers and put her dirty tea cup in the refrigerator, spoon, saucer, and all. I heard her feet on the hallway floor—flap, flap—and then the first creaks of the threadbare carpeted stairs. I sat watching the blue jays harp on blue jay woes, and wished on the blurry edge of the pale morning moon that Kilroy would come back soon.

chapter twenty-one

The next day, I went for my six-month check-up with Dr. Early.
These middle visits were quick, unintrusive, reassuring. She marked
my steady weight gain, took my blood pressure, measured my belly, listened to the baby's heartbeat.

"So, what's new, Leo?" she asked, after I'd sat back up on the table.

"Not much." I pulled down my shirt. "My tomatoes and zucchinis
have sprouted. I'm kind of amazed. I was sure I had a black thumb."

"Tell me something else," she said. "Tell me what you had for
breakfast."

"Toast," I said. "I always have toast."

"Creature of habit, are you?"

"Yes."

"Butter? Marmalade? Jelly?"

"Just butter."

"Nothing else?"

"Tea. With lots of milk. I've given up coffee. It makes my hands
shake." I looked up at a drawing of A GIRL WITH WINGS FLYING IN
JELLO AIR. "How's your granddaughter?" I asked her.

"Mad." Dr. Early sighed. "She's writing hate mail to her mother. And her mother is sending it to me. She says I've turned Halley against her, that it's all my fault. Part of me is up at arms, and part of me feels guilty. Figure that one out." She looked up at me. "Toast and butter?"

"Butter and toast."

"Here I am, Leo, telling you all of my family problems, and all I can get out of you is buttered toast and zucchini."

"You've seen me inside out." I lifted my hands. "What's left to know about me, except how my garden grows?"

Dr. Early folded up her stethescope and put it in her coat pocket. "I worry about you, Leo. So many tough things all at once. I don't know what came before all of this, what goes on with your family or your work. Maybe it's my nature. But I worry. So reassure me. Tell me something else."

"I just graduated from the Beacon Conservatory of Music," I said.

"Congratulations," she said, gesturing to my violin on the floor. "I'd love to hear you play sometime."

"Sure." I swung my legs over the edge of the table. "Sometime."

Dr. Early jotted down some notes in my file. "What happens with your music after the baby's born, Leo?"

"I keep at it," I said. "I have no choice, really. It's what I do. It's what I am."

"Do you have help?" she asked "Family? Friends? Someone to take care of the baby while you work? I know some people I could recommend."

I was frightened by the mention of a real and looming future, as frightened by the notion of taking care of my baby as I was by the idea of leaving it with someone else, of being with my music forever as letting it go. I didn't want to have to make more decisions, more plans. I wanted to wander forever in a summer haze, unencumbered, uncommitted. But Dr. Early wasn't about to let me.

"I'll just jot down some names." She took out a pen and put it to her prescription pad, started scribbling. "Very reliable sorts. This one even took care of my daughter when she was little. She must be ancient by now. Quite a character, but the real McCoy."

I stopped her pen with my hand. "No," I said. "I'll be all right, Dr. Early. Thanks."

"Okay." She clicked her pen and put it away. "Just one more question, Leo. And then I'll shut up."

"What?"

"Is there someone who'll be with you through all of this? When the baby's born. After. Your mother, maybe?"

"My mother can't really help out much."

"Is there a man, Leo?"

"Do I need a man?"

"No. Of course not. It's just the way things have gone for a long, long time," she said. "That's why I ask."

"There is a man," I said. "Sort of."

"Will he be with you? she asked. "With you and the baby?"

I looked up at Halley's drawing of TWO MONKEYS WITH THEIR FINGERS IN THEIR EARS WHO DON'T LIKE TO LISTEN TO PEOPLE TALKING SO MUCH. I thought of Kilroy walking away from me in the garden, off to chess heaven at the Biltmore. "I'm not sure," I said.

"And the baby's father? Is it hard without him?" Dr. Early asked me. "Do you miss him, Leo?"

"I miss something," I said. "Some way he made me feel. It's not sadness, really. Just a pain I get sometimes."

The flash of anger left as quickly as it had come, giving way to a dull throb at my temple. How dare Danny abandon me, to answer all of these questions, to sort out all the mess? He'd been my lover and he had died, and those cold truths would chill and shape me forever. But day in, day out, I didn't miss Danny McPhee. That was a fact. That was something.

When I got to the fish market, Po hugged me. "Work here forever, Leo," he said.

"Forever's a long time," I said. By then I was able to touch him without a jolt, to feel the soft red and not the rough sand of Danny's head when I tousled his hair.

"Not for everyone," he said.

"That's true," I said. "I won't ever go anywhere you can't find me, Po. I promise."

"I'll be here forever," he said. "So we'll both always be where we are."

"Why does that make so much sense?" I asked him.

"Because I said it." He beamed.

I looked down at Po's face. The fish market would be his world—busy, orderly, complete. The work would pull and shape and round him, and he would grow. As the elder son, Danny had been prepared to take over the business, but for as long as I'd known him, he'd had a running argument with his father about his future. Danny wanted to step in right after he graduated, but his father, still a young man himself, had started to grow more ambitious for all of them.

"Business school, Daniel," he'd started to say. "Go to business school. And then you can take care of business."

"I know enough about business," Danny would say. "The business of fish, that is."

And his father would shake his head and mutter, "The business of fish," and Danny would storm off, furious, every time, to have practicality mistaken for defiance, loyalty for laziness. Who knows where he might have headed if fish weren't his fate, his obligation, how he might have reinvented himself over time.

Po handed me a clean apron. "Here, Leo," he said. "Put this on. And then kiss it. Three times."

I did as I was told, tied the apron in the back and brought its bib to my lips. Kissed it three times. "Now," I said. "Tell me why I did that."

"Because now you're good luck," he said. "Now the good things will keep happening."

I'd never been anyone's good luck charm before. Po didn't blame me for what had happened to Danny. He of all people understood that I'd given his brother some small measure of pleasure, even peace. And because I'd held some small power over Danny, Po endowed me with others that weren't really mine. He imagined it was me who'd brought summer and the end of school, who'd made Rose's baby come early and swept his mother away where she was needed more, where she wouldn't hover over him so and turn him back into a boy who could do nothing. Po somehow thought I was responsible for the long hours working alongside his father, for the great surge of business at the market.

"Business is booming," he told me as I adjusted my apron around my huge middle.

"We may have to expand soon," Mr. McPhee said.

"Leo will help," Po said. "Leo's good for business."

"How's that now, Porter?" his father asked.

"She told Mrs. Merson about Beethoven. Mrs. Merson never talks to us. But she talked to Leo."

"She did now, did she?" Mr. McPhee said, losing the battle to a rising smile. "How'd you crack the old bird, Leo?"

"I heard her humming the Ninth Symphony," I said. "The rest was easy."

"Now she'll come back," Po said. "To talk to Leo. To buy more fish. That's good business."

"Leo won't have time to be mucking about with fish and little boys much longer."

"I'm not little," Po said scornfully.

"My mistake," Mr. McPhee said. "You're a great, huge, towering lad. King of the fish pile, you are."

"I'll always have time for the McPhees," I said.

"Yeah," Po said. "You're making one."

"Who's making what?" The grandmother's voice flew across the room.

"Calm yourself, Mother," Mr. McPhee said to her. "We'll always take care of you. Don't you worry."

"You take too good care of me, Sean," the grandmother said. "I've got nothing left to do."

"Don't be pitying yourself, now, Mother," Mr. McPhee said. "Think back on harder times. And then do as you please."

"I can't remember," she said. "What I like to do or how to do it."

"A fine thing," Mr. McPhee said.

"Only one person didn't treat me like an invalid," she said. "And that was Daniel. He waltzed me around this floor in my slippers and I might have been the queen. He knew how to treat a lady."

"We all miss Danny, Mother. God rest his soul."

The grandmother shook her head. "I couldna understood how anyone could be so smart and so stupid at the same time."

"Danny wasn't stupid," Po said.

"Not stupid up here, child!" The grandmother said. "Just down here." Her fist pressed against her chest.

"You're wrong," Po went three steps closer and hissed at his grandmother. "Danny wasn't stupid anywhere!"

Mr. McPhee taught me the cuts of fish and the quirks of the scale, how to arrange the filets and write the specials on the board. The work was rhythmic, satisfying. I kept the cases and the counters clean, packed the fish in ice, marked the price tag sticks in black ink. I learned how to hold the fish on a piece of paper in my palm under the customer's careful eye, saying, "fresh just this morning, Mrs. Abagoni," how to wrap the packages neatly with sharp corners and no stain, snapping off the string with a flourish and tying a tidy knot.

The grandmother fell silent, except to utter the names of the fish as the customers came and went—"halibut . . . sole . . . tuna . . . crab." Once, she jabbed a finger my way and called out, "What's she doing here?" squinting her eyes, trying to place me. "She has the look of an O'Connor. Is she Liam's girl?" What's she doing here?"

I made the round of her chair, brought my face close to hers. "I was Danny's girl," I whispered into her good ear. "I danced with him, too."

I worked at the fish market the last two weeks of July and into August. Business was steady and Mr. McPhee made plans to knock down the storeroom wall. Solemn and watchful, he kept his eye on the door, his ear to the phone. When he saw me starting to rub my back or lean on the counter, he'd pull over a stool and I'd work the register. "Soon you should be off your feet altogether, Leo," he'd say. "Don't want you popping your cork too soon. Like Rose."

Mrs. McPhee swung back and forth from the hospital, but never to stay. She came as purveyor, inspector, collector—to scan the fish cases and counters, pluck the cash from the register drawer, pass her eyes over my growing belly, which she now did unflinchingly. She didn't question my presence in the market, at least to my face. But still, she wouldn't speak. The new baby seemed to have put the spark back in her eye, if not the sparkle. Rose had developed an infection and was still in the hospital. The incision site was sore and she couldn't nurse the baby or spend much time with him. And so it fell to Mrs. McPhee, who didn't think much of hospitals beyond the god-like acts of surgery and transplants, to rescue tiny Patrick from the din of the pre-emie nursery, the hot lights and the stocking caps which fell over his tiny eyes, to change his diapers and keep his bottles warm and full, to give him sponge baths and put alcohol on the stump of his umbilical cord, ointment in his eyes. I listened to the details of these rituals, ter-rified to think I'd soon possess a set all my own.

"Patrick's out from under those hot lights today," Mrs. McPhee would report to her husband. "Thank God, they were baking him like a fruitcake." Or, "Still won't take the breast, though with all that poi-son they're pumping into Rose, who can blame him. He'll take the bottle all right, but only from me. The name's fitting. He's as stubborn and ornery as my father ever was, God rest his soul." And at the men-tion of God, or the baby, or the Father, the grandmother would cross herself and make a low, rasping sound in her throat.

Rose and the baby came home one hot August afternoon. The tiny bundle was passed around, jellyfish pale and perfect in sleep. Rose held him out to me. She still looked pregnant, swollen and stiff, moved slowly, as if in pain.

"Come on then, Leo," she said. "You'll be needing the practice."

I took the baby in my arms. He weighed no more than the swordfish I'd just handed to Mr. Mishkin, Buddha doll face pushing out from the folds of his tightly wrapped blanket. The baby suddenly opened his eyes wide, wrinkled his nose, and made a noise which I took to be a sneeze.

I handed him back to Rose. "I didn't wash my hands," I said. "Maybe he doesn't like the smell."

"He'll get used to it soon enough," Rose said. "After all he's a McPhee."

"He's going to work for me." Po jabbed his chest with his thumb.

"Aye, you're the big boss now, aren't you, Porter?" Rose tousled her brother's hair. I saw in her face a gentle ferocity, a new restraint.

We stroked Patrick's downy face and uncurled his tiny fingers, passed him around again and again like a diamond on a velvet pillow. And when he screwed up his face and started to roar, we scattered to the four winds. I went for the diapers in the car, Mrs. McPhee fished for the diaper rash cream in her purse, Po laid out a blanket on the counter, and Mr. McPhee said it was about time to knock down the storeroom wall and the Lord only knew, there was no time like the present.

The "closed" sign swung on a nail on the door of the market. Mr. McPhee went down to the basement and brought up a sledge hammer and saw. Po and I put the fish away, cleaned the counters, and closed down the register. Patrick's diapers got changed. Mr. McPhee lifted the hammer and made the first dent in the wall.

"Go on now." He hit it again. "Go on, get out of here, all of you." He took another whack. Plaster bits trickled onto the tile floor. "Take the baby upstairs," he said. "Put a chicken on to roast, Moira. Come back in two hours and see what an old man and a little elbow grease can do."

"I want to help," Po said. "Let me help you."

Mr. McPhee looked over at me. I read the plea in his eyes.

"Let's go out, Po," I said. "Do something fun. Just you and me. To celebrate Patrick's homecoming."

"Off with you then, Porter," Mr. McPhee said, more gently. "Go with Leo and have a bit of fun. There'll be plenty more to do when you get back. Let me and this wall here have a few words. We've been meaning to all these years."

He swung the sledge hammer up over his shoulder and made another crashing hole through the wall, and then another. It was Danny he was having words with that day, each rise of his powerful arms a question, each blow a stab at an answer. The why's of Danny's discontent, of his temper, of his recklessness, of his dying. The pride grown thick and hard between them fell in plaster chunks to the floor. The rising swirls of dust were the tears that had never been shed. Po and I stood in the middle of the fish market and stared.

"Are you deaf then?" Mr. McPhee cried out. "Get on with you! Get out!" His voice trembled; his eyes teared. I felt a trace of the heat that had made and shaped, and maybe, in the end, worn Danny thin. Po and I reached the door just as Mr. McPhee raised his sledge hammer again. We heard the explosion of metal meeting plaster, and the fury in Mr. McPhee's cry.

And as the door of the fish market closed behind us, the wall came tumbling after.

Po and I took the subway to the Public Gardens and bought crackers to feed the ducks. We waited in line to buy tickets for the swan boat ride. Po wanted to talk about Danny, and so we did.

"He brought me here once," Po said.

"Me, too," I said.

Po looked at me hard. "Danny took me to all his hockey games," he said.

I nodded. "My feet always got cold," I said. "Did yours?"

"No." Po snapped a cracker in half, looked up at me. "He took us to the same places."

"Sometimes," I said. "Is that okay?"

"Yeah," he said, as we stepped off the dock onto the swan boat. "I don't know. Maybe."

"Hey," I said, putting my hand on his arm. "You were his brother."

"I know." Po slid along his seat to the water's edge, leaned his head back against the curved wooden slats. "Anyway, ducks are stupid," he said.

"Or maybe they know a good thing," I said. "All these people to fuss over them and feed them, able to pick and choose. See, that one won't even eat my cracker." I pointed. "He's waiting for caviar."

"What's caviar?"

"Fish eggs."

"Yuk. If he's waiting for that, he *is* stupid."

Behind us, the pedaller's feet spun furiously. Sweat laced his pimpled brow. The boat glided up to a small island in the pond.

"I'm thirteen, now," Po said.

"You are?" I looked over at him with surprise. "God. I can hardly remember what it's like to be thirteen."

"What grade were you in?"

"Seventh, I think. Mrs. Fuentes was my teacher. I liked this boy named Thadeus Fletcher. I tried to pierce my ears. I guess I do remember."

"How'd you do it?"

"With an ice cube," I said. "And a needle."

"Did it hurt?"

"A little," I said. "I only made one hole. It got infected." I showed him my scar, a slight, ragged lump in my right ear. He reached up and felt it with his finger.

"Did you get in trouble?" he asked me.

"No," I said. "I just got sick." The lily pads were thick and covered with a layer of yellow fuzz. "How's school, Po?"

"It's summer, Leo."

"I knew that," I said. "Just testing you."

"How could you forget it's summer?" Po adjusted his baseball cap with a jerk. "It's so damn hot."

"It is hot." A seagull perched on a rock on the island squawked, scaring away the line of ducks at our side, as we made our way back to the dock. "Don't swear, Po. Unless it means something."

"Danny did," he said.

"That doesn't make it right," I said.

"You sound like my mother," he said.

"Maybe," I said. "But I'm not."

We walked through the public gardens and found the ice cream man. I licked my creamsicle and Po bit off chunks of his fudgsicle, making my teeth ache. We counted people wearing red as we made our way back to the subway. "Danny's twenty-three," Po announced as we walked.

"He would have been," I said.

"July 5th was his birthday," Po said. "Seven days ago."

"Did you celebrate?" I asked.

"I brought him a picture of Bobby Orr," Po said.

"You visit Danny, Po?"

"Every Sunday."

"You talk to him?"

Po nodded. "Me and Danny talk about stuff."

"What stuff?"

"What to do at the market. How to pitch a fastball. What to do with my mom and dad. Stuff like that."

I turned to him, momentarily confused about who was the grown-up and who was the child. "Does Danny ever talk about me, Po?" I asked.

"No way." Po licked his fudgicle sticks clean and stuck them in his back pocket as we hit the stairs underground. "Danny and I made a rule, Leo. We never talk about girls."

chapter   twenty ~ two

A few hours later, after I'd left Po back at the fish market, I went out to the garden to water and weed, to try to remember more about being thirteen. As the moon slid up into the sky, I felt a night shadow at my back.

"Still here?" a voice asked.

I looked up into a strange, bearded face, the face of a man who'd fallen asleep at his chessboard. "Kilroy," I said, You're back."

He knelt down in the dirt and put both hands on my stomach. "How's little Bo?"

"Bo?"

"I heard a lot of Bo Diddley in New York," he said. "It's a good name, don't you think?"

"Bo Baye?" I said. "Bodina? I don't think so."

"Maybe it's not so good." He whistled low as his hands traveled the breadth of my stomach. "Wow. You've gotten so big, Leo."

"And you've gotten so hairy." I put my hands up to his bearded face. "I can't see you in there."

He laughed. "Okay, I'll shave. How are my popcorn plants doing?"

I pointed to a row of tiny shoots "See what can happen in nine days?"

"Nine days?"

"You're four days late," I said. "How was the tournament?"

"Great," he said. "I always forget how much I like playing chess."

"I hadn't noticed that you'd forgotten," I teased.

"I mean how much I really like playing chess, Leo. How I could do it all the time."

"You *do* do it all the time, Kilroy," I said.

With a slow nod, he let go of the neck of a paper bag he'd been holding. "I got you something," he said.

Out of the bag came a store-wrapped gift with striped silver and green paper and curling purple ribbons. I uncovered a small music box, an Empire State Building perched on a round pedestal, filled with people and dogs and bushes and trees. I turned the key in the back and the pedestal started to turn. The people and the taxis bobbed up and down as they twirled, serenaded by a Billie Holiday song, "Strange Fruit."

"I love this song," I said. I felt a coil of embarrassment snake around me, for all the attention I'd received by way of this gift over time—Kilroy's choosing it, the saleslady's fingers wrapping it, its journey in the paper bag, in the train, from Kilroy's hands to mine. "It's beautiful," I said. "Thank you."

"For the baby, maybe." Kilroy smoothed dirt with the trowel. "It's such an amazing building, Leo. A hundred and eight stories high. An airplane crashed into it in 1945, an Army bomber lost in a thick fog. It made an eighteen by twenty foot hole in the building and started a raging fire. Thirteen people died."

"Lydia never told me." The music slowed and life on the pedestal slowly froze in my palm.

"What?" Kilroy asked in a puzzled voice.

"Where've you been, Kilroy?" I said. "You said five days."

"When I left, you didn't seem to care."

"But I was listening," I said. "And I was counting. You said five days."

231

"You missed me," he said, visibly pleased.

"After the fifth day, I pictured you in a ditch."

"You did? That's great."

"No, it wasn't great. I was worried."

"I met a grandmaster at the tournament," Kilroy said. "He lived in the Village. A few of us went back to his apartment after the tournament ended and just kept on playing. I didn't sleep for three days."

"Neither did I," I said.

"I kept hearing that music you played at the audition," Kilroy said. "You blew the roof off that place, Leo. You blew me away."

"I blew you away." I reached up my hand to feel his lips in between the mustache and the beard. "But you came back."

Kilroy woke me three times in the night to make love. He couldn't stop touching me, stroking me, trying to find the places that might sing to him, make his breath slow. "God, I missed you," he said. "God, I missed this." Near dawn, we lay awake, groggy and spent, having no more than catnapped all night long. The grey light crept in from the widow's walk and filled half of the room. I looked over at Kilroy's dark face.

"What are you thinking about?" I ran a finger against the rough grain of his eyebrow and back again.

"Chess," he said.

"What about it?" I said.

"You really want to know?"

"I do."

"Well, in the end," he said. "Time equals material."

"What do you mean?"

Kilroy rose up on one elbow. "Time, space, material," he said. "The three basic elements of chess. I'll show you some time." He flopped back down on his back. "Tal didn't care much about material."

"Tal?" I brushed the hair off his forehead.

"World Chess Champion. Nineteen-sixty. He's still around. Still making his mark. He's a salty old Russian. He plays boldly, but never stupidly." He reached up to touch my face. "He's a gambler. People like that in him. He puts on a show."

232

"Are you a gambler?" I asked him.

"Not on the chessboard," he said. "I'm more of an Petrosian, I'd say."

"What's a Petrosian?"

"The turtle. Not the hare."

"How about off the chessboard?" I asked him.

Kilroy thought for a while. "I'm careful," he said. "If I lose something, I like to know why."

"I never ask," I told him. "Does that make me a gambler?"

"Depends on what you have and how you lose it." Kilroy turned over on his side. "What it meant to you, or if you ever really had it to begin with."

The fish market closed down for renovations in late August. Once again, I was in limbo. At Cobb's Hill, the garden lay tidy and smug. I looked over the neat rows of shoots one morning and set out to make a trellis for the morning glories, which already wove a low tangled web on the sticks I'd pounded into the ground to support the vines. I found my old toolbelt in the attic, a broken hammer and some rusty nails in jars I'd labeled and filled as a child, now covered with dust turned to sticky film. But I found no wood, no saw.

I took my first trip in many years to my father's hardware store in Davis Square. The #49 bus let me off in front of the Dunkin' Donuts. I breathed in the smells of coffee and sugar and lard. Burrows Hardware was a few blocks down, sandwiched in between a furniture store and a Chinese restaurant. Bells jangled as I opened the door. Once inside, the smells of childhood and my father came rushing at me— paint, plastic, metal and wood. "IF YOU DON'T SEE IT, JUST ASK." The faded sign still hung just inside the door. It was my father's job to keep track of inventory and stock, to keep the shelves tidy and full. Full was a word my father understood, but tidy wasn't, and he was the only one able to find anything in the clutter.

My father had brought me to the hardware store a few times as a child, always cautiously, steering me clear of his boss, the younger Mr. Burrows, a huge, overflowing man. I'd pick out something special for myself—a flashlight or a keyring or a tape measure, a see-through box of screws and washers. My father would always pay before we left, even though his boss would say, "No need to drag out your cash, August. I'll just take it out of your next paycheck." But my father would insist on paying, waving me away to the front of the store while he took care of the small business.

The last time I'd been there, I was about eleven or twelve.

"Let's get a look at that kid of yours," Mr. Burrows called out. "What's she got, anyways, leprosy? Always hiding in the aisles. Come on over here, girly. And tell me your name."

"Leo." My voice rose up over the paint cans as I walked to the back of the store, where Mr. Burrows, Jr., was eating his way through a box of donuts, splayed across an old, checkered arm chair. "It's Leo," I said again.

"What kind of name is that?" he asked. "Like Leo, the lion?"

"No," I said. "Like Leonardo da Vinci."

"Da Vinci?" He looked me up and down. "She a good worker?" he asked my father. I saw the folds of his stomach piled one on top of the other, straining the fabric of his shirt, the sweat stains at his armpits, the dull shine in his eye. I thought he might reach out to feel my skin, or tell me to open my mouth so he could examine my teeth, like a horse. "Your father could use a little help, honey. On Saturdays, maybe. You want to make a little pin money?"

"No," my father said quickly. "Leo has schoolwork. And music lessons. She has to practice."

"Prima donna, eh?" Mr. Burrows said. "Too good for a hardware store, are you, little miss? The princess of a pauper."

My father ushered me out of the store as if from a house of plague. Mr. Burrows was the only person I'd ever seen turn him cold, enraged. Mr. Burrows, Jr., was the only person I could say that my father ever hated. After that day, on the forms I had to fill out in school, I wrote that my father was an inventor, instead of a retailer, which is what I'd been writing ever since I asked my first grade teacher, Mrs. Halligan, what they called a guy who just worked in a hardware store.

Burrows Hardware had changed little over the years, except for a moldy smell and an uneasy silence. Dust motes swarmed in the late morning light. A fan whirred on a shelf, with a click and a moan every rotation. The store was nearly deserted at the noon hour —no rustlings, no clinkings, no leisurely discussions of pipe or caulking or paint colors. Donovan's, the new hardware store up the street, was slowly squeezing Burrows out of business. I looked up and down the aisles, at the rolls of chain and the paint cans and the key station and the dusty curtain rods, and knew the place was not long for the world. I made my slow way to the back of the store, where my father sat slumped in the checkered armchair, his head tilted backward, snoring softly.

I stood still and watched, more surprised than anything else to finally be a witness to my father's true slumber, the slack jaw and tilted head, eyelashes pressed against his cheek. In sleep, he looked young and helpless, limp in the arm and the ankle.

Just then, the door swung open and the bells jangled loudly. Mr. Burrows, Jr., grown only bigger and older, stormed into the store, shouting, "Baye! You in here? Wake up, Baye! Wake up, damnit!"

My father came to, startled, his hands gripping the sides of the armchair. He raised his head and looked around, slowly gathering his wits about him. He took it all in—the sputtering, red-faced Mr. Burrows, the time on the Coca-Cola clock—12:08—and, finally, me.

"Leo," he said. "Is everything all right?"

"Everything's fine," I said. "I just came to get a few things for the garden."

"What a nice surprise." He smoothed down a wispy patch of hair.

"To hell with all that, Baye," Mr. Burrows fumed. "I just met Charlie Axlerod out on the street. He said he came in here a few minutes ago to get some paint thinner and you were fast asleep. Said he didn't have the heart to wake you. He was on his way to Donovan's. Charlie Axlerod's been doing business here for thirty years, Baye. We can't afford to lose customers like Charlie Axlerod."

"I must have dozed off," my father said.

"Must have dozed off," Mr. Burrows jeered. "Third time in two weeks, Baye. I'd say that's three times too many."

"Two maybe," my father said.

"I must be out of my mind to keep you on here," Mr. Burrows said. "I could pay a high school kid half of what I pay you to do twice the work. If I hadn't promised the old man . . ."

My father got up and raised his hand. "Let's leave him out of this," he said. "Let's just say, you and I, that this thing has run its course. In memory of your father, let's just say . . ."

"Let's just say . . ." Mr. Burrows sputtered.

"I quit, Abe," my father said quietly.

Mr. Burrow's jaw dropped. His eyes pulled tight at the corners. "Clear out, Baye!" he said. "I've done what I could for you. I must have been nuts."

"I've often wondered," my father said.

"Get out. Now, before I . . ."

Mr. Burrows flung some boxes of Chinese food out of a brown paper bag splotched with grease stains. Clear, rectangular packages of soy sauce and hot mustard tumbled to the dirty floor. He bent down, but was unable to reach them, lost his balance and fell backward on his rear. My father bent over and picked up the packets of sauce, placed them carefully on the seat of the armchair. But he didn't offer to help Mr. Burrows to his feet.

"You can send me my last paycheck at home, Abe," he said. "Minus the three times I fell asleep, call it a half hour each, plus the cost of Charlie Axlerod's paint thinner, which is $2.20 at Donovan's, fifty cents cheaper than ours." We left Mr. Burrows speechless on the floor, legs outstretched, mouth agape, like a baby robbed of his candy, getting ready to roar. "Come on, Leo," my father said. "I'll take you to lunch."

Out on the sidewalk, my father and I sat down on a bench at the bus stop.

"Don't ever let anyone treat you that way, Leo," he said.

"Why did you?" I asked him. "For all these years."

"I thought I had no choice," he said. "But of course, I did. There've been so many times, Leo, when I've lacked imagination."

"It's a common affliction," I said.

My father took out his wallet and opened up the cash slit, brought out three worn dollar bills. "Won't be much of a lunch, old girl, I'm afraid."

I dug in my pockets, brought out the money I'd brought for the garden tools. "I have a little money," I said. "I got a job."

"A job?"

"At Danny's fish market. I sell fish."

"You sell fish?"

"I sell fish," I said.

"Well, I'll be damned," he said.

We went next door for Chinese food and then to Donovan's for a coping saw and lattice and nails. When we got home in the mid-afternoon, Lydia looked up from her book and said. "Five-thirty, already? You're back so soon?"

I got the same answer both times I called Lamaze—you should have someone to come with you to natural childbirth classes—a coach, the woman said.

"A coach?" From Danny I'd learned a healthy distrust of coaches. He'd spent his whole life being whistled at, yelled at, slapped on the back, given his game plan. "I don't need a coach," I told her.

"Call it a partner if you like," the woman said. "People prefer different terms—husband, helper, enabler, call it whatever you want."

I didn't want any of them. "I'm going to have the baby alone," I said.

"That's not unusual," the woman said.

"Lonely mothers?" I don't know what it was about the woman that brought out the sarcastic in me, maybe her relentless calm, the way she seemed to know more about what was going to happen to me than I did.

"Lots of single mothers come here," she said patiently. "We all know it takes two to make a baby, and only one to have it, but still, we recommend that you have a support system, including someone to assist you at the birth. We call that person the coach."

"The father's dead," I said.

"It doesn't have to be the father." Her voice stayed calm, but lost its edge. "Just someone with whom you feel comfortable, whom you trust, someone who'd be good in a crunch. It can be your mother, your sister, the mailman for that matter."

"But ghosts are out," I said.

"Right." In the end, we jested. "No invertebrates, no aliens," she said. "And, ideally, no ghosts."

I went to the Square that August day in a heat so thick and dense it gave license to be slothful. People lolled in various states of undress, sleeves and pant legs hiked high, buttons freed from their holes, shoes slid from the heel, stockings rolled down to the ankle. Shoppers, strollers, street vendors, students—they moved slowly in the rippling heat, licking ice cream cones, sweating, slouching, sipping drinks. Papers crackled and simmered. Somewhere an explosion waited. A bag and bottle man sorted through his collection in front of the Brigham's storefront, sweat dripping from his brow. A woman drew a picture in colored chalk on the sidewalk of a man in jail. People stepped carefully around his afro, around the prison bars. The right-to-life man, with his W. C. Fields nose, paced up and down in a dirty suit jacket in front of the Coop, sandwich placard slung over his shoulders.

"Murderers!" he shouted in between mutters. "Stop the baby killers! Save their lives! God love you missus," he hailed me as I passed by. "God love you and your baby!"

I crossed my arms over my belly, wanting to sever any connection he'd made between us. He waited for a word or a smile, some sign of solidarity, but when he saw that I could give him nothing, he turned away and began his rant again.

At Holyoke Center, Kilroy's chair was empty. I sat down with an apple and a glass of iced tea and watched the people in the courtyard. Styles had changed, or maybe it was just me. There was a new absence of color, shape, and give. Black, grey and olive green clothes ripped just so, at the knee, over the elbow, dark and drab and never mind the weather, tattered cutoffs, trenchcoats over bared, thin bodies, pale, tatooed, the slender swirl of cigarette smoke the only softness, dyed hair streaks the only brush of color. Hair was cut severely, standing in spikes or shaved to the scalp, hanging in curtains like sheets of rain over one eye. I looked in vain for one curl or curve, one soft blue or shimmery gold. Bleached, darkened, asexual, forlorn. Like half-finished statues, they lolled on the pedestals they'd found—on steps and low walls, against street lights and benches. They perched with heavy lids in difficult, studied positions, knees tucked up, legs splayed at improbable angles, holey black Converse high tops resting on flipped-up skateboards with gilded edges and tar strips, sluggish, watchful, lizards sunning on hot city rocks. Blameless, shameless, completely harmless. If they stayed still long enough, they'd never do anything that might cause them trouble or give them pain, anything that might come back later to haunt them.

I used to be one of them. But they couldn't see.

I took off my shoes and sipped my iced tea, ate the apple down to its core. This was where I lived. My city. My home. Kilroy lived here because he liked it. I lived here because there was no other place I knew. The cars rumbled by and the whistles of a policeman directing traffic punctuated the din. I lifted my stretch pants up off my swollen, sticky belly. The outdoor tables of the Cafe Troc were littered with bottles and cans, half-full ashtrays, half-eaten croissants and muddy-bottomed coffee cups. The stone bricks were hot under my feet. I took a long, deep breath. Kilroy walked cool out of a crowd.

"Leo, what are you doing here?"

"Just out on the town," I said.

"Lazarus was right," he said, brushing my head with his hand.

"Lazarus?" I looked up at him. "Lazarus, who rose up from the dead?"

"No. Lazarus, who plays chess at the next table over. He was asking me, 'Who dat sexy potato you been keeping time with, Kilroy?' And I've just now seen the potato in you. For the very first time."

"Everyone's comparing me to fruits and vegetables these days."

"Potatoes have eyes." He kissed me on the mouth. "They see everything."

"I came to ask you a favor."

"I do sexual favors. For potatoes only."

"Ha ha. I need a partner for natural childbirth classes."

Kilroy sat down in his chair. "Partner?" he said.

"A coach, they call it. For the birth. Someone who's dependable and not faint of heart." I recited the virtues described by the woman on the phone. "Someone who's calm and supportive. Someone I can trust. Someone who's good in a crunch."

"Man. Sounds like Mother Theresa to me."

I reached out and touched his arm. "It sounded like you to me," I told him.

"Me?" He ran his hand through his hair nervously. "Wow. What would I do, Leo? What would it mean?"

"You'd help me get the baby born. It wouldn't mean anything."

"You need help?"

I shrugged. "They say I do."

"Would I actually be there?" The wheels started spinning in his brain. "Could I watch the baby being born?"

"That'd be the fun part," I said. "First we'd have to go to birthing classes, once a week for seven weeks." I watched Kilroy's face for reaction, proceeded softly, on cat feet. "We'd learn breathing techniques and what happens during labor. Toward the end, we'd visit the hospital. Then you'd come to the delivery room with me. You'd help me with the breathing and feed me ice chips, let me squeeze all the blood from your hand. It might take one hour. Or it could take forty."

"I'd be right there with you?"

I nodded. "At the end, I might get weird, Kilroy. I might yell at you, or even bite you. I might tell you to shut up when you're just trying to be nice. I might scream bloody murder. Some women lose it." I felt woozy when I talked about the end, when the baby would lunge forward and split me open wide. I took a sip of iced tea. "I don't want to lose it."

"Do they know I'm not the father?" Kilroy asked me.

"They don't care."

"What about you?"

"I don't care either."

"Do you want me to be there, Leo?"

"I'm asking you."

"That doesn't answer the question."

"I wouldn't want you to do this for the wrong reasons," I said.

"What would a wrong reason be?"

"Pity, duty, curiosity. Something you've had on your cosmic list."

"Watching a baby get born—it's on there, for sure." He ran his hand through his hair curly hair, over and over again. "I just didn't know I'd get to it so soon."

chapter twenty-three

"Welcome to your last trimester!" The Lamaze teacher greeted us with a handful of pamphlets and a gold-toothed smile. She was small and compact, not pretty but surely once unbearably cute, an elf escaped from a fairy tale and left to fend for herself in twentieth century Cambridge. She was dressed in a leopard skin shirt and black leather pants, dangly giraffe earrings and a shark-tooth necklace. "The penguin parade!" she cried. We waddled into the class with pillows under our arms and our partners trailing behind. "You all look wonderful," the elf in black leather kept saying. "Positively . . . pregnant!"

"Brilliant," I whispered to Kilroy, as we settled on a corner of the rug. All around us, on the walls, were huge diagrams of fetuses at different stages of gestation, from swimming tadpoles to lima bean ghosts, to furled up babies at zero station, waiting to descend. I leafed through the pamphlet, a woman in a pastel nightgown on its cover, beaming down upon a baby at her discretely covered breast. Inside, page after page, were pictures not so pretty—of the uterus and dilated cervix, birthing positions and breast pumps. I opened up to the E page of the index. ENCEPHALITIS. ENEMA. EPIDURAL. EPISIOTOMY. I closed the pamphlet, slapped it into Kilroy's palm.

"You all look gorgeous!" The teacher corralled us into the room. We clustered in our groups of two, looked each other over, up and down. It was a lie. They said we were the most beautiful creatures on the face of the earth. But we knew better. We had hemorrhoids, indigestion, insomnia. We had stretch marks and varicose veins, gas and swollen ankles. Our stomachs would never be the same. We had backaches, nightmares, heartburn to kill. At that moment, in that carpeted, air-conditioned room, as we saw these truths in one another's gargantuan bellies, we grew collectively scared.

"My name's Candy." Our teacher's loud voice pulled us back to center. "Officially, Candace. I can never figure out which is worse. Whatever you do, please don't give your child this terrible name. I've survived, but it hasn't been easy. I'm sure your parents were all much kinder. Let's hear who you all are. Fat ladies sing first."

Candy consulted her list. We were to say our names, our due dates, a little bit about ourselves, our interests, how we were feeling about the pregnancy so far. I swung back to grade school, felt my ribcage contract around my heart. Every Tuesday, in fifth grade, we'd had to stand up and speak in front of the class. Who were we, in forty words or less? What had we done on our summer vacations? Every Tuesday, I'd blushed and mumbled my way through another edited chapter of my life. Who ever would have believed the whole truth? Who would have understood? I'd watched the "Collapsible Treehouse" collapse on my father, knit my snake, Charlie, a sweater. Once, my mother once didn't speak for a month. And I couldn't say why. Who was I? A girl who'd once swallowed a fly. For months I'd wondered if I'd sprout wings, or if I'd die.

"Leo? Leo Baye?" Candy found my name on the top of her list. "Let's start with you."

"Well. I'm Leo," I said. "My due date's on Halloween. I'm a musician, a violinist, and I'm feeling pretty good, pretty huge. Pretty strange." I looked around at the group. "Pretty scared."

Round the circle we went. Marcia. Karen. Alison. Two Mary's. Even a Joy. Most of the couples referred to themselves as husband and wife early on. All were first-time parents. "We never mix the primas with the paras," Candy explained. All of us were expecting to "go," as Candy put it, near or around Halloween. Everyone was very excited, very nervous, starting to feel very uncomfortable. We nodded our heads as our stories rolled forth, sitting in the pool of facts we'd spilled. We were having trouble sleeping. Bladder problems. Skin problems. Mood swings and cramps. A lot of us liked reading, music, gardening. Candy nodded her head, as if each story were unique, as if she hadn't heard it a thousand times before. We were all unnervingly the same.

Next, Candy went around the circle of partners, all of them men except one of the Mary's, most of them tongue-tied and nervous. "Last but not least . . ." She landed finally on Kilroy, looked down on her list. "The man with the 'Stairs to Nowhere' t-shirt. I don't have a name here. You're . . ."

"Kilroy." He swept his fingers through his hair. "I play a lot of chess," he said. "My due date, well, Leo's due date. . . ." Everyone laughed. "Is Halloween. Trick or treat. I feel pretty good." He looked around the room. "And I wasn't at all scared. Until I got here tonight."

Everyone laughed again. I looked over at Kilroy, felt a warming in my belly. Everyone liked him. Trusted him right from the start. No one knew he wasn't the baby's father. And the woman on the phone had been right. No one cared.

For the next hour, Candy sat in the lotus position, motorcycle boots at her side, and talked. She spoke knowledgeably and with care, weaving fact into anecdote and fear into fiction. I forgave her the gleaming smile and magenta fingernails, her loud voice and fondness for animal garb. Candy had what we craved—information. She was a nurse and a mother of two. She'd attended hundreds of births; she knew how we were feeling.

"It's no wonder you can't get comfortable, that you pee trickles all night for what feels like should fill buckets, that you kick anyone you might find in the bed, that you get full after two bites, that for heartburn, you could kill."

She scrawled key words on the blackboard. AORTA. INSOMNIA. CONTRACTIONS. ANXIETY. BLOATED.

"Your hormones have gone off the deep end," she said. "You alternate between sheer terror and joy, right? You cry at the drop of a hat. You are Hercules and the spider both. One minute you don't have enough strength to lift even a finger, and the next, you're scrubbing the kitchen cabinets. These babies are milking you, ladies, and it's more than a pun. Milking you for all you're worth. Remember that when they come out and you're afraid of breaking them. They're tough!"

We lay on our backs on our pillows and practiced deep breathing, first the long, even inhales and exhales we'd use during early labor, the cleansing breaths. Candy told our partners to massage us—starting from the tips of our toes and moving upward to our scalps.

"Tell 'em what feels good, ladies!" she bellowed. "And tell 'em what doesn't." Even in the crowded room, with Candy directing us in her booming voice, Kilroy's touch on my leg sent a ripple upwards.

"Relax!" Candy kept saying.

Kilroy's hand moved up my thigh. "You heard her," he said with a grin. "Relax."

"I can't relax," I whispered. We were probably the only ones in the room who'd started making love after the baby was made, still hot and blushing in the seventh month. Kilroy's hand slid down the inside of my thigh. "What are you doing to me?" I whispered.

"I'm feeling you up," he said.

"Well, feel me back down." I laughed and pushed his hand away. "God!"

"Okay, everyone, now just lie back and close your eyes," Candy said. "Hands at your sides. Let everything sink to the bottom. Imagine yourself in your most favorite, peaceful spot. Go to the place you'd most like to be in the world. Or any other world for that matter. Money and cares no object."

I lay on the pillow and closed my eyes, flew on fly wings to the island where I'd escaped as a child, to Bora Bora, where the breadfruits grew like weeds, to a coral beach drenched in hot, bleached light, where the palm trees swayed as they said palm trees did, where Lydia would never be cold or confused, where my father could putter with

stones and reeds and the branches of trees to his heart's content, reinventing simple things important in a simple world—levers and wheels
and knives. George Moustaki sang a French lullaby on Candy's tape
player. I dug a hole in the hot sand for my belly and lay with it hanging
freely. The sun beat down on my back. The tide came in and lapped at
my swollen toes, leaving pools of warm water at my feet, bits of white
coral and pearly pink shells stuck to the backs of my calves and in my
hair. I was nearly asleep when Candy came around softly, tapping me on
the shoulder. "Back to the real world," she said. "See you all next week."

Two weeks later, after the third Lamaze class, Kilroy drove away from
the health center, away from Cambridge, along Storrow Drive towards
the lights of the city.

"Where're you taking me, devil?" I asked.

"I'm kidnapping you," he said.

"Okay."

"Don't you even want to know where you're being kidnapped to?"

"Sure."

"New Hampshire," he said.

"New Hampshire?" I looked over at him. "You're kidnapping me
to New Hampshire?"

"Let me guess, Leo. You've never been to New Hampshire before."

"It's true. I've never been to New Hampshire before. And I can't go
now, Kilroy." I stuck my hand out into the muggy air. "It's way too
late. Way too hot."

"It'll be ten degrees cooler in New Hampshire," he said. "I want
you to meet my father, Leo."

"Your father?"

We climbed the ramp to the Tobin Bridge. I looked down over the
harbor and the shipyard, suspended in the night sky, the bridge's
arches spanning high above us. I filled with the panic all heights and
water brought me then, looked over at Kilroy's solid profile to steady
myself. "All right," I said. "I'll meet your father."

"Great." He said, putting his hand on my knee. "That's great, Leo."

"God. What will he think of me?"

"No telling," Kilroy said. "You know, for someone who doesn't be-lieve in God, you sure invoke him a lot."

"Invoke him? I don't even know what that means. And who's to say, even if there is a god, that it's a he." I brought my legs up underneath me in the lotus position. "What should I say to him, Kilroy?"

"God, or my father?"

"I don't talk to God," I said. "For me, God's a figure of speech. Nothing more."

"Really." Kilroy tossed a quarter into the basket at at the toll booth. The gate lifted, wobbly and slow. "Say whatever you want, Leo."

"I mean about the baby. And Danny and all. How much should we tell him?"

"He knows everything, Leo."

"Everything?"

"Don't worry. My father's only religion is tolerance."

"You're his only child." I stroked Kilroy's shifting arm as we came down off the bridge into Charlestown. "He may think I'm a waste of you."

"Come on, Leo."

"Danny's family did," I said. "His mother still won't even look me in the eye."

"So, why do you work there?" Kilroy asked. "Why do you put your-self through that, Leo?"

"I don't know," I said. "For Po maybe. For the baby. It's important, somehow."

We curved onto the dimly lit highway north. From Danvers to Newburyport, we were quiet. In Portsmouth, I reached over and rubbed the inside of Kilroy's thigh, up the ridge of his jeans, from his knee to the base of his zipper. His foot jerked off the gas pedal and the car swerved.

"Easy," he said, with a grin.

"Where did you go, Kilroy?"

"When?"

"During the relaxation exercise. In Lamaze class."

"Into a chess match," he said. "Alekhine and Capablanca. Buenos Aires. 1927. Alekhine came out of nowhere. He changed his style of play completely. Fired all his seconds. Gave up smoking. Took up exercise. Switched gears. He beat the great Capablanca. Nobody ever had before."

"Doesn't sound very peaceful." I slid my hand under his t-shirt, ran my palm along his belly, tugged at his belt.

"It was. Jesus Christ, Leo. What are you doing to me?"

"Go on," I said. "Explain. The chess match. How was it peaceful?"

"In its clarity." Kilroy planted his hands on the steering wheel. "Alekhine had such a solid plan. He knew exactly what he was doing. He studied his opponent and he studied himself. He was completely prepared. He met his goal."

"What's yours?" I slid my hand around to the small of his back.

"Good chess. What about you? Carnegie Hall, maybe?" He arched his back and groaned. "God, you have great hands."

"Good music," I said. "A spot with a symphony. First fiddle maybe, if I push." I unsnapped the top button of his jeans.

"And that would be no better than good enough?"

"That would be good," I said, lifting the metal pull of his zipper. "Halfway decent."

Kilroy's stomach heaved. "I can't take much more of this, Leo."

"Don't then," I said.

Kilroy pulled over to the side of the road into a small opening in the woods. He jerked the car into neutral and fell toward me. I hiked up my dress and put my arms around his neck. And in the pitch black of night, as the car purred and rumbled, we lay down on the sticky leather seats and did what teenagers did in parked cars.

"Halfway decent," Kilroy whispered, as he pushed deep inside of me. "Just the way I like you."

I woke from a catnap to find us on a small road hugging a river, passing by an old railroad station and several abandoned mill buildings. The wooden planks of a covered bridge shook and clattered as we passed through into a small town. We drove down the main drag, the movie marquee lit up, one engine in the fire house, two men outside smoking cigarettes, music swirling out of a bar in an old train caboose, grease smells wafting from a diner, a 7-11 shining bright on the outer edge of town, pickups slamming into the dusty parking lot, teenagers lurking, trees shivering in the wind.

Leaving the town behind us, we drove in the dark along a crumbling road that hugged the riverbank for miles. We passed more abandoned buildings, a few motels and take-out restaurants, a drive-in movie theater, its lot dotted with cars, screen lit up with two lovers clinging. Turning off the river road into darkness, we drove through the woods on a dirt road until we nearly ran smack into a small, one-story house. No yard, no driveway, just the house perched on the edge of blackness, an old truck tilted in the weeds, a stack of wood in a lean-to shed. The porch light went on. A thick arm opened the screen door. Moths scattered. Mosquitoes hovered. I pictured Lydia making the same gesture back at Cobb's Hill, beckoning a lover of mine with a slender, long-gloved arm.

Mr. Brimmer appeared on the steps. He could well have been Kilroy's father if picked from a line-up in an empty room—dark and of sturdy build, with Kilroy's broad shoulders and strong chin. But he was a more ordinary looking man, missing Kilroy's full mouth and thick, curly hair, delicate hands and coffee-colored skin. In Mr. Brimmer, I'd expected to find Kilroy's calm, his gentleness, his even-tempered way. But the man holding the door open was edgy and crisp, almost hard with a shake of a hand that stilled the blood in my fingers and a clap on the back that made Kilroy stumble, a cheerfulness not false, but charged.

"Well, well, Leo," Kilroy's father said. "It's about time."

"Nice to meet you, Mr. Brimmer."

"No, no. None of that. It's Martin or nothing. You guys are late. Baby class run over?"

"You were expecting us?" I gave Kilroy a sideways glance.

"Kilroy didn't make any promises." Martin rubbed his bald head. "But he's always been a pretty persuasive guy. Come on in. I've got spaghetti water boiling. Couldn't go wrong with spaghetti, I figured."

"No," I said. "You really can't."

"Just eat what you like, Leo," Kilroy said. "He's a bit of a Jewish mother."

249

Martin's house was cluttered, just as Kilroy's cabin was, signaling the same insatiable interest in everything, from marbles to mangoes to *Maus*, and not enough room for it all, not enough time. I saw snowshoes, cameras, hammers, schoolbooks, papers, fruit, photographs, a chess set on the kitchen table.

"Do you play chess, too, Martin?" I asked.

"Who do you think taught this wise guy to play?"

"Mom did," Kilroy said.

"She did?"

Kilroy nodded. "Well," Martin said. "Who do you think taught him everything else he knows?"

The tomato sauce was thick and homemade and good and I was glad to be able to say so and eat three helpings.

"Where does she put it all?" Martin kept asking Kilroy. "She's so tiny."

"Tiny?" I laughed. "I feel like a hippopotamus."

"Best looking hippopotamus I've come across in a long time," Martin said.

"Just eat, Dad," Kilroy said.

"Right." Martin turned to his spaghetti, twirled some on his fork and took a bite. "Kilroy tells me you're a musician, Leo."

"I play the violin."

"Wait until you hear her, Dad," Kilroy said. "She'll knock your socks off."

"What a great way for a kid to start out," Martin said. "Surrounded by music. Phoebe—that's Kilroy's mother—Phoebe used to say that he'd kick in the womb every time she played the 'Emperor Concerto.' For a while, she was hot on naming him Ludwig. But I said, come on, Pheebs, how you gonna call the kid in for dinner with a name like that. I couldn't do that to you, son."

"So instead you gave me a nice, normal name." Kilroy served himself some salad. "Like Kilroy."

"Is it a family name?" I asked.

Martin shook his head. "Know anything about the Second World War?" he asked.

"Don't get him going, Leo," Kilroy said.

"My father was in the war," I said. "He doesn't talk about it much."

"Don't blame him," Martin said. "Most of it was an atrocity. But there was this fellow named Kilroy . . ."

"He's basically the guy who invented graffiti," Kilroy said. "Only he did it in wartime, all across Europe."

"No one knows much about him," Martin said. "The story goes he was a riveter, a shipyard inspector who used to sign his work. Slowly, his name spread all over Europe—on the sides of ships, lampposts and bombed out walls. Everywhere you went, you saw, 'Kilroy was here.' The message gave people a sense of unity, a sense of hope."

"Just one man?" I asked.

"One spirit, anyway," Martin said.

"What was he like?" I asked.

"No one ever met him, far as I know," Martin said.

"Some people say that he wasn't real," Kilroy said.

"Not true." Martin got up to clear the table. "He was real all right. He was real."

Kilroy touched my leg under the table. I'd eaten too much spaghetti. My belly ached. The night had grown chilly. Martin brought me a sweater. Kilroy washed the dishes and I dried them.

"Should we sleep together?" I whispered to Kilroy. "Will your father mind?"

"What's the worst that can happen?" Kilroy smiled. "You've already been knocked up."

"He seems kind of old-fashioned."

"I sleep in your bed," he said. "And your parents don't mind. And they're old-fashioned."

"Oblivious," I said.

"You talk about them sometimes like they were . . . aliens," he said.

"Do I?" I slid the dry plates onto a shelf. "I just don't think it would ever occur to them to be shocked about anything."

"Are you saying they have no values?"

"I'm not sure they've ever really needed them," I said.

"Everyone has them, Leo," Kilroy said. "Everyone needs them."

We were quiet for a while. Martin sat out in the living room on the couch and read the paper while we finished cleaning up in the kitchen.

I listened to the night's noises, water running, crickets clamoring, dishes clattering.

"Have you ever done this before?" I asked Kilroy.

"Washed the dishes?" he said. "Yeah, once or twice. I try not to make it a habit."

"No. Brought someone here, I mean. Slept with someone in your father's house."

"Come on, Leo." He pulled a soapy finger out of the dishwater and scratched his nose.

"Have you?" I blew the suds off his nose. I wanted to be able to talk openly with Kilroy the way Martin had, about his ex-wife and days gone by. I wanted to know everything, so that nothing could take me by surprise.

"Once I did," Kilroy said.

"You came here with a girl?"

Kilroy nodded. "She was a girl."

"What kind of girl?"

"Just a girl."

"Tall? Quiet? Smart? Shy? A girl you liked a lot?" I was both fascinated and jealous of the girl who took Kilroy away from the sink for a minute. "She was tall," he said slowly, "and smart." He handed me a dripping plate. "She definitely wasn't shy." He smiled. "And I did like her, more than she liked me."

"What happened?"

"She dumped me."

"She broke your heart?" I slid a dry plate back onto the shelf.

"A little piece, maybe," Kilroy said. "She was older than I was, six years. But I kept forgetting that. I was the one who wanted to settle down. She wasn't ready. The age difference bothered her. She thought I'd up and leave her, just when she was getting used to me. She didn't know me." He pulled the plug from the drain and took me in his arms. "I didn't know her."

"Oh, it didn't work out with the tall girl," I teased. "So now you'll settle for me."

"You don't come to me exactly unattached," he said.

Martin came in through the swinging door, caught us twisting out of an embrace. "You kids take my bed," he said. "I'll sleep on the couch."

"Are you sure?" I asked him. "We're comfortable anywhere."

"She's lying," Kilroy said. "She's hardly comfortable anywhere these days. Thanks, Dad. We'll take the bed."

"Thanks, Mr. Brimmer," I said.

"Martin," he said sternly. "It's Martin or nothing."

I slipped half naked under Martin's cold sheets. Kilroy looked through the books on the shelf for a while before coming to bed. This was the kind of luxury I'd missed with Danny, these moments of nothing in particular—after dinner, during a lull, before the touch. I crossed my arms behind my head and watched Kilroy. A chicken wing bone stuck out of his back as he scratched his shoulder. His hair stuck up on one side. And by God if he didn't, out of the blue, start to whistle "Clementine."

"What is it with that song?" I asked him.

"Beats me," he said with a shrug. "It's a catchy tune."

Kilroy undressed and came to bed with a chess book. I put my nose to his warm chest, for the first time knowing him to be the most familiar body in a foreign place—the language of his arms and legs all part of my lore now, one hand propping up his book on his chest, the other punching his pillow, trying to get comfortable, his big toe digging for my shin.

"You need the 'Automatic Page Turner,'" I said.

"What's that?" he murmured.

"A fabulous invention," I said. "That will soon rock the world."

"Great," Kilroy said. "I'll wait." He put the book down, flicked off the light and turned toward me on his side. I curled up to fit the S fold of his body. He clasped his hands around the huge swell of my belly. We lay in a lumpy embrace.

"So what do you think of my father?" he asked.

"I like him," I said.

"He liked you. I can tell."

"How?"

"He sang to you and he talked too much. Telltale signs." Kilroy wove his fingers through mine. "And he told you the Kilroy story. He doesn't tell just anybody the Kilroy story."

"It seems sort of sacrilegious, doesn't it?" I said. "Sleeping in your father's bed?"

"I was probably made here," he said. "So maybe it's fitting." The pressure of his fingers tightened on mine. "I told you about the tall girl, Leo," he said. "Tell me more about Danny."

"Everything with Danny was spilt milk," I said. "A mess."

"Did you love him?"

"I thought I did."

"Why?"

"The reasons don't seem so good anymore," I said. "He was strong and beautiful. He was troubled. For me, that was an irresistable combination somehow."

"Did he love you?"

"In his way. I can see now. I didn't ask for much."

"If Danny hadn't died," Kilroy lifted my hair, blew on the nape of my neck. "If I hadn't come along. Would you have stayed with him forever?"

"Probably," I said. "We would have lived above the pizza parlor, in Inman Square, eating fish till we grew gills. We kept trying to hurt each other. I don't know why."

"Bastard," he said. "Did he ever? . . ."

"No." I untangled my fingers from his. "He never did."

"He was right on the edge, Leo. I saw it that night. He was wasted, out of control. He really could've hurt you."

"You saw him at his worst," I said. "I told you. He usually . . ."

"Bastard," Kilroy said again.

"No." I brought my knees tighter into my chest. "He wasn't a bastard, Kilroy."

"Me thinks . . ." Kilroy's hold on me slackened as he yawned. "You doth protest too much."

"No, I don't," I said. "No, I don't."

Before Kilroy drifted off, one last thought escaped him. "Think of a sentence, Leo, with five thats in a row. A straight string. No other words in between . . ."

I would have lain awake for those hours anyway, in that creaky, old bed in New Hampshire, listening to the wind and the cranky hoot of an owl and Kilroy's even breathing, having it out with a buzzing mosquito, having it out with the tall girl. I was glad for the silence, and the darkness, for the riddle Kilroy had left me with, his warm body stirring beside me.

"That that is spelled t-h-a-t." I got two right off the bat.

"That that that I used in the sentence was underlined." Three came after a while.

The night passed slowly in Martin's house as I turned the words over and over in my brain. "That that that that man used in the sentence was spelled incorrectly." In the nether hours, I found four.

"I had to point out that that that that that man used in the sentence was spelled incorrectly."

By the crack of dawn, wide awake and triumphant, I'd gotten five.

chapter twenty-four

*T*he sun pummeled the earth by day and the rain fell silently at night, leaving a fresh wash on the dusty earth each morning, like the buckets of water Danny used to splash over the sidewalk before he opened up the fish market. My garden ran riotous, the morning glories thick and fluted on their trellis, the tomatoes red and bursting, the impatiens pushed up in bunches against the side of the house, a perfumed crowd waiting for the doors of Filene's Basement to open. The popcorn plants held steady with no fruit. The breadfruits' spindly stalks were still fragile.

Each day, I wore one of three cotton housedresses I'd bought at Woolworths, that covered me respectably enough, but still let me breathe. I stared at the mother-of-pearl hairbrush from time to time, but only when the purplish glare of its backside stared me down did I pick it up and brush my hair, which now crept down my back in a thick black tangle. I wondered if they'd let me in at the hospital when it was time, unsure of what I might give birth to on one of their sterile, back-rising beds. My breasts were huge and tight, my stomach an arid, veiny planet. My feet were cracked and dirt-stained, tough as they'd been when I was a child. Ankles thick and tender, tongue forever dry.

We were cloistered up there on Cobb's Hill —my father, Lydia and I—like monks left to wander an abandoned monastery. My father was home all day now. We didn't speak of what had happened at the hardware store, or Anton, or Danny, or the baby, or what might come of us all. But my father must have told Lydia about quitting his job. One morning, at the breakfast table, she said, "Well, Claire, I'm glad your father finally got out of that place."

"What place?"

"The hardware store." She'd grown newly impatient with my caution. "He never liked it there."

"Why do you think he stayed?" The words flew out of my mouth on hornet wings to sting.

"He had no choice, Lydia said.

"Maybe he did," I said.

"Your father works too hard," she said. "He always hated it there."

"It wasn't the place he hated," I said. "Just the fact of having to be there. The time it took away from his inventions. From us . . . From you."

"Me?" Lydia held the thought for a minute, then let it fall with a brush of her hand. "And that boy," she said. "I never liked that boy."

"What boy?"

"I told your father to quit after Abraham Sr. died."

"And do what?" I asked her.

"Anything but work for that boy. That boy was greedy. He had no love for his father."

"Dad was just trying to take care of us," I said.

"We'll manage," Lydia said. "I'll send August up to the attic. We still have a few things to sell. The Byeworths thought I married down, but I wasn't swayed."

"There's nothing left up there, Lydia," I told her. "Everything's gone."

"There must be a few more things," Lydia said. "Your father will find them."

But my father was out of touch, out of reach. He only sometimes came to the breakfast table anymore, and spent his time there brooding or buried in a book, then wandered off back to the invention room. After I took him coffee one morning, I went up to the attic to scrounge. And sure enough, there were, amidst the overturned boxes and crinkled newspapers, a few more treasures—a gold-leaf cigarette holder and a silver ashtray, which I took to the pawn shop in Harvard Square to turn back into toast.

I watched Lydia carefully in those days, examining her from different angles, in different lights, as if she might pass on some secrets which would otherwise be hard-won, costly in time or psyche. She was after all, my mother. I sat as living proof. And she seemed well enough, by then, plumbable. I wanted to take everything I could from her, everything she could newly offer. And yet I couldn't help but be wary, too, of this changing Lydia—her clear eyes and comebacks, her bright, new clothes. I had long sensed that any rise on my mother's part would somehow mean my fall. As the anchor of Lydia's illness was lifted, wouldn't I be the one left to drift? Any dime-store psychiatrist might have told me what crept up over my toes like a cold, Bay of Fundy tide, that the new Lydia could not help but be a disappointment to me. From a greater distance, anyone might have seen how much of my love for her had been steeped in her mysteries, her tragedies. Anyone else might have seen right away how the real Lydia would turn out to be so much more ordinary and less complicated than the mother I'd invented over the years—the one who would someday return to me from wherever she roamed—how much plainer she'd appear face to face than from the remove of illness and longing. Who ever could have measured up to the mythical figure I'd created over time? Anyone but me could have seen how my feelings might slowly twist like pipecleaners in the hands of a lonely, anxious child.

And so, despite my vow to confront Lydia about Anton, I kept my distance. Where she hovered, her arms cast a long, warped shadow. I turned my belly aside as she passed, closed my eyes when she opened her mouth to speak. I crossed my fingers when she started to spin a tale of doom, as if she were Cassandra, the prophetess, or a jinx, as if all of her weaknesses might choose that moment to creep inside of me and come alive—Lydia's demons evicted, on the loose, in search of a new home, and what better vacant lot than me? I'd made the choice. I'd come back to this house, the house that wrapped its arms tightly around you and wouldn't let you go.

Po and Kilroy came and went, sometimes staying for hours, sometimes just to sit on the bench by the chestnut tree or stretch out in a slice of shade. Kilroy brought books and a chess set and Po roamed the yard as I once had, in search of backyard creatures or lost in games of jungle travel. He'd lean over Kilroy's shoulder at the chessboard to watch and one day he said, "teach me how to play, Kilroy." We brought a rickety card table out into the yard and shoved bark under its legs to steady it. Kilroy taught Po how to play and I listened—how the bishops ran on the diagonal, how the knights made their crooked hop, how the pawns moved only one space at a time, always straight ahead, in quiet defense and pursuit. I'd come to love the language of chess, numbers and words ricocheting off one another in an intricate dance—pawn to f6, Queen's Gambit Declined, an open g file. As Po learned the moves, I focused on the ideas as Kilroy explained them. Lydia pulled up a chair one day and started fingering the pieces, asking questions.

"Couldn't the bishop have gone there?" She took it all in, quickly, with a clear eye. "The knight's better off here, isn't it, Kilroy?"

"Lydia's the smartest," Po observed. "She learns the fastest."

"I'm the oldest, Po," she said, matter-of-factly. "I have the least time."

The chessboard stayed out all day and night. We ate dripping peaches and plums and fresh bread that Kilroy brought from the Cafe Troc, tearing off hunks and digging in as we tried to figure out how to get a knight, say, from the g2 square to the b6 square in six moves, how to mate in three. Kilroy left us with visions and glimpses, riddles and puzzles. Soon, we played among ourselves.

From time to time, I'd bring food or coffee up to my father on a tray. He'd nod his thanks and wave me away. The invention room was strewn with sand and fabric, the sand stuck all over his arms and hair, patches of him often wet. He was more dissheveled and unkempt than ever. The Rambler was often gone for hours at a time. Some days when I asked him where he'd been, he'd say, simply, the beach. I had no way of knowing if this was madness or metaphor. I had to wonder if he was slowly easing himself over the edge of a cliff into a warm sea of folly or dementia. The coffee cups disappeared one by one from the kitchen shelves. Every few days, I'd collect them from the invention room, their bottoms covered with speckled, brown crud, wash them and put them back in the cupboard. My father didn't speak of what he was doing, and we didn't ask. It was his turn, after all those years, to be secretive, withdrawn.

We sat in the yard like chess pieces on a summer chessboard, waiting to be moved—by a whim or a pang or an urge—to the bathroom or the kitchen for whatever we might scrounge—carrots, water, apples, crackers—to the garden to weed or pluck, into the tall grass to play. Lydia often traveled without her radio now. She came and went from the kitchen to the yard, from her room to the living room, brewed tea in the sun, often in sporty new clothes she'd ordered from catalogs, with no real intention of keeping. She'd wear them once or twice, and send them back, saying they weren't quite right, or had a small defect. The company would write back that it couldn't have been so, ma'am. Inspector #467 had found the merchandise without flaw. She'd write back again, courteous, firm—the seam was weak, one sleeve longer than another. It wasn't her color, her style. She wouldn't be able to use it, after all. She'd take the lavender corduroy jacket instead, the peach-colored hat. The packages came and went. And over the young mailman who delivered and took these packages from her hands, Lydia cast an old and powerful spell.

Lydia's elegance was not gone, but lost in dazzling confusion—mixed devotion to the old styles and a burning curiosity about all that had come and gone in the fashion world since she'd retreated. Dignified and comical in her old button-up boots and a new purple polka-dotted top, Lydia sat regal still on the sofa. Not unlike the way I dressed, I realized. What Danny had called "prom-queen, bag-lady" style.

"Strangely enough, Claire," Lydia told me one day in a puzzled voice, "I seem to have nothing to wear."

I pointed to the hallway closet. "What about all your old clothes?"

"They're quite outdated now, aren't they? Some day I'll make a pile for Goodwill. Someone still might want these old things. I can't imagine who . . ."

"I'll help you, Lydia," I said. "Anytime."

But time moved slowly in our house, as it always had, at the pace of an addled snail.

Watching Lydia on those hot summer days from the garden, as she came and went, I began to feel some new feeling of attachment to my mother that carried with it a slow, leaking pain. This Lydia who took chances, who wore loafers and ventured half a joke, the Lydia who made eggs and took walks and flirted with the mailman—this Lydia might land in a hole, might make a fool of herself, might catch a cold. I watched her and I worried. If my mother were finally going to show her true colors, then I'd have no choice but to reveal mine. If our old selves were truly perishing, then we'd have no choice but to forge new ones. And as terrifying as this was, neither of us could afford to pass up the chance for reincarnation.

Lydia started to bring things outside with her into the yard—books, newspapers, knitting. And though she never really read or wrote or knit anything, she often made a show of doing so, even resting some old reading glasses on the bridge of her nose. She'd count the stitches on her needles, read me a line of poetry, Dickinson or Poe, an item from the paper, and not always news of earthquakes or floods or a child caught under the beam of a falling building, in the blade of a threshing tractor, anymore.

Some days she'd tell me about a white sale at Jordan Marsh, or a movie I might like to see, with one of the Redgrave girls, triplets conceived in a petri dish, an actor she'd once known, now starring in a play downtown. He must be quite a bit older by now, that actor, quite accomplished. She'd like to see that play, she said, before it moved on. Dvořák was playing at Symphony Hall. She'd rehearsed there, long ago. She'd gotten to know the janitor, a sweet young man with a stutter. Perhaps not so young anymore. Stutters, like hairlips and fears, never really died. Fate played favorites, but sometimes time was kind to the sufferers, to the stutterers. He'd been quite smitten with her, quite sweet, a schoolboy crush. A tiny young man with beautiful eyes. Lydia was sure that janitor was still there, still working, still listening to the music behind the velvet curtains with closed eyes and curling lashes—still there. One day, as I hoisted the laden tomato vines up onto a stick and secured them with twine, I thought I heard Lydia humming, but who knows. The birds were used to us by then and noisy once more. It was probably just the birds.

A cool August night found Kilroy, Po, and me whizzing down Storrow Drive in the Rambler along the river, headed for Fenway Park to watch the Red Sox play the Yankees. The river was dotted with white sails. The CAINS sign formed, letter by letter, in neon orange and green, against rolling pink clouds, and then disappeared.

"Why didn't Lydia come?" Po propped his arms up against the back of the front seat.

"She was busy," I said.

"No, she wasn't," Po said. "She was just sitting in the kitchen. She wasn't doing anything."

"Lydia doesn't go out much. You know that, Po."

"But she loves baseball."

"It's true," I said.

"Next time we'll bring her," Po said. "Next time she'll come."

At the Citgo sign, we turned off at Kenmore Square. Parking in front of a basement pizza parlor, we walked through the square, following the crowds and the misty shine of the ballpark lights, the calls of the street hawkers selling banners, dolls and caps, eating peanuts as we went.

My belly got stuck in the turnstyle and the ticket taker had to help me through. Po laughed.

"What's so funny, wise guy?" I asked him.

"You are, Fatso."

"Fatso?" I grabbed Po from behind by the collar of his shirt and brought his grinning face close to mine. He was finally and so clearly Po, this freckled imp, and not Danny, so full of crooked glee. In the cavernous spaces underneath the stadium seats, my voice echoed in a wicked whisper. "Would you like to share your little joke with the rest of the class, Mr. McPhee?"

"Yes! No!" he shouted gleefully. "You can't catch me, Leo." He danced on the bottom step. "You can't catch *anybody!*"

I chased him up the wide, concrete steps out into the summer air, suddenly lifted into a hushed world of green velvet and shimmering mist, the smell of popcorn rising in the dusk, the muffled slap of balls hitting the pockets of leather mitts, murmurs and squeals coming from the loudspeakers, band music playing somewhere. Po and I froze, looked at one another, waited for Kilroy to come from behind with the drinks. What had we been thinking? How could we have come? And yet how could we have stayed away? We both remembered; we both knew what was wrong. This was Danny's world. And we'd never been here without him.

When Kilroy caught up, we climbed to the bleacher seats, banged on the great green wall for good luck. The game started up and we hailed the vendors as they roamed the stands, downing popcorn and hot dogs and pizza and ice cream bars. The players came up to bat, one by one, the pitchers winding up time and time again like well-oiled machines. Po filled in the score card. He and Kilroy pulled change out of their pockets and made bets—who'd strike out first, who'd hit a home run, which pitcher would take off his cap first in the bullpen.

I leaned back against the wall and remembered the night I'd come here with Danny, the summer before, my first and only other ball game. In a flash, I'd seen why it was a national pastime, why it could have been more—an institution, a cult, a way of life, a game that stilled time, turned men back into boys. I'd been instantly bewitched by the surreal green world, with its mossy bottom and tidy diamond infield, the uniformed men who drove the little baseball-shaped carts, the players in their spiffy uniforms and tight-socked calves, the Oz-like echoes from the loudspeakers, the murmurs of the crowd, slack pitches in the bullpen, the tobacco chewing and hunched shoulders, the gentle male hubris of it all—kids with baseball mitts poised, the banter, the auctioneer voices of the food vendors with their trays slung low on their bellies, a man in a suit and a mask crouching low in the dirt, fingers dancing between bent knees, the lazy pace of the unfolding game, the crack of the bat and the frenzy of the crowd as it rose to its feet, the lope of the outfielders inward at the end of an inning, the bright lights and the silhouette of a man who straddled the Marlboro sign out in left field above the Expressway, riding it like a bronco, a baseball glove in one hand, waiting for a soaring fly ball, and Danny beside me, suddenly softened, opened wide.

"Classic Leo," Danny'd said. The smile only rose on one side of his face. "Never eaten a hot dog. Never drunk hard liquor. Never been to a baseball game." These omissions in my life seemed to please him, make me pure in his eyes in some way. Danny showed me how to keep score, marking the strikes and balls and errors and home runs. He taught me the language of baseball and I only wished we could speak it always. If my gaze wandered, or if I missed a play, he'd nudge me, and point to the tip of my perfectly sharpened pencil. I watched him in profile, so beautifully chiseled and almost serene on that warm night. He was as close to happy as I'd ever known him—in his element, anonymous, glad to have me beside him, willing and unwise in baseball ways, at some small disadvantage. We sat among 33,000 others, our feet sticking to the Coke-soaked ground, a record crowd, the loudspeaker boomed. But all I could think about that night was that Danny and I were doing something together, just the two of us. For once, we were alone.

The breezes blew and idle chatter passed between us. Danny wolfed down his popcorn, knuckles leading, reaching over to paw my blue-jeaned knee from time to time. A comfortable feeling settled in, one we'd never known before and would never know after. I thought how I could have sat there forever in the soft breeze, how amazing it was that Danny's beer lay flat and practically untouched, that my legs were red from his squeezing, my head aswirl with statistics, how the lovemaking might change for a night like this, how nothing made me feel better than Danny feeling good and how that wasn't quite right, but how it all might somehow work out after all, if I could only keep Danny in a baseball park forever, if I could only keep him happy. I'd sat beside him as the air cooled, as the bat cracked and the players ran around and around the bases, eating pieces of popcorn one by one, imagining a home we might make, the children we might have—all the while mistaking this for a love of baseball.

The Sox went ahead three runs in the fifth. Po bounded down to the bullpen two steps at a time to get Frankie Amanzo's autograph. The Yankee pitcher came away from the mound in the baseball-shaped cart, satin jacket slung over his shoulder.

"Frankie Amanzo says that's all she wrote." Po came back breathless, a signed ticket stub clutched in his hand. "Frankie Amanzo says, sit back and enjoy the rest of the show." Kilroy and Po plunked down more coins on the metal bleachers. The bets got more outrageous, which way the wind would blow a paper cup, how many times the Goodyear blimp would pass overhead, which Yankee would scratch his crotch first in the dugout. In the sixth, the Yankees lost heart and the game got even more lopsided. People began drifting home.

"Want to head out?" Kilroy got up for the seventh inning stretch. "Beat the traffic home?"

Po shook his head. I leaned back against the wall. "No way," we said at the same time.

"What is this?" Kilroy said. "Some sort of pact? Some sort of mutiny?"

It was Danny's rule. You didn't leave the ballpark until the game was over, no matter what the score, no matter how dull the play, how cold the fingers or bloated the belly. Kilroy sat back down and sighed. We reached for the scorecard, tilted our pencils, focused our eyes back on the field. We sipped sickly sweet cocoa and polished off one last piece of doughy pizza. We would stay, until what was almost a bitterly cold end, bound in loyalty and memory, and Fenway Park indigestion.

* * *

I stopped in the next day to the fish market, where big plans had led to bigger plans. Po and his father were painting the walls, putting down tile. Mrs. McPhee was planning a chowder corner, a small café with tables for soup and sandwiches. A huge blackboard lined one wall. On the counter sat a new cash register, one that told you how much change to give the customers.

"This sucker's going to do my math homework for me next year," Po told me, pressing a button that made the cash drawer open with a zing.

"No, it won't. You'll be using your own brain, Porter McPhee," his father said. "You taking care of yourself, Leo?"

"There's nothing to take care of," I said. "Nothing to do but wait. Put me to work. Please. I want to do something."

"No time for you to be hefting fish, Leo. You go home and rest."

"I can't go home," I said. "I can't rest."

"For the baby, then," he said. "Do it for the baby, Leo."

"You sure you don't need any help?" I checked with Po.

"Nah, Leo," he said. "We got it all covered."

chapter twenty-five

*B*ack on Cobb's Hill, as August slipped away, the house began to feel its age. The drainpipes leaked and the gutters were clogged. The doors swelled and scraped the jambs. The good weather held and the garden was dry. I brought pails of water out from the kitchen and doused the plants. Po made a scarecrow from a broomstick to keep the crows away. Whoever passed by the garden stopped to weed. Kilroy played long hours of chess at Brattle Court. Dollar bills filled his pockets. He'd stuff them into the glass bowl on the hall table at Cobb's Hill, hush me when I tried to stop him, to thank him. We'd fall into bed, make love, sleep fitfully and hard.

Sex had become more challenge than pleasure. I came easily, at the drop of a hat, almost as soon as Kilroy's hand touched a vulnerable spot, a crease in my thigh, a ridge of bone. For Kilroy, the climax seemed to get harder, more studied, more out of reach. I wondered how it would be when the baby came, where it would lie, how much it would cry, how needy it might be, how much touching we'd still do. We'd always made love with the baby in between us—a buffer, a witness, a third spinning wheel. How would it be when we lost our center? Would we stare at each other shyly and start all over again, shift positions, scraping skin and bones? When the baby took to its own bed and left us alone in ours, would we know what to do with each other anymore? Or would Kilroy have found another body by then, another bed?

Kilroy woke early each morning, to take care of business at the reservoir before he started his chess day in the Square. He'd drag himself out of dawn sleep with a groan and fiddle with his chessboard for a while, before he rolled over onto the floor to do push-ups, groping for a sock, reading a page of a book, reaching out to touch some part of me, dragging out the leaving—dragging. Danny had slipped away from my bed stealthily, like a cat burglar, leaving no traces or fingerprints, no memories, no regret. Kilroy left half-heartedly, slowly, left his books and his chessboards and his socks and loose change and his scent and his reluctance and his kisses and his confusion strewn all about. And I'd hold them all hostage, until he came back for them, came back for more.

I woke up one night to the touch of a sweaty hand and brow, hot breath on my neck, a chill whisper.

"Danny?" I reached up in the dark to feel his wet brow. "Did you win?"

"Danny?" the voice said. "Did I win? What are you talking about? Jesus Christ, Leo. It's me, Kilroy. It's not Danny."

"Kilroy?" I felt for the ridge of his jaw, the rough grain of his cheek. "Is that you?"

"Yes, it's me, Leo," he said. "It's fucking me."

"Don't swear," I murmured.

"Why not?" he asked, starting to undress. "He did, didn't he? Everything was fuckin' this and fuckin' that with him, wasn't it? I didn't think they encouraged that kind of language at Harvard."

"What's wrong, Kilroy?" I blinked my eyes to see his face more clearly.

"I don't know." He started to rub his forehead with one hand. "I'm just tired, I guess. I don't know."

I made room for him on the bed. We arranged ourselves carefully, back to back, and drifted off in silence. Kilroy slept restlessly, talked in his sleep—wait, no, now, can't—the words were clipped, hard and slurred. He woke with his t-shirt twisted, his hair standing up on end.

"I'm not long for my job at the reservoir," he told me the next morning as he got ready to leave. "The money's drying up. And I'm not really supposed to be living in the cabin. It's against city regulations. Against code. Some guy came poking around the other day, asking questions. I tried to play dumb."

"Not easy for you," I said.

"My boss says I should start looking for another place soon," Kilroy said. "Another job."

"Ettore says endings are just beginnings in disguise."

"But what's there really left to be, Leo?" he said. "After you've been the Keeper of the Golf Course?"

I heard the edge in his voice. "Are you okay, Kilroy?"

"It's time to start thinking on another plane," he said. "That's all."

I reached out to touch his arm. Another person in my life, on his way to another plane, and me not sure I could follow.

"Take me with you," was what I couldn't say.

Came the night that Kilroy stopped touching me. He lay still at the farthest remove of the mattress. All that night. And then the next. He was distant, kind, almost polite, in a way that made me feel he couldn't forgive me for something and it wasn't the sex. We'd crossed over some line, which, even in hindsight, I couldn't see, couldn't name.

I left the bed one night while Kilroy slept and went out into the garden. A while later, he came to find me.

"What are you doing out here, Leo?"

"I couldn't sleep," I said.

Kilroy sat down beside me, wrapped his arms around his chest.

"Why won't you touch me anymore?" I said.

"I'm sorry," he said.

"Sorry for what?" I steeled myself. He was going to leave me there,

269

up in my garden on the hill, leave me with my parents and my thirsty plants, all my terror and my unborn child.

"I'm sorry for being scared."

"Scared?" I couldn't hide my relief. "You're scared, Kilroy? That's all?"

"I'm scared of everything." His hands flew up in the air. "I'm scared of you. Scared of the baby. Scared of me. I get worried. What if it's not enough, for any of us?"

"I don't know. It's a good question. Just keep talking, Kilroy."

He started to rub his temple with one hand. "I'm tired of talking, Leo," he said. "I'm just so damn . . . tired."

As I watched him, sitting there slumped in the dirt, eyes closed, something came into my mind from the Lamaze Manual. I was amazed to find I could recite whole chunks of it, in litany, by heart. I remembered the page, a drawing of a man with beads of sweat pouring off his brow, question marks popping out of his brain.

During the eighth month, your partners may begin to experience anxiety. They may feel increasingly alienated and useless, neglected, impotent even. They may suddenly be more aggressive, or passive, more distant. Where have they gone? Just into their own heads for a while. Don't worry. Let them go. They'll be back. Stronger. Rested. Ready.

"You don't owe me anything, Kilroy," I said, reaching out my hand. "You're not the father."

"You keep reminding me."

"The last thing I want you to feel is trapped."

"I don't feel trapped," he said. "I feel . . . swamped. I feel marooned."

"Why?" I said.

Kilroy gave his forehead to his hands. "Who knows?" he said. "It's you. It's the baby." He began to run one hand through his hair, the way Danny used to, over and over, like a mouse on a treadmill. "You're one and the same. You're attached. I never knew you when you weren't. I wish I had."

"The previous me was not that admirable," I said. "I was weak, Kilroy, unsteady. I didn't know what I wanted. I couldn't stand my ground."

"I don't believe it, Leo," he said. "All this talk about strength and weakness. You're tough as a kangeroo hide."

"You've felt one, of course."

"I have," he said.

"Come on." I reached out my hand. "Let's go back up to bed."

"No." Kilroy ran a finger down the stalk of a breadfruit plant, barely upright and in peril. I leaned forward and kissed him on the mouth, brought my hands up under his shirt, pressed my body up close against his.

"All right," he said, catching his breath, sliding his hands down onto my hips, kissing me back. "Okay. God, Leo. Yes. Okay."

I hadn't been listening, or watching carefully. I'd missed the silences, the breaks in rhythm, the tightening of words, the slip of gesture. I hadn't seen it growing—Kilroy's distance, his malaise. I'd missed the third-day growth on his chin, the dirty t-shirt, the clench of his jaw in sleep. When we went back to bed that night, he was hard, almost rough. He didn't take care to steer clear of my stomach or be gentle with my bursting breasts. He pressed hard against me, tugged at my jersey. "Take this damn thing off, Leo," he said.

"No, I'm cold, Kilroy. I want it on."

"Take it off." He yanked the jersey up over my belly. "Get rid of them, will you? Get rid of all his fucking shirts." I pulled the jersey back down. Kilroy's forearm pressed into my stomach and I pushed him away. In the struggle, Kilroy fell off the bed and landed on the floor with a thud. For a while he lay silently, face turned away, naked, arms propped up by his side, belly flat to the floor.

I sat up on the bed, swung my legs over the side. "You've got to tell me, Kilroy," I said. "What's going on?"

"Nothing." He spoke to the wall.

"Don't say nothing."

"But what if it's the answer?" Kilroy picked himself up from the floor and sat on the floor by the bed. "Your body's here, Leo. I enter it from time to time. But the rest of you is somewhere else and I can't get there. You're like a stone. You're not grieving. You're not dealing. You barely seem to remember the accident. And I can't forget for one god damned minute."

"What are you talking about?" I said quietly. "All I do is remember."

"You never talk about it."

"There's nothing to say. It happened, Kilroy. I'm trying to move on. I'm trying to forget."

"But how can you possibly forget," he said. "Until you remember?"

"I told you, that's all I do."

"Truth is stranger than fiction, Leo. You went down to Hell and came back up. In the beginning, I admit, it was a turn on. You were mysterious, heroic. Tragedy made you beautiful. But now, I'm in deep. So deep." He turned his head away. "I feel like we're floating in this crazy dream, dragging Danny's body behind us."

"No wonder you can't look me in the face," I said. "When you say something like that."

"I don't know what to do." One of Kilroy's hands sliced the air. "I don't know where I fit in, Leo. I feel so detached, so . . . beside the point. You watched your boyfriend die . . ." I heard the tremor in his voice.

"The word never even applied," I said.

"Okay, the guy you went to parties with, the guy whose hockey games you went to, the one who drove you home and you screwed with on a regular basis." Kilroy wiped his nose on the back of his hand.

"Oh, god, don't cry, Kilroy. Please."

"Why shouldn't I cry?"

"Because I won't know what to do," I said. "I won't know how to make you feel better."

"You don't *have* to make me feel better, Leo. That is not a requirement of this relationship. You went down with him. You went under. You came back up and he didn't. Part of you must still be in that car with him. I understand that. I accept it. It's a place I'll never be able to go. I want to be with you. Here and now. But you're so vague, so tightly wound, so incredibly far away sometimes." In horror, I heard Kilroy describing Lydia. "Even when I'm with you, Leo . . ." He threw his hands up into the air. "You're not here."

"I *am* here." I pressed my knuckles together, tried to speak calmly, even as the steam of panic rose up through my throat—to give reasons, defenses, answers, in a clear, rational voice, the way Lydia had never been able to do. "I'll be right here, Kilroy, any time you look—in this house, in this bed, at the kitchen table, or at the Conservatory, at the fish market, out in the back yard." I heard my voice, even and calm. My heart raced uncontrollably, beating, "liar, liar." "I *am* here," I told him again, and this time my voice trembled. "*Here*."

"How did it feel in the water, Leo?" Kilroy reached over and took my arm. "When they pulled Danny out. At the hospital? When they told you he was dead. How did it *feel*?"

"Awful." I flung his hand away. "It was terrifying, sickening. I puked. All over a nurse. All over myself. I was sick for weeks."

"Tell me about it."

"It was the worst thing that ever happened to me," I said. "For a while, I wished I were dead. What else can I say? Nothing so terrible can ever happen again. I thought I was dealing with it pretty well."

"Maybe too well, sweetheart." Kilroy said.

"Don't call me sweetheart," I said. "Eddie Quintana called me sweetheart."

"Eddie Quintana, by the way, is a slime bucket."

"He loved Danny like a brother."

"Is that the way you love me?" Kilroy said quietly.

"What?"

"Is that the way you love me, Leo? Like a brother?"

"I never had a brother, Kilroy."

Kilroy clenched his fists then, desperate to drag something from me, like an old chain from a riverbed. I truly didn't know what he wanted from the muddy bottom of my soul, what to offer up of the sick fish and rusty cans and useless tossed out bits of hardware that had gathered there over the years. I knew he'd leave, and I didn't know what I could say to stop him.

"Tell me what you want, Kilroy. Please."

"I just want to know how you feel about me, Leo. It's not so complicated. It really shouldn't be this hard."

"I need you, Kilroy. Please don't go away."

"You need me," he said quietly. "You need me." He stood up and pulled on his t-shirt inside out, his pants in one jerk, in such a hurry to reach the door, he forgot his shoes, so mad he never came back for them. "But do you love me, Leo?" he asked, his hand on the knob of the door. "Do you fucking love me?"

"Kilroy," I said, as he opened the door. "Don't go."

"He made your baby, damn it. He was drunk out of his mind and he never even knew. Where's the justice in that, Leo?" Kilroy turned to me one last time before he left. "Why the hell couldn't it have been me?"

chapter twenty-six

September came stealthily, killing the grace of August. The heat dropped one morning out of the bottom of the sky. Cool winds lurked. Trees shivered. Lydia showed up for breakfast in a wool jacket and the old mother-of-pearl combs in her hair, a worried look in her eye. The radio was back on some days. I was hopelessly big and tired of suspense. The baby had taken me over, nearly knocking me out of my chair one day with a hard kick to the groin, stealing me once again from sleep. My father was mired in the invention room, working on an idea which he couldn't share but which I could only imagine would fail. And Po was back in the fifth grade again, kicking and flailing, in the clutches of a certain Mrs. Farglass, who expected even less of him than his mother, and didn't love him nearly as well.

"I'm going to screw it up even more this time," he said.

"No, you won't, Po," I told him.

"Yes, I will, Leo," he vowed. "Yes, I will."

The new fish market got ready to open for business.

And Kilroy disappeared.

All around me, paranoia started to swirl. Suddenly it was clear. I was doomed. I was the one—who'd catch the stray bullet, stumble into a tornado's eye, be struck deaf, dumb or blind. The whole world order would change while I lay senseless on a birthing bed. Po had gone, not to fifth grade again, but to spy school. The fish market was a front. Kilroy had left to carry out the plot Danny had begun that night, on the ride home from Eddie's, when we crashed. Lydia and my father were lovers again, no longer the odd, gentle robots of my youth. Each day stretched before me, a dark, twisted maze. Everyone, and everything, was out to get me.

When my father did come to the breakfast table, he had eyes only for Lydia. He leaned over her, placed his square hands on her broad shoulders, and folded her up to the jaw, kissing the back of her neck. She reached one hand back, without turning, to pat him, the way you would a cat that comes to rub against your legs. The bedroom door was often closed now at night. I closed my eyes, felt the crunch of burned toast under my teeth. Lydia raised a tea cup to her thin lips. They'd always been in love, I saw it then. I saw how over time, my parents had become creased, as old clothes will do, how they filled and drained one another, and how now, slowly, the balance was shifting. As my mother grew stronger, my father was beginning to let go, to weaken, left to wonder not only what Lydia would have left for him, but what he had left for himself, after all those years, all that devotion, all that struggle. I saw how sex made primary things secondary, how it devoured you and puffed you up, left you raging and purring, how it killed the child in you, and brought it back, time and time again.

Once again, I felt sexless, an amorphous mass, with no corners or niches or folds, no distinctly shaped contours, no private parts, no place to call undiscovered or my own. It didn't matter where one part of me ended and another began. In my bed, on Cobb's Hill, I lay distended, immobile, the baby lying heavy on my aorta, trying to imagine how on this earth, physics and gravity being what they were, a hole so tiny could possibly grow big enough for a baby's head to fit through. Mine, I was sure, would be the first cervix not to dilate, the first baby to go on strike, to opt for life inside the womb. My baby would be stuck inside me forever, a laughing dwarf of a joker, playing the stock market on a microscopic phone which I'd swallow for the purpose. I'd always be huge. I'd never be a mother, only the shell, the hotel, the barn, the house.

I began to dream again, terrible dreams, about the baby. It was born with three arms or no face. It came out of me no bigger than a thimble. I knew something was wrong because there was no blood, no pain. No one came to see us; there was no celebration, no joy. The baby wouldn't cry, wouldn't smile, wouldn't grow. I let it slip down the drain of a sink, plucked it out again with tweezers. It was neither masculine nor feminine, only thin and primordial, translucent, wide-eyed and silent. I'd run off to exotic places, invited by a handsome stranger to play music in a lush, hot land—lured by beauty, myth and smoke. I'd pack my violin gently in its velvet case and whisk myself away, forgetting all about the baby I'd left on a sun-lit mantle or counter top, and then I'd return home frantically, brown breasts overflowing with coconut milk and rum and guilt, to find the baby dead on the surface on which I'd lain it, left it with a piece of burnt toast and a thirsty plant, with my list of things to do before I left, things to take care of. Plants, dishes, baby. Plants, dishes. Baby. The baby would be shriveled up, dessicated, sardine-like, and hollow-eyed. Dead as a doornail. Dead.

Desert dreams. Dry. Gasping. Choking. No water in sight. Cups of overflowing sand, stuck on my father's eyebrows, pouring off the ridges into my parched throat. Dreams of neglect. Horror. Incompetence. Impossibility. Flight. Waking dreams. Dreams that wouldn't let me sleep. All mine. Dreams where the baby cried and cried for water and there was none. I licked my parched lips, looked frantically for a drink, begged even for Danny's hands to break the dam and let the river water gush my way. I'd have gulped it gladly in my dreams— blood, guilt, oil and all. But Danny's hands lay crossed across his chest, placed there by the divers, occasionally rising up to meet in prayer. Desert dreams. Windswept. Sandblown. Parched. No water. No ice skating rinks to melt. No rivers or seas. The earth and the mind gone dry. My body, hotter, bigger than the sun.

* * *

The fish market reopened on a gray September morning. There was no ceremony, no ribbon cutting, just the new doors opened wide. The McPhees had hired a distant cousin, just arrived from Ireland. They called me in to help out for a few days, while the cousin was being trained. The market was sparkling and clean.

"Congratulations," I told Mr. McPhee. "It all looks wonderful."

"Well, it was high time, Leo," he said. "Wasn't it now?"

"High time?" It was one of Lydia's favorite expressions. As a child, I'd fixed on the word *high*, imagined how time could rise and hover above me, how I might slip away out from under its shadow.

"High time we moved on, Leo. High time we all moved on."

The air in the market was hopeful but grim. We worked silently side by side, tired, on edge. Rose and Mrs. McPhee took turns upstairs with baby Patrick, who was still not strong, needing oxygen on and off. All day the baby's thin cries filtered down the stairs, mixing with the shrill, clashing voices of Rose and Mrs. McPhee, as they changed the guard. The Irish cousin was serious and dour, one of those reliable, all-purpose relatives. If I'd been a true widow, they might have called him over to mop up the mess of Danny's death and marry me. Mrs. McPhee didn't speak; Mr. McPhee merely grunted. And some mangy old cat had got Po's tongue.

"How's school going, Po?" It took me hours to loosen it.

"It sucks," he said.

"Why?" I said.

"Stupid Farglass won't leave me alone. She treats me like an idiot."

"So, what are you going to do about it?" I asked him.

Po held up a book, *Ben and the Big Bug*. "I'm going to read these stupid books," he said. "So I can get out of that stupid class." He started to read out loud, jabbing each word with his finger, "It-is-fun-to-rob-a-wig," then slapped it back down on the counter. "Stupid book. It is not fun to rob a wig," he said. "It is *stupid* to rob a wig. Unless you're bald."

"Or unless you're a wig collector," I said.

"Yeah." He smiled. "Or unless you're just plain nuts."

"Yeah," I said. "You're reading, Po."

278

"Dear Leo," the postcard read, a postcard of a giant potato resting on the roof of a house. I ran my hand over the crinkled ridge of the stamp, tried to read the blurry postmark. Boston? Braintree? Buffalo?

"I haven't fallen off the earth," it read. "I just need time to sort things out. Love Kilroy."

I smoothed my hand over the glossy back of the card. Love Kilroy, who had not fallen off the earth, who just needed time, who was somewhere near a place that began with B, sorting out his crowded brain.

Love, Kilroy.

Rack and ruin hung over Cobb's Hill like a wet tarp. The leaks in the roof were bigger, the floor atilt, the plaster falling in chunks off the walls, the plumbing on its last old pipe legs, the windows cracked and a winter chill hovering in the chestnut tree. When the top and bottom of your house were in trouble, well then, so, surely, were you. It was only a matter of time, I could see, before a piece of the roof caved in, before the house slid off its center, or sunk into it, before we had not one sock without a hole, or one more tea bag to our name. Before the utility company came to shut off our lights, to cut the gas lines, yank out our phone. I made one last trip to the attic to scrounge for one last treasure, but the cupboard was truly bare. The eave room was now a mess of scattered empty boxes and crumpled up newspapers, broken trinkets and china, dustballs and brazen moths. I could not find us, poor dogs, even one small bone.

Tuesday came and I went to the fifth Lamaze class alone.

"Where's Kilroy?" Candy asked.

"I don't know," was all I could tell her.

"Everything all right, Leo?"

"Fine," I said. I simply knew no other answer to this question.

Candy sat near me, patted my arm as she started up the class. The partners hovered over their pregnant women, touched them, watched them with careful eyes. I decided that if Kilroy didn't come back soon, I'd ask Candy to be my coach in the delivery room. In a crunch, I thought, she'd help me.

"Okay, folks. This is the heavy class." Candy's voice was subdued. "The what-can-go-wrong class. Complications. Risks. Odds. I couldn't call myself a good teacher if I gave you only the candy-coated version of this business, forgive the pun. The pain of childbirth is real. And as with anything else that falls into the category of a miracle, there are risks. For a small few, it can be a rocky road."

Risks. I wanted to run. Complications. Heartbreak. Pain. I stayed near Candy and breathed. We worked on the hoo-has and the hut-huts, the fast, intense breathing of active labor. I breathed so hard I hyperventilated, then recaptured my breath in a paper bag. We talked about pain and medication—epidurals and gas and locals, needles, needles everywhere, in the cervix and the thigh and the spine. We talked about what could go wrong, what did go wrong—tangled umbilical cords and babies that refused to descend, twisted limbs, meconium in the baby's lungs, oxygen deprivation in the birth canal.

Risks. On the way home I stopped at the Broadway Supermarket to buy bread and milk. In the checkout line, I leafed through the *National Enquirer*. An eight-year-old girl had given birth to Siamese twins, and a woman had been raped by Elvis's ghost. Meanwhile Jesus Christ's younger brother had been found reincarnated as a pretzel vendor in New Jersey. I handed the cashier my money. He looked at me as if I'd come from another planet, then down at his palmful of change, as if what I'd given him wasn't legal tender. I put the paper back in its rack, saw my own headline flash. "*Alien Baby Abducted at Birth by Dead Father.*"

By mid-September, the cupboard was truly bare. I hadn't fully appreciated the kindnesses Po and Kilroy had shown us over the summer, the gifts of fish and fruit, bread and cheese left in paper bags on the kitchen table, out in the yard. Neither Lydia nor my father asked from where sustenance came. They both seemed to need so little. But I was ravenous again, as I had been some days as a child, so hungry I could eat a house, or a horse, and no house or horse in sight. Once again, I was trying to manage, for all of us. But my limbs were shaky, my resolve spare. I was in no better shape than they were. I could no longer keep the lid on my family's boiling pot. It was time for Lydia's voice to come back, for my father to invent a money tree, for Kilroy's mind to clear. Danny was dead. Kilroy was gone. Summer was over and I was about to have a baby.

It was high time.

Kilroy missed the next Lamaze class, too. I breathed myself deeply off the bus in front of the health center. Candy showed us a movie of three natural births. The women in the movie were strong and brave. They sweated and breathed and pushed until their veins popped out of their skins, smiling all the while. Exhausted. Triumphant. Dripping with sweat and tears, they reached for their newborns with strong arms. I watched and waited. Where were the screamers? The weaklings? The ones who begged for a needle? Where was the woman who pushed her baby away and said, no, not now, not just yet. Take him away. I'm not ready yet to be a mother. I need to be myself. Please. Just for a little while longer.

Candy had lied. It wasn't really all right to be afraid, to cry. It was weak, undignified, selfish. Like Danny, we'd be called upon to be saints and martyrs. The movie terrified me. It seemed to give the others strength. As the film flickered to a close and Candy turned on the lights, the excitement rose. An eerie pep rally began in the carpeted room. The women cheered. They rose up and rubbed their bellies. They were euphoric. Geared. Ready. The Mary's. Marcia. Karen. Alison. Joy. Everyone, it seemed, except me.

The chatter rose in sunflower stalks around me. My heart skipped a beat, and then another. The details of their lives hit me like stones of hail. The nurseries were painted, the "Goodnight Moon" posters framed. Bassinets were lined with bumpers. Plush hippos and monkeys dangled on mobiles, smiling moons and stars hanging overhead, playing "Over the Rainbow" with each swing of a star. The powders and diapers were ready, the blankets folded, the shower gifts in place. The lawns were mowed, the cupboards clean. The in-laws hovered and fussed. The two Mary's had even opened a savings account for their baby, little bits of money they'd been squirreling away over the years. They were all ready, and I'd done nothing. As Miss Young, my fourth grade teacher had said, I had a good head on my shoulders, but wasn't always prepared.

"All they'll need is love." Candy was in good form that night. "Spray 'em with the stuff and they'll flourish. Douse 'em in it, and they'll grow."

I drank my punch and lay my hand on my belly. A tiny foot poked up under the skin.

"Okay, baby," I whispered. "I'm listening."

But what could I tell this person inside me about love? Who, on the face of the earth was less qualified? What if, after all, I had no feelings for my baby? What would I answer to the question, "did you love my father?" I could say yes, that I'd loved Danny, and it wouldn't be a lie, but nor would it help to explain. Did I love my own father? I wasn't even sure anymore who my real father was, and that wasn't supposed to matter, but in the end, of course, it did. Did I love Kilroy? Did Kilroy love me? Should I be calling him, trying to find him? Should I be angry at him, or ask for forgiveness? Should I be fighting for him? Or letting him go? Did I love my mother? And, if not, did a person who didn't love her mother have any business becoming a mother? Would I be loved as a mother? Was that love earned or bestowed?

More than ever, I wanted what I'd never had—a mother of my own making—one who'd sit beside me in the buttery dark of a movie theater and tuck me into bed at night, who'd stroke my hair, light the candles on a birthday cake she'd made for me the night before, sing softly and fiercely to me, *of* me. I would have believed that mother. I could have loved her back so hard.

In the end, as I waited for my baby to be born, I had to wonder— had I confused the desire to *have* a child with the desire to *be* a child?

For a while I chose to call what happened in my garden, love. I watered the plants, weeded them, fed them, built supports and sunshades to see my three remaining fragile breadfruit plants through a week-long drought, harvesting the tomatoes and the zucchinis, leaving only Kilroy's popcorn plants to fend for themselves. Laughingly, they didn't suffer from my lack of care, braving the smothering heat with no rain. If anger really did have anything to do with love, then maybe I did love Kilroy. There was more between us than silence, and it must have been anger, because I was so mad. Mad to have been abandoned. Mad to have let him go. Mad not to know how I felt, how he felt. Mad as blazes.

In a calm and rational moment, I could understand. Kilroy'd had enough. He wanted out. Or had I wanted him out, chased him out? He'd scared me with his vision. The stony, vague presence he'd described—so out of reach, out of touch—was Lydia, not me. I'd struggled my whole life not to have family history repeat itself, to establish my voice, cement my shadow, imprint my name. How could Kilroy have left me? Danny, too. Rosalie, Lydia, my father. How could they all have left me? My head spun with laughing deserters, round and round and round. I was used to the people around me doing vanishing acts, used to being the only image left in a once-filled frame. I was used to doing things my own way, to being left alone. In the end, maybe I wanted it that way. I didn't blame Kilroy for leaving me on the tracks. We'd both known the train was coming. I just hadn't realized that my foot was stuck.

The annual outdoor chess master's tournament started up at Brattle Court. I knew Kilroy had been invited weeks before to play. Tables were set up outside the Cafe Troc, banners and lights strung up on the spindly trees. A scoreboard rose on the first evening, and cups of ice water were placed on the tables at dusk beside the six boards. Voices quieted when the heads of the players bowed. Kilroy sat at the third table. I watched him from afar, planting myself in a hushed crowd. The chess clocks ticked away. Onlookers hovered, nodded, whispered and pointed, put their fingers to their chins. Kilroy studied the board and tapped his foot, moved his pieces, patted the stray dogs.

After the third night, Kilroy had two wins and a draw. After the fifth, he was tied for first place. On the sixth night, he won the tournament. It was an upset, a victory. He'd been the underdog, one of the lower rated masters in the group. I went to watch the last game. Both players were in time trouble; Kilroy's rook dominated the board. When his clock ran out, Kilroy's opponent held out his hand in concession. Kilroy shook his hand and smiled. I folded myself back into the crowd. The manager of the Cafe Troc came out and awarded Kilroy a trophy and a certificate for a year's supply of coffee and croissants. The applause started out quiet and polite, and then grew loud. Kilroy's hand rose in a wave of thanks, as people cheered for him. I felt the tremble, the slip of the locked knee. I saw Danny on the ice, after scoring a goal, gliding back to the blue line to be slapped on the butt and the back and the head by his teammates. Everyone wanted to shake Kilroy's hand, to congratulate him, to ask him how he'd done it, to talk chess, strategy. To talk victory.

A girl with long black hair and a silver belt and sandals, a girl I'd seen there before on other nights, one whose eyes had followed the play with understanding, bent over and asked Kilroy a question. He answered her with his hands, moving the chess pieces around the board, but his eyes kept sliding sideways to her silver-cinched waist, a waist so slender, his hands could have spanned it, could have wrung all the juices with one squeeze from her pores. I watched the tips of her long, silky hair brush the board and Kilroy's hand as it reached out to touch the queen she'd just moved. I closed my eyes, crossed my arms over my stomach and held my legs together tight. It was another hot, hot, night, and I hadn't the faintest idea how to keep from melting.

Mr. McPhee called me early the next morning to come work last minute at the fish market. He was short-handed, was all he would say. He needed help. Could I spare a few hours? The day was fine, a warm breeze blowing, and puffy, rushing clouds. I took the bus to Inman Square. The baby kicked five times in one minute, hard. It had become so still of late; I'd worried. I took the kicks as a good omen and didn't bite my nails. I'd had a fair night's sleep. The baby had dropped and my heartburn was suddenly gone. I was happy for Kilroy and hoped he might come back soon so we could talk. I remember the beginning of this day in the clearest detail.

Po and his father were working alone in the market. I crossed the threshold and the bells jangled. The fish lay in the cases; the grandmother sat in her chair by the window. The floor was swept, the windows clean. The tile floor gleamed and the plaster of the new walls glistened. The smell of rich chowder filled the air and the clock said a little past nine. All of this I took in. Mr. McPhee's voice said, "hello, Leo," and went on to explain to Po how to cut swordfish, on an angle, with a sharp, unhalting slice. Po's eyebrows knit as he listened, trying to take it all in, to get it right.

"Where's Conor?" I asked, for that was the Irish cousin's name.

"We missed the delivery this morning," Mr. McPhee said. "I sent Conor down to the wharf to pick it up."

"Missed the delivery?" I looked around, suddenly aware of tension, erratica. "Where's Rose, and Mrs. McPhee? Why aren't you at school, Po? It's Friday."

"Patrick's sick again," Po said. "He's going to die."

"Hush, Porter," Mr. McPhee said. "We talked about faith, remember."

"Faith." Po spat out the word, as if it were made up, then spelled it angrily. "F-A-T-H-E."

I felt fear flood over me, as if Po were spelling out the fate of all babies everywhere, as if Lydia's radio had just plugged itself back into the socket, to announce that we were all doomed. The grandmother sat by the window. "He won't make it this time," she said.

"Enough from the two of you," Mr. McPhee said, turning to me. "The baby was having trouble breathing in the night, Leo. He's back in the hospital, on a respirator. We don't know any more than that. We're waiting to hear. Moira will call when she can."

"Moira will call," echoed the grandmother. "It may be too late."

"What's going to happen to him?" I asked.

"He's in God's hands," Mr. McPhee said. "Either way, Leo. Patrick goes with God."

"God has no hands!" I said. "What do the doctors say?"

"They're doing everything they can." Mr. McPhee took my arm. "Calm down, Leo. Hysterics never did anyone any good. And we've got fish to sell. This is a business, after all."

"Fish to sell," the grandmother said, raising a finger. "Haddock's fresh today."

Fish to sell. The business of fish, that is.

I saw Danny, alive and among us, taking in the news about baby Patrick, steam shooting up the shaft of his chest into his throat, another act of God over which he had no control. I saw him opening the cases, grabbing the fish by the tails and flinging them through the new plate glass window, shattered glass raining down upon the sidewalk, a mess of gills and eyeballs and tails. Somewhere in the back of my throat, my breath backed up. I caught myself in the middle of the mistake I'd made, coming back here one time too often, to Danny's fish market, haunting Danny's old haunts, taking over Danny's old tasks, wearing his apron, reading with his brother, arguing with his father, cradling baby Patrick in my arms.

The smells hit me first and hard—the damp salty smells of fish and sawdust, the faint scent of the sliced lemons sitting pretty in a bowl. The dizziness rose to form an eddy and choke me at the neck. The winds of my lost mind roared in my ears. I put my hands up to my ears, to dull the noises as they rushed in to get me. The garbled chatter of three women who'd come in to buy fish grew into a screech. "Swordfish! Have you got any swordfish, I say!" Their eyes grew large in their sockets, their tongues slid out of their mouths, dripping slimy, fishy words—scrod, filet, flounder, skate.

The sunlight strode in through the window, blinding me as I tried to focus on Mr. McPhee behind the counter, who was calmly lifting a heavy pink gray bleeding silver-laced chunk of fish and holding it before one of the witch's eyes, grinning, as he shed years and turned into Danny before me, the sparse grey hair growing dark and thick, the skin of his face growing taut, the jaw line firm, the muscles in his back tensing. Dorian Gray in confusion. Swordfish run amok. *"You must eat a lot of fish. You come in here a lot."* Danny grinned. I was in his fish market, his tomb. He hadn't really wanted to spend his life here, any more than he'd wanted to spend it at a hockey rink. He'd wanted out of his chilled, fishy fable, a way off this briny, slippery planet. He'd passed his fate on to me.

I looked for the door and saw Danny's grandmother slide her chair in front of it. I couldn't move or speak. I saw the drawn gray face of Danny's father and the pale slabs of fish in the cases. I saw spidery crystals of frost on the window that couldn't possibly have been there on a warm September day. I saw the red leave the blood smear on Po's white apron and his lips, and the green disappear from the middle of his eyes. All color left the world. My knees buckled. Po reached for my apron and it fell from its hook before he was able to catch it, just as I fell from mine. I spun down, helpless to stop myself, trying to clutch the rungs of newer and better memories, Kilroy, the baby, the sun, Bora Bora—paradise—it *did* exist, even if I'd never set foot on its shores. The last thing I saw was the gleam in Danny's grandmother's eye as she stood guard at the door. She was the mastermind, after all. The grandmother sitting still and watchful in the chair. The power in her fingers made men shrink and buildings fall. She waited for these moments. She made them happen. It had all been a sham, this summer of healing and calm. Nothing but a sham.

I remember hearing a cry, although I didn't know it was mine, confusing it with the cry of a baby. My throat was parched; I couldn't speak. Danny's hand formed a fist, and came at my belly.

"Why didn't you tell me? he said. "Why didn't you fucking tell me, Leo?"

"I didn't know, Danny," I said. "I swear. How could I tell you, when I didn't even know?"

On impact, the river water came blasting through the dam of my skin, over Aurelio's waterfall, the music rushing shrill in the background as the water swirled and rose up above me, catching me in the cone of its swirl as I gasped for breath. Danny called out to me, "Leo! Get out!" and reached down to pull me out of the car before he floated away, missing my hand by a whisper, by an inch. The tide shifted and the moon rose. And then, because Danny hadn't been able to save me, I died.

c h a p t e r   t w e n t y - s e v e n

*B*ack on Cobb's Hill, having once again been rescued by my father, I slept the rest of that day and lay awake long into the night. The door to the widow's walk was opened wide. The crickets were mournful, the cats ahowl. I lay still—sild back in time. All I could think about again was the accident, and Danny. I'd felt the hard press of guilt that morning in the fish market, and buckled without a whimper beneath it. It was clear to me, then. I hadn't grieved properly, long enough, with enough pain. No sooner was Danny buried than I'd jumped into Kilroy's bed, found pleasure and comfort in his arms. I was an imposter—of daughter, widow, lover, mother-to-be. I belonged in one of the frames on Mrs. McPhee's rose-covered wall, on the side reserved for dead people and saints, the ones who'd never really had to prove themselves, who'd never been tested.

The hindsight demons had come to call —the taunting should've's, would've's, could've-been's. I should've insisted Danny stop drinking at Eddie's party. I could've made him talk about his outburst at the chessboard, tell me what was really bothering him. I should've told him to slow down on the road. I could've seen what was happening in the car, when Danny made the turn, grabbed back the wheel in time. We would've made it safely across the bridge, gone back home to Inman Square, climbed the crooked stairs. I should've held my breath longer, gone back down one more time . . .

I'd always been bewildered by Danny's notion that he hadn't suffered enough. "That's crazy," I used to say. "Be glad."

God forgave the sinners, Danny said, but kept the cinch circled around their waists, ready to tighten it with a jerk, for the slightest lapse, the slightest betrayal. That's what kept you in line, he said, the taut, testing pull of that divine, unbreakable rope.

"That's medieval," I told him. "If that's true, and there is a God, then he's a sadist."

"Maybe so," Danny said with a shrug. "But for thousands of years, that's the way it's been. And, for whatever reason, by God, it works."

That night, lying in my bed at Cobb's Hill, I tried to put back—piece by piece—the dark puzzle that had been Danny's and mine. I tried to remember everything that had happened, from the moment we'd met in the fish market until the moment he died—every word, every nuance, every gesture—from the damp patch at the back of his neck to the way he said "car" with a flared Boston A, to his last words—"*that guy knows something, Leo . . . oh shit.*" I struggled to remember the tenor of Danny's voice and the reach of his arms, the fabric of his skin, the bumps on the back of his elbows, the smooth, hairless chest. The physical evidence was nearly lost, all confused, by then, with Kilroy's warm brownness and the dents on his shoulders, the big dipper birthmark on his calf, his smells of coffee and wet earth.

All that remained real of Danny to me was the desperate, reaching way he'd had, even in what were supposed to be the good times—full-tilt, surrounded by his family on his birthday the summer before, blowing out his candles with a gust of anguish that had nearly sent the icing and its curly, congratulatory letters sliding off the cake, accepting a hockey trophy and holding it limp by its silver handle, as if it were a dead cat, anathema, twisting a cap off a beer bottle after a game, throwing the sour, fizzy stuff down inside of him and waiting for deliverance, the hard, frantic press of his body against mine. He'd dug in with his knuckles, pressed them against my throat, into my ribs. The sounds that came from him weren't so much moans as brays. Sex hadn't felt good to Danny unless it drained, shook, blasted him inside out. It hadn't felt good unless it hurt him—maybe, I considered that night—unless it hurt me too.

For the next few days, I stayed upstairs in my room. It seemed to be the only safe place left in the world. I sat in bed, propped up by three pillows. The baby protested if I lay any farther down. My father came with books and food. I remembered how far away he'd wandered over the summer, and was grateful for his return. Lydia brought me cups of tea and read to me from *Jude the Obscure*. I hunkered deep down into fictional tragedy while Lydia rose gingerly up to embrace reality. She rummaged in my bureau drawers, folded, sorted, tossed old clothes onto the floor into piles which she then left to settle, to fend for themselves. I was grateful for her presence. I didn't speak. I didn't want to have to talk to anyone, but I panicked when I was left alone.

Kilroy had been gone for so long. His silence teased me, double-dared me, told me so. I'd become the person he'd described that night when he left—remote and vague, ill in that terrible, nondescript way, no bruises or bumps or blood, nothing to show for it but inertia, the worst affliction of all—helplessness. And Danny was back. Back to haunt and test me—dragging my fear behind him like a comet's bright tail.

How long would I be able to count my mind my own? Soon, they'd start making decisions for me. They'd take my baby away, maybe trick me with some story of a stillbirth that I could never disprove, try to appease me with a scrawny, bleating kitten wearing a bright red bow. I'd be told what to do, have no choice but to obey. I'd be at their disposal, their mercy. I had never spoken loudly enough, out there in the world, never staked my claim. No one knew where I was. Who could I really trust? I thought to call Eddie Quintana, until I remembered the feel of his sweaty hands running up my sides, as Danny lifted a rook from the chessboard and looked on without expression, until I remembered that Eddie didn't exist for me without Danny—apart from

Danny—or I for him. No one would understand what had happened to me, that I was still Leo, still of sound mind, that trauma had not rendered me stupid, just exhausted, and stunned. She comes from that family, they'd whisper. No surprise.

My parents came and went, sometimes alone, sometimes together, with anxious faces and reaching hands. They smiled and fussed over me. They urged me to get up, to start doing this or that. They'd get me a jigsaw puzzle, a thousand pieces, they said, or we'd take a little walk. It would be easy. It would feel good. To take a shower, brush my teeth, walk downstairs. I know, I told them. I knew all of this. I'd written this book—for Lydia—time, after time, after time. It *would* feel good, to walk out of the house, across Five Moon Fields, to smell the earth and buy a grapefruit, play a symphony, look up at the stars. It would feel good. It would be easy. Soon, I'd do those things again, I told myself. I could. If I chose to. Anytime I wanted. The thing was, I didn't want to anymore.

On the fourth morning, a Tuesday, I woke up restless and chilled. Downstairs, I heard the screen door slam. Getting up out of bed, I went out onto the widow's walk. I leaned over the railing and saw Lydia walking out to the bench, a cup of tea in one hand, a book in the other. She looked up at the trees, but didn't see me. I watched her take her place in the overgrown yard. A shadow passed by slowly, tall and distorted. I heard voices, a deep cough, the shriek of a crow. A shiver ran through me.

Back inside, I realized that I'd broken a sweat, that my mouth had gone sawdust dry. They were all around me, but I couldn't feel or touch them. Were they the spirits, or was I? Either way, I had to get out. I reached for a dress and fumbled for my sandals under the bed. I had to get out of this house, had to place myself back on the rock-hard earth. I would atrophy here, curdle, suffocate, die. I reached for my desk calendar, on which I'd been marking the days and weeks of my pregnancy, noting progress and changes, my appointments with Dr. Early. My hands trembled as I put my finger on the calendar square of the Friday before, the day I'd gone to the fish market and collapsed. "Baby kicking again," I'd noted early that morning. "Tired but okay. Where's Kilroy?"

I'd missed an appointment with Dr. Early on Monday, just the day before. ONE MONTH TO GO, I'd marked on the calendar. The home stretch, Dr. Early had called it. She said she'd want to see me every week during that last month, to check for signs of readiness or change. I made my way to the trickle shower next door. Dr. Early would help me. She was the healer in the white lab coat and silver barrettes. She knew me. She knew all about me. She'd talk to me. Calm me down. Look me over. Tell me what had gone wrong, and what remained right. She'd give me a pill, a number, a name. I needed the voice of reason and sanity. I needed one of Dr. Early's lists.

I pulled a brush through my snarly hair and went out into the hall. To my right, the door of the treasure room was opened wide. And there, inside, amidst the dusty mess, in what was completely a modern outfit, fitted pants, slim leather belt, tan tucked-in blouse and white sneakers, was Lydia, cleaning and sorting and tossing out old newspapers and boxes, sweeping cobwebs and making piles, creating the primitive beginnings of order, a kerchief holding back her silver hair.

"You're up, Claire," she said. "You must be feeling better."

"I am," I said carefully. "Weren't you just outside, Lydia? Outside in the yard?"

"In the yard?" She held up an old shirt of my father's. "We've got to get rid of some of this old stuff, Claire," she said. "I can't think why I saved it all these years."

"Neither can," I said, turning away.

"Where are you going?" Lydia asked.

"Downstairs." I stepped carefully, spoke carefully. "I thought I might go out for a while. If it's not too cold."

"It should warm up soon," Lydia said. "Highs in the sixties. No wind to speak of. Go on downstairs, Claire. Have some toast. You'll feel better if you do. I'm sure."

"Who's here, Lydia?" I rested my hand on the banister to steady myself. "Who else is in the house?"

"Just you and me. And your father, of course. Were you expecting someone?"

"I saw a shadow in the yard, Lydia. I heard a voice. Who was it?"

"It was no one, Claire," my mother said, in a voice like silk. "No one at all."

Dr. Early would be with patients until noon, Sheila, her secretary, told me. Would I like to wait? Or could she pass along a message?

"No. Thanks. I'll wait," I said. It was only ten-thirty, but I couldn't go back outside. I felt like a creature chased off the screen of a horror movie, cornered in a temporarily safe place, the blob climbing the walls of the building and the clock still ticking. I sat in the waiting room with a pile of magazines, more beaming mothers staring out of their covers. *"Your bundle of joy: when euphoria turns to exhaustion." "Breast-feeding: Love it or leave it?" "Resuming sex after the birth: Will he still want you?"* I put the magazines down and looked instead at Halley's drawings on the wall, a new crop—Dr. Early changed them religiously, like rotating the psalms. LIGHTNING IN THE BACK YARD THAT HITS A LITTLE BIRD. A CRAB EATING MARSHMALLOWS THAT STICK TO HIS CLAWS. All around me were pregnant women, tidy, relaxed, composed. I was suddenly aware of how I must look—hair wild and tangled, sandles unbuckled, my stomach straining the weave of a thin cotton shift. People came and went, murmured and smiled, fished in their purses, sat down gingerly, leafed idly through the magazines. I kept my eyes downward and pretended to read.

At a little after eleven, Dr. Early came out with a patient, patting the woman's arm, steering her toward Sheila's desk to make another appointment. I was jealous of that pat, of that confidence, the gruff tenderness I'd come to think Dr. Early reserved only for me.

"Thank you, Dr. Early," the woman said. "I feel so much better now."

Dr. Early's eyes passed over the waiting room, caught me in the corner. "Leo. Are you all right?"

I nodded. "I need to talk to you."

"I have a break at noon. Can you wait?"

I looked over at the windows and doors, bit my trembling lip and managed a nod. "Yes," I said. "I can wait."

* * *

Dr. Early led me through one of her office doors into the living part of her house. We landed in a bright, cluttered kitchen, which looked out onto the brick wall of the apartment building next door. In the middle of the room stood a wooden table with a blue oilcloth, a bowl of fruit at its center. The floor was red and black checked linoleum. I made the move of a knight on the chessboard floor.

"I'll make lunch while we talk," Dr. Early said. "I've got to start up again at one o'clock." She opened a can of soup and put it in a pot on the stove, then brought bread and sandwich makings to the table where I sat.

"Hungry?" she asked me.

"Starving," I said.

"Good," she said. "Sheila's been trying to reach you, Leo. You missed your appointment yesterday."

"I know. I'm sorry."

"Doesn't anyone answer the phone in your house?"

"Not always. It's a big house."

"I was worried." She spread mayonnaise on a thick slice of brown bread. "Is everything all right?"

"No," I said. "It's not. I think I'm going crazy, Dr. Early."

"Call me Eleanor, please." She put down the mayonnaise knife. "Why do you think you're going crazy, Leo?"

"I had a breakdown."

"What?"

"First, you should know, that my mother had one," I said. "When she was twenty. She's been a recluse for years." I played with the lid of the mayonnaise jar. "She was an opera singer. She collapsed during a performance. She completely lost her nerve."

"And now you've lost yours?"

"I lost something," I said. "I went to the fish market last Friday. And I passed out."

"Fish market?" Eleanor sliced tomatoes thin as silver dollars with a serrated knife.

"Danny's family owns a fish market in Inman Square."

"You've been in touch with his family?"

"Yes. I've been working there on and off since June."

"You have?" Eleanor looked up at me, snapped a hunk of lettuce in half. "What happened at the fish market, Leo?"

"Danny's oldest sister had a baby in July. He was very premature. He's been sick. They told me he was back in the hospital, that he might die. Something snapped. I lost it. I passed out."

"Ah, Leo," she said, laying the tomatoes on a bed of mayo. "The last straw."

"My baby's about to come," I said. "And I'm not ready. Not at all. I'm back in the river again, floundering around, trying to find my way out. I stayed in bed for four days and there's nothing wrong with me. I'm hopeless and I'm scared, Eleanor. Helpless. Like my mother."

Eleanor handed me a sandwich. "I don't know your mother, Leo," she said. "And I don't know you all that well. But you are neither hopeless nor helpless, and I can tell you why."

"Why?" I asked.

She tilted her wrist to look at her watch. "I have to get back to work soon. Can we talk later?"

"When?" I asked.

"Come back tonight," she said. "Come back for dinner and we'll talk. Do you have plans?"

"No." I bit into the sandwich she'd made me, grateful and relieved. "I have no plans."

chapter twenty-eight

*T*hat night at Eleanor's, we talked as we ate. She told me more about her granddaughter Halley, named after the comet that had come in 1910 and was expected back in 1985, how she liked peanut butter and potato chip sandwiches and could add four digit numbers in her head, how she was a child who'd understood too much too soon and maybe not enough too late. I threw her more questions, stalling. How many teeth had Halley lost? Was she funny? Was she shy?

"Halley's a wonderful child and a good excuse for many things," Eleanor said. "But let's talk about you, Leo. Start from the beginning. Tell me how you began."

"I began . . ." I threw up my hands and took a deep breath. "In total confusion."

I gave short answers, reluctant to let go of too much of myself. I felt an old breastplate rise in defense. Eleanor wouldn't understand. You didn't swoop out of a tarnished lamp like mine and not arrive a queer and crooked genie. In my world good deeds counted as acts of survival. Feelings were not so much allies, as stalkers. Language was more a means of marking time than connecting. I separated the facts and events of my life without emotion. I could only hope that in the course of talking with Eleanor, my feelings might reveal themselves. She made me talk about Lydia, about her singing and what I knew of the breakdown, what she did with her days and nights. She made me talk about my father, which was even harder—his work, my feelings for him, past and present. I dug up varying shades of adoration, frustration, revulsion.

"Who are you more like, Leo?" Eleanor asked.

"In many ways I'm like my father," I said. "We're both inquisitive, quiet, introspective. But I'm bound to end up like Lydia."

"Why, because of the music, or because you're a woman?"

"Both. And because I'm afraid. I'm slowly turning into her and I don't know how to stop. I just sat in bed for four days. Doing nothing."

"That's probably what you needed to do, Leo."

"*Nothing*," I said again.

Eleanor made me talk about Danny. "Was he unhappy?" she asked.

"No, he was more . . ." I tried with a twist of my hands to describe the brooding, the anguish, the edge. "Frustrated. Angry, sometimes. Overwhelmed."

"Resentful?" she asked.

"Of what?"

"What was expected of him?"

"Maybe."

"Was Danny a dreamer?"

"No, more of a realist."

"I meant night dreams."

"Oh. I don't know. He thrashed in his sleep. He never talked about his dreams to me. But then he never really talked about much of anything."

"Did Danny drink?"

"All the time. In between games. After practice. To warm up. To cool down. Hockey players drink oceans of beer, oceans of whiskey." My brain loosened; words began to spill more freely. "Alcohol is one of their religions," I said.

"How did Danny's behavior change when he drank?"

"He grew more of all that he was . . ."

"Which was?"

"I told you—moody, withdrawn."

"Aggressive?" Eleanor's bushy eyebrows arched.

"A little bit. In spurts. He had a temper. When something was bothering him. He always felt bad afterward."

"Hangover or humility?"

"Both."

"Did Danny ever hurt you, Leo?"

"Hurt me?" I thought of the jab, the press, the rope—the next-day aches and bruises I'd sometimes borne. "He was a rough lover sometimes," I said. "But he never meant to hurt me."

"But he did sometimes."

"Not badly. Not on purpose. Sex was an outlet for Danny. He was under pressure from so many sides—his family, his teams, Harvard . . . from me, too, I guess. It all spilled out in bed. It was the only time Danny opened up to me at all, the only place he let go. So I didn't mind."

"You didn't mind being hurt?"

"I didn't see it that way."

"How *did* you see it?" Eleanor asked gently.

"Danny was in more pain than I was," I said. "I thought if I could help him by letting him get it out, it was worth it."

"Worth what?"

"Worth what I got back."

"Which was?"

"Gratitude, relief," I said. "It was the only time Danny let me give him anything."

"And what were you giving him, Leo?"

"Consolation, support. An outlet, I thought."

"I think you were giving him license."

"To do what?"

"To be violent and destructive. To himself and everyone around him. Not to deal with his feelings, or what was on his mind."

"He tried," I said. "I really think he tried."

"Was Danny jealous of you, Leo?"

"Jealous?"

"Of your strengths? Your independence, your music, your mind?"

"He had all of those things," I said. "Except the music. He had no reason to be jealous."

"Was he aware of his own strengths?"

"I don't know."

"Do you think Danny might have felt that it would be hard to share anything other than a bed with you—a family, a secret, a whole life? That you might never understand him, that your backgrounds and characters were just too different? Did you ever talk about any of this?"

Backgrounds. Intentions. Values. We'd never crossed rivers so deep. I hadn't thought about much of anything when I was with Danny.

"What was Danny giving *you*, Leo?" Eleanor asked me.

"I thought he was giving *me* license," I told her. "License to be me."

The next night, we ate pizza together, and talked about the night of the accident.

"Okay, Leo," Eleanor said. "Take it slowly. From the top."

I told her about the hockey game, about Eddie's party, about the drinking and the dancing, about my getting sick. I told her about the chess game and Danny's outburst, the ride home, the crash. I wound my way calmly through the story, as if it were someone else's, and by then, it almost was. I felt so much disdain for the person in black boots and a white lace blouse, who'd gone to Eddie's party and sat with a paper cup full of bad wine and no spirit. I thought so little of the person who'd sat alone and simply waited— for it to be over, for a chess game to play out, for a man to take her home to bed. It was me, who'd sat so passively on the couch, who'd gulped gin and spun in a moondance for revenge. It was me.

"Okay." Eleanor opened the second pizza box, green peppers limp and curling, red onions twirling on hot cheese. "Those are the facts. Now let's look inside the cracks of the night. How was Danny feeling after the game?"

"Relieved, at first. He won it for Harvard. The final game, the biggest victory of all. He was glad it was over. He told me on the way home. Danny always had to be the hero. They depended on him, and that put a lot of pressure on him. He hated the attention. It embarrassed him. But it just kept coming his way. He didn't think he was good at anything besides hockey, and he knew it wasn't enough. He was tired of games, he said. I told him I was too. Danny was giving up hockey that night. And I think he was scared."

"Anything unusual happen during the game?"

"Danny scored the hat trick—three goals. The last one won the game. He got a penalty for roughing and then got kicked off the ice by the referee. He stomped off to the dressing room. He was wearing a cowboy hat. It was red."

"Roughing?" A strand of cheese stretched from the pizza to Eleanor's lips.

"Hockey's a tough sport. Danny always had cuts and bruises."

"How did you feel about that?"

"It was barbaric. I didn't like it. But who was I?"

"Good question," Eleanor said. "But for another time. What else, Leo?"

"Danny was in a bad mood after the game. The best times were the hardest for him. He didn't think he deserved any of it—victory, praise, happiness."

Eleanor looked up at me. "Or you?"

"Me? He could've had anyone he wanted, Eleanor. Like that girl at the party said, he was to die for."

"But you weren't willing to go quite that far."

"No."

"Was Danny faithful, Leo?"

"I think so. I don't think he knew any other way."

"What happened after the game, at the party?"

"Danny got drunk right away. He and Eddie played Cardinal Puff. Budweiser and shots of Jim Beam. I was feeling sick to my stomach. I thought it was the wine, but it was morning sickness. I didn't know it then. Danny was playing chess."

"Danny played chess?"

"A little," I said. "He was playing with Kilroy."

"Kilroy."

"He's a chess player. A master. And you might as well know. He's my lover."

"What? He's the man? No, wait." Eleanor raised her hand. "Let's not get sidetracked. More about the party, Leo. Danny and Kilroy were playing chess."

"I was dancing with Eddie, swigging gin, getting drunk."

"Was Danny mad about that?"

"No. He knew I'd never let Eddie go too far. And Eddie knew that Danny would've killed him if he did. They didn't cross those lines."

"What next?"

"I left Eddie on the dance floor and went to the bathroom and got sick."

"And then you interrupted the chess game."

"Danny wanted to finish. I looked at the board and saw that he was beat."

"Did you tell him so?"

"I did. *That* was different. Another time, I probably would've kept quiet."

"Did you say it in a way that might have offended Danny, upset him when he was drunk and down?"

"No. I just said it. I felt so sick. All I wanted to do was leave. Danny was upset. He kept wanting to go over the game."

"What happened then?"

"Kilroy told him to take me home and he knocked all the chess pieces off the table."

"Danny took the loss hard, then," she said. "Winning was a big deal."

"He wasn't used to losing," I said. "But this was different. He didn't expect to win the chess game. He didn't think he had the brains. But he was trying to figure out something that night on the board and it was hard for him."

Eleanor pulled a slice of pizza from the pie. "The car ride home," she said.

"Danny was mad."

"Why? Because you were sick or because you'd dragged him away?"

"Neither, I think." I leaned back in my chair. "He was tired and drunk. He'd passed his limits and he knew it. He wouldn't admit it, but he was embarrassed by what he'd done. And he kept thinking about the chess game, something Kilroy was trying to explain to him right at the end."

"Do you play chess, Leo?"

"My father taught me when I was young. And I've been playing again, this summer. With Kilroy."

"Did you understand what Kilroy was saying to Danny that night?"

"I was only half listening. Now I might understand a little better. When Kilroy starts talking about chess, he's in another world."

"But Danny was listening, trying to understand, and it was important to him in some way."

"Yes. But he only came away with a piece of it. Kilroy has a way of thinking out loud. Sometimes you just catch the middle part of a thought, and you can't make sense of it. Danny hadn't gotten a hold of what Kilroy was saying, and that frustrated him."

"You admire Kilroy?"

"Yes."

"That was something you and Danny agreed on."

"We would have. I didn't know Kilroy then."

"Would Danny have been jealous, of your admiration? Of your attraction to Kilroy?"

"No." I reached for another slice of pizza. "Danny didn't believe in jealousy. Or people belonging to people. I sometimes thought he'd be relieved to have me love someone else."

"Or no one else at all?"

The pizza was gone. We crunched the ice bits left in our water glasses. "What was it that Kilroy said to Danny about chess?" Eleanor asked. "After the game was over. Exactly, as best you can remember."

"Something about objectivity," I said. "About the attack, and the counterattack, how the more careful idea always prevailed. Kilroy said nothing is ever as good or as bad as it seems."

Eleanor nodded, slowly repeating the words. "Not as good or as bad," she murmured, "as it seems."

* * *

Eleanor started asking Mr. McPhee's questions. Was it wet that night? Slippery? Were there any other cars on the road, any witnesses? Seatbelts on, doors locked? I told Eleanor more about the tension between Danny and me, my churning stomach, the lit cigarette, the slippery turn, the crash into the guardrail, flying through the air, our last words, the pressure of the water, coming up for air, trying to go back down to get Danny . . .

Eleanor raised her hand. "Stop. Rewind. You went back down to get Danny."

"Yes. I tried. But I couldn't stay under for more than a minute. I couldn't see."

"You may have been a fish in another lifetime, Leo. But not this one."

"I know what you're saying, that at least I tried, that it should be enough. But it isn't."

"How much power do you think you have, Leo?"

"Very little."

"So why did you expect more of yourself on this night?"

"It was life or death. I should have been able to do something. I should have had the strength."

"You did have the strength, Leo. Strength to move, to think, to act. How would you be feeling if you hadn't tried to go back down?"

"Worse, if that's possible."

"How long before someone came?"

"I don't know. Ten, maybe fifteen minutes. The police came first, then the ambulance. Then the divers."

"Was Danny dead when they pulled him out?"

"Yes." I swallowed a hard lump as I remembered touching Danny's face on the roadside. That was the only moment that still had the power to take my breath away—his flesh still warm, the mouth in random half smile. "He was dead," I said. "No one needed to tell me."

"Danny was strong, athletic, wasn't he?"

303

"Yes. God. He was."

"So if he'd been able to get out, don't you think he would have?"

"Yes."

"Did you see him moving, struggling?"

"No, but I couldn't see anything. I couldn't use my eyes. I remember thinking, this must be what it's like to be blind. How strange," I said, "that I even had time to think that."

"You know, Leo," Eleanor said. "It's possible that Danny was already dead when you tried to go back down to get him. He may have hit his head when the car crashed. Or sustained internal injuries that were just too severe. It's possible no one could have saved him."

"It's possible," I said.

"You weren't responsible for Danny's life at that moment, Leo. You were only responsible for your own. You took care of yourself. Your survival instincts were at work. You saved your life and you tried to save Danny's. You did all there was to do."

"That's what Kilroy says," I told her.

"He's right, Leo. Listen. You were two separate people, sitting in two separate seats, two different lives, two different minds. You knew that. Instinctively, you disassociated. Your reflexes went to work. You didn't panic. All of what I'm saying flashed through your brain. You weren't the least bit confused in the water. The fact that this ended so badly for Danny is not a measure of your sanity, or your strength. You knew just what you had to do, and you used all of your power to do it." Eleanor drained her cup of its last drops of water. "And that is why, Leo, you are neither hopeless nor helpless."

The lid to the empty pizza box closed. "It's late." Eleanor's voice came to me from a far-away place. "I'm going to Texas tomorrow, Leo. I better get some sleep."

"You're leaving?"

"Just for a while."

"To visit Halley?"

"Yes, and my daughter, too."

"How long will you be gone?"

"About a week. Don't worry. I'll be back before your baby comes. I'll try to leave before things get out of hand with Susan. They always do."

"Why are you going, then?" Kilroy's words echoed in my head. "Why do you put yourself through that, Eleanor?"

"Susan's my daughter," she said.

"What's she like?" I looked up at a drawing of A GIRL WITH HER FACE ON BACKWARD.

"Susan?" Eleanor said. "Well, the apple doesn't fall far. Susan's as stubborn and ornery as I am. We'll come to blows, as usual. She'll tell me to stop interfering."

"Maybe she just can't see it yet," I said. "That all you're trying to do is help."

"She's angry," Eleanor said. "And she has her reasons, Leo. I wasn't a very good mother. I've been a better doctor, I think."

"You are a good doctor," I said. "And a good grandmother."

"You don't get points for that," she said. "It's easy to be a good grandmother. You have distance. And perspective. You have your sleep. Righteousness comes easily to grandparents. I'm trying to remember that."

"You are remembering," I said. "And no one's keeping score."

"Susan's the keeping score type," Eleanor said. "And I'm just the kind of person who believes in hanging onto a kid until the kid lets go of you."

"She isn't going back to Halley?"

"Every other weekend." Eleanor shook her head. "I just can't bear it," she said. "For Halley to be an every-other-weekend child."

"Maybe it's only temporary," I said. "Until she gets back on her feet."

"No," Eleanor said. "Susan's relinquished custody. She says she can't cope. She's anemic, depressed, hypoglycemic. She's wheat-sensitive, and possibly manic. She may even be bisexual, she tells me. She says she needs to get in touch with her id. I suggested she try putting a K in front of it and she got furious."

"Id," I said quietly. "Kid."

"Susan really thinks she's doing what's best for Halley," Eleanor said. "But I just can't believe that having a screwed-up mother isn't better than having no mother at all."

I waded through the double negatives, looked back up at the girl with her face on backward.

"No," I said. "I don't think I can either."

"You've tried."

I nodded. "In the end, only your mother can validate you, make you believe that you're real." I looked back at Eleanor. "And vice versa, I think."

Eleanor nodded. "Susan's real all right," she said. "And so am I."

I reached out to touch her sleeve. "I've never really thanked you, Eleanor. For . . ."

Eleanor raised her hand, gruff once more. "No need for thanks, Leo. No need for anything at all. Just have the baby and get on with your life. Get on with your life, that's all."

At the door, after I'd gotten my coat on, Eleanor handed me an envelope. As my fingers went for the flap, she stopped them. "No," she said. "Don't open it now."

"Why?" I asked, stuffing the envelope into my coat pocket. "What is it, Eleanor?"

"Just something to think about while I'm gone," she said. "Not now. But later. Go home and get some sleep, Leo. And take good care."

chapter twenty-nine

The next morning, Lydia sat at the kitchen table, having breakfast, she said, although there was no food in front of her. She appeared in the kitchen ritualistically at mealtimes now, whether or not it was her intention to eat. I pulled out a loaf of Anadama bread, but there was no point in making any more toast. Neither of us was hungry. Neither of us could cook. So much bread had been wasted in that kitchen already, toasted and buttered and left to cool and harden. We sat alone, across from one another, with not even the smell of toast as buffer.

"You've been to the doctor, Claire." Lydia continued to know things I'd never told her. "Is everything all right?"

"I suppose you could say that." I ran my hand over the smooth grain of the oak table. "If you were sitting in that chair, if you saw only what you chose to see. Then you could say that everything was fine."

"What do you mean?"

"Everything's fine, Lydia," I said. "I'm tired, that's all. The doctor said everything's fine."

Lydia took out her notebook. "Did you know, Claire, that more babies are born in January than any other month?"

I did the math. Made sense. Spring sex, winter baby. "Where did you hear that?" I asked her.

"'Baby Talk.'" Lydia pointed to the radio by her side, not plugged in, but within reach. "Mondays from ten to eleven a.m. It's a new program on WBZ. You might want to listen."

"I might."

"Where's Kilroy gone, Claire?" she asked.

"I don't know," I said carefully. "I wish I did."

"He comes and goes, doesn't he? I guess that's what young men do. I'd gotten quite fond of him. He'll be back, won't he?"

"You haven't seen him, Lydia?" I took a black-eyed Susan out of the vase on the table. "Kilroy isn't staying here?"

"Here?" Lydia said.

"I thought I saw him. I thought I heard him," I said. "Talking out in the yard."

"You must be hearing things, Claire."

"No." I pulled the petals from the black-eyed Susan one by one, looked Lydia in the eye. "I'm not hearing things."

"The program also said that more babies are born on Tuesday than any other day."

"Why?" As with a three-year-old, this seemed to be the only question left worth asking.

"Doctors go away for the weekend," Lydia said. "They induce on Monday. The Caesarean rate is too high in this country. Babies are too big. Women are overnourished. We've overstepped the bounds of nature."

"We have?"

"It won't end well, Claire." Lydia shook her head.

"Why are you telling me these things, Lydia?" I asked her.

"Because you're going to have a baby," she said. "And because today is Tuesday, isn't it?"

I crumpled the waxy flower petals in my hand. The terrible thing was, neither of us was really sure.

* * *

But the calendar confirmed—that it *was* Tuesday—the day of my last Lamaze class. I set off at dusk, wearing black sweat pants and the pink sweatshirt Kilroy had once borrowed. My stomach looked like a joke, a stuffed basketball hanging low. In those final days, I liked to flaunt it. I'd decided either to ask Candy that night to be my coach, or to make my peace with having the baby alone. Either way, I'd be ready.

The door of the health center sprang open, as I stepped on the rubber mat. Candy was downstairs in the lobby xeroxing some papers for class.

"Leo," she said. "I thought we might have lost you, until Kilroy showed up."

"Kilroy's here?"

"He's upstairs." She caught the upswing of my voice. "He's been here for almost an hour. Is everything all right, Leo? I don't mean to keep asking you that, but . . ."

"I don't really know, Candy," I said. "It's always so hard to tell."

Kilroy was sitting in the corner we'd always claimed as ours, in a flannel shirt and black jeans. He looked beautiful and crumpled, heaven-sent. I forgot that he'd left me, forgot why, forgot when, forgot where.

"Hi." We greeted each other shyly, like secret lovers at a gathering of mutual, unknowing friends.

"I had to come, Leo," he said.

I nodded.

"Last class, folks!" Candy started up. There were only three couples left, Joy and Bob, the two Mary's, and Kilroy and me. "You're dropping like flies," Candy said. "Three more gone this week. Here's the baby news. Jack and Marcia had a boy, Benjamin, eight pounds, two ounces; Alison and Paul a girl, Emily, six pounds, thirteen ounces; and Randy and Karen a girl, Laura May, seven pounds, thirteen ounces." We all clapped and cheered.

"Before we celebrate," Candy said. "There's one last order of business. Line up fat ladies. It's belly-reading time."

She moved along the line of us, drill sergeant style, hands clasped behind her back, inspecting our stomachs.

"Boy," she announced to Joy. "The testosterone's flying over here.

Another guy who's not going to stop to ask for directions." Joy looked over at her husband, Bob, and smiled.

"Girl here," Candy said to the Mary's. "I feel a delicacy, an inner strength and calm." The Mary's nodded.

Candy stopped before me for a long time. In the end, her eyes rose from my stomach to my face. "Boy," she said softly. "Baby boy here."

"You don't sound so sure," I said.

"At first I felt boy, but then girl vibes took over. I think I was feeling the tail end of the Marys' girl. I'll go with my first instinct."

"How do you guess the sexes?" Kilroy asked.

"No clue," Candy said. "I sense it somehow. My record speaks for itself. Eighty-eight right out of the last one hundred and two. But please." She held up her hands. "No lawsuits if I'm wrong."

Candy pulled up a chair. We gathered around her.

"So, it's the people's choice tonight," she said. "We've covered it all, all that fits into the books, at least. Now, I open up the floor. Let's talk about anything you want, whatever's left on your minds."

We brought our chairs closer to the middle of the room in our diminished circle. We didn't talk about birth—forceps, episiotomies, breeches or twisted cords. Instead we just talked about babies—plump, cooing babies that had already been born, powdered, kissed, diapered a hundred times, babies we'd known and touched, who'd come safely through the birth canal and landed earthlings, learned to walk and talk. Kilroy described a little girl singing "Shoo Fly" on the bus ride over. One of the Mary's told about her two-year-old nephew who did Elvis impersonations, tucking his hands into the front of his diapers and saying, "sank you, sank you berry much." Candy told us about how her toddler used to eat ants and I found myself describing baby Patrick on the first day he'd come home. The hour wore thin. We exchanged addresses, and said our goodbyes. Out in the lobby, I slid a dime into the pay phone and called the fish market to see how Patrick was doing. He was still in the hospital, Mr. McPhee told me, still hanging on, the little peteen. In the end, he just might be the toughest of us all.

* * *

"How are you?" Kilroy asked me. We sat in the kitchen at Cobb's Hill later that night after class, at a safe distance, the table between us, eating raisin toast.

"Bigger," I said, looking down at my stomach and then up again. "Better."

"Good," he said. "Bigger is good. Better is better."

"Déjà vu, Kilroy. I'm hearing my own echo. Where've you been?"

"Away." He took one of my hands and put it up to his face. "Here. Not here. Away. No good answer."

"I thought I saw you in the yard one day."

He nodded. "I came a few times. To see how you were doing."

"You won the chess tournament."

"How did you know?"

"I came a few nights," I said. "To see how you were doing."

Kilroy smiled. "It was good chess."

"Good chess." I took back my hand. "Is that like good sex?"

"God," he said. "I hope I never have to choose. I've been living chess, Leo, day and night."

"And I've been living baby."

"It's getting close, isn't it?"

"It is."

Kilroy's brow creased as he leaned forward. "What happened at the fish market, Leo?"

"I lost it, Kilroy. I passed out."

"Let's get married," he said.

"Fine thing," I said. "Now that I've cracked up, you want to marry me."

"I'm glad you only cracked up," he said. "I thought you might explode."

"Maybe I did." I turned my head away, spoke to the plate glass window. "Or maybe I'm about to."

"I love you, Leo," Kilroy said.

"Don't be confused," I said.

"I think we could be good together. I think we could be a good family."

"A good family?"

I looked over at Kilroy. His lips were full and still. His voice was earnest, his crisis nearing an end, maybe thanks to the coming of mine. But he was too close, too calm, too sure. He'd forgive and love and protect me too well. It would be *our* life, before I'd even gotten a hold on my own. Memories were still so jagged and blurred—Danny sailing through the air, Kilroy appearing in the garden at dusk, my father asleep in Mr. Burrow's armchair, Lydia in a feather boa, fingers raised to her pale cheek. Kilroy couldn't see. I could have no part in his happy ending. I had no clue. I didn't know how to be part of a family.

"We can't get married, Kilroy," I said. "Not now."

"Okay," he said softly. "We can't get married now."

"Don't go," I said, reaching out to him. "Please. I don't want you to go."

"I won't go," he said quietly. "I'm not going anywhere, Leo."

"If you've changed your mind about being my partner . . ."

"I haven't changed my mind," Kilroy said. "I meant it, Leo. I want to marry you, spend my life with you."

"It might be easier if I did this myself."

"Of course it would," he said.

"It's not fair to put you through all this, Kilroy. I can't . . . That night, when you left. You wanted to know . . ."

"Listen." Kilroy lifted his palm. "I went to stay with my father for a few days, Leo. I told him I was confused. He asked me about what and I said I didn't know. He asked me what mattered. And I said, chess, you, family."

"Ah, the Cosmic List." I smiled. "I've arrived."

"My father asked me which of those goals were attainable, and I said all of them, theoretically. 'Even her?' he asked, meaning you." Kilroy reached out to lift a clump of my hair. "I said I didn't know if you wanted to be attained and my father said he thought you looked as if you might, if I played my cards right and then he asked me if I loved you." Kilroy let go of my hair. "And there was no question in my mind, Leo. I told him I did."

"What does it feel like?" I asked.

"Not convex, like I expected. It's concave. Quiet."

"That's not what I had with Danny."

"Good," he said. "I want what you have with me."

"But is it enough?" I said. "That was your question, remember?"

Kilroy lifted his hands. "It is what it is," he said.

"If you went away again," I said. "I'd be scared. That's not love."

"Fear's part of it," he said.

"What about desire?" I reached out to touch his face.

"Definitely desire."

"Confusion?"

"Confusion is key," he said. "Really key."

"It's not much of a romance, Kilroy. You should be with someone normal, someone's who's not so screwed up. The tall girl. The smart one who dumped you. Maybe she's still on the loose."

"Too late now. The tall girl missed her chance," he said. "I want you, Leo."

"What about the baby?"

"I want the baby, too."

"You'll take us?" I said. "You'll take us the way we are?"

"I will," Kilroy said. "I do."

Out on the widow's walk, the moon hung a sliver in the western sky. I remembered how I used to go out there as a child on fall nights, to make that very assessment of the moon, to feel for the first real nip, the first cold ripple in the wind.

"Let's bring the mattresses outside," I said. "Put them end to end."

"It's freezing out here," Kilroy said, wrapping his arms around his chest.

"Think warm," I told him. "All you have to do is think warm."

I brought out socks and sweatshirts. We lay head to toe on the mattresses, staring out through the railings of the widow's walk at the city lights and the clouds that gathered to warm us. I buried my feet in Kilroy's thick hair and he took hold of one of my ankles.

"You said you were better, Leo," he said, tilting back his head. "How? Why?"

"I've been talking," I said. "With Eleanor."

"Who's Eleanor?"

"My doctor. We've been talking. She's been getting me to talk."

"That's good." Kilroy let my ankle down, rubbed it gently. "Talking's good, Leo."

We slept a little. We lay awake. We took turns looking through the telescope, chasing shooting stars across the sky. Kilroy told me how Lasker played the man, and Fischer played the board. I told him what he'd missed in Lamaze class. We talked about pain, with or without purpose or end. I told him how Aurelio had once broken his own bone to fix a crooked finger. He told me the story of the baseball pitcher with one arm. We practiced the hoo-hut breathing until we nearly floated.

"You won't marry me?" Kilroy asked as we drifted off, curious now, nothing more.

"Not now."

"Will you have a baby with me someday?" he asked. "Or two? Or maybe four?"

"Maybe one," I said, rubbing my belly. "Maybe later. Maybe much later."

"We could get married when the kid turns five," Kilroy said. "On that island you've always wanted to go to. Underwater, maybe."

"Or maybe when we're eighty," I said. "At the top of the Empire State Building. Then we'll know we're really an item."

"What is marriage, anyway?" Kilroy said. "When you think of it, what other mammals get a blood test, go to city hall, and mate for life?"

I laughed. In the end, it wasn't the answer that intrigued us, so much as the question.

Danny's voice, hoarse and ragged, reached me that night in a dream. He called out my name. Over and over again. I woke up in a cold sweat, looked over at Kilroy on his mattress, tried to even my breathing

"Kilroy." I shook him gently. "Kilroy, wake up."

"What?" Kilroy sat bolt upright. "What is it? The baby?"

"No, it's not the baby," I said. "I have to go back to the bridge, Kilroy."

"You have to go back to the bridge?" He scratched his head and yawned. "Now?"

"I have to go back and see where it happened."

"At two in the morning?" Kilroy mumbled as he looked at his watch. "You have to go back to the bridge and see where it happened at two in the morning? This couldn't wait?"

"No." I fumbled with my sweater, handed him his shoes. "You tried to tell me, Kilroy. It's already waited too long."

We slid out into the night. The Rambler lay sleek in the driveway, with its gleaming chrome and red leather seats, dashboard lighting up with arrows, dials and gauges, when Kilroy turned the key. The old car filled me with longing for a time when my father and I used to spin off in a cloud of Cobb's Hill dust, to escape everything we couldn't change, when there'd been just the two of us, and the car and the hill and the road.

Kilroy started down the hill and turned onto the river drive. The lights of the city buildings blinked low.

"Head for Boston," I said. "On Mem. Drive. The bridge is . . ."

"I know where the bridge is," Kilroy said quietly.

I turned to him. "You do?"

"Everyone knows where the bridge is, honey," he said. "Everyone's been back there to see it. Except you."

Honey. Still, to me, the stuff that bees made, that ran thick from a jar, sweetened tea and toast. "Have you?" I asked.

He nodded. "Twice," he said. "Once before I met you, kind of as a tourist, and once after that first night in the cabin. I went to remind myself what had happened to you, how serious falling in love with you would be. Anyway, by then it was too late." His hand reached over to touch my leg. "Are you sure you want to do this?"

I nodded. "Some day, I'm going to find myself on that bridge," I said. "Some day, I'm going to have to cross it. If I wait too long, I'll forget. I want to see it, Kilroy. I want to remember."

* * *

I expected to be swallowed by a dark corner and so at first didn't recognize the well-lit bend in the road as the place where the Buick had swerved. The shoulder had been widened, with room for an all-night diner now. A new triple-slatted guard rail scaled the river bank and rose up several feet. Anybody who took that turn wrong now would have rippling steel to deal with, and not the river. A neon sign flashed three messages, in succession: SLOW, BRIDGE, DANGER. All people nearing disaster should have such bright, orange warning, I thought.

A highway shrine. Atonement. If in fact the road had been at all to blame, it had tried to make amends. Kilroy pulled over on the shoulder and put on the safety blinkers. I walked out onto the bridge and tried to make out the water through the slats of the new railing. Closing my eyes, I felt the car swerve, tip and soar. Danny's voice called out again —"Leo!" The car sank slowly down in an explosion of bubbles. Running my hand over the metal railing, I twisted the rope of danger into a safe, tidy coil.

Our legs freed like mousetails from a trap, Danny and I shot up to the surface and swam to shore. Danny, mad more than anything, muttered to himself the whole way.

"Good fucking move, McPhee. I can't believe you just drove the Buick into the river. What an idiot. The old man's going to be rip shit about the car."

On shore, we found a phone booth and called Eddie to come and pick us up. Safe back in my apartment, we took a hot shower and made love standing up as the water rushed over our goose-bumped skin, slippery with soap and relief.

"That was a close one," Danny said, excited, now that he was no longer scared. "Man. That was a close one, Leo. We almost bought the farm."

Danny crunched me down as he shot up inside me, bit my purple lips with his chattering teeth. I felt myself slip and start to fall. He pressed me up against the tiled shower wall and rammed me again, as the hot water grew warm, and then cool, and my belly tightened and we went to bed shivering as we'd come, pruny and spent. The bruise on my thigh would be a bit longer to push its colors from pink to blue to yellow and gray, my insides a bit more twisted and sore, the night a bit longer. But for once, Danny would wake softened and smiling, grateful for sleep, grateful for the morning. For once,

316

he'd kiss me goodbye. He'd slip away into the dawn, and I'd reach sleepily for my violin. We'd be very much alive.

Walking off the bridge, I slid down the embankment to the water's edge. The river water was sluggish, tepid as Lydia's tea. I looked around on the ground for some object, something to throw, found a piece of broken glass from a beer bottle and held it up to the moonlight. The cross section of one sharp edge gleamed limpid and green, the color of a gumdrop after the first bite. Holding it gingerly, I laid the glass flat on my belly, then held out my arm and let it fall. I heard the faintest plunk as it hit the water. I felt the splash on my cheek and thought it was river water. I imagined the piece of glass as it sank, twirling, floating, spinning.

"*You're still down there,*" I said. "*I know. You've been waiting for me, Danny. I'm here. I came.*"

I went over the accident again, as it had really happened. We tipped, we sailed, we sank. I got out, swam up to the surface. I tried to go back down, felt my lungs press in on themselves. I heard nothing, saw nothing. I shot back up to the surface, swimming as fast as I could. Every action had been borne by the one before and followed by the one after, a cartoon strip drawn frame by frame. Leo not able to lift her head until Danny's arm had moved, not able to break the surface until it had been reached, not able to submerge until her lips had drawn air, not able to reach or see or feel. Danny stuck, stuck in the death frame. Ink dried black even as the water gushed into the car. I'd known instantly, sickeningly, that he was gone, that there was nothing I could do. But the pen of life had been on me. I'd lifted my arms. I'd had motion. I'd flown.

"*What happened down there, Danny?*" I whispered. "*I got out all right. Why couldn't you?*"

The beam of headlights hit me at the neck and shoulders. Kilroy's arms were suddenly wrapped around me from behind. A car made a screeching turn onto the bridge. I saw a girl's arm outstretched, fingers flexed to the wind, the tips of her hair whipping horizontally. The car regained its balance on the straightaway and sped across the river.

"What are you doing down here?" Kilroy said.

"There was no way, Kilroy. No way I could have saved him."

"I know." He held me tightly, burrowed his face in my hair.

"And there was no point," I said. "No point in both of us dying."

"No, there wasn't," he said. "It's true."

I looked out across the water, felt the tight grip of Kilroy's arms. "It wasn't your fault, Leo," he whispered. "It wasn't your fault."

chapter thirty

"Y̶ou know," Kilroy told me a few nights later as we walked through
Five Moon Fields. "August and I . . ."

"August and I?" A firefly wove a thread of light in the distance.

"Your father and I were talking."

"Talking's good," I teased.

"I'm going to open a chess bookstore, Leo," he said. "And I've asked
your father to help me run it."

"You and my father? A chess bookstore?"

"Why not?" We reached the edge of the woods. "We're birds of a
feather. We both go our own way. This way, we can keep it all going. I'll
have chess, August can keep working on his inventions, you can play
your violin, and we'll still have the family."

"The family."

"Yeah, the family, Leo."

I stopped in a puddle of moonlight. "You don't understand about
this family, Kilroy. It's broken."

"We'll fix it," he said.

"You can't fix it, Kilroy. We have no money, no real jobs. How can we start a business?"

"August and I just put money down on a storefront on Ash Street," he said. "My father cosigned a loan. It's a good location, right outside the Square. The warm weather will hold for another month. I'll play chess. Your father and I will fix up the store and the business will start to bring in little bits. We'll open the café. You can play your violin. Maybe Lydia will sing."

"You don't get it, Kilroy." I ran my hand along the bark of a birch tree. "Lydia's been living inside a wall for almost forty years. She's better now. But she's still ill. She can't sing for you."

"She told me she'd think about it," he said.

"What?"

"If she's not too busy with her piano lessons."

"What are you talking about, Kilroy?"

"Lydia has three students lined up. The piano tuner's coming on Friday."

"The piano tuner's coming on Friday?" I said. "I don't believe it."

"Believe it, Leo," Kilroy said. "It's true."

The next day, my father called out to me while I was working in the garden.

"Leo! Come upstairs!"

I shaded my eyes with the edge of my hand, looked up at the window. "Why?" I yelled.

"Don't ask questions," he said. "Just come upstairs."

Slowly, I climbed the tilted stairs. The invention room was a mess, swept by a monsoon of brainstorm and neglect, a swirl of sand and cloth and bottles, the sweet and sour smells of sweat, coffee and suntan lotion mingling. My father's face was flushed. Sand was plastered to his hands and hair and face. The work table was piled high with the accumulated junk of years, but at one end, a bright island in the storm, was a neatly folded beach towel

"Behold, Leo," my father said, handing me the towel. "An ordinary beach towel."

I unfolded the towel and draped it over my shoulders like a shawl. "Sure enough," I said. "An ordinary beach towel."

I gave the towel back to him and he spread it evenly on the floor. Flipping up the tails of an invisible tuxedo, he splashed cupfuls of water onto the towel until it was soaked in big, dark patches. He then took handfuls of sand from a bowl and threw them all over the wet towel, rubbing in the sand with his hands, and his feet, one handful, and then another, until the bowl was empty. Gathering up the gritty, sodden towel, he began to shake it. The sand fell in sheets to the floor. When he was done, the towel hung wet and heavy from his hands.

"Now, Leo, touch it again," my father said.

I came close, put out my hand, buried my fist in a clump of wet cloth.

"What do you feel?"

"Dampness, terry cloth." I ran my fingers along the vertical stripes, searching for more of an answer. "I feel towel, Dad. All I feel is wet towel."

"Exactly," my father said. "All you feel is wet towel." He drumrolled two coffee spoons on the table. "Ladies and gentlemen," he said, the 'Sandproof Beach Towel.' Leave the sand where it belongs..." Another drumroll from the spoons. "Back on the beach."

"'The Sandproof Beach Towel.'" I felt a grin split my face from ear to ear. "Oh, my god. You did it."

And from some hidden reach of the mess, my father conjured up a bottle of real champagne.

I started to talk in my sleep. To dream ungodly, earthly dreams. The baby was real—red-faced, kicking and wailing. Needy. Furious. Hungry. I opened my eyes in the middle of the night in a panic, breathless, seized, lost. My body sizzled and pumped as if an electric charge ran through it. Sweat soaked my neck and arms. Where would the baby sleep? Where would it go to school? Who would take it skating, take its temperature, tell it when enough was enough? Who would stop it from crying, teach it algebra, rock it to sleep? These were talents and instincts I lacked, the ones that would make the beds and dry the tears and build the volcano for the science fair. Kilroy had them all. He was a born mother.

"I found a crib in the *Want Ad*," he told me one day. "I'll pick it up after work. Strip it down. Fix it up. Put it in the green room on the south side. Lots of sunlight for the baby. Vitamin D. It's crucial for the early development of the psyche. Babies who are light-deprived don't want to go to kindergarten. They're depressed already. What do you think, Leo?"

"I think you're incredible." I ran a finger over the pulse point of his temple. I hoped he understood, that I was grateful, beholden. He was going his own way, as well as mine. He was taking care of the little things. And the big things. He was taking care.

The next morning, I saw Kilroy bare-chested out in the yard with the crib, dipping a rag into a bucket, stripping off the old paint. When he saw me through the kitchen window, he waved, put down his rag, and came in to see me, kissing me once on the mouth, then again, and again.

"What are you doing?" I laughed. "Why do you kiss me so?"

"It just hit me," he said. "We're going to have a baby. Maybe today. Maybe tomorrow. It's really going to happen."

As I ran my hand over the rippling skin of Kilroy's warm back and leaned forward to kiss him, I knocked over the milk carton. The white liquid gushed over the edge of the table and made a puddle on the floor. I got a sponge and knelt down to clean it up. Kilroy took it from me, wiped a splash from my leg. "Let me do that," he said. "Let me do that, Leo."

"God. Is it really going to be all right?" I asked him.

Kilroy knelt with the wet sponge, bare to the waist, mopping up my toes, and told me that it was. And how could I do anything but crouch in the puddle of milk and hang onto him, and believe him?

The "Sandproof Beach Towel" was patented—divined, by my father, a world where sand knew its place and a towel could still breathe, where a body could stretch out on the beach on a soft bed of cotton and not have to shake or scratch. Clean car rides home. No sand in the laundry. Or the bathtub. Stores would clamor; people would flock. And every time money passed hands—for every grain of sand that stayed at the beach where it belonged—my father would get a little something for it.

He came home one night with a copy of the patent and chocolate letters for everyone—the first initials of all our names. He grinned the fluted grin of a real inventor, and Lydia patted his arm and said of course he'd done it; she'd always had faith in him. Kilroy and Po played chess as the night settled in. We made dinner out of bananas, fried noodles and half-iced tea. We sat around the old dining room table, which I'd set with as much finery as I'd been able to dig out of the pantry, a motley collection of chipped china cups and plates and tarnished silverware. I'd found an old can of furniture wax, broken it into hunks and polished the table. It gleamed mahogany under the flickering light of Lydia's silver candlesticks, one of those possessions, along with her piano and the portrait of her grandfather Byeworth, that she'd always said she'd rather walk the plank than part with.

I watched my father take his seat at the head of the table in a "Plough and Stars" t-shirt and wispy hair. I pictured him as a young boy, seen but not heard in a time gone by, sitting with clean hands folded, wool shorts and bangs combed wet to the side, a slice of rubbery roast and a tablespoon of shriveled peas set before him, mind churning with the marvels he'd someday invent—a lima bean evaporator, a robot friend, a machine that made your parents forget all the rules.

Kilroy and my father made plans for their store, "The Chess Corner," they'd decided to call it. I listened to Po and Lydia, chatting like magpies. I'd never known that Lydia once had a parrot that said, "No dice, bub," or that her mother would never let her grow her hair long, terrified she'd get lice. Who knew that ponds froze from the middle outward, that Po's grandfather had been a backgammon champion in Ireland? Who would have guessed that of all things, Lydia hated corn?

My father yawned and tried to catch Lydia's eye. Po and Kilroy told jokes. No soap radio. To get to the other side. Who's the first Irishman to come out in the spring? Patio Furniture. Ha. Ha. My father laughed. The big questions went unanswered. But still and always, hallelujah, the punchlines flew. The salad was dressing. The elephant sat on a fence. How did you make time fly? You threw a clock out the window, or was it the other way around?

The baby kicked. I ran my hand over my belly. "Okay, baby," I said. "I'm listening."

Soon, I, too, would have a cohort at this table, someone to bend my ear—bugs, bats, boogers, bums, bad guys, burps and braces. Hush little baby. Don't you cry. Something about a mocking bird, I remembered. A mother who kept buying more and more things to keep her baby from crying, rings that turned brass, a dog that didn't bark, a cart that broke. I hoped it wasn't like that, that there were other, simpler ways of connecting. Hush little baby. Don't you cry. That ghost sitting in the chair in a hockey jersey is just your father, the one who made you. He'll come as a breeze to stroke your cheek, as a song to comfort you. You may feel the press of a hard word sometimes, or the spray of ice as he passes. But he'll never hurt you. I won't let him. I promise. He made you but he can't keep you. He's not even real. Hush little baby, don't you cry. Your real father's the guy with the chessboard at the end of the table, telling jokes. He'll tell you the answers. He'll make you laugh. Listen.

"Okay, here's another one," Kilroy said to Po. "Why did the chicken cross the road?"

"To get to the other side, Dumbo," Po said.

"Hey, who you calling Dumbo?" Kilroy rolled his fists and popped Po's jaw. "All right. I got another one for you."

"It better be better than the last one," Po said.

"Okay, here it comes," Kilroy said. "Why'd the *elephant* cross the road?"

"Because he was in love with the chicken?" Po laughed and laughed.

"No," Kilroy said in mock disgust. "He was definitely *not* in love with the chicken."

"Okay, then. Because he thought *he* was a chicken." Po lifted his hands. "I don't know. Why *did* the stupid elephant cross the stupid road?"

"Because it was the chicken's day off," Kilroy said. "Dumbo."

After supper, I felt a surge of energy so strong it took my breath away. I washed the dishes and put contact paper on the newly painted cupboard shelves. I scrubbed the stove top and cleaned out the trash can, opened all the windows wide. Lydia drifted off to bed and my father followed. Kilroy drove Po home and then went off to lay carpet in the baby's room. I swept the living room, cleaned out the hall closet, went through the racks of old clothes—gowns and jackets and blouses and gloves and hats—making piles for Goodwill. Still not tired at midnight, I roamed the house from room to room, breathing in the smells of fleeing must and autumn air, listening to the silence. As I went, I set up all of the chessboards Kilroy had scattered around the house— knights and bishops ready, pawns in a line, queens strong and silent, on their own colors.

The next morning, the sky filled with the darkness of a coming storm. It was hot and humid. I was out of sorts. My father and Kilroy were nowhere in sight. Lydia and I sat at the breakfast table—me with a cup of tea, she with a piece of toast.

"Why do you play with your toast that way, Lydia?" I said. "It makes such a mess."

Lydia rose up in her chair. "I often wonder, Claire, why you treat me like a child."

"Treat you like a child?" I steadied my eyes to meet her gaze. "How could I? I don't even know what it's like to be treated like a child."

She didn't say she deserved that; nor did I say I was sorry.

"It's not all it's cracked up to be, is it, Claire?

"What?"

"Childhood," she said.

"I treated you the way I thought you wanted to be treated," I said. "The way Dad treated you."

"No." Lydia shook her head. "You father never pitied me, Claire. Or blamed me. Your father isn't angry with me."

"I'm not angry with you," I said.

"Of course you are," Lydia said quietly.

"Why?" My voice cracked. "Why am I?"

"You've never forgiven me, I suppose," she said. "For being . . ." I held my breath, waiting to hear the words she'd choose. "Distant. Incomplete. You've always protected me, Claire. My weaknesses made you strong. I didn't mind. I didn't have much else to offer."

"I was just trying to take care of you," I said.

"That wasn't your job," she said.

"I thought it was," I said.

"You misunderstood, Claire," she said quietly.

I picked up the salt shaker, looked Lydia straight in the eye. "My name is Leo," I said. "Why won't you call me Leo?"

"Is that what you want me to do?"

"It's my name, Lydia." I banged the salt shaker down on the table. "It's my name. After all, you gave it to me."

"No." Lydia shook her head. "Your father gave it to you."

"My father . . ."

"Yes," she said. "Your father."

"Who *is* my father, Lydia?"

"What?"

"What's his name? What's my father's name? My actual father."

"Actual father? What other kind of father is there?"

"Fake. Pseudo. Ersatz. Whatever word you want to use."

"You're talking like the Cheshire Cat again, Claire."

"*Leo. Leo.* Tell me about Anton, Lydia. Tell me everything. I want to know."

"Anton?" Lydia's hand rose to her cheek. "I haven't thought of him in so long. How strange."

"You went to his house to sing." I threw the breathless words at her, afraid she'd lose hold of the memory. "Just before I was born."

"I did," she said. "For eight months and sixteen days. He accompanied me on the piano. It wasn't nearly enough time. And then . . ."

"What happened, Lydia?"

Lydia's back straightened. Her mouth set itself in a grim line. "We went to the funeral, Claire. We were the only ones."

"Dad went to the morgue."

"It should've been me."

"He didn't want you to get hurt."

"I already was," she said.

I took what was left of Lydia's toast from her hands, tried to level my voice. "Was he your lover, Lydia? Was Anton your lover?"

"Anton?" I could tell by the way her head jerked back, by the slackening of all the features in her face, that the idea shocked Lydia even more than it did me. "My lover?" she said. "No. You don't understand. No one did." She closed her eyes. "Anton loved a boy, a student, a young flutist."

"What do you mean?"

"It was terrible," Lydia said. "Hopeless. The parents accused him, though of course he'd done nothing at all."

"Anton was gay?" I said again.

She looked up at me, confused by the word. "They took everything away," she said. "How could they?"

"The child," I said.

"They took Anton's job, his music, his dignity. There was nothing left. He killed himself. He saw no other way." Lydia held her hand up to the light. "I often thought there was nothing left for me, Claire," she said. "And then I had you."

"People shouldn't have babies to save themselves," I said.

"That's not why I had you."

"Why did you have me then?"

"I had you because I wanted you." Lydia took the salt shaker from my hands, tipped it over, and let it pour in a steady stream onto the table. "Because I knew, that once you were here, no one could ever take you away." The salt piled up slowly, a tiny mountain, soft and white. "Because as long as you were on the earth . . . Leonarda . . . then there was proof, you see . . ." Her eyes shone bright. "That so was I."

chapter thirty-one

*I*n the predawn hours of the next day, there was a thunderstorm. The rumbles came on the lightning's lit tail, shaking the earth. The wind rose and blew in ragged gusts and then the rain came in rippling sheets, battering the already battered roof and parched ground. Kilroy played chess in bed with a flashlight. I rolled in and out of stormy, dream-laced sleep, turning with every crack in the sky, every shift in the wind.

I woke to a sodden quiet. Kilroy lay a heap of twisted blanket and sheet beside me. Downstairs, I heard hammering and the plunking of piano keys. It was Wednesday. Still two weeks to go. After breakfast, I went out into the yard. The storm had brought down several small branches. I got down on my knees to collect them. Near the chestnut tree, I came across a dark and lumpy form. Clearing away the debris of branches and wet leaves, I found a cloth drawstring bag—Po's bag, I knew right away, the one he'd hidden in the crook of the tree the spring before. I didn't touch the bag. I made order around it and tended the garden, pulled up the last of the tomato plants and the herbs for drying, raked the earth in the garden plot smooth. The popcorn plants had never flowered, and one lone breadfruit stalk remained. After I was done in the garden, I went over and stood above Po's bag and stared, but when its curves and lumps began to take on human form, like the tiny feet and fists that lurched through the skin of my belly when the baby moved, I went back inside to call Po.

I did everything, that day, it seemed, and got nothing done, stirred the paint but never set the brush to a wall, sorted old music but never got the piles back onto the shelves, left half-washed clothes in sinkfuls of grey, dingy water. The storm eased and hovered. I went out to look at Po's bag from time to time, as I might a dying bird. By the time Po came in the late afternoon, the bag lay shrouded on the autumn ground, covered once again with the rubble of the storm—dirt, wet leaves, tangled vines and branches.

"Where is it?" Po arrived breathless at the front door in a Roadrunner t-shirt and jean shorts, his red hair frazzled from the wind. "Where's my bag?"

"Outside. On the ground." I led the way through the kitchen.

"Did you open it?"

"No, I didn't touch it, Po. I promise."

Po slammed the screen door and went outside to scoop up the bag. He brought it back in, clutching, pulling at its strings. "Got it," he said.

"Good." I tried to talk slowly, calmly. "Are you hungry?" I tried to keep Po there with me in the kitchen, slow him down, fill him up, keep him from flying away. Outside, the dark, swollen clouds slid noiselessly by.

"I'm starving," he said. "School lunch sucks. Mystery meat and cardboard potatoes, boiled-up slop and burned grilled cheese. I can't eat it."

"You're in a good mood."

"I had to stay after."

"What happened?"

"Me and this other kid put gum on this other kid's chair."

"Why?"

"He punched out this other kid for no reason and didn't even get in trouble. So we gummed him."

"Seems fair," I said. "How're his pants?"

"Gummy." Po grinned. "He's gonna stick to every chair in his house."

"Serves him right," I said. "How's Patrick, Po?"

"He's home from the hospital," Po said, looking up at me. "Maybe he won't die."

"He'll probably live to be a hundred," I said. "Do your parents know you're here?"

"Nope." Po pulled up a chair and swung it around to straddle it backwards. "I might as well eat something before I get yelled at."

"Aren't you supposed to be working at the market?"

"Conor's there."

I shook my head. "You should've told them, Po," I said. "You'll get us both in trouble."

"You're a grown-up, Leo." Po snorted. "You can't get in trouble."

"Wanna bet?" I got out two slices of bread. "Peanut butter okay?"

"Sure." Po adjusted his baseball cap, tugged at the strings of his bag.

"So what were we talking about?" I spread the thick brown paste against the nap of a stale heel of bread, kept my eyes on the bag.

"You were asking me how school was," Po said. "You're always asking me that, Leo."

"I'm interested. I really am. I had a hard time in school, too, Po."

"Well, I showed them I could read," he said. "So they took me out of that old hag's class. I got a man teacher, now. He's pretty cool. He shoots hoops with us at recess. But he puts grease in his hair. And he's got a girlfriend. Miss Isaacs, the gym teacher. She's a dog."

"Women aren't dogs, Po."

"Miss Isaacs is."

"Most dogs are beautiful," I said.

"Well, Miss Isaacs isn't. She's a dog."

"Okay. Okay. How's stuff at home?"

"Well . . ." His mouth was clogged. I brought him a glass of juice. "Since Patrick came home, my mother isn't acting so crazy anymore."

"Funny," I said. "Mine either."

"Lydia's not crazy," he said.

I looked up at him. "Another sandwich?" I said.

"Sure."

I slathered the last piece of bread with peanut butter, cut it down the middle, and gave us each half. I sat down with Po at the table. He held the bag in his lap, tapped his sneakered feet on the old tile floor.

"What's in the bag, Po?" I finally asked.

"Just stuff." He leaned back in his chair, swung the bag around in a circle by its string.

"Stuff?" I chewed slowly, trusting that I'd stop when and if I'd gone too far. "What kind of stuff?"

"Just some of Danny's old junk." Po took a gulp of juice and his voice cleared. "I took it out of his room before my mother cleaned it up. She made it into a guest room. I don't know why. We never have any guests. I just grabbed some stuff before she threw it all away."

Stuff. The peanut butter lodged in my throat. A bag full of Danny. Artifacts. Things he'd used, touched, things that maybe still carried his smell or his mark. I understood how dangerous opening the bag might be, like waving an open bottle in front of a ex-drinker's nose. I understood and I didn't care. I had to see what was inside, had to chase the baby back in time to the first glimmer, the first time I'd laid eyes on Danny at the fish market, the first time my heart had stirred. I ran my hand over my belly. So dim had the picture of Danny grown in my mind, so confused by then with the different clones that came to me, in spirit, voice or dream—saint, brooder, skater, tease. I was frantic to touch the things he'd once touched, to bring him back into focus, to remember the feel of his ice-smooth chest or the hammer-shaped scar on his thigh. How terrifying and thrilling it would be, to touch what Danny had unwittingly left behind to describe him at the kitchen table, unaware that he was about to disappear into a deep blue void.

Po chewed slowly, tipped back on the legs of his chair and rocked, twirling the bag around and around on its string. I might have lunged. I might have hurt him, had he not met my eyes just then and yanked open the bag, his fingers working quickly, as if he sensed danger. As he emptied the bag, I closed my eyes, felt the blood drain from my upper half and my heart slow to a standstill. We stared as the objects came to rest. Po might just as well have flung Danny's ashes across the worn, pine table. The baby kicked low and hard. As Po let his brother's ghost out of his bag, I let myself understand, in the dark of my eyes, that Danny McPhee had not been just my lover, but my addiction.

It was just a bunch of stuff, as Po had said—a chewed-up number two pencil, a hockey puck, a sports patch for a sports jacket, some notebook papers.

"Can I look?" I asked. "Can I touch them?"

Po nodded. I reached for the hockey puck first, knowing it would be the most tangible thing, wanting it to fill my hot palm with its cool black weight. I wrapped my fingers around the puck's battered edges— dented and chipped from countless blows, against Plexiglas walls, net, bone, and teeth. I felt the sweat on Danny's hair after a game, the racing pulse, the heat of his gleaming, bloodshot eyes.

"It's the puck Danny slammed into Xavier Roland's net at the Princeton game to win the division title," Po said. "Remember, Leo?"

"Just barely." Or maybe more than I knew. Po and I had sat together in the stands and cheered. His whole family had been there. After a victory party at Eddie's, Danny and I had gone back to my apartment. He was too drunk that night even to make love. He started to climb on top of me, lost his balance and fell flat on his back. I remembered a fat lip and a groan, a slew of empty beer cans on the floor beside the bed, the limp Danny who'd come outside of me in my grandmother's bed, writhing and mumbling until he fell asleep. As I ran my hand along the mottled, pockmarked edge of the puck, I remembered for one brief instant what it felt like to run my hand down the flagging muscle of Danny's pickled arm.

The papers were folded and creased, stained with blurring ink from the rain. I unfolded them, smoothed them out one by one on the table, a patchwork of swollen letters and bleeding, crooked lines. The sight of Danny's bold, uneven handwriting was as painful as the sight of his little brother had once been to me.

"College stuff," Po said. "I got it from Danny's desk."

His final economics paper, just the beginning of the project that had so frustrated Danny the fall before, the one that had waited for him in the wings after the championship game. The paper started off neatly, Danny's name, student number and date, January 4, 1982—in the right hand corner, title centered.

THE SMALL BUSINESS IN AMERICA: MAKING IT OR BREAKING IT

The small business in America is in peril today. Nevertheless, as long as there are neighborhoods, and families, there will remain a place for the family business in our culture and economy. If we don't fight to save small businesses, we risk losing families and neighborhoods as we know them. This is simply too big a price to pay.

The paper went on solidly, logically, even-keeled. Danny gave a brief historical background, expanded on his hypothesis, began his defense. But midway down the fourth page, the writing began to change, flowing larger, more urgently.

You want to know how to run a small business? Come down to the wharf at five in the morning. I'll show you a buying session. Come to the fish market some afternoon. That's where I'll be. Every. Single. Day. I'll cut you halibut, scrod. I'll show you the books, balanced to the penny. I'll show you the bend in my father's back and the cracks in my mother's hands. You'll see how they can't even look each other in the eye any more. And you'll ask, what the hell ever happened?

The writing grew sloppier, more agitated.

I'll show you how to mop the floor and keep the fish cases clean, how to make the fish look good, certain cuts and angles, sliced lemons and sprigs of parsley. I'll show you how to wrap a filet. It's like making an origami bird. Business is partly an art form— big business, small business. You learn by watching, feeling, asking, sensing. You learn by *doing*. It's not something you sit in a classroom and learn about for four or six or ten years, but who the hell is counting—all the time you waste and the money you spend, in debt your whole life through. And for what? Your whole God damned life through. You do what your father did and his father did before him and you try to do it well. You try to accept it. And if you can't, if you fail . . .

Business is common sense. It's sweat. It's bone. It's boredom. It's ritual. It's family. It's people. It's survival. If it's a good business, it's a way of life. If the business gets out of hand, so can the life. And if the life gets out of control, so does the . . .

The last words grew wild and barely legible, taking up half of the last page.

My life is out of fucking control . . .

Po read slowly over my shoulder.
"Why did he say that?" he said.
"I think Danny was having trouble holding on, Po," I said.
"To what?"
"His center," I said. "Everything he cared about. He thought he had to figure everything out, all at once. And he didn't want to let anyone down. Danny was always in a hurry, wasn't he, Po? He wanted to do it all."
"So do I," Po said. "I want to do everything. I want to be the boss."
"You already are," I said, reaching out to rub his head. "Don't you know that, Po? You already are."
I put the economics paper aside and picked up a drawing of a hockey player, sketched on lined school paper, frayed at the edge.
"Danny drew this?" I asked Po.
"Yeah. He drew lots of pictures."
"Hockey players mostly?"
"Hockey players, and birds," Po said. "He wanted to fly."
"Like Leonardo," I said.
"Who's Leonardo?" Po asked.
"Da Vinci," I said. "A great scientist and inventor."

"Is he still alive?"

"No," I said, studying Danny's drawing. "He's dead, too." The sketch was so good, really, a few lines drawn just so. It captured the stalking, bear-like stance of the player at the face-off, as he waited for the ref's whistle to blow—the heft of the stick, legs bowed slightly for balance, the swing of the heavy, gloved arm, the rocking motion, the unblinking eye. "Are there more of these, Po?" I asked.

"No, Danny threw most of them away. He said they were only good for wrapping up fish guts." Po pointed to the number on the drawn player's jersey. "Sixteen," he said. "That was Danny's number."

"I know."

"I can't even skate," Po said disgustedly.

"Have you ever tried?"

"My mother won't let me. She says I got brittle bones. She says I'll break them."

"I'll take you skating sometime," I said.

"You're having a baby, Leo."

"We'll bring the baby."

"Babies can't skate. You'll be too busy. And you'll be too tired. You won't take me."

"I will," I said. "I promise."

"Mothers break promises," Po said.

"They don't mean to," I said, smoothing my hand over Danny's drawing. "Would you mind if I kept this, Po?"

Po looked at the drawing and then away from me before he answered. "I found it, Leo," he said.

"You did," I said, holding out the drawing. "You keep it."

Last in the pile was a pageful of words, arranged in groups of three, and some doodling. "What's this?" I asked Po.

"Lists," Po said, taking the paper from my hand. "Danny made lists. These words all begin with L. I can read them. Listen." He began to read. "LIFE. LIMB."

"Limb," I corrected him. "The b is silent."

"Limb? What's a limb?"

"An arm," I said. "A leg."

Po started off again.

"LIFE. LIMB. LUCK."

I looked over his shoulder as he read.

"LUCKLESS. LOW. LAME."

"LISTEN. LORD. LICK."

"LIMP. LATE. LOVE."

"LESSONS. LEO. LOST."

The bottom of the last letter, T, trailed off into an inkstain blur.

"Hey, look," Po said. "You're in there, Leo. Leo begins with L."

"There I am." I took the paper and ran my finger over my name. I might have felt comforted or validated, tucked away in Danny's list of L words. But somehow I could only think how much better I'd have felt if I'd never asked Po to see what was in the bag, if my name had at least been in the group with love, if lost hadn't been the last word.

We drank orange juice to unstick the roofs of our mouths. The sun fell low in the sky. Po gathered Danny's things and put them back in the bag. "You still visit Danny?" I asked him.

"Every week. After church," he said.

"Where's he buried?"

"St. Ann's Field," Po said. "Next to my grandfather. And my other dead brother."

"What other dead brother?"

"The one that came out dead. After Rose. Then my mother got the twins, because of the one that died. Maybe you'll get two, Leo. Because of Danny."

"No," I said. "There's only one." I put the peanut butter away on the shelf. "Where's St. Ann's Field, Po?"

He shrugged. "Up on a hill somewhere."

"In Cambridge? Can you take a bus?"

"I don't know. We always drive."

"What's it near?"

"A flower shop. Next to McDonald's. We get lunch on the way home."

I knew the place. There'd been a big to-do about putting the McDonald's there, on the rise above the river. I pictured the McPhees visiting Danny's grave, then going off to lunch without him, seven Big Macs instead of eight, flowers wilting on his grave.

"Come on, Po," I said. "I'll take you home."

"No way." Po wiped a smudge of peanut butter from his mouth. "I'm going with you, Leo."

"Right." I slipped on my sandals under the table. "We'll take the bus. I'll bring you home."

"No. You're going to the cemetery," Po said. "And I'm coming with you."

I looked into Po's green eyes, hardly recognizing him as the slow, crooked boy Danny had left behind, no more a mute, tripping shadow, but now a boy who ran strong up a hill and stood up to bullies, had no fear of a storm or the wrath of his parents or even a graveyard at dusk. Danny's death had given Po permission to grow, painfully and slowly, but surely and in his own time, in a way that might never have been possible had he always remained Danny McPhee's warped little brother, just as I might have forever stalked the earth as Danny McPhee's strange, skinny girlfriend.

"Come on then." I grabbed an old vinyl jacket that had been kicking around the closet since it failed to become the "Reversible Raincoat" in 1973. "Let's go while we have the daylight. I think Phil's bus goes that way."

We made our way down the crumbling sidewalk of the hill. Po kept by my side, hands stuffed into the pockets of his jeans, bag slung over his shoulder, face smudged with peanut butter and dirt. He steered us clear of puddles, pulled back overgrown branches to let me pass, cleared rubble from my path.

"City oughta do something about this hill," Po said, in a voice that Eddie Quintana, once and future mayor of Cambridge, might have used. "It's a real mess."

chapter thirty-two

"Not planning to have that baby on my bus, are you, Stradivarius?" Phil asked me, as we boarded.

"Why not, Phil?" I rummaged in my coat pockets for change. "Can't think of a better place to start out."

"Don't you dare," he said.

"I got it, Leo." Po plunked two quarters into the fare box. "She's just kidding, Phil. Don't worry."

"Okay, Mr. Gotrocks," Phil said, pulling away from the curb. "Where you two headed?"

"St. Ann's Field." I slid into the seat behind him. "You go anywhere near there, Phil, after you leave the Square?"

"Not too far," he said. "Taking up gravedigging, are you?"

"No, just visiting," I said.

"It's hard to watch the old folks go."

"He wasn't old," I said.

"He was twenty-two," Po said. "He was my brother."

"I'm real sorry to hear that, Porter."

"Yeah," Po murmured. "Hey, Phil. Do you live on this bus or something? Every time I see you, you're on this bus!"

"Fancy that!" Phil laughed. "No, I'm usually home by now, Porter. I'm just putting in a few extra hours this month. My wife and I finally got the last kid out of the house. Twenty-five years we've been married, and we're finally planning a vacation." He drove carefully, never taking his eyes from the road. "Jerome just went off to college. Vassar College in New York. Used to be all girls. Now, they want Jerome."

"My brother went to Harvard," Po said.

"Smart guy," Phil said.

The bus took a wide turn onto the river drive. The sycamores towered over us. We rode in twilight to the end of the bus line, past the hospital and the boathouse, up near the boy's prep school at the bend in the river.

"There's St. Ann's," Phil said, pointing upward with his chin. In the distance, I saw gravestones sticking up from the ground, white wafers on a clouded hilltop. "Don't stay too long, you two," Phil said. "They say this storm's not done with us yet."

The bus pulled over to the side of the road. As I reached for the pole by Phil's shoulder, his eyes swung to my ring finger.

"I'm not married, Phil," I thought to tell him. "The baby's father died. That's who we're going to visit."

"Hey, none of my business," he said.

"I'm the uncle," Po said.

"Lucky kid," Phil said.

As I went down the steps, I turned back to Phil. I had a sudden worry that I knew too much about him and he not enough about me, that I might never see him again.

"I'm going to be a good mother," I told him.

"You bet you are."

"And my real name is Leo, Phil."

"Leo?" Phil scoffed. "Nah. Doesn't fit. You'll always be Stradivarius to me."

"And you know. Stradivari *made* violins. He didn't play them."

"Is that right?" Phil said. "Well, he made good ones, didn't he?"

"Yeah, he did, Phil," I said. "He made the best."

Po and I walked through the iron gates of the graveyard. He led me to Danny's grave. I saw his name carved in the cool, speckled granite, the ruts of the letters smooth and deep. Beside him lay his grandfather Patrick and the brother who'd come out dead, Thomas Paul. In the distance, a lily pond lay pollen-frosted and still. Sunday's flowers were limp and strewn. A huge branch had ripped off a nearby oak in the storm and lay twisted on the ground. This wasn't where I would have put Danny, in a field where teenagers came to neck and throw beer bottles, where lightning struck to the roots, time and time again, and flowers wilted when you turned your back. Where the silence was bottomless and the dark of night pitch.

I would rather have kept Danny in an urn in a corner of a sun-baked room, next to a pile of newspapers, in my kitchen, enveloped by the smell of toast, out of harm's way, within reach. But it is a mother who buries a child, not a lover. Danny's mother had ushered him out of the world just as she'd brought him in, remembering how he'd squirmed his way out of her belly, taken his first steps, spoken his first word. It wasn't a time to remember the way a child grown into a man had slid his tongue around the insides of your mouth, how he'd bored into you in the night, how he'd sweated and clutched and moaned. The final act of intimacy belonged to the mother. Only to the mother.

I traced the rutted letters of Danny's name with my finger. In horror, I found myself trying to imagine what he actually looked like at that moment, wondering how you could come to this place week after week and sit peacefully, remembering the living, breathing Danny and not conjure up the dead, decaying Danny, or the Danny in ash. Either way, how could you leave thinking anything other than, what a waste?

Po propped a pile of baseball cards up against the gravestone. "There's a Louis Tiant in there, Danny," he said. "You remember Louis Tiant?"

"He remembers," I said, bending down to pick some dandelions.

Po leaned back against Danny's gravestone and read my mind. "He's in there, Leo," he said. "Just rotting away."

"What about heaven?" I said.

"His spirit's in heaven, Leo," he explained. "Not his body."

"Ah," I said. "That helps me to understand it better."

"My mother wouldn't let Danny get burned."

"Cremated," I said. "I'm sure she did what she thought was best."

"He wanted to be burned," Po said.

I looked up at him. "How do you know?"

"This guy on tv once had his ashes dumped out of an airplane over a mountain he used to climb. Danny said when he died, he wanted his ashes thrown out on the hockey rink and rubbed into the ice by the zamboni. He said that would sure give his coach a scare."

"A mother doesn't know these things," I said.

"I told her." Po traced lines in the dirt with a stick. "I told her what Danny wanted, but she dressed him up in a stupid suit like he was going to church and she buried him in the ground so he could just rot away."

I laid the bunch of dandelions next to the baseball cards and looked around to see Danny's neighbors—a Frank Carter, faithful husband and father, a Harriet Moss, who'd only made it to the age of seven. "It doesn't really matter where they put him, Po," I said.

We looked at each other. Danny was with us still, under our tongues and in the creases of our eyes, tucked into the folds behind our knees. We hadn't been ourselves with Danny. We'd neglected and submerged those selves. Still, we'd loved him best, Po and I. And we'd have given anything to call him back, for just one more baseball game, one more touch, promising even to be our old, selfless selves, if only he wouldn't be so silent, so still.

A gust of wind blew the dandelion bouquet apart and sent the stack of baseball cards flying. We got on our knees and rearranged them, found rocks to weigh them down.

"All the boys die, Leo," Po said.

"What do you mean?" I looked up at him.

"All the boys in my family. They die." He shot his fingers up one by one. "Thomas Paul. My Uncle Rory. My cousin Timmo. Then Danny." His fingers pulled back into a fist. He looked over at me and said, "Maybe I'm next, Leo."

"You're not going to die, Po," I told him. "Not for a long, long time."

"Will Danny still be there when I do? Can I be with him?"

"Yes."

"Will he still be young if I'm old?"

"I don't think it will matter much any more."

"What if I'm the only one, Leo?" Po said. "What if I'm the only one who *never* dies?"

"You will, Po," I said, reaching for his head. "I promise. You will."

As I looked out over the lily pond, it turned slowly to ice. Danny rose up out of the smoke in a genie tailspin, in his hockey skates, without the pads or masks or helmet, without the sweat-soaked brow and the killer look in his eye, bruised cheek and bulging mouth. Danny skated, graceful and strong, in shorts and a t-shirt, what he might have worn to the ball park on a summer's night, making circles and looping figure eights, his hair blowing, the ice tearing into shreds of showering crystals around his feet, eyes soft and clear, smile untwisted—no goals to score, no axes to grind, no bones to pick, no scores to settle—just the thrust of strong legs on smooth ice, around and around and around, the circles getting smaller and smaller, until Danny disappeared back into a spin that rose up into a spiral of smoke as soft mist and drifted away.

We went back to the fish market to face the music, which wasn't sweet. I passed Po over to his grim-faced mother in the dark.

"I'm sorry he's home so late," I said. "It wasn't his fault."

"Whose was it, then?" she asked me.

I stared at her, felt anger rise up in me hot, like a fever. "The day got complicated," I said. "We didn't have a chance to call." Whose fault was it? she kept wanting to know. I turned away, held my head up high. I would not, I would never say to her—that it was mine. I said goodbye to Po and the door was closed upon me. I walked down Cambridge Street to the bus stop, feeling oddly fearless, floating in the dark.

* * *

Later that night, back at the fish market, Mr. McPhee went up to Po's bedroom and looked him square in the eye.

"*Your mother tells me you were gone all day, Porter. That you never came home after school and missed dinner, too. And through it all, not a word.*"

"*I went to St. Ann's.*" *Po pulled his knees up to his chest and traced the stripes on his pajamas with one finger.* "*With Leo.*"

"*You knew I was off on business,*" *Mr. McPhee said.* "*And who did you think would be minding the market this afternoon?*"

"*Conor was here. I thought. . . .*"

"*Conor is an employee,*" *Mr. McPhee said.* "*And you are my son. Do you see the difference?*"

"*Yes.*"

"*There's work to do, Porter. There's been too much larkin' about.*"

"*Leo wanted to visit Danny. She's never been. I didn't want her to go alone.*"

Mr. McPhee rubbed his forehead and sighed. "*I think it's best you don't see Leo for a while, Po. Or her family.*"

"*Why?*" *he said.* "*Why not?*"

"*It's your own family needs attention now. We're on the mend, Porter. Finally. And we've recently traded our souls to the bank. The only way to get them back is to work. Work hard. Stick together. God knows, your poor mother's had enough to bear.*"

Po looked off into the distance. "*I remember,*" *he said.*

"*Remember what?*"

Po looked out the window. "*What it was like before Danny died.*"

"*It's our life still, Porter, with Danny here or gone,*" *he said.* "*God looks out for the living and the dead.*"

"*No.*" *Po shook his head.* "*It's different. You don't go out bowling any more. Mom doesn't make cakes. Rosie's mad all the time. And the baby cries. All day long.*" *His voice grew loud, almost frantic. He put his hands to his ears and yelled,* "*I'm the only one who remembers. I'm the only one who remembers when I had a brother.*"

"*Brother or no brother,*" *Mr. McPhee said.* "*You're still part of this family, Porter.*"

"*I'm part of Leo's family, too,*" *Po said in a trembling voice.* "*I'm the uncle.*"

"*Aye, you won't let us forget it, will you? We need you here, now, Porter.*"

"*Leo needs me, too.*"

Mr. McPhee shook his head. "*I can't let you see Leo anymore, Po. I don't mean for-*"

343

ever. Just until the baby's born, until the waters calm." He took Po by the shoulders and shook him gently. "It's just too damn hard," he said. "Do you understand me, son? Do you understand what I'm trying to say to you?"

Po looked his father straight in the eye. "No," he said. "I don't understand you at all."

Back at Cobb's Hill that night, after Kilroy had fallen asleep, I went out onto the widow's walk and sat down in the armchair he'd brought out a few days before. The sky was dark and smoky; the second shift of the storm still held. I could see the lights of the city in the distance. An owl hooted in Five Moon Fields. I put my hands into the pockets of my coat, the one I'd worn to Eleanor's the last night we'd talked over pizza, just before she went to Texas. Burrowing my hands in its pockets, I pulled out the envelope Eleanor had handed me at the door. I'd forgotten all about it.

"Read it later, Leo," she'd said. "Some time when your mind is open and you're feeling strong. There's often a time, before a baby comes, when you feel this way, calm and clear."

I opened the envelope and turned on a flashlight. On a page of her prescription pad, Eleanor had written:

> Dear Leo: I'm thinking of you and hope you are well. When you read this, if it seems like a good idea, go over the night of the accident once more. Slowly. Step by step. As you go, think carefully on this question, but not too hard. *Is it possible that Danny was trying to kill himself that night?*

What was different about the night? Go over it again. And again. I turned off my flashlight and closed my eyes, dipped into that January night once more. The nuances rang and vibrated like single notes on a harp. My temples pounded. Danny wore a dark blue t-shirt, one breast pocket on the left side. He was stewing, at odds, as usual, but softer somehow. When he looked at me out on the sidewalk, after the party, after he'd flung Kilroy's chess pieces to the floor, his face had filled with ragged concern. He'd taken my hand, put his coat over my shoulders, led me to the car. *Taken my hand.* How strange. How sweet. I'd felt too mad, too sick to even notice the rare gesture. I was different, too, that night—quiet, but harder somehow. I'd drunk bitter gulps of gin, let Eddie lead me out onto the dance floor. I'd spoken up at the chessboard, pointing out Danny's lost position, for the first time not calculating how what I said might make him feel. His flinging the chess pieces of the table was nearly the last straw. I was sick, frustrated, fed up, close to telling Danny we couldn't go on. He'd sensed it and bristled. In the car, there'd been silence, raw jokes and jibes. Danny and I both knew that something had to give, but neither of us had the slightest idea of what or when or how. He'd been trying to tell me something that night, but I couldn't listen anymore, couldn't hear.

"*Hockey's over, Leo,*" he'd said. "*What the hell am I going to do now?*"

"*Do whatever you have to do,*" I said. And I'd meant it, that he should do whatever it would take, no matter how extreme, how wild. Anything to get us off the ledge we were stuck on. I'd as much encouraged him to jump.

"*Just as well,*" he said. "*I'm sick of games. I'm almost a quarter of a century old and all I've done my whole life is play games.*"

"*I'm sick of games, too, Danny,*" I told him.

"*Break my fucking bones . . .*"

We'd driven home from Eddie's house a hundred times. I wasn't much of a navigator and rarely paid attention to the road. But we always passed the Polaroid factory, and we didn't pass it that night. We turned right on Putnam. That was different. We usually took Western Ave. to the Drive. Danny locked the car doors with a flick of a switch, took out a new pack of cigarettes and pulled the cellophane tab. He didn't smoke a lot, mostly when he drank. I asked him when he was going to quit. He said now that hockey was over, he could afford to slack off. He could suck a butt or two if he damn well felt like it. What was the big, fucking deal? Life was short, he said. Shorter still, I said, if you keep smoking. Chess, he said, changing the subject. Now there was a game. It was more than a game. He gestured with his hand, trying to explain. That guy Kilroy was onto something.

"Anyone can play chess, Danny," I said. "Anyone can learn. It's free, what that guy's onto. And you don't even have to wreck his chessboard or beat him up to find out what it is."

"No. That guy knows something the rest of us will never know," Danny said. "Something big, Leo."

"How big?" I'd asked wearily.

"Big," he said, reaching for the matches. "Just believe me, Leo. It's big."

My head rested back against the seat, eyes half closed. Danny lit up his cigarette. The first rush of smoke came my way. Before I could even tell him it was making me feel sick, he told me to open my window.

"Open it wide, Leo," he said. "All the way. Let's get some air in here."

I opened my window. Wide. All the way. As the cool air rushed in, I felt the improbability of our love. A flash of warmth grazed my cheek as the smoking match whizzed past my face, on its way from the tip of Danny's cigarette—

through the air,

past my face,

out my window.

out *my* window.

Danny had told me to open my window.

But he'd kept his closed.

The wind shifted and the clouds began to clear. I sat in the armchair and folded Eleanor's note into smaller and smaller squares. Inside, on the bed in my room, Kilroy slept on. I was shocked by the question scribbled on the paper, not only because I'd never considered it before, but because the answer was, at once, so clear. Of course, it *was* possible that Danny had been trying to take his own life. He'd thought so poorly of it, valued it so little. It wasn't something anyone would ever know as fact, or be able to prove. I'd been the only witness. Mine was perhaps the best guess.

I shifted my weight in the armchair, trying to find a comfortable position. Suddenly crystalline was the balance of fact and reason. Danny hadn't earned himself sainthood or absolution by dying, no more than I had by saving myself, by staying alive. Down in the river, we'd both been merely playing out that one moment of our lives. I was only as responsible for Danny's death as he might have been for mine.

No more. No less. Eleanor was right. There, in the water, plunged by recklessness or fate, we'd only been responsible for ourselves.

I saw then how it might have been. I saw how Danny, at a low, dim, moment, lost on a chessboard, hockey stick snapped in two, economics paper unfinished, love just another battle, might have felt exhaustion start to creep through his bones. I saw how at the end of that long, lost moment, that last, deep drag of his cigarette, after he'd heard the edge in my voice and the hollowness in his, when he felt the wheel slip under his hands and knew he'd taken the turn too fast, when the car tilted—in that fraction of a split second when fate crushes like tin under steel—he might have imagined that death was as good a place as any to find answers. And maybe, as he rounded the last curve of that thought and blew smoke out his nose, he'd given in to the slope and lean of the car, hadn't turned the wheel back quite far enough to center the car on the bridge, or put his foot hard enough on the brake. I couldn't remember any screeching, no lurching forward, no smashing glass. My head hadn't hit the windshield. It was a clean takeoff, a smooth sail.

Was I right in remembering that when Danny said, "oh, shit!" he said it with a certain euphoria, the same exhilaration as when he watched a spectacular baseball play, or a speeding shot to the net, blind and deaf to the rest of the spinning world, never hearing my "I love you" at all? Maybe, as the water started pouring into his lungs, Danny made a bargain with death in one blink of an eye. Maybe he didn't try with all his might to open the car door. Maybe, as I scrambled for the window, he didn't try at all. Maybe, in that one split second, as it was offered to him down on the river bottom on the cracked leather seat of a '78 Buick, death seemed as good and final a resting place as any—where he'd have to answer to no one or no creed, no standards, no desires. Where he wasn't stared at, where nothing was expected of him—winning hockey games or looking out for Po, smiling for his mother's camera—nothing to do except complete the coping tasks of the dead, whatever those might be—haunting the living, teaching them, warning them, pulling the plugs on the rain-filled clouds. Death, as Danny's god had promised him from day one—a safe haven, a soft place to lay down his aching head—Harvard out of sight, no crowd cheering, no

Eddie to one up or save, no women to fuck or love, no father to tussle with or please, no mother to honor and revere, no Mary on the Half Shell to tap, coming or going, no grandmother's hard feelings to waltz around a room, no feelings, no earthly obligations at all. Death, where no decisions had to be made, no pride upheld, no future planned, no body aroused, no violence felt, no mind to empty or fill. Heaven. That alluring, promised kingdom of oblivion. Where you finally pressed up against your shadow and became one. Where maybe there really was a god, where higher powers really did intervene, where you were forgiven your trespasses, as you forgave those, where you were not led into temptation, where life was finally taken our of your clumsy, aching hands . . .

Where it didn't smell like fish.

The armchair filled with the weight of my sorrow. It made good and terrible sense. Danny *had* been trying to kill himself. Maybe not that night, not in one fell swoop, but slowly, surely, over time. And I couldn't help but see one of many dark shadows that lurked in the corners of this truth, that if Danny had been trying to kill himself, he might have been trying to kill me, too. Maybe he'd pictured me going down with him. Maybe he'd seen his chance that night, on the wet road. We'd had words. We'd argued. I was sick. And tired. He was drunk, and beat, afraid of what he was feeling, what I was feeling. Terrified, like the rest of us, of all we couldn't bear or grasp, of the dark unknown. Take her with me. Take her down. Take her with me. Love her. Make her suffer. Serve her right. Love her. Take her down . . .

At the last minute, Danny lit the cigarette. Open your window, Leo. Open it wide. Let's get some air in here. Give you a way out. I love you. And I don't know what the fuck to do about it. Take you with me or let you go. *Take you with me. Or let you go.* In the space of those few minutes, a death sentence and a reprieve. Maybe this was the twisted sense Danny had finally made out of the love he felt for me—enough to take me with him, enough to let me go. Just after we crashed, I said, "I love you." He'd been testing me. He wanted to know, just as Kilroy had, if I had it in me, if it were true. It was a fair question, one whose answer had, for so long, left me at a silent and terrible loss. There in the water, as I shot up to the surface, I'd given Danny his answer—too late—and I'd given myself—just in time—one last chance to prove it.

chapter thirty-three

"*L*eo." I woke up in the armchair to the sound of a voice, the feel of someone shaking my shoulder.

I gripped the arms of the armchair, looked for Kilroy's face and found my father's. The sky had cleared and the moon lay low in the sky. "What's wrong?" I asked.

"Mr. McPhee just called," my father said. "Po's run off. They had an argument. He's not in his bed."

"Oh, my god." I struggled to sit upright in my chair, stiff and sore. "What time is it?"

"Four in the morning," he said. "Lydia's missing, too, Leo. I've just searched the house."

My father helped me to my feet. I passed Kilroy sleeping on the bed, thought for a minute about waking him, but covered him with a blanket instead. We pulled the Rambler out of the driveway and started down the hill, weaving through the last purple flashes of darkness.

"She's out there somewhere, Leo," my father said, as we drove. "I'm worried. She can't handle it."

"How do you know?" I said. "Did you ever give her a chance?"

"What do you mean?"

"After Lydia's breakdown," I said. "Did you ever get her any help?"

"I tried," he said. "I made an appointment once, with a psychiatrist. I told Lydia we were both going, just to talk. I was relieved. She seemed to take it so well. But later that day, I found her in the kitchen, pouring boiling water from the teapot over her hands. I spent all that night icing the burns, calming her down. All those years, and with one phone call, I'd lost her. I had to start all over again."

I looked over at him, shook my head.

"After that, I couldn't risk it anymore," he went on. "I was the one person she trusted, Leo, and I'd betrayed her. I promised I wouldn't make her go back out again. Not until she wanted to. Until she was ready. I promised her that I'd take care of her. That was all I knew how to do."

I reached over and touched his arm. "You took good care of her, Dad," I said, looking over him. "And you took good care of me, too."

"I had to take care of you, old girl," he said. "You were my best invention."

We drove to all of the haunts we could think of—to the hockey rink and Harvard Square, to the Common and the car barns, landing back at the fish market at dawn with no clues. Mr. McPhee sat in his bathrobe in the grandmother's chair, waiting by the phone, staring out onto the dark, empty street. The police had been of no help. Po and Lydia wouldn't be missing persons for forty-eight hours. Until then, they were runaways, pranksters, cavorters.

My father and I drove back to Cobb's Hill. He went upstairs to lie down. I sat out in the yard on the wrought iron bench as dawn broke, raw tangerine. Somehow, I wasn't worried. Po was with Lydia and Lydia was with Po. They'd look out for each other. They'd taken to one another right from the start, stories flowing between them like gentle breezes—from the leaping dog to chestnuts to babies and baseball stars. Snippets of their conversations raced through my mind. At the dinner table the night we celebrated the "Sandproof Beach Towel," Po had been telling Lydia about the janitor at his school, a guy who dressed like Elvis and wore blue suede shoes. Lydia was reminded again of the janitor at Symphony Hall, the tiny young man with blue eyes and a stutter, who used to leave roses for her in the wings of the theater after rehearsals. She'd been thinking about that man lately, her last admirer, maybe, out there in the spinning world, the only one who might still remember her as she'd once been, regal, vibrant, star-dusted. He was probably still working there, she'd told Po—keeping the railings gleaming, the seats cleaned, the curtains dusted. He'd taken great pride in his work, had a true love of the music. Some day, Lydia told Po, she'd take him to Symphony Hall, to meet that janitor, to see the great stage.

My belly barely fit behind the wheel of the Rambler. I hadn't driven a car since before Danny died. The light was rising. It was just after six o'clock. There was no traffic. I lurched down Massachusetts Avenue, through Central Square, crossed the river into Boston, down past Commonwealth Avenue and the Christian Science Church, hailed by a drunk as I pulled up in front of Symphony Hall.

"Have you seen an older woman with silver hair?" I asked, getting out of the car. "And a little boy? A redhead?"

"Sure. I saw 'em," he said. "They came a while ago." He pointed with a wobbly finger to the door. "What's going on in there? I don't hear nothing. I don't hear the music." The drunk took a swig from his bag, cupped his hand to his ear and waved to the door. "Go on in," he said, waving his arm. "Go on. All of you. Get the hell outta here. And, hey. God bless."

I banged on the locked front doors for a while, then went around to the back of the building and found a door propped open with a mop, a bucket of dirty water beside it. I slipped inside, made my way down a dark basement corridor past the overhead pipes and the furnace until I found a flight of stairs. The stairwell was silent and cool. Upstairs, the lobby sparkled, mosaic tiles gleaming and chandeliers glistening, red carpet soft and newly vacuumed—Milk Duds, Twizzlers and Jujubes lined up in cases of shining glass. I stole into the auditorium through a side door, slid gingerly into a corner seat in the last row. And there, milling statues on the stage, were Lydia and Po.

"Ghosts," I heard Po say. "There are ghosts in here."

"A few." Lydia pointed up to the domed ceiling, where the new light flickered through. "They're harmless, though. They fly around up there with the angels."

Po looked up at the ceiling, where three painted angels floated in a circle. He threw back his head, cupped his hands to his mouth and called.

"Hey, Danny! You up there, Danny?"

Nee, nee, nee, his echo answered.

"He's here," Po said. "I can feel him. He's skating. He's coming in from the blue line. He steals the puck. He shoots . . ." Po jumped up, shooting an invisible puck with an invisible stick. "He scores!"

Lydia clapped and laughed. "He scores!" she said.

"Did you ever sing here, Lydia?" Po reached out to touch the velvet curtain.

Lydia went center stage, lifted one arm. "I stood here one night," she said. "All alone. All dressed up in a crimson gown. There were hundreds of people sitting in those seats, waiting to hear me sing. Can you imagine?"

"You must have had to sing real loud."

"I never did sing, Po."

"Why not?"

"Something happened," Lydia said. "In that one small moment, my whole life changed. And I still don't know why."

"What happened?" Po asked.

"It was almost as if my voice . . . fell out of me," Lydia said. "All of a sudden, I was so scared."

"Of what?" Po asked.

"Everything," Lydia said.

"I used to be scared of everything," Po said.

"Did you?" Lydia said. "And are you now?"

"Not so much." Po grabbed his bottom lip with his teeth and shot another invisible puck into the curtains. "What were you scared of, Lydia?"

"I was scared that I wouldn't sing well enough," she said. "That they wouldn't like it, or maybe that they would. I was afraid that my heart would stop beating, or that I'd start to scream. I was afraid that I'd have to do it all over again. And again. Everyone thought I could. But I couldn't. Everyone thought I loved it. But I didn't. Not the music. I loved the music. But I hated all the rest."

"Did they make you sing again?"

"Twice," Lydia said. "Two more times. Then they gave up. Then they left me alone."

"Were you glad?"

"At the time," she said. "I could only be glad."

"Sing now, Lydia," Po said. "I want to hear you sing."

"Oh, I can't sing anymore, Po. It's been far too long."

"Yes, you can. Nobody really took away your voice. You've still got it, Lydia. Sing."

Lydia ran her hand down her throat. "No," she said. "It's impossible."

"*Sing!*" Po shouted, as he took another swing with his hockey stick on the gleaming, wood floor.

I sat on the edge of the theater's last seat, last row, bathed in the shadows of fading starlight and red velvet. Lydia clutched her hands together and opened her mouth. Out came a wrinkle of a note, without tenor or form, which slowly smoothed itself and gathered strength, gradually finding balance and pitch in a middle register. Lydia started up the scale, then back down, up another octave, a trill in B flat major, until she reached a fragile, quivering high C.

The note floated toward me, gaining volume and speed, wrapped itself around me, hot and tight. The baby kicked low and hard. Once. Twice. Then again. Lydia's C note took off into an Offenbach aria from "The Tales of Hoffman," and finally released me. As I let go my breath, the dam inside me burst, the baby's sac of bathwater split open wide with a final, walloping kick. I clutched my legs together as the warm liquid spilled out of me and down my legs. A clear puddle formed at my feet and rolled down the slope of the hall toward the stage. Candy's voice reached me through some dark tunnel of my mind. "If your water breaks, get thee hence to the hospital, kiddo. Fast." But Lydia's singing voice drowned out all the others that followed—Kilroy's, Eleanor's, my father's—the voices of caution and reason. The voice from the stage gathered power and sheen, rose clear and strong, "*elle a fui, elle a fui,*" until it filled the room like sweet, spring air.

I noticed the pains then. They might have been coming for some time. I fell to my knees. The contractions came close and hard, so hard that my head spun, one so strong I had to catch my breath before I could give it instructions. I'd once asked Eleanor how much it hurt to have a baby and she'd said a lot, probably more than anything had or would ever hurt me again. But it was pain with purpose, she said, pain with a gift, and so it didn't compare. But was it physical pain? I asked. Like a cut or an ache? Yes, she said. It was physical, bodily pain. I didn't believe in the absoluteness of pain, I said, or anything else for that matter. I told her the story of the farmer and the cow. She didn't believe in my not believing. She didn't like barnyard comparisons. Halley talked to a pretend chicken. And it talked back. It would hurt, Eleanor had said. Hurt like hell. Let it hurt, Leo, she'd said. Give in to the hurt. Give in to it. And breathe.

The pain twisted through me like a vine and I worked to untangle it, breathing in and out as the contractions rose and fell. As the pain got stronger, so—strangely, slowly—did I. I listened to Lydia's voice singing Offenbach, traveling a long forgotten road, and I breathed hard and long and deep. The music sailed me through each contraction. I worked at syncopation, ending the breath on one note, beginning with another. When there was no space left between contractions, I crouched low and dug my hands into the seat in front of me and began my fast breathing. Lydia's voice rose to a crescendo. I knew I must be in active labor, and that it was no longer a matter of pain, but will.

Hut, hut, hut, hut.

The baby bore down against my bones. My legs felt welded to the floor. I wasn't supposed to push, not until the very end, and it was up to me to decide when that end was. There was no time for taxis or telephones. No one was there to feel my cervix or check my pulse. I couldn't ask for drugs or ice chips or a clock to watch, for a needle or a hand to bear down on. All I could do was breathe and hunch and feel, listen and breathe, and clutch and gulp and feel. Lydia's voice flew and trembled. From out of the corner of my bulging eye, I saw her long arms rise and sweep the stage. Her voice swooped and bled. I listened for a long time. I knew I should do something—move, reach, cry out. But I couldn't move, couldn't stop listening, because it was such a mystical and powerful sound, Lydia's voice, and I'd waited so long to hear it.

When the aria was done, I clapped my hands, once, maybe twice, raising my head from the seat in front of me, wet to the waist with a weeping sweat. Somewhere in between breaths, I found a groan and blew it out, brayed it out like an animal. And as my head sank down on my hands again, I saw Lydia and Po rush toward me, following the trail of my broken water. Upward.

Later, Kilroy and I would sit around the kitchen table and tell the others the story, Kilroy tossing in details a bit sadly, a bit on edge, because he'd missed it all, still scrunched up, rumpled and restless, on the attic bed at Cobb's Hill, as I lay down on the floor of Symphony Hall and Po took off his jacket and Lydia rolled up her sleeves to deliver the baby. The story didn't need embellishment, though it gathered adornments over the years—the shine of the stage floor, the gold tassles on the curtain pull, the length of the aria. It was, all by itself, a magical tale, a robust fable, a gallant ode. What was the best part? Each of us lay claim to our own. When Lydia said, "now," and I pushed four times with four contractions, when Uncle Po spotted the baby's dark, slippery head and Lydia slid the baby into the world, singing softly all the while, soothing, strong hands, handled like a pro, Eleanor later told her. Or was it when Uncle Po took off his shirt and wrapped the baby as best he could and placed the baby in my arms, or how the three of us huddled together in the empty theater, as the world around us woke up and came to life, amazed that we'd not been disturbed, that we'd been left in peace, savoring the moment, the place, staring at the baby, watching, rejoicing, mourning, all of it—the lost time, the lost voice, the lost brothers, the lost lover, the lost summer . . .

What was the best part? How we waited for the baby's cry, but what came out first were bird sounds. How we said nothing through it all, nothing out loud, every thought expressed through our senses— with a look, a touch, a breath. How we watched the tiny baby for a while, covered with goop and blood and a fine layer of ivory vernix. Wide, tiny blue eyes, the bluest of blue. How we watched the baby reach and squirm, until the big doors clanked open wide as we'd known they would, until they burst in upon us and came with a stretcher, moving quickly, wearing white coats and guarded smiles, to take us all to the hospital.

What was the best part? How the photographer's bulbs flashed in our eyes, how the clatter rose up to the angeled ceiling. How we were on the front page of the newspaper the next day, the four of us up on the stage. How the baby and I got carried off on the stretcher, still attached, belly to belly, how, as I left the hall I saw the janitor standing at the door, a rose in his hand, which he handed to Lydia as we passed by, a shriveled old man, watching Lydia, always watching, half-remembering, the tiny, proud man with the beautiful eyes. How Lydia gave him the melting smile of a queen and went the wrong way, not out toward the exit, but back towards the stage. How the janitor went after her and pulled her gently back on track . . .

The janitor must have heard the singing. He must have closed his eyes until the aria was done, then called for the stretcher, gone for the rose. The siren blared as we took off in the ambulance down Mass. Ave., by then come alive with suited men and high-heeled women, radioed teenagers, a few lost souls. What was the best part? Maybe how, as the ambulance flew across the city, Lydia sang the mockingbird song to the baby in a soft, creaky voice, and Po joined in, not missing a word, or a beat—every note perfectly in tune.

When the light and noise of the hospital hit the baby, her lip trembled and she roared the cry of all creatures freed from a place too small, a place she'd been kept too long, become more attached to than she should. I held the baby on what was still the mound of my middle, no longer hard and fit to burst, but loose and rubbery, like a balloon losing air. When I started to hum, she stopped crying. After I'd had a good look at her in the harsh, neon light and knew she was mine, I let them take her again, to weigh and measure her and put ointment in her eyes.

Soon, they were all around me—Eleanor, just back from Texas, Kilroy, my father and Po, who'd been waiting in the solarium, Mr. McPhee, who came alone, with flowers from the hospital gift shop, and Ettore, on his way over from the Conservatory. Eleanor wrapped the baby tightly in a receiving blanket, wiped some leftover goo from the corner of her eyes with one finger, and announced her exquisite.

My father took the baby without a second's hesitation or fear. "I remember now," he said. "You smelled like bubble gum and yeast." He shifted the baby in his arms. His eyes lit up as the wheels of invention started turning. "There ought to be some kind of sling," he said. "Something you could hoist . . ."

Po took the baby and set her in quiet motion. "The Rocking Sling," he said. "You could make it out of a blanket, to keep her warm."

"Put velcro on the sides," Kilroy said.

"Velcro?" my father said. "What's velcro?"

"Little nylon hooks and loops," Kilroy said. "It keeps things together. Like zippers."

"Ah, hooks and loops," my father said. "I almost invented that."

Mr. McPhee cradled the baby's head carefully, this one of so many he'd held, the first one, Danny.

"She's a strong one, Leo," he said, taking the baby's finger. "A strong one, to be sure, just like her father."

The baby took to Kilroy right away, as people did. He bent his face close to hers and spoke to her, maybe about chess or a paradox or some plan he'd made for them already, as if she'd been around for a good, long while. He pulled her stocking cap down over her ears, no more than a segment of bandage cut and bunched together and taped at the top, one of so many that were lopped off from a roll at the hospital, day in and day out, for all new babies born. Kilroy would always have some special feeling about that hat, some ache that would make him keep it planted on that little girl's head all of that first cold winter, even as she grew round and fat and her ears popped out of it, as if the hat would keep her from harm. The next winter, I went out and bought the baby a real hat, one with ear flaps and a chin strap that wouldn't chafe or slide, but she pulled it off every time, with a kick of her chubby legs and an angry flap of her hand. And even though Kilroy kept reminding me that you lost eighty percent of your body heat through your head, I gave up on hats altogether.

The door suddenly opened and Lydia was escorted into the room by a hospital orderly in a white coat.

"Lydie!" My father's head jerked up. "Where on earth have you been?"

"Walking," she said. "Just walking, August."

"I found her on the sixth floor," the orderly said. "Is she with you folks?"

"Yes, she's with us." My father told the man indignantly. "She delivered this baby. At Symphony Hall. She's the grandmother." He went over to Lydia and took her hand. "Are you all right, Lydie?" he said. "We were in the solarium. When did you leave? I didn't even realize you'd gone."

"I went for a walk, August." Her hand rose to her face. "There are so many sick people here. So many people."

"Come hold your granddaughter, Lydia," I said.

Lydia came over to my bedside and took the baby from my arms with the same bewildered look that must have been on my face an hour before when she first held her up to me, pink and slippery. Lydia held the little pointed face close against her shoulder and walked over to the window.

"What an odd little prune," she said. "I'd forgotten." She stared out the window, at the city and beyond, searching for a familiar place. The baby slept on Lydia's shoulder. Slept and slept. My father took her again. Then Po. Then Mr. McPhee. They held her and passed her around, murmuring and stroking. The baby didn't protest. She didn't cry. I wanted her back suddenly, and when I got her, I wondered how I'd ever let her go—climb a ladder or cross a street or go to school, how I'd ever let her grow up and become someone apart from me.

For a moment that crystallized in the lingering beams of the sun, they were all occupied—Lydia arranging flowers in a plastic pitcher by the window, Po playing with the buttons on my electric bed, my father adjusting the venetian blinds to let in some more of the dusty light, some new idea dancing on his fingertips. Mr. McPhee framed a snapshot of the baby with his camera, one that might never make it up onto the flower-covered wall, one that might lie hidden in a wallet or a drawstring bag for a good, long while to come. He gathered up his things and gestured to Po that it was time to leave, but Po waved him away, saying, "I'll be back soon, Dad. I'll be back before the market opens."

"All right then Porter," he said. "I'll be expecting you."

A voice came over the loudspeaker. "Dr. Early, Dr. Eleanor Early. Please report to maternity, Room Twelve." Eleanor went off to deliver someone else's baby. Kilroy settled back into the chair by my bedside and pulled out a pocket chess set.

I looked down into my daughter's tiny, wizened face, a face so young, it might be confused with the face of one as old. She had a small round mouth, upslanted, almond eyes. She knew herself completely. She knew about beginnings and ends, so close was she to both, in the Möbius strip of time. She'd been down there with me and Danny, down in the water. She'd ushered him into the warmth of darkness, and shown me the way back up to the surface, to the light. She still understood in a visceral way about time and reason, faith and space. Her mind was empty of all earthly clutter and ready to be filled. She'd reinvented and encompassed us all.

A slight breeze rustled my ear. Danny sailed into the room and sat down in the empty chair beside me.

"Bunch of nut cases you ended up with, Leo." Danny said. "Too many brains."

"No such thing," I said. "You had brains, Danny. Big brains."

"Mixed-up brains," he said, pointing to the baby. "Hope she didn't get them."

"Don't stay if you can't be nice."

"I'll be nice. You just tell that guy to take good care of my kid."

"He will," I said. "That's Kilroy. The chess player. He knows something, Danny. Something big. Remember?"

I stared and stared at the baby. I needn't have worried. She was strong and beautiful and completely her own self. I looked around at all the people in the room, lost in their own swirling thoughts, on the verge of scatter. Po leaned over my shoulder and stroked the baby's head. Lydia clung to the light and warmth at the window. My father played with the strings of the venetian blinds, scribbled something on a hospital napkin.

"It's time to go now, August," Lydia said suddenly. "Time to go home. I've been gone so long."

"All right, Lydie," he said, letting go of the blinds. "Let's go."

Kilroy looked up from the chessboard, at me and the baby, and back to the chessboard, whistling softly, his eyes too busy, too full, ever really to land. Back in my garden, the last breadfruit plant fell from its stalk to the cooling ground. I looked at the sleeping baby in my arms, and decided that of all of them, with her full lips and remarkable calm, in her infinite, quiet wisdom, Clementine most resembled Kilroy.